'I want back what I'm owed,' he said reasonably.

'Your dowry is what your grandmother wants me to have to pay her debt,' he continued. 'I'm not too proud to take it.'

'But you know it won't come unconditionally,' Elizabeth jeered. 'I'm surprised at you, my lord. You'll stoop to take a sullied woman to wife just to lay your hands on her money? For a short while this evening, when I saw how well you live, I deemed you a gentleman of some standing.' She paused to sniff. 'It's all show, is it not? Now you want to procure my portion to squander!'

'Will you marry me, Elizabeth?' he asked quietly.

Dear Reader

Bad boys can be fascinating. With this in mind I decided to write about some, and the result is a quartet of Regencies that commenced with MR TRELAWNEY'S PROPOSAL. The novels feature heroes, linked by family or friendship, who are definitely rogues. Wickedly charming, wryly humorous, dangerously attractive…good girls can't resist them. But innocence can be as captivating as sophistication: the heroines are more than a match for their jaded suitors.

In this story, you'll meet Ross Trelawney, the brother of Luke (who starred in MR TRE-LAWNEY'S PROPOSAL). Ross is an adventurer who has been newly ennobled to Viscount Stratton by the King. Viscount Stratton generously lends Lady Elizabeth Rowe's grandmother money, unaware that the only way she can repay him is with Elizabeth's dowry. That means Elizabeth and Ross must marry—a prospect which does not appeal to either of them—at first!

As the separate stories unfold in this quartet, the couples battle through a maelstrom of action and emotion. I hope you enjoy their passionate skirmishing, the laughter and tears that pave the way to harmony and happiness, as much as I have enjoyed writing the novels for you.

Mary Brendan

The previous titles in this quartet are:

MR TRELAWNEY'S PROPOSAL
A KIND AND DECENT MAN
THE SILVER SQUIRE

A ROGUISH
GENTLEMAN

Mary Brendan

To Amazing Grace
Also for Elaine, Doreen, Jane, Amanda, Marie and all the
other Friday-nighters at 2-HOD

*First published in Great Britain 2001
Harlequin Mills & Boon Limited,
Eton House, 18-24 Paradise Road, Richmond, Surrey TW9 1SR*

© Mary Brendan 2001

ISBN 0 263 82725 9

*Set in Times Roman 10¼ on 11 pt.
04-0401-89047*

*Printed and bound in Spain
by Litografia Rosés S.A., Barcelona*

Chapter One

'Elizabeth!'

Lady Elizabeth Rowe turned in the spacious hallway of her grandmother's elegant townhouse to see the elderly lady bearing down on her, nose pinched between thumb and forefinger and what was visible of her face, behind her podgy hand, set in a grimace of utter distaste.

Elizabeth understood. Sheepishly she glanced down at her hem. It *was* suspiciously clogged. She sighed and shrugged an apology. It was possible the stains were mud from the hedgerow she had skipped over moments ago on alighting from Reverend Clemence's gig. Unfortunately, she suspected, as did her grandmother, that it was rather more offensive detritus. Probably ordure from the gutters in Wapping where she'd been assisting the vicar in teaching at Barrow Road Sunday School.

'Look at you!' Edwina Sampson shrieked at her granddaughter, jewels flashing on her fat fingers as they flicked floorward in disgust. 'There's no mistaking when you are home. I simply follow m'nose!'

'Don't nag so, Grandmama,' Elizabeth said mildly. 'There are worse things in life than a little muck. I have just been amongst poor wretches who live with the stench daily in their nostrils as well as beneath their feet.'

Edwina Sampson bristled. 'Decency and hard work is

what's lacking! Shut that door!' she suddenly bawled at a tall, stately man who was standing by the draughty aperture, steely eyebrows slightly elevated as he phlegmatically assessed a trail of dung on formerly pristine marble. 'Quickly, man! Do I warm this house simply to let it out and encourage vagrants to congregate on m'step? Do you know the cost of a sack of coal? A cartload of logs?'

'Indeed, I do, madam,' Harry Pettifer calmly responded. 'I have just this week settled the fuel bill.'

'Is that insolence, Pettifer?'

'I am never insolent, madam,' her butler informed his mistress, inscrutable of face as he regally paced the hallway poker-backed. One bright blue eye disappeared as he passed Elizabeth and she stifled a smile at the unobtrusive wink.

Harry Pettifer had been in service to the Sampsons for almost thirty years. In the few years Elizabeth had lived with her grandmother in this quiet part of Marylebone, she'd witnessed far more entertaining exchanges between the short sexagenarian and her statuesque butler.

As Elizabeth carefully eased off her suspiciously slimy shoes, she noticed the commotion had drawn other servants to gawp at the spectacle. With supreme aplomb, Pettifer clicked his elegant fingers at mobcaps. 'Brush… mop…hallway…now,' was his brusque instruction to them to dispose of the mess.

Edwina Sampson frowned at his back. 'For what I pay him, I could take on two footmen, or pay m'butcher for a twelve-month.'

'I think not, Grandmama. I doubt poor Pettifer's salary would even cover your confectioner's bill.' She teased her grandmother's fondness for marchpane with a meaningful nod at her sizeable girth.

Pettifer allowed an appreciative smile to touch his lips, prompting his employer to snap, 'Less of your sauce, miss! I might have a sweet tooth,' she admitted while twitching Elizabeth's skirts this way and that, her smooth, plump face a study in revulsion. 'And why should I not? A woman who's worked her fingers to the bone is entitled to a little treat in her twilight years.'

Elizabeth padded to the stairs in her stockinged feet. 'You know very well that we need Pettifer…far more than he does us, I suspect. I hear that Mrs Penney is stalking him again. She's keen to lure him away to her Brighton townhouse,' Elizabeth warned.

'Is she? Who told you?' Her grandmother's lips compressed into a tight, indignant line, her pale blue eyes narrowing.

Elizabeth removed her bonnet, dropped back her ash-blonde head and laughed while the hat swayed on its strings. 'I shall just freshen myself, then join you in the parlour and share some gossip regarding Pettifer's popularity. Meanwhile, perhaps you ought go and curry a little favour with him, lest he really is tempted to go this time,' she taunted over her shoulder as, grimy skirts held high and shapely ankles displayed, she ran easily up the curve of stairs.

Moments later, in her lavender-fragrant chamber, Elizabeth grimaced down at her hem, then up at her maid. Josie distastefully wrinkled her small pert nose, shook her head and gingerly helped her mistress step out of the serviceable garment before bundling it away for the laundry.

Her grandmother was right, Elizabeth mused while bathing her face with petal-scented water. It *was* the stench that disturbed the most. Even when home and decked in fresh clothes, the reek of the slums would haunt her nostrils.

She'd been assisting at Barrow Road Sunday School every week for some thirteen months. In all that time, it seemed that the air never got sweeter or more foul. The fortitude of unwashed humanity, seething middens and the proximity of the docks contributing salt and tar spillage, remained stoically unchanged. Even the recent heat of summer seemed to make little difference to rank poverty. Only the flies came and went. As did the school's pupils.

At times a gap would appear on the rough pew on which the boys and girls sat, slates balanced on tattered laps.

'A'workin' t'day, m'm. Ailin' t'day, m'm,' would gruffly answer any enquiry as to where was the absentee. 'Dead, m'm,'
on one occasion was the toneless reply to the condition of a
sickly child.

The philanthropic owner of a spice warehouse had allowed
a spare, bare corner to serve as a classroom to a score or more
local urchins, aiding their escape from a little petty larceny
along the wharves or watching young 'uns on the Sabbath to
scratch out scripture instead. On arrival at the premises on
Sundays, a mass of skeletal arms and legs would jostle and
elbow for a place on a splintery bench as determinedly as
they doubtless fought for a portion of what was available to
eat or earn. The weakest would sink cross-legged to the cold,
stone floor.

Seating herself on her velvet dressing-table chair, Elizabeth
studied her well-nourished appearance. As Josie worked pins
from her hair, pearl-blonde tresses sinuously spiralled to
bounce either side of her oval face and slender column of
neck. A healthy flush was still rimming her high cheekbones
from the brisk walk earlier.

Each Sunday, she and Hugh Clemence hurried through a
maze of narrow alleys to reach Barrow Road. Even a clergyman who was afforded a respectful nod or word from ragged parishioners never chose to tarry in such an area. Their
route never differed. Winter and summer, lines of greyish
washing crisscrossed overhead between grimy tenements.
When the air froze in front of their mouths as they talked and
walked, the rags hung stiff and unmoving; at other times a
tepid oily breeze might flutter the tattered flags of a commu-
nity surrendered to its fate. Dead-eyed women and rickety
children crowded the dank doorways or squatted on the cobbles sifting through the rubbish for something useful.

Elizabeth closed her violet-blue eyes and relaxed into the
chair as Josie gently but firmly drew a brush through her
blonde tangles. She sighed as she thought of the children. Was
it enough to simply suspend reality for them for a while on
the Sabbath? What were they really thinking as they gazed,

glassy-eyed, at her and rubbed at streaming noses or chapped skin? Their empty bellies? The chores they had just come from or were soon returning to? The nonsense of hearing tales of a Benevolent Father when in their short lives most had experienced nothing but hunger and harshness?

'If but one child escapes the ravages of the gin house or the bawdy house through our work today, I shall die a happy man,' Hugh Clemence had once expounded his philosophy on it all. Enduring the stench of poverty in her nostrils once a week was a paltry price to pay to help just one poor soul.

'We must make it two,' she had answered him, and he had taken her hand to hold. And she had allowed him to…for a few seconds, before extricating her fingers.

'Ah, that's better,' Edwina Sampson praised the sight of her granddaughter's pretty, petite figure. Elizabeth entered the cosy, flame-flickering parlour, dressed in rose-pink crepe with her shiny blonde hair piled elegantly atop her head, making her look taller than her five feet three inches. 'Now you look and smell more like my sweet Lizzie.'

'On the subject of odours, Grandmama…have you been smoking in here again?' Elizabeth quizzed, wrinkling her small nose. 'It reeks of a gentleman's gaming room,' she chided, fanning a space in front of her with a small hand.

'And how would you know of such places? Have you lately *been* in a gentleman's gaming room?' her grandmother shot back distractingly while the heel of a slippered foot sent a dark stub skidding under her chair.

'You know Papa and his cronies could set up quite a fug in the blue salon at Thorneycroft when playing at Faro. I am well used to identifying tobacco smoke.'

'Hmmph,' Edwina rumbled. 'I thought perhaps you'd been spending time with a real man instead of that whey-faced clergyman who limps after you.'

Lady Elizabeth Rowe sent her grandmother a prim look. 'Hugh is a very conscientious and kindly gentleman, and I cherish him as a good friend.'

The demure description was dismissed with one plump hand while the other dived into a silver dish and extracted a piece of marchpane. Chewing and eyeing her granddaughter speculatively, Edwina demanded, 'Has he yet proposed?'

Elizabeth sank daintily into a fireside chair opposite her grandmother's seat. Holding her hands to the glow in the grate, she allowed a small smile. 'No, he has not. Neither will he. Hugh is well aware I have no fondness for him in…that way.'

'Thank God for that!' her grandmother muttered. 'I live in dread of you arriving home with some paltry bauble on your betrothal finger to announce you're to move into some roof-leaking rectory in a godforsaken part of town.' With a finger-wag, she added, 'That's not to say I've given up on your nuptials, miss. It is far and away time you were wed. You are soon to be twenty-nine and can't live with your old grand-mama forever. I might soon get notice to quit and first I must know you're settled.'

'You're as robust as ever and as like to see a score more years. And you're well aware that I shall never marry. Now then,' she speedily changed subject, 'are you interested in learning how I know that Mrs Penney is again batting her lashes and her banknotes at Pettifer?'

'You shan't sidetrack me that easily, m'girl. I meant what I said. I'm sixty-five years old and often afflicted with a pain right here.' She thumped a spot beneath her ribs. 'It could be a serious malaise; it might see me off!'

'It's indigestion,' Elizabeth mildly reassured her. 'And as like to disappear if you cease eating for…let's see…one hour a day?' A cheeky smile made her look no more than nineteen, and immediately melted her grandmother's indignation.

'Elizabeth,' Edwina wheedled. 'You are a beautiful woman and need a husband. You can't let a tragedy that occurred a decade ago blight your entire life. It is forgotten. People have forgotten.'

'I haven't forgotten! Neither have I any wish for a hus-band…especially not a gentleman from the *ton*. Were I to marry, I would choose a kind, caring man such as Hugh, which would rile you greatly and have you ranting of a *mésalliance*. After all, I *am* the daughter of a Marquess and poor Hugh comes from a long line of impoverished men of the cloth. So please, no more of it.'

A theatrically languid hand displayed despair as Edwina flopped back in her chair. Her fingers began straying comfortingly towards the silver dish. 'Tell me then why that cat Alice Penney is after Pettifer.' She resorted to sighing in a martyred tone.

Elizabeth smiled winsomely. 'I imagine it is because he is so handsome.'

'Pish! He is an old codger: a year older than me!' emerged through a mouthful of marchpane.

'He is still a very sprightly and handsome man, despite his age. According to Sophie, many a matron in Mrs Penney's set would like him to greet their guests and grace their hallway. They are to have a wager, so I hear, on who can steal him from under your nose. I believe a great deal of money is in the pot.'

'A *wager?*' Edwina spluttered. 'On who can steal my *butler*? He's been my man for nigh on three decades and my man he will stay. I'll…I'll never give him a character if he leaves me.'

'I rather think he might not need one,' Elizabeth chuckled. 'I'm sure Mrs Penney will snap him up without.'

Edwina shook her salt and pepper ringlets back from her plump cheeks, her eyes narrowing, her mouth twitching angrily. A gleam appeared in her light blue eyes. Wager? If there was one thing Edwina liked as much as a good gobble, it was a good gamble. She'd give those wanton alley cats a run for their money!

Harry Pettifer was a fine figure of a man and he had noble blood in him. Had it not been for his idiot father, Sir Roger Pettifer, taking the family into penury through his love of hazard, his youngest son might have had an inheritance to smooth his path through life. Instead, fate decreed he take up a position as butler to a friend.

Harry and her late husband had been chums, even though, at one time, Harry had been frowned upon for keeping company with a lowly 'cit'. For Daniel Sampson had made *his* tidy fortune through commerce, progressing through hard work from humble mercer to retail baron, dealing in all manner of luxury commodities. At that time, Harry had been an eligible bachelor who lived off a generous allowance. Then bankruptcy came; no more funds were forthcoming for the Pettifer sons and Harry would not hear of a loan from Daniel Sampson being written off. So his services were taken up, half in jest, half in earnest, for Harry had always been a proud man. What ensued was an employment lasting half a lifetime. On her husband's death some thirteen years ago, Harry had stayed on. She hadn't expected him to: her relationship with her husband's friend, confidant and man of all trades, had at times been quite prickly.

Edwina had never been generous or mean in her dealings with him. Since his financial obligation had been cleared, Harry had drawn a reasonable salary. Edwina had always paid him an acceptable rate: what was fair. And now, if he wanted to go, she had no right to detain him. In the past, when she had casually interrogated him for his opinion on their status quo, a slightly quizzical look would sharpen his blue eyes. Politely he would assure her he was content. Perhaps he no longer was content. Perhaps he missed not having a wife, children of his own. Perhaps he regretted only ever observing family life rather than engaging in it himself. Perhaps, Edwina mused with a leaden feeling in her stomach that she knew was nothing devoured, she regretted that she had never rewarded her loyal gentleman butler with gratitude and generosity instead of a remote fairness. Annoyed at the melancholy that the possibility of losing him evoked, Edwina suddenly barked irritably, 'What time are we to go to the Heathcotes'?

'At eight,' Elizabeth confirmed the hour of the quiet soirée planned at Sophie's parents that evening. At twenty-two, Sophie Heathcote was six years her junior. Her closest friend was an attractive brunette who possessed a sharp wit she refused to disguise. That rendered Sophie far less attractive in the eyes of the *beau monde*. Sophie was a blue-stocking, an odd creature who was happier pursuing knowledge than an eligible man. Which was as well, for no man would want a wife whose intelligence was superior to his own. The two young women were outcasts in a society which despised and isolated women who didn't conform to an accepted ideal. Since Elizabeth moved to town from the countryside when her father, the Marquess of Thorneycroft, died, some few years ago, she and Sophie, both lonely yet lively, had gravitated towards each other and become firm friends.

'Would you mind terribly if I cried off tonight, Lizzie? You know it is all a bit dull for my taste and I have an invitation to Maria Farrow's salon. Josie can accompany you there.'

'No, I don't mind. I shall not stay too late, in any case. There is a visit to Bridewell planned tomorrow—' Her grandmother's snort of disgust cut her short, making it clear she had no interest in learning any details of her visit to the correctional institution, with Hugh Clemence and some other charitable ladies. Elizabeth, undeterred, ploughed on, 'Actually, Grandmama, we are hoping for some kindly people to donate—' She got no further.

Sixty-five years old and portly, maybe, but Edwina was out of her chair in a flash and soon at the door. 'I have told you, young lady, I have no spare fortune to be squandered housing foundlings and fallen women!'

'I am not asking you for a fortune, Grandmama,' Elizabeth sighed. 'A few pounds would be very welcome. It would buy cloth for the women so they can make things to sell: pinafores, handkerchiefs…'

'Had they not stolen such articles in the first place, they wouldn't now be stitching scrappy rags to while away the time till their release!'

Elizabeth sprang to her feet and glared at her grandmother. 'One mistake in their miserable lives—perhaps to put bread in their children's mouths—and they should pay forever? I made a mistake once; have you forgotten that? I made a bad mistake. But I refuse to feel ashamed. I, too, was wrong for the right reasons. Some of those gentlemen you would like to see come a'courting are the worst immoral riffraff. If one or two of them still loiter about me, it is for far less honourable reasons than proposing marriage!' Her small oval face flushed with anger, her fingers clenched. After staring stonily at each other for a moment, Elizabeth sighed and gestured apology.

'I'm sorry Grandmama. I had not meant to shout. But…' She dredged up a weak smile, reseating herself. 'I have been meaning to ask you for some weeks now…' She paused, striving for coaxing words to unlock her parsimonious grandmother's purse. 'The portion you have put by for my marriage is money likely to stay untouched. I shall not marry. But if you really intended it to benefit me, I beg you allow me just a small sum from it so that I can—'

'You are right in one respect, miss,' her grandmother interrupted tightly. 'The money is for *your* benefit. If you think I will pass over some of my hard-earned cash—from the days when I worked dawn till dusk in your grandfather's mercery—so you can then transfer it to such drabs as used to rob us blind the moment our backs were turned, you are much mistaken! Never a week went by but a pair of gloves, silk stockings, handkerchiefs and ribbon went missing from our first shop. And now you want *me* to support those miscreants' descendants in their thievery?'

'No, Grandmama,' Elizabeth reasoned wearily. 'So it can assist such poor wretches to perhaps gain employment, a little self-respect; to help them start a new life. Just one hundred pounds…please? It is my money and it would make such a difference to so many; children as well as their mothers.'

'I'd as lief hand it straight to your husband to squander at dice.'

'And the men you would see me wed would do exactly that!' Elizabeth snapped bitterly. 'Perhaps I shall wed the vicar after all, I'm sure I might persuade him to give it me straight back!'

'Hah...you think I've not thought of that? No clergy. It states in the terms. Marry a clergyman and the dowry is forfeit.'

Elizabeth threw up her hands in despair. 'I love you dearly, Grandmama, but your misanthropy disgusts me.'

'And I love you dearly, granddaughter, but your misplaced charity disgusts me,' was flung over a plump satin shoulder as Edwina quit the room.

Lady Rebecca Ramsden raised her glorious turquoise gaze from the paper and stared into space. It couldn't be true! Luke surely would have said! She shook the page to straighten it, dipped her golden head and read the paragraph again. It *was* true! It was there in black and white! Springing from the chair, the paper clutched tightly in a hand, she sped for the door. Out in the hallway she gasped at their aged butler, 'Have you seen my husband, Miles?'

'Er, no, Miss Becky,' Miles returned with a frown at his mistress's agitation. Neither of them were in any way put out by him addressing her so informally. Miss Becky she had been prior to marriage to Baron Ramsden and Miss Becky she was now to all old and trusted servants at Ramsden Manor, who had known her since childhood. Now approaching his seventy-seventh year, Miles would never think of her as anything else but little Miss Becky. In all other respects, Lady Ramsden was accorded every respect due to her station as the much-loved chatelaine of this grand house.

'I expect he's about the stables, putting young Master Troy through his paces on his pony,' Miles added helpfully.

Rebecca had already reasoned that and, with a laughing wave of the crumpled *Gazette*, was off again. She ran in mellow late-afternoon sunlight towards the stables. 'Luke!' she called breathlessly as she hurtled into the cool, musty building.

Only a few young stable-hands, toiling at one end of the

brick-and-timber building, were within. They looked curiously at her. 'I think his lordship be in the barn wi' young master. Right tired he were after his ride, m'lady. Practic'ly a'snoozin' on his feet,' the more gregarious of the grooms told her.

Rebecca nodded in appreciation of the information and was gone. She pushed open the barn door and located her husband at once. Against the yellow straw his dark breeches, white cambric shirt and jet hair were a striking contrast. He looked up as a shaft of warm, mote-ridden sunlight bathed him. Earth-dark eyes locked on to his wife's curvaceous figure, silhouetted by hazy golden light. He smiled slowly in that special intimate way that quickened her heart. A finger beckoned her in, moved to touch his lips, then indicated their small son, curled up on his side on soft straw close to his father.

Rebecca sank gracefully down onto her knees close to her husband. Even casually reclining on his side, dark head propped on a hand, one black knee raised, the powerful masculine lines of his body were immediately apparent. She shook the paper at him and hissed in an undertone, so as not to wake their sleeping son, 'Why did you not tell me? Isn't it wonderful news?'

Luke frowned at the paper, removed a stalk of sweet straw from between his even white teeth and said softly, 'Whichever marriage you've seen announced...I've no knowledge of it, Rebecca. I've not yet read the paper today. And don't be cross if I'm not about to be as enraptured as you at the prospect of some acquaintance's impending nuptials.'

'No...no, not a wedding!' Rebecca chided in an excited squeak. Then her turquoise eyes were sparking mischief. 'You've not seen it? Guess, then, what I have just read,' she teased, standing up and whipping the paper behind her back, out of reach. 'I promise it will interest you. It should delight you...'

'Enough...I'm curious,' her husband growled, snaking a powerful hair-roughened forearm about her slender blue silk figure to catch at the paper.

'No! Guess!'

A peaty-brown gaze swerved to his son, then raised to his wife's beautiful flushed complexion. His hands jerked her forward and his mouth approached a rounded hip close to his face. Slender fingers wound into long dark hair, holding his hot trailing mouth against her midriff as she insincerely discouraged, 'Oh, Luke, not here…not now; Troy might wake and…'

'Give me the paper, then,' her husband whispered in a throaty growl against warm silk. 'Or I'll have no option but to wrestle it from you…'

Heat flooded Rebecca; her fingers tightened in his hair, but, with her eyes on her sleeping son's profile, she again sank, with an expression of very ironic submission, to her knees.

Demurely she handed over the paper, pointing at a paragraph before resting back onto her heels and watching his face.

Luke Trelawney, Baron Ramsden, slowly pushed himself upright, a slow grin moving the lean dark planes of his handsome face. 'I didn't tell you, my love, because I didn't know,' he emphasised for Rebecca. 'Only Ross would keep quiet the fact that he's being gazetted as a peer of the realm.'

'Viscount Stratton! How noble it sounds,' Rebecca said on a musical laugh. 'You had no idea?' she quizzed her husband. 'He had said nothing?'

'Not a word. But then I've not seen him in six months. Neither, I imagine, has Mother or Katherine or Tristan.'

'Oh, but it's too bad of him, Luke! He really should have written to let his kin know of such an honour.'

'*Ross? Write a letter?* My little brother is more likely to turn up unexpectedly after half a year's absence than he is to pen a couple of lines.'

Rebecca flung her arms about her husband's neck. 'It's such wonderful news. Viscount Stratton of Stratton Hall in the County of Kent. Ross must be so proud.'

'Is Uncle Ross coming soon?' a small voice quavered from beside them.

Rebecca relinquished her husband to stroke her son's silky black hair. 'No, my love. But your uncle Ross is now a nobleman. The honour has been bestowed by the King. Uncle Ross is now a Viscount and will be Lord Stratton.'

Troy Trelawney looked singularly unimpressed by this news. He fully opened his sea-green eyes and looked at his mother from beneath black curly lashes. 'Will Uncle Ross still play pirates with me?' he asked with all the gravity of his six years. 'Now he is so important?'

Rebecca stifled a laugh and looked helplessly at her husband. Luke gave his son a lop-sided smile. 'I think that's still very likely,' he gently reassured Troy while a stray thought acknowledged that, at thirty-three, his recklessly intrepid brother still looked and acted like a dashing young buck. 'Besides, if he doesn't, then I shall.'

Again Troy Trelawney looked unimpressed. 'But you're not such a good Blackbeard, Papa, as Uncle Ross. He teaches me to fight with his sword. The one with the silver hilt, not a pretend wooden one…'

'Now I think it's time a certain sleepy man was snuggled up,' Rebecca hastily interjected, on noticing her husband's murderous look. Her brother-in-law might never live to enjoy his new rank.

'Excellent suggestion, darling,' Luke murmured. 'Tend to Troy first, though.' In a lithe movement he was on his feet and tousling his son's glossy raven hair with long fingers. 'Come back here when he's settled so we can enjoy the sunset?' he quietly requested.

Rebecca took her son's hand, picking stray straw stalks from his hair, before she met her husband's gleaming dark eyes. She smiled, then murmured on a virginal blush that never ceased to enchant Luke, 'Yes. I want to…'

Within fifteen minutes, Rebecca, Lady Ramsden, having seen her eldest son safely within the nursery and settled close to his sleeping infant brother, was again speeding over the vestibule flags, blue silk skirts scrunched in her palms, on her way to rejoin her husband.

'Dinner is served in ten minutes, my lady,' Judith called at her back as she rushed lightly past.

Rebecca came to a halt and spun about at her housekeeper's words. 'Oh…oh…' She looked towards the open great doors. An orange ball was visible, dipping low on the horizon. 'Lord Ramsden and I have…er…a few estate matters to discuss, Judith, while we…er…enjoy the sundown. Will dinner keep awhile?'

'Twenty minutes?' Judith offered on a smile.

Rebecca looked into middle distance and frowned, unsure.

'Thirty?' Judith amended neutrally. 'I know these estate matters take time.'

'Yes,' Rebecca said. 'Thirty. Thank you, Judith.' She spun away and was gone in a flash of blue silk.

Judith looked after her and grinned. Eight years married, two handsome sons tucked up in the nursery, and still they pulled together like magnets. It was the longest honeymoon of any couple she'd ever known.

'What's that you're fiddling with?' Edwina barked at her companion as they rocked together in her cosy old coach en route to a private card evening with Mrs Farrow.

Evangeline Filbert held up her knitting so the light from a passing gas lamp illuminated it. 'Stockings. I've finished ten pairs so far for Lizzie. She's taking them tomorrow to Bridewell for the inmates.'

Edwina Sampson snatched the needles and threw them onto the seat. 'Not you, too! Is everyone now with attics to let over these misbegotten felons?'

Evangeline looked mortified, her lips started to quiver.

'Oh, for God's sake, don't blub. Here.' Edwina plonked the knitting back on her lap. 'Finish a few more rows if you must. Just don't blub or I shan't again let you accompany me to m'friends. You shall sit at home alone.'

'Oh, I like to come,' Evangeline whispered. 'Your friends are all so…so…'

'Yes…?' Edwina snarled. 'So?'

'Exciting. And glamorous. And thrilling,' Evangeline expounded in wonder. She was a spinster of forty-three who had led a very quiet and careworn existence tending her ailing mother. When that lady—who had been a long-standing friend of Edwina Sampson's—finally accepted the notice to quit delivered some years earlier, Edwina had kindly taken Evangeline under her wing. The arrangement suited them both: a few times a week Evangeline escaped boredom and solitude, and Edwina gained an unpaid and unaware companion to accompany her to some of the unconscionable venues she favoured.

Tonight their hostess was an exceedingly glamorous widow, fêted for being the Duke of Vermont's current mistress. She was more notorious for cuckolding him quite openly with any lusty young buck who caught her eye. Still the ageing duke remained besotted. Mrs Farrow ran an exceedingly fine salon, Edwina judged, if a little *demi-monde*. Certainly more interesting than sitting with her granddaughter on the Heathcotes' sofa and listening to young Sophie spout about the position of ploughs and bears and how the planets might form a conjunction and alter one's fate.

Despite Maria Farrow being some twenty years her junior, the two women had a lot in common. They *were* common. But now Edwina had mighty connections: her late husband had hobnobbed with the gentry. Their beloved daughter had married an aristocrat. She had a beautiful granddaughter, sired by the late Marquess of Thorneycroft. Edwina frowned. What she really would have liked was a grandson. But her daughter had fallen foul of an icy winter before producing further children. It galled her greatly that, when the Marquess had remarried, desperate to produce an heir to prevent his detested cousin gaining the entailed estate on his demise, the sour-faced cat of a second wife had produced an heir within the first year of the nuptials.

A grandson-in-law was still an option, despite dear Lizzie's protestations that she had no wish to wed. A decade had passed since that fateful midsummer evening when she'd been compromised. When all was said and done, it had been no more than a silly little slip.

Chapter Two

'It's hot enough to roast an ox in here, Maria!' Edwina expostulated with her friend, feverishly fanning her sanguine complexion.

'Lawks, Edwina, but you'll have to make do with the veal pies,' Maria quipped. 'Spitting an ox, even for you, dearest, is totally too…mediaeval.'

Edwina gave her comrade a playfully indignant knock with her fan.

'The blaze in the hearth is for his Grace's benefit,' Maria confided, inclining her auburn coiffure in the direction of a sparse-pated, august gentleman engaged in a rubber of whist at a nearby table. 'Charlie, bless him, is keen to keep me warm since he discovered that young Carstairs had overnighted here last week. I pleaded it was so chilly in my chamber I was doomed to freeze to death a'bed lest a hot-blooded member of the regiment slide in and warm me. Next day, a forest of logs had sprouted in the gutter outside.'

Edwina chuckled, then gestured with her glass. 'What in heaven's name is this foul potion? Has he spent so much on your fires that the wine cellar's gone begging? It tastes like infant's cordial.'

'His Grace is keen for sober company tonight.' Maria sighed. 'Yesterday, I over-imbibed and he couldn't wake me.

Not that it mattered to me. I'd as lief the old goat got on with it while I'm unconscious.'

Edwina smothered a guffaw. Maria floated daintily away to greet some new arrivals, a vision of virginal loveliness with her alabaster skin and fiery tresses, and her willowy body draped in white muslin.

Edwina inclined her head at some acquaintances and smiled serenely, but she was vexed. Her enjoyment had been spoiled before it had begun, yet the company, the food and the music seemed as fine as ever. Even the stifling heat was just bearable. It was another matter which had dampened her humour.

On drawing up outside Maria's modish address, she had noticed Alice Penney's carriage stopping at a house along the street. Mrs Penney had made a point of loitering and simpering very deliberately in her direction on alighting from her barouche. Now Edwina could concentrate on little else but what that snide look signified. She'd concluded a wager was won: Harry Pettifer was to quit her service for pastures new. His resignation letter might, even now, be awaiting her, and she felt irritably inclined to rush home to discover if her gloomy prediction was correct.

With her lace fan whizzing before her ruddy countenance, Edwina was oblivious to Evangeline huddled in a corner seat, needles flying through the wool in her lap. Knitting her brows, she marched towards doors that led to a terrace, seeking refreshing night air. She stalked over stone flags to the iron balustrade that overlooked the lawns, gripping at it as though she'd reshape it with her bare hands.

'You look fit to do battle, Mrs Sampson,' drawled a voice from one side of her. 'Have you been sucking lemons to perfect that sour look?'

Edwina's brow smoothed, her eyes peeked sideways as she grinned in delight. But, despite that husky baritone sounding so familiar, it probably wasn't who she'd thought. Having clawed back some awesome fortune for the King's hungry coffers by confiscating a shipload of smuggled gold bullion destined for the continent, her favourite scoundrel, so she'd learned, was now much in favour with Georgy Porgy and very welcome at court.

The new Viscount Stratton was unlikely to be sitting alone in the dark on a mature courtesan's terrace, even if the lady did run a damn fine salon and her aristocratic lover was present tonight. Edwina didn't imagine the Duke of Vermont and Viscount Stratton were chums: there was a score or more years' difference in their ages and a vast discrepancy in their energy. Stratton was always up to carriage racing, pugilism and cavorting with enthusiastic strumpets; his Grace sometimes left unfinished a game of whist and a brief romp with an indifferent woman. Were it indeed the Viscount, even as plain Mr Trelawney, there would be an ambitious young female loitering somewhere hereabouts, keen to turn his head.

A cigar glowed in the night to one side of her. Edwina raised her lorgnette strung on the pearls that were lost in the folds of her neck. 'Is that you, Trelawney? Slumming this evening, are you? Taking a little break from the Carlton House Set? Must I curtsy?' Edwina ribbed. She chuckled delightedly as a tall, dark and exceedingly handsome man pushed to his feet from the stone bench he'd been resting on and strolled into the shaft of weak light filtering through the french doors.

'I accept your congratulations, Edwina,' he commented drily. 'And how have you been?'

'I have been better,' she snarled, suddenly recalling what had brought her out here. 'I'm in high dudgeon, Ross. But it's good to see you. It must be…' She looked reflective, trying to recall the last time she and this man had socialised.

'Two years or more, as I recall,' Viscount Stratton supplied. 'At Vauxhall two summers ago. I don't get to London as much as I used to.'

'And when you do it seems you skulk about in the dark. Are you grown shy all of a sudden?' she laughed.

'I'm always shy when a woman has commitment on her mind; especially when I figure in her delusion. That's not the real reason I'm out here,' he admitted, with a flash of a white smile. 'The whole house is hellish hot, is it not? I wasn't sure whether to drink that odd brew being doled out or throw it on the fire.'

'I sympathise on both counts,' Edwina said, peering distastefully at her glass, but her eyes were narrowing thoughtfully. 'So you're still unwed…I imagined some young minx must have cornered you by now.'

'They do, Edwina,' he agreed wryly. 'But not well enough that I might submit.'

'You're a heartless rogue,' Edwina chided, her mouth aslant and gimlet eyes sparkling with a crafty light. 'Of course, I understand why these flighty young misses straight out of the schoolroom don't appeal. Why…you must be thirty-three if you're a day. You're a sophisticate who would suit a more mature lady. Someone older and wiser in the ways of the world…'

'Are you proposing, Edwina?' Ross asked with studied gravity.

Edwina tutted, rapping her fan on his arm in mock outrage, but her pale eyes were veiled behind her lashes and her mind whirred.

'So what's set you so glum-faced this evening?' Ross asked idly. 'Apart from the lack of a good cognac to be had, of course.'

Edwina looked shrewdly at him. 'Well, I'd like very much to tell you actually, Stratton. I need a friend to confide in. It's all about some underhand thievery in the offing, so I'd value your expert advice on the subject,' she teased with a wicked smile. 'You must visit me tomorrow; we shall dine and catch up on all our news. You can impress me…and m'granddaughter…' she mumbled on a cough, 'with all your heroic exploits.'

Ross frowned, and ruefully moved a hand as he mentally sifted through prior engagements.

When he seemed unsuspecting, Edwina hurriedly encouraged, 'It's time you met m'granddaughter…' At his slow, speculative look, she hastened on, 'You'll find the tale amusing...very droll. And perhaps there might even be a little side bet in it for you. You know you and I always manage to make a good wager. There was that two thousand guineas we shared when the Duchess of Marlborough didn't survive the Duchess of Cleveland...remember? It was strange fortune indeed that day; you'd needed a doctor y'self and it happened he'd come straight from her sick-bed. How are those old wounds?' she asked, prodding maternally at his arm through his jacket as though testing his fitness.

He allowed her ministrations for a moment before extricating his arm. 'Those are forgotten, Edwina. I've added a few more scratches since that have also healed well.'

Edwina shook her head and started a lecture on the necessity of early stitching that had barely begun before it was rudely interrupted.

'I've been searching for you, Lord Stratton. I thought we were to go elsewhere in search of a real drink...'

Ross looked about rather than responding to Edwina's fussing.

'I hadn't realised you were with your grandmama.' The young woman placed apologetic gloved fingers over her rouged mouth. 'Oh, dear, *is* she your grandmama?' Cecily Booth was lounging against the door frame, the candle flame behind clearly outlining her voluptuous figure beneath diaphanous voile.

Edwina squinted through the gloom at her firm, youthful face, guessing her to be barely twenty. But she *was* polished and confident—probably already had several years as a kept woman beneath her tiny belt. Glancing enquiringly at Ross, she saw he was laughing silently. Her scowl prompted him to give an easy shrug.

Striding regally for the door, Edwina glared at the young woman until she moved aside. 'Yes,' she purred, with curled top lip, 'I might be his grandmama. But what, pray, might you be, I wonder?' Thin, sooty eyebrows winged disdainfully. Her lips twitched in triumphant satisfaction as Cecily's mouth knotted into a rouged rosebud. Peering down her nose, Edwina turned with a sniff and a raised shoulder. 'I'll expect you tomorrow at seven then, Stratton. Don't be tardy. Reheating game makes it tough. A soufflé doesn't like to wait and neither do I.' With that she marched through the stuffy, crowded salon, barked at Evangeline to find her cloak, and within five minutes was hoisting herself with a footman's help back into her carriage.

Cecily peeked sulkily up at her lover. She angled her brunette head, and pouted at him. Ignored, she trailed a fingernail lightly back and forth on the lean dark hand resting idly on the iron balustrade. When he still gazed, starstruck, into the night, a possessive hand slipped through the crook of a muscular arm. 'Who was that fat lady, Ross?' she finally sighed.

'A good friend.' He drew on the stub of his cheroot, then sent it in an arc of glowing ash into the darkness.

'I told you yesterday evening that I was to be abroad today, Grandmama.'

'Yes…yes. Well, I forgot. It is important you are back to dine. We rarely have guests and today we do.'

'Do I know them?'

'Er…no. It is just the one guest. He is a…well-travelled gentleman. A friend of mine of some long standing who I've not seen in an age. We used to play cards and have a little flutter during the years you lived at Thorneycroft with your papa. You would not know him. As I say, he is…an adventurous gentleman who has sailed the seas and has tales to tell. Presently he is in great favour at court.'

Lady Elizabeth Rowe pulled on her gloves and straightened her bonnet over her smoky-blonde hair. 'Well, I dare say he has a deal more enthusiasm for your company than mine and will never miss me. It is good you are to see one of your old friends again. If we are early back from Bridewell, then I shall be happy to meet him.' She smiled at her grandmama, pleased that their tiff yesterday seemed forgotten. 'He sounds great fun…' she added amiably on wandering off to the window and pulling back the curtain. 'Oh, Hugh's gig is just arrived. I must hurry.'

Edwina followed, hot on her granddaughter's heels, into the hallway. 'Seven o'clock. Tell the Reverend I expect you home by that hour to dine with Viscount Stratton…'

Elizabeth skipped lightly down the stone steps and allowed Hugh Clemence to help her alight. He politely raised a leather-gloved hand at Edwina. She scowled back a greeting.

Elizabeth settled herself on the seat, then slid forward again. She indicatively shook the carpet bag she had dropped to the floor. 'Twenty pairs of knitted stockings, a roll of twill donated by Mrs Heathcote, four of my own woollen shawls and three quite serviceable kerseymere gowns that my grandmother is grown too large for.' Elizabeth gave him a sparkling amethyst look. 'She doesn't know I have purloined them, but she will never miss them. She believes she is the same size, but the dresses are shrunk from the laundry.'

Hugh Clemence's eyes lingered on her sculpted, ivory profile. 'Did Mrs Sampson mention Viscount Stratton? Or was I mistaken in hearing that name?'

Elizabeth's smooth brow puckered in a frown. 'No. I believe that is the name she mentioned. She tells me he is an old friend of hers who is to visit and dine later. He sounds rather an intriguing character!' At the protracted, crackling silence, Elizabeth studied her companion's twitching jawline. 'Is something wrong, Hugh?'

He forced a tiny, prim smile. 'No. I realise your grandmother is a little…eccentric in her ways and the company she keeps is at times a little…bizarre. I have to own to surprise, though, that she and the Viscount are acquainted.'

'Why?' Elizabeth asked with idle curiosity.

'He…he is a bachelor of a…a certain reputation, Elizabeth. Perhaps you might know of him better as Ross Trelawney. He has recently received honours from the crown. Did you not see it gazetted?'

Elizabeth frowned and shook her head. Then her eyes widened and she gave an incredulous little laugh. 'Not the Trelawney…the pirate? The Trelawney from Cornwall…who is always in some fight or scandal? The robber bandit?'

'A clan of marauding smugglers rather than pirates or bandits, I believe.' Hugh sniffed. 'Now, of course, he is fêted as a smuggler catcher and has recovered over the years for the crown some fortune in currency and contraband. It is why he has been ennobled. Dark deeds indeed have shrouded that man over many years…' he added ominously.

Elizabeth stared into space. 'It cannot be,' she muttered in a tone that harboured horror and humour. 'Why, I'm sure I heard a ridiculous tale that Ross Trelawney cut out a foe's liver and fried it for breakfast.'

'I think that's a little *too*…fictionalised an account of his villainy. But villain he is, without a doubt. And young ladies who cherish their virtue would be well advised to give he and his friends a very wide berth!' He reddened at his evangelical zeal, fiddled with the reins, then sent them undulating like leather snakes over the horses' backs. 'Don't make an ironic comment, Elizabeth, as to your own reputation,' he gently charged her. 'You know I judge a person by deeds. In my estimation, never was there a more virtuous and charitable lady than sits beside me now.'

Elizabeth smiled on a frown and turned her head. 'Thank you, Hugh. Now, please don't forget that Sophie is to join us later when she has finished attending the lecture on Nostradamus at the Taverners' Hall. I have said that she can travel home with us, if you have no objection.' But her mind was not on Sophie; or the Reverend's compliments, as he assured her he was more than happy to escort her friend home to her door. It wasn't even at Tothill with Bridewell and its wretched inmates. Time and again she ruminated on the intriguing possibility that, if it wasn't all a case of mistaken identity, her grandmother was intending to dine later with an infamous rogue. And she had said that he sounded fun!

If gossip was to be believed, the new Viscount Stratton was as hardened a rake as her worst enemy, the repulsive Earl of Cadmore. But whereas the Earl was a youngish dandy about town, Ross Trelawney rarely set foot in the metropolis and was more likely to feature in tales of far-flung places. Perhaps a coast in Kent or a port in Bristol. Or even on foreign shores. She believed it was in France, during the war, that he was rumoured to have dined on liver. She stuffed a fist in her mouth to stifle an hysterical giggle, wondering whether he'd managed to uproot a Gallic onion to make it more palatable. As Hugh said, it was too outlandish to be true.

But why was her grandmother keen for her to return and dine with a disreputable old sea dog she'd known for years? She gave a delicate shudder. He probably talked with his mouth full of food and guffawed at inappropriate moments, showering the table with peas or wine. And if he was anything like the portly Mr Hollyrood…! The noises emitted by that ancient gentleman over the canard a l'orange had been accompanied by such a sulphuric smell that Elizabeth had been forced to quit the room, pleading a migraine, for fear of bursting into very unladylike laughter in front of him.

If only half she had heard gossipped about Trelawney was true, he was hardly fitting company for a spinster of gentle birth. Her grandmother would enjoy his salty tales, of course: Edwina liked a little raucous talk.

Elizabeth had been so relieved when it seemed that there were to be no long silences, no frosty-faced looks from her grandmother following their quarrel yesterday. Perhaps something had occurred to sweeten her so quickly. She'd been known to sulk for three days following an altercation. *I want you settled*, her grandmother had stressed yesterday and with more finality in her tone than usual. Why was she seeking to introduce her to this old friend? A moment ago Hugh had said he was a bachelor. The reprobate was now a peer of the realm. Perhaps he was keen to complete the transformation from villain to gentleman by acquiring a high-born wife. Did his unsavoury history render him unnacceptable to respectable ladies of the *ton*? Despite his newly acquired title and lands, perhaps he was cold-shouldered by the *beau monde*. Perhaps

her grandmother believed he might be persuaded to settle for
a consort whose reputation was as sullied as his own.

Or perhaps she was just being ridiculous, she exhorted herself as she wriggled against the upholstery. The man was possibly as old as her grandmother. If he was a decade younger,
he would still be in his fifties and unlikely to be desperate to
saddle himself with a wife. Besides, he was a renowned rake
who probably had offspring scattered around the countryside.
He must like one well enough to nominate as his heir. With
that safe, inspiriting thought, she gave Hugh such a sweet
smile as made him almost swoon. Scrambling for his wits, he
madly shook the reins at the horses while clicking and clucking with his tongue at the startled animals.

'Wager you can keep him, then bribe him to stay on,' Ross
remarked, then sipped from his glass. 'That way you can recoup his bribe from your winnings if he agrees to go along
with it.'

'Yes. I considered doing that,' Edwina said waving a fork
full of pheasant at Ross. The meat soon disappeared and she
chewed and looked thoughtful. 'I'm sure that Pettifer would
not be averse to an early retirement gift. Problem is, Stratton,
that I've little cash I can quickly lay hands on. If I'm to keep
m'butler, and lay down some wagers that will wipe the floor
with that slut Penney, I've to act without delay. By the time
I've sold a little stock, that bitch will have made of me a
laughing stock. I need a fairly substantial amount... Have
some more red currant jelly,' she offered through a mouthful,
sending the silver sauceboat skating along the polished table.
'It's m'own recipe, fortified with a little orange liqueur.'

Ross arrested the flying dish and carefully positioned it by
the ornate candelabra. He glanced about the cosy, elegant dining room, wondering what odd fancy had prompted him to
do this old termagant's bidding and dine with her tonight.
True, the food could be relied upon to be excellent; true, Edwina was entertaining company. But so was Cecily, who had
the added advantage of being far easier on the eye, and she

could be relied upon to divert him over the dining table with
an altogether more sensual banquet. Instead, he was spending
a substantial part of the evening with a woman in her sixties
and suggesting ways and means for her to outwit her cronies
over some old cove they all fancied.

Perhaps he'd spent too long at court in George's company.
The King was renowned for favouring ampled-bodied mature
women, yet even he chose them a little less long in the tooth
and broad of beam. His own preference was for lively young
women who enjoyed a roistering good time as much as he
did and never grew possessive or tearful when he disappeared
to carouse elsewhere; which made his choice of current paramour rather an enigma. He smiled privately at his loaded
plate. Cecily liked slavish attention and lavish payment. In
return she was liberal with her body and her devotion. Although happy enough with the former, the latter was becoming tedious. He didn't want her to unexpectedly materialise at
his side every evening. He enjoyed being unattached while
with male friends and spare women and was growing irritated
at being constantly stalked.

He glanced at Edwina, to see her ladling more vegetables
onto her plate. He smiled. He'd come here this evening, he
realised, because he thrived on diversity. And there was something exceedingly diverse about a woman lacking in vanity
and at ease with her appetite, and him. There were no devious
games, no arch looks while hinting at putting commitment
into what he regarded as a casual liaison. No allusions to
trinkets favoured. No requests for cash so non-existent family
paupers could be saved from starving. Edwina wanted only
his company, his advice and a little reminiscing. And they
had aired some extremely amusing anecdotes over dinner. He
picked up his knife and fork again, feeling content and amiable. 'This is a fine house, Edwina. You don't look to be short
on blunt.'

Edwina shot him a hasty look. 'Oh, I'm not. Never better.
But I like my money accruing. Investments should be where
they can't easily be got. I'm charier than you, Stratton. I know

you've always a little on hand for those necessities of life which thrifty mortals like me class as luxuries. That's why I'm a little…er…embarrassed for liquid funds, right now…'

Ross smiled at the fire roaring away at one side of him. Then he laughed ruefully in comprehension. He'd been uncharacteristically naïve in congratulating himself on having found a female companion who wanted nothing from him. 'Edwina…why don't you just ask?' he drawled wryly.

'Twelve thousand…and you'll have it back within two weeks, plus a nice rate of interest,' she immediately responded, wiping her mouth with a snowy napkin and eyeing him shrewdly over it.

'Twelve thousand?!' he repeated slowly, in disbelief. 'I thought you wanted to keep your butler, not set him up in a residence with a staff and carriages of his own. Are you sweet on him, Edwina?'

Edwina flapped a dismissing hand, but couldn't prevent a girlish giggle. 'It's not all for him, you fool! Harry Pettifer would be as pleased as punch with a tenth of that amount. The balance is to be used wagering against Alice Penney…once I've contrived to convince her she's every chance of snatching Pettifer. Bertram Penney left her ten thousand a year and a sizeable estate in Surrey to go with that mansion in Mayfair and the townhouse in Brighton. She can afford to lose a little face…and a little cash…and deserves to.'

Ross leaned back in his chair, raised his glass to his lips and looked at Edwina over the rim. She was aware of his perusal despite her eyes being fixed on her busy cutlery, and fidgeted beneath his calculating gaze.

Ross studied her thoughtfully. He had been expecting some stout, plain young woman to be blushing and giggling at table while they ate. Since his peerage had been gazetted, it seemed he couldn't venture out of the house without some matron trailing a younger version of herself, accosting him on street corners, reminding him of some short acquaintance they'd enjoyed years previously. In this instance it seemed his fears for his bachelorhood were unfounded. 'Where is your grand-daughter this evening?' he asked idly.

Edwina choked, thumped herself on the breastbone. Damn! She'd been confident he had forgot! It was only when rumi-nating on her strategies an hour before his arrival, that she realised she wished she'd never mentioned dear Lizzie to him at all. And she was also hoping her headstrong granddaughter wouldn't have an uncharacteristic fit of meekness and rush home to obediently join them at dinner. If she stayed out late this evening it would be a blessing. Things had been going so well... Now he looked...too cynical. And this wasn't a man you played for a fool...

'Oh, she's off doing good deeds,' Edwina gasped, still ham-mering at her ample chest, making the satin undulate. 'No interest in anything else, don't you know. Spends all her time with bores and vicars. You wouldn't like her,' she dismissed with screwed-up face and wrinkled nose. 'Now don't change the subject, Stratton. You owe me a favour. There was that time I paid your marker at Almack's when you were fifteen hundred down and due to be carted to the Fleet. Then there was that other time when I took your place for over an hour while you disappeared for a snooze. You'd sat at that gaming table all night and couldn't keep your eyes open, let alone your credit.'

'All right...I give in.' Ross laughed. 'What the hell? It's only money. But ten thousand tops and for just two weeks,' he said soberly. 'I can no longer afford to be as liberal as I might have been. I've a cash-eating country estate to restore and a few dependants. You aren't the only one with old re-tainers to keep happy, Edwina. Stratton Hall's also saddled with the quaint aspect of allowing one to stargaze from the comfort of one's bed. I'd guess the roof hasn't had a full set of slates for almost a decade.'

'Well, make a little side bet with me and you can buy your roof out of your winnings. Come, you know I'm good for the money,' Edwina purred persuasively. 'We've known each other some fifteen years. When you were first in London as

a callow youth, I took to you at once…treated you as my own
kin. I would have liked a grandson. Still would…' she rumbled to herself. 'Even at eighteen you could charm the birds
from the trees,' Edwina chattered on.

'I remember you were good to me, Edwina,' Ross said on
a smile. 'That's why I'll lend you the cash. Send your man
to Jacey's in Lombard Street tomorrow and he can collect a
contract for signature.'

'A contract?' Edwina barked. 'Don't you trust this old
friend who once saved your miserable young hide from a rat-
infested cell in the Fleet?'

'Of course I do, Edwina,' Ross smoothly said, dazzling her
with his fabled charming smile. 'For I've a notion you've no
liking for the Fleet any more than I, and would hate our
friendship to founder at such an establishment should things
turn awry. The contract is as much for your benefit: I might
come to my senses and try to renege on such lunatic generosity.'

Elizabeth put down her teacup and glanced at the clock on
the wall. It was approaching nine-thirty and she was tired and
ready to leave this little gathering of members of the Society
of Friends. Following their weekly visits to Tothill Fields, the
members who'd attended the correctional institute for women
and children usually congregated at Mrs Martin's residence
for light refreshments and earnest debate. Usually the lively
talk held her attention. Tonight she had barely contributed a
word.

The whole afternoon and evening had been dominated by
her fascination with Viscount Stratton. She'd seen pictures in
books of dark-visaged men with tangled, dusky locks and
wicked grins. Did he sport a gold earring or a gold tooth,
from his smuggling days? Or keep a parrot and a monkey as
pets? Part of her wanted to rush home now, and find out, and
part of her wanted to linger here as long as possible, lest she
returned too soon, and did.

Hugh intercepted her next glance at the clock as it chimed

the half-hour. He inclined towards her. 'Are you ready to leave, Elizabeth?'

She smiled and sent Sophie a meaningful look. Her friend understood the signal and nodded. Elizabeth had decided. She *did* want a glimpse of this intriguing scoundrel. Perhaps, if they were back in Marylebone before ten, he might still be at her grandmother's house. After all, from past experience, she knew that Edwina's guests could linger over some score or more dishes.

'What's your opinion on the usefulness of the treadmill as a deterrent for felons, Elizabeth?' Hugh Clemence conversationally enquired as they jogged along. They had five minutes ago dropped Sophie off at her home in Perman Street and were now making good time past the new gas lamps towards Connaught Street, where Elizabeth lived.

'It's a soul-destroying contraption,' she opined at once. 'When used to grind corn or draw water, I suppose it gives some purpose to the discipline; but to make the poor wretches step it simply to beat the air! What a stupid and inhuman exercise! It's more likely to produce bitter recidivists than reformed characters…' Her words tailed off. Hugh's gig had turned into Connaught Street and her stomach fluttered excitedly as she noticed that fine matched greys were approaching along the street at the head of an elegant carriage.

Hugh was agreeing with some of her comments and tendering his own but she was barely listening, for within that glossy coach might be… The horses drew level and, heart pumping exceedingly slowly, she slanted a wide-eyed violet glance from beneath her bonnet brim at the carriage window.

She had the impression of staring at the top of an ebony head. A flare of a match illuminated a cupped hand and a cigar pointing towards it. A hard lean profile was momentarily gilded by sulphurous light, and strands of hair slipped forward to soften a strong jaw and planed cheekbone. Abruptly the man's head snapped back with an inherent shake that took the obscuring locks away from his features. A slash of white teeth were visible, clenching on the newly lit cheroot, then his sensual mouth moulded around it. Aware of the gig, his idle glance strayed sideways, skimming casually as he extinguished the match with a hand flick. A second too late he was aware of glossy wide eyes and whitish curls peeping from a dark bonnet. His eyes ricocheted back, but the vehicles had passed.

Chapter Three

'What on earth is up, m'dear? You look positively peeky,' Edwina exclaimed, looking up from her novel. 'You really must stop visiting the prisons, Lizzie. I swear you look more forlorn each time you return. And I go in fear of the gaol fever creeping within these doors…or the lice.' A shudder undulated her purple satin bosom.

'Has Viscount Stratton just left?' burst from Elizabeth as she snatched her bonnet from her dishevelled fair hair and paced back and forth.

Edwina looked curiously at her. 'Yes, not more than a few minutes since. You have just missed him.' Relief lilted her tone at that realisation. 'The dinner was fine; Stratton enjoyed it…'

'What age is he?' Elizabeth interrogated. 'You said you had a long-standing acquaintance. I imagined him to be old…as old as you.'

'Why, thank you for making me sound a veritable decrepit dodderer,' Edwina huffed drily. Discarding her novel on the sidetable, she absently picked over pieces of marchpane in the silver filigree dish. 'I have known him some fifteen years, but he was probably only eighteen or nineteen when first we met. He ought to have been sent down, you know. He was hardly scholarly…always gallivanting…' She frowned at her restless granddaughter. 'Do stand still, Lizzie! You're turning me giddy, wheeling about like that. Why are you so concerned about any of it?' A knowing glint narrowed her eyes. 'You caught sight of him in the street, didn't you? Handsome devil, is he not? Is that what's vexing you? You're now wishing you'd forgone that whey-faced vicar's company and dined at home? Well, you're not the first young woman to be overset by his good looks. With my own eyes, I've seen shameless hussies in a pretended swoon at his feet just so he might pick them up.'

Elizabeth's violet eyes flashed at her grandmother, her colour heightening. 'I am overset, Grandmama, because you were half-right in your description of *his Lordship*! By all accounts, he is, indeed, a devil. Even I, out of circulation for so long, have heard gossip of Ross Trelawney. You conveniently omitted to mention that he and Viscount Stratton are one and the same. Hugh Clemence told me and was as shocked as I that you would know such an individual, let alone invite him to dine with us.'

Edwina flapped a dismissive hand. 'Don't be priggish, Lizzie. Do you think I give a fig for that milksop clergyman's opinion? Do you think Stratton would care?' A shrewd glance at her granddaughter preceded her declaring, 'You're showing a deal of interest in a man you've only ever heard tattled over and only ever glimpsed in passing. Did he see you?' she demanded.

'No…I don't know.' Elizabeth was flustered, still pacing about. 'It was dark and the vehicles had passed so quickly. He might have glanced my way, I think.'

'Good,' Edwina muttered to herself with some satisfaction.

Elizabeth slanted a frown at her grandmother. 'From what I could distinguish of him in the half-light, he resembles a Romany…a heathen. Which is what he is, by all accounts.'

'He has dark colouring, it's true. But he's not unattractively swarthy. And never fret over all those ludicrous tales of marauding on the high seas and eating Frenchies' offal and so on,' Edwina scoffed through a sweetmeat. 'Now he's so sought after by the *ton* I expect there'll be more wonderfully concocted fables of his warrior habits: maidens in distress either spoiled by his virile lust or saved on a romantic whim. He won't bother denying any of it. I think, beneath that cool, detached air he has, he deems it all faintly amusing.' Edwina grinned widely. 'Besides, now he's the King's favourite and so eligible, he could spitroast a street urchin for his dinner in Pall Mall and still be invited to Lady Conyngham's ball. If he bothers to attend, he must bring along his cane…to beat off the petticoat set.'

'I don't see anything amusing in it,' Elizabeth admonished tightly, fingers dragging through her thick, pearly hair. 'Wretched street urchins are not a case for banter. And there's always a grain of truth in gossip.'

'You of all people should know that's not necessarily so, miss!' Edwina brusquely reminded her granddaughter. Noting Elizabeth's wince and flush, she gestured apology with a plump hand. 'Stratton was good enough to ask after you,' she added, with every intention of alleviating the tension.

'*Me?* He doesn't know me!' Elizabeth squeaked in protest, renewed agitation sending her in another turn about the room. Inwardly she prayed, *Please don't let such a man know of me or my misfortune, especially if he's going to be a regular visitor to Connaught Street. I receive more than enough lecherous looks and whispered propositions from Cadmore as it is.*

'I told Ross I now live with m'granddaughter and he politely enquired after you. He is cultured and mannerly.'

'He is a rogue, Grandmama, and well you know it.'

'Rogue, maybe, but he's a gentleman too. He has excellent connections. His eldest brother is a baron and has a large estate in Brighton. His father amassed a vast acreage in Cornwall which another brother now administers. They have business interests embracing mining and shipping and banking which extend the globe. They are an exceedingly wealthy and influential family who are on good terms with other important aristocrats. Sir Richard Du Quesne and Lord Courtenay are but two of his close friends and business associates. Ross courts danger and excitement from choice, not financial necessity.'

'In that case, Grandmama,' Elizabeth stressed quietly, 'surely it behoves us to studiously avoid the company of such a madman.'

Their conversation ceased as Harry Pettifer entered and bowed. 'Excuse me, madam; may I lock and bolt now that Lady Elizabeth is home?'

'Ah…indeed,' Edwina said, a little flustered. 'And, Pettifer…'

Harry Pettifer pivoted politely, poker straight.

'I should like to speak with you before you retire—' Edwina broke off to bid her granddaughter good night as Elizabeth pecked her cheek and informed that she was ready for a warm bath and a soft bed. As the door closed behind Elizabeth, Edwina shifted her purple satin bulk in her chair and looked up at the tall, imposing man standing close by. He seemed relaxed, yet she had stiffened with tension while fiddling with small buttons on her cuffs, and it needled her. She forced her fingers still. 'Am I right in thinking I've treated you fairly over many, many years?' she burst out.

'Indeed, madam,' Harry Pettifer replied, inclining his pewter head.

Edwina stared at him, hoping he would contribute more. He didn't, merely watched her with a clear, untroubled gaze. But amusement lurked far back in his bright blue eyes, she was certain. She shifted again in her seat. The silence protracted. 'Are you perhaps keen to discover if the grass grows greener in Sussex?' she hinted, irritated by his composure and how stately he looked: all grey and black and rigid-backed. She bit her tongue to prevent herself simply snapping out that she knew he was planning to quit.

'Would you like me to tell you whether I intend to take up Mrs Penney's offer of employment at her Brighton town-house? Or accept a similar offer from Mrs De Vere or Lady Salisbury?' he blandly offered.

'You know dam' well I would,' Edwina gritted through her teeth, abandoning any attempt at nonchalance. Flinging herself against the chairback, she grabbed a handful of sweetmeats and chewed ferociously.

Harry inspected his immaculate shoes. His mouth twitched. Then his eyes levelled on his fiery-faced employer.

'I have not yet responded to those ladies' offers, but I have little desire to…er…investigate the shade of turf outside London,' he said solemnly.

'Why not?' She eyed him suspiciously. 'I know, without you telling me, all those…*ladies*—' she spat on a sneer '—have offered you more than I pay you.'

'Money isn't the first consideration, at my time of life. I have adequate funds for my needs, and a little to spare. I have no wish to leave Lady Elizabeth…or you.'

Finished with the sweetmeats, Edwina chewed her full lower lip, eyeing him thoughtfully. 'You have a deal of fondness for Lizzie. I've noticed a rapport strengthening between you the few years she's lived with us. You would spoil her as a child when she visited with her papa: bring her titbits from the kitchens.'

Harry Pettifer bowed his head. 'As you say. I have a great fondness for Lady Elizabeth…and her family,' he added quietly. 'I have been employed by Sampsons for a long while now. I believed you deemed me loyal.'

Edwina fidgeted and grew hot at the gracious reproof. A finger commenced twirling absently in the silver dish. She suddenly lifted the bowl and proffered it, by way of reparation. 'Have a sweet,' she said, shaking the dish. 'Come… take one…' she cajoled with a coy smile.

Harry Pettifer approached and his long, patrician fingers selected a small piece of marchpane. Edwina watched as he carefully chewed.

'It seems to me, Pettifer, we both want the best for Lady Elizabeth. I imagine you, as much as I, would like to see her happily settled, before we are grown too crotchety to hug her children. She is in her twenty-ninth year, you know, and no nearer to swallowing her pride and socialising properly than she was immediately after the…um…delicate situation.'

'I understand the predicament, madam. Lady Elizabeth, I think, is proud. And not without reason. She is of noble birth and character. Of course I crave to see her happy.'

'You think she's not happy?' Edwina pounced.

'I think she is at times a little…wistful,' Harry said, choosing his words carefully.

Edwina nodded slowly, eyeing him thoughtfully. 'Yes…wistful…that's it. It is time she was wed…not wistful.'

'I heartily concur, madam. Lady Elizabeth would make some fortunate gentleman an excellent wife.'

'And children would never find a better mother,' Edwina added. 'She has a lot of affection going begging. Succouring waifs and strays is no substitute for having a husband and children to love. Mayhap she just needs a little nudge in the right direction…to realise it.'

'I think those are very wise words, madam. My sentiments exactly,' Harry said, emphasising his approval with a movement of his steely head.

Edwina's flushed visage cocked to one side; she watched her plump fingers pleating the satin of her skirt. 'It was nice to see Trelawney again after such a long absence, don't you think?'

'Indeed, I do, madam. In all the years I have welcomed that gentleman into your houses, he has never grown too coarse or too fine to speak to me and ask how I do. To my mind, Viscount Stratton is an altogether grand fellow, for I always judge as I find.'

'I think those are very wise words, Pettifer. My sentiments, exactly,' Edwina said, an affable look slanting from beneath her lashes at him. 'It seems we share a deal of common sense where m'granddaughter and the Viscount are concerned. I wonder if there's a way in which both might benefit from it?'

*   *   *

It was when her grandmother described him as cool and detached, yet given to a latent amusement, that something far, far back in her mind started to stir.

Relaxing back into warm, scented bathwater, Lady Elizabeth Rowe allowed corners of banished memories to pierce her consciousness. People…events…conversations…trickled in, pulled together to surface from a deep well of pain.

Agitated, she pushed jerkily upright, causing the towel turbanning her newly washed hair to unwrap and flop into the tub. Tutting impatience, she wrung it out, then dropped it onto the mat while her loose topknot of damp platinum hair uncoiled. Her creamy, narrow back and firm rose-tipped breasts were soon screened by sleek pale tresses falling to float on soapy water.

A decade ago, during a summer that had seemed unremittingly hot and humid from the months of May to September, she, her beloved papa and her grandmother Rowe had moved to London. Her maternal grandmother and paternal grandmother detested each other in equal part, so Edwina Sampson had immediately removed herself from the City to avoid breathing the same air as the Dowager Marchioness, and spent the summer in Harrogate with her sister.

On her eighteenth birthday, in May of that year, Elizabeth was presented at court and thus began the most memorable, the most thrilling, the most devastating period of her young life. But in May, when all was heady excitement, and all she and her dear papa rued was that her mother hadn't survived to see her looking so blissful and beautiful, it seemed that nothing could mar the utopia. She was blessed with everything any young lady could want: beauty, vivacity and an indulgent and doting parent.

A popular debutante, the daughter of a Marquess, a descendant of one of the noblest, if no longer the wealthiest dynasties in the land, gentlemen had vied for her favours, sighing that her silky silver hair and violet eyes were incomparable. She was that season's rage. Constantly besieged by gay, modish acquaintances gathering at her father's Mayfair townhouse, constantly plied with invitations to the most lavish balls, the smartest soirées, she had attracted the attention of many eligible partners: one duke, two earls and three baronets. In all, nine and a half offers of marriage were forthcoming in one month. The half, her sweet papa had gently joked, was from one blushing young admirer who, having stuttered and suffered through an earnest speech praising Elizabeth's loveliness, had then stumbled away, too embarrassed to deliver his proposal.

With youthful vanity and an arrogance borne of her spoiled and privileged upbringing, Lady Elizabeth Rowe had flirted a little with each devoted beau, broken at least a half-dozen hearts and deemed it all so trivial and amusing, for secretly she had made her choice within a month of arriving in London. Despite the Dowager Marchioness's eagle-eyed vigilance and chaperonage, Elizabeth had fallen madly in love. With all the naïve idealism of youth, she was adamant trusting to her heart must be the only right way.

The man she'd loved had not been *a catch*. He had impressed upon her that her relatives would tell her so, and that, ergo, they must proceed stealthily. Blinded by infatuation, buoyed by the self-assurance of her youth and inexperience, she'd entered into the spirit of the romantic adventure, oblivious to the havoc her behaviour might wreak. She chose badly, acted rashly, tasted a little of her own medicine. But what really hurt was that in the doing of it she'd shattered and shamed her papa, besmirched his illustrious name and broken his heart. That she had degraded herself beyond redemption, too, seemed of less consequence in the face of her beloved father's despair.

She tossed her head aside, clamping shut her eyes, not wanting the sorrow to knife her insides. She forced her concentration to another man instead. A tall gentleman with hard, dark features who had never figured amongst her languishing suitors, but he did figure in her memories. They had never spoken but she had espied him during that sultry summer.

Roistering on the fringes of the ton were young rakehells: Corinthians who mostly shunned conventional socialising in favour of their own riotous assemblies. They rarely bothered entering Almack's stately portals where a marriage mart took place under the guise of fusty regimented assemblies. Neither were they lured by lavish balls arranged by fond mamas with nubile daughters and an ulterior motive in mind. If they did deign to show at such insipid venues, within an hour or so of arriving, they were gone in search of more bacchanalian entertainment. Arrogant and affluent, their spendthrift ways were legendary. Gambling large amounts of money on a whim was rife. Bets of hundreds of pounds might be made on the most ridiculous eventualities: whether a drunk would fall before he reached the end of the street. If he did, whether he would topple forward or backward. Whether an acquaintance with pockets to let would pawn his silver ice pails, or sell on his Spanish mistress. Those were just a few of the outrageous wagers that she could recall.

Apart from the customary sporting activities of fencing and boxing at Gentleman Jackson's, more hazardous pursuits drew them: racing high-flyer phaetons had resulted in the death or maiming of more than a few daring young bucks. Duelling over the favours of immoral women—whom genteel young debutantes such as she would never have acknowledged existed—had taken several others…either to the grave or to a sojourn abroad until the scandal died away.

An especial amusement of younger sons with no stately pile or peerage to polish was the sorrowful sight of impecunious heirs found planted amongst the pillars in Almack's, loitering to barter a title for a fortune and perhaps buy back freedom and licentiousness with a dowered bride. Elizabeth recalled thinking that marriage to such a selfish debauchée must be hell. And when her thoughts ran that way, the enigmatic man with a rugged, gypsy visage and long chestnut hair had dominated her mind. Languour hooded his hazel eyes, yet his muscular physique was testament to a regime of regular, punishing exercise.

Indolent amusement had hovered on his hard, handsome features when he glanced at her and her friends. But then he did so rarely, for he was in demand elsewhere. On the few occasions fate had manoeuvred them close, he had seemed insolently unmoved by her blonde beauty and petite sensual figure hemmed by a throng of fawning admirers.

Once or twice as she'd sneaked a fascinated peek through seething humanity at that group of distinguished men and their exuberant female companions, her amethyst eyes had tangled with his. Captured, held fast, she recalled how his golden-glinting mockery had burned. Flustered, she would eventually drag her eyes away, feverishly indignant that he dared laugh at her. Yet, piqued, too, that he didn't notice her more often.

Since she had turned fifteen and her chubby body began dipping and curving in exactly the right places, she had come to realise that men liked to look at her. In her naïveté, she had revelled in the power her femininity bestowed. At eighteen, her face shed its youthful plumpness, and wide-honed cheekbones sculpted her countenance to a symmetrical, classical loveliness. Her blue eyes deepened to violet, her lashes and eyebrows darkened, while her hair retained its light pearly sheen. It was as though time and nature had conspired to perfect her looks in readiness for her first outing in society.

Even strangers told her she was beautiful. She already knew it…and used it. She'd enjoyed knowing that male eyes followed her when she left a room, then observed her return. She'd been amused by the compliments, by the gifts, by the constant attention, and had fostered it. But it wasn't until it was too late that she had understood that male interest could be dangerous as well as gratifying, and her gentle birth and innocence was no guarantee of kindness or respect. Now when men sidled looks at her, her chin might tilt, but it was in undefeated pride, not vanity. Once she might coquettishly have sought eye contact with an admirer—now she studiously avoided it. What had unsettled her so this evening was the momentary glint of interest that had whipped Ross Trelawney's eyes back to hers as their carriages passed. Yet, if truthful, she couldn't deny she'd hoped to catch his eye…

Elizabeth sank lower in her bath, drank in the soothing scent of the lavender-scented water as she dwelt on the memory of a less-menacing man: Guy Markham had kept company with that wild set. His father, Sir Clive, had been her papa's friend. The baronet would often grumble to the Marquess that he feared his heir would turn out bad because of the company he kept. She wondered what Guy Markham might be doing now. She had quite liked him. On the few occasions she had met him through their fathers' friendship, he had seemed civil and amiable. Now that she was out of circulation she had no idea, nor did she care, what occurred in the *beau monde*. She imagined Guy to be much as he ever was, for she knew from her grandmother's casual chatter as to what went on that Sir Clive was still enjoying robust health and seemed unlikely to relinquish his baronetcy yet awhile.

Her thoughts veered, unbidden, back to Viscount Stratton. Never once had she made the association between him and the scandalous rogue, Ross Trelawney, whom the gossiping matrons used to whisper about. Perhaps if her come-out had not been curtailed, fate might eventually have remedied that…

'You should allow me to do that for you, my lord.'

Ross half-smiled. 'If there's one person I would allow to hold a blade to my throat, it would be you, Henderson,' he told his valet as, slowly, he drew a razor carefully up the column of tanned neck to his square, shady jaw. He dipped the soap-edged steel into warm water, then angled his head and proceeded to shave the other side, his eyes on the mirror. At a gruff laugh, Ross's eyes strayed to another man's reflection.

Guy Markham was standing by the window of the dressing room, shaking his head in amused disbelief as he observed an entertaining spectacle in the street below. Moments ago a pickpocket had caused havoc by fleeing straight across the path of an elderly gentleman. Having overset that man, who in turn accidentally brought a matron to her knees, the lad, now sure he was free and clear, had turned and was making an exceedingly lewd and triumphant gesture. Having given chase for two yards and decided the sport too arduous, the fallen woman's companion instead began shaking his cane at the taunting, dirty-faced urchin. The gentleman on the floor was rolling about clutching a leg, the tumbled matron was trying to preserve her modesty by rearranging her skirts, and the lady who had been robbed of her reticule, but managed to keep to her feet, was prancing on the spot and squealing, red-faced, for assistance from any who would listen. And it did seem that the majority of Grosvenor Square's residents were a captive audience: people were either craning from windows or emerging onto elegant front steps to investigate the hullabaloo.

Ross glanced at his friend's profile as Guy's head tipped back and he guffawed at the ceiling. 'Did he get clean away?'

Guy grimaced disappointment through his smile. 'I'm afraid so…'

Ross continued shaving with one hand, his other extended meaningfully.

Guy stepped away from the window and, having foraged in a pocket, dropped a note into his comrade's damp palm.

The bank note was deposited on the dressing table and Ross's attention returned to his toilet. 'I think I'll take a place in Cheapside,' he mentioned drily, swirling the razor in water again. 'I've paid a premium for a salubrious address and genteel neighbours and what do I get? Daylight robbery. Dockside manners.'

Guy returned to the window to watch the injured parties hobbling away, no doubt in search of a Bow Street runner.

'I bow to your superior knowledge of daylight robbery and dockside manners, Stratton,' Guy chuckled.

Henderson was still hovering behind his master, dipping this way and that in time with the blade's movement as he judged Ross's dexterity with the razor.

'A close shave is much appreciated by the fair sex,' Guy informed the limber valet with a suggestive wink and a nod at his friend. Henderson responded to this piece of information with a sniff and an extremely old-fashioned look. He straightened his back and shoulders, stalked to the four-poster bed and busied himself with extricating discarded shirts and breeches from amongst the blankets.

Guy took out his pocket watch. 'Well, it's after noon. Speaking of the fair sex: I imagine the delectable Miss Booth might be even now loitering outside. You've been out of her clutches some twelve hours,' he warned Ross of his young mistress's increasingly determined pursuit.

Ross examined his lean features in the mirror. His angular, clefted chin rested in the fork of a hand as long fingers and a stroking thumb tested the smoothness of his skin. He raised his eyes to his friend's laughing expression. 'Sit down,' he ordered, as he pushed himself to his feet and dried his face with a towel. 'Maybe it's time I gave you an equally close shave. It might help you do better than last night's lanky strumpet.'

Guy put out two defensive hands. 'No, thanks; I'll stick with last night's strumpet, and stubble.' A hand wiped across his bristly jaw as he moaned, 'God, I'm ravenous. My belly's complaining my throat's been cut and I've been nowhere near a razor.'

'Toast…crumpets…tea?' Henderson offered over a starchy black shoulder.

'Yes, thank you, Henderson,' Guy Markham enthused, rubbing his hands together and smiling as his stomach loudly endorsed its ability to do justice to the breakfast selection.

With his long, dark fingers busy at his neck folding a sepia silk cravat, Ross strolled to the window and looked out over

Grosvenor Square's resumed gentility. Smart vehicles thronged the street, people strolled and a few liveried servants could be seen weaving busily between the gentry. To a newcomer, the fracas a moment ago would seem unimaginable.

Ross inwardly sorted through his business affairs. There were several matters to finalise before he journeyed later to Kent; several messages to relay: Luke and Rebecca were bringing his mother to London to visit and wanted confirmation from him that it was convenient to arrive this week. A few good friends were also soon due in London, keen to personally congratulate him on his elevation to the peerage. It was incumbent on him to throw some sort of celebratory party for them all, he supposed. His younger sister Katherine had written to say she wouldn't be travelling to London because she was still confined after the birth of her son. But he was to be godfather. Yet possibly what occupied him most was that a fortnight had passed and no repayment had been forthcoming from Edwina Sampson.

Before he left for Stratton Hall it would be prudent to pay her a visit and remind her of her contractual obligations regarding his loan. Not that he wanted to harrass her; but commencing restoration of his very own stately pile was a pressing concern. Besides, he smiled inwardly, he was still intrigued to know the identity of the blonde who had been peeking at him as she passed in that rickety gig. He'd caught a brief glimpse of the man beside her: he'd looked like clergy. It would be his luck to lust after a vicar's wife…or daughter. He hadn't seen enough of the man to guess his age. Perhaps they were neighbours of Edwina's. It might be interesting finding out, especially as something in her shy stare had seemed to stir memories…

'White's or Watier's?' he asked Guy while shrugging into the tan tailcoat his valet had laid out. He was adjusting spotless cambric cuffs just as Henderson reappeared with a silver salver rather than the breakfast tray he had been expecting.

'Watier's…the food's better,' Guy decided, having given the matter a moment's thought.

'Are you attending Maria's rout later? She's promised the comely Clarke sisters are to be there. I imagine the King's favourite contraband-catcher might do rather well with one or t'other…or both. If you can escape Cecily's eagle eye, you're guaranteed a pleasurable evening. You could travel to Kent in the morning.'

Ross shook his head. 'No, I want to reach Stratton Hall this afternoon. There's an architect I've to see…' he muttered in explanation, taking the letter Henderson was proffering on the salver.

Guy frowned at him. 'You're becoming a building bore, Ross. You sound like my father. Renovate this wing…pave that terrace…sweep those chimneys… You'll be holding forth on cooking ranges or roof pitches next.'

'Well, when it's all yours, you'll know why,' Ross said with a grin.

As Ross turned his attention to the missive and broke the seal, his valet cocked his head as though he would read it too. Green-flecked hazel eyes levelled at the servant. 'Thank you, Henderson,' Ross said, mildly amused at the man's inquisitiveness. 'You may organise breakfast. A pot of coffee, too, if you please.'

Henderson pulled a supercilious long face on turning for the door.

Guy settled himself before the dressing mirror and, unwinding his canary-yellow cravat, picked up the razor.

Ross strolled back to the window to read his letter. Seeing the elegantly scripted address at the top of the parchment, he smiled. Trust Edwina to come good before he needed to chivvy her about the loan. She'd been a good friend and a good business partner on occasion. He had owed the old harridan a favour or two and had felt obliged to help her out. But he knew she could be trusted…

It was some moments later that the silence made Guy stop shaving and look curiously at his friend. Ross was staring at the letter, his face an inscrutable, granite mask. Slowly, he crushed the paper in a powerful hand. His lips strained back against his teeth, then formed an inaudible blasphemy.

'Bad news?' Guy asked quietly, the razor poised over lathered skin.

'Bad move...' Ross said softly with a smile that chilled his friend. 'Very bad move, Edwina,' Ross expanded on a humourless laugh and, leaving Guy staring after him, quit the room.

Chapter Four

'Calm yourself, Mrs Sampson…there is no need for panic.'

'Calm myself! No need for panic!' Edwina parroted in a hiss. 'M'granddaughter shouted at me not two hours since that she never again wants to see me…doesn't give a fig if I end in the Fleet catching rats for m'dinner! Loathed by m'own flesh and blood and after I've taken her in and boarded her these past few years when that sour-faced bitch turned her out. And now Trelawney is come and you say he has a face like thunder! It is all gone awry! How can I be calm?'

'You must expect Lady Elizabeth to be overset at first, she is…independent…strong-willed. Such news would naturally come as a shock. And I described the Viscount as thunderous, not thunder-faced; there is a subtle difference. Outwardly he appears unperturbed, but inwardly…ah…inwardly he is turbulent,' Harry opined with a nod, his customary reserve lost to admiration. 'I must say he conceals his anger exceedingly well. There was some coolness in his request to know how I do today.'

Edwina stared at her manservant, recognising again the wry humour lurking in his eyes. 'It is not a matter for jest!' she snapped testily. 'I am in a tizz over whether I am a fit grandmother. Dearest Lizzie has no other close kin, apart from the hag of a Dowager Marchioness and her little stepbrother who can do her no good turn as he is but seven years old. Perhaps

I should not have meddled, but let well alone. What if Lizzie never forgives me? I might get notice to quit before it all comes right! What if Stratton rejects her? Oh, what will I do then?' She whirled about, displaying some stamina as she marched away, then speedily stomped straight back. 'And do you realise what sort of man we are dealing with? This is not a fool to be trifled with. Oh, no! And now I have forgot what I must say to him.' She flapped a hand and, eyes closed, waddled around in a circle, rehearsing inaudible lines.

'Of course he is not a fool. He is a fine fellow: a lesser man might be making matchwood of your stair spindles, instead of demolishing his shoe leather in the hallway. Lord Stratton must have covered a mile over marble since arriving. Yet still he remains self-possessed. It should greatly reassure you that, if all goes to plan, Lady Elizabeth's future well-being is entrusted to worthy hands.'

'Do you imagine I would have risked her to anything less?' Edwina squealed, puce-faced.

'No, of course not, my dear. Calm yourself, please,' Harry Pettifer soothed. To obscure the casual endearment, he pressed on steadily, 'I simply congratulate your choice. But you must have expected that the Viscount would be…miffed, on receiving your note.'

'*Miffed?* You think Trelawney is *miffed* to discover he cannot have back his ten thousand pounds and a little extra? I think the Viscount, self-possessed or no, is a deal more than *miffed* with me,' Edwina emphasised, bulge-eyed. 'And so is m'granddaughter! My sweet, dear Lizzie is fair spitting mad. Are you sure her chamber door is secure?' she demanded, prowling the cosy drawing room searching surfaces for a dish of sweetmeats. Finding none, she resorted to chewing on a fingernail. 'If she should bolt to that vicar, she'll wed him just to spite me. But…I shouldn't have done it. Locking her in her room like a naughty schoolgirl will guarantee a fit of the sulks.'

Abruptly she ceased perambulating and summarised matter-of-factly, 'Lady Elizabeth has long needed to be properly settled. All this loitering in slums and prisons makes her vulnerable, as does her…unlucky past. Cadmore sent another letter only last week. I wish to heaven I had managed to intercept it. But she had received the post on her way out to meet Sophie. If I was younger I'd shoot the blackguard down dead! She needs a man to care for her. A man other fellows respect and will not dare cross. I can't imagine any man…unless he is moonstruck…attempting to cuckold Stratton, can you?'

Edwina received a smile and gesture of absolute agreement. 'Just for a moment I s'pose m'nerves had the better of me. It is all too late for second thoughts, anyhow. The deed is done; and done for Lady Elizabeth's own good. Should I turn up m'toes impecunious, she'll never need to beg a living from that miserly crone of a Dowager Marchioness, or her vinegar-faced daughter-in-law. Stepmother to Lizzie?' She snorted in disgust. 'She's never shown the dear girl a jot of affection. So, I must set to, rally m'courage and cut this crazy babbling…'

'I'm happy to hear that, Mrs Sampson,' drawled a voice from the doorway. 'I'll admit I was beginning to fear for your sanity, too, when I received your letter. My apologies for the intrusion, but I find myself a little pushed for time. I think we should…*set to*…right now,' was added in a deceptively mild tone that brooked no refusal.

Edwina smoothed her skirts, then strained her generous lips into a welcoming smile. 'Come in…come in, Stratton. Good of you to respond to m'note so quickly. Tea, Pettifer,' she ordered with a hand flick. 'And don't be tardy. You heard the Viscount: he is a busy man and must fly off before he is properly arrived.'

Harry Pettifer arrowed a glance at the tall, imposing man just inside the door. The Viscount's narrowed hazel eyes were most definitely upon him, too. An almost imperceptible movement of Ross's dark head acknowledged the butler's neat bow.

'Oh, and Pettifer…' Edwina said casually. 'Don't forget you were to attend to m'granddaughter…'

Harry Pettifer inclined his head, tacitly indicating that nothing had slipped his mind.

Elizabeth yanked at the door again. She rattled at the knob, peered into the keyhole, then banged angrily on the panels with two small fists. After a moment spent glaring at the wood she turned, marched back into the room, her blonde head flung back, and closed her eyes, trying to calm herself. It wasn't her grandmother's fault…was the mantra that echoed in her aching head. She must not blame Edwina. In her own idiotic way no doubt the woman truly believed she was securing her a nice future. Her grandmother must have been swayed by that…Elizabeth's soft lip curled into a sneer, her violet eyes glittered…*roguish gentleman,* as Edwina was wont to quixotically term him.

Walking on stiff legs and with rigid fists at her sides, Elizabeth moved to her bedroom window and looked out over the gardens. She forced her humour to lighten; made herself appreciate the dazzling late summer flowers in the borders, the laurel hedging glistening grass green in the noonday sun. A small smile unclamped her compressed lips. Such a ridiculously transparent plot, too, she dismissed on a faint laugh. Between them, they really ought to have managed something slightly more plausible. But then her grandmother had let slip that the Viscount had been keener on gallivanting than studying in his youth: he was no doubt a dullard who relied on his fabled charm or his fists to get by.

In the two weeks since Ross Trelawney had dined here, all Edwina had seemed to talk of was the Viscount: his future prospects, his past heroics, his good connections. Yet to Elizabeth's knowledge he had not paid a return visit. Had he again set foot over the threshold, she was sure the honour would have been brought to her notice…many times.

She was surprised by Edwina: her grandmother had a sharp, quite devious mind when it suited her. Now she appeared to be held in thrall by this villainous acquaintance of hers. Perhaps her grandmother's advancing years were unhappily telling on her now. Perhaps she was beginning to lose sense and logic and was allowing herself to be manipulated.

Elizabeth managed a sour smile at the azure sky. Her own reason, however, seemed never more acute. It transpired that her thoughts on the Viscount seeking a consort of good birth to cement his aggrandisement were sound, almost prescient. Two weeks ago, she had been prepared to dismiss the notion as fanciful. Now, according to her grandmother, she was to soon receive a marriage proposal from the upstart.

Obviously Edwina had let slip her granddaughter had a pedigree and a portion, then fallen in with his mercenary plot because she was keen to see her granddaughter wed. Well, they were both about to find out that *she* refused to be manipulated. She had no wish to marry but, if she must, it would be preferable to wed a comfortable friend rather than a disreputable stranger. And if that meant the dowry was forfeit, so be it. With a little encouragement, Hugh would propose and they would live, hand to mouth, in that dilapidated vicarage her grandmother had scorned. Better that, than endure the ignominy of having a husband bought for her…especially a coarse ruffian with pockets to let and no interest in her other than filling those pockets with her grandmother's money.

Ross placed his teacup down carefully and leaned back in the chair. 'I hope that's a joke, Edwina,' he said softly.

'A joke! You think I would joke about such a thing? I've no more liking for the way things have turned out than you. I can't keep the man here against his will longer than to work a month's notice. He's accepted another position and I've lost m'wagers. I even made some more to try and get you your cash back. I've never been so out of favour at the tables. Whatever I tried…Faro, Hazard, Picquet…all duds. Unlike me, too…you know that, Stratton. I bet you'd have wagered on me turning up trumps. I'm not a pauper, but neither have I adequate funds at present. I've some merchandise on a trader returning from the Indies and due to dock in a few months' time. Once that's sold you will be welcome to the profit. It might prove a little short of ten thousand...' She flapped an impatient hand, flounced her pudgy visage away from him. 'Oh, you simply must wait a while, that's all.'

'I *must* do nothing of the sort,' Ross corrected in a tone that sent a shiver down Edwina's spine. 'I want my money. Our contract states repayment was due yesterday. I've builders, bricks, timber and slates on their way to Kent and I've no intention of cancelling any of it.' He watched her plump hands clasping and unclasping in her lap. He knew she had other funds. So did he...but he didn't see why he should damn well use them. Unravelling a maze of joint business ventures held with friends and family would take time. He also was loath to present himself as some sort of gullible fool to those gentlemen when they questioned his reasons for selling out, when by right he should have adequate liquid funds pooling in his business account.

Edwina was one of the richest widows in London, if chary of advertising that status. She was certainly one of the canniest. Why she was lying was beyond him. Some instinct told him that she wasn't intending to defraud...just delay; deceive him for her own benefit. But he felt too preoccupied with other matters to be bothered dissecting the workings of the female mind for probable motives. What he did allow himself to indulge in was utter irritation. Not only directed at her, but himself.

Perhaps the whole sorry state of affairs had come about because she was getting senile and he was getting soft. His attitude to money had always been too cavalier...as had his attitude to women. Now he was reaping the cost of that double folly and at a time when he was least able to afford it. A few weeks an aristocrat and he was already done with *noblesse oblige*.

'We've been friends a good amount of years, Edwina. I'd hate this to end badly between us.' A charming smile accompanied the remark but it failed to soften the glitter in his golden eyes or the hard line of his lips.

'There's only one tidy amount of Sampson money going begging,' Edwina quickly spluttered. Her mouth felt dry, her tongue clumsy, her complexion fiery beneath his astute observation. She and this man had never before crossed swords, other than in banter. She knew he had a savage, ruthless side, of course, but was certain it was directed only at deserving foe. She had never anticipated experiencing it personally.

Her needling fears subsided. Pettifer was absolutely correct. Stratton had every right to give vent to the frustrated anger she could sense seething below his suave exterior. Yet he was ever the perfectly mannered gentleman. He was, she realised with a burgeoning serenity, exactly right for provocative, proud Lizzie. As she slanted a sly look at his handsome, rugged features, for the first time it occurred to her just how wonderfully well they would complement each other: Elizabeth with her fragile, pale femininity and Ross with his dark, virile strength. But looks apart, their temperaments and characters would mesh too. She was growing impatient to get them in the same room. Sparks might fly…in fact, she would wager on it. But the blaze they ignited might just warm them through a lifetime.

'The cash is tied to terms and conditions, Stratton,' Edwina snapped, defensively brusque on realising she had been quietly brooding too long.

Ross elevated dark brows, wordlessly demanding to know what they were.

Edwina fiddled with her salt and pepper ringlets. 'There's a trust fund for m'granddaughter that was set up some years ago: fifteen thousand lump sum and ten thousand a year to be paid each January for her lifetime.'

'Why didn't you say so at once?' Ross sighed, peeved at the circuitous route they had taken to achieve a settlement. 'Surely you didn't think taking some chit's inheritance might trouble my conscience? I'm confident you'll replenish her fund…when your ship comes in,' he reminded her ironically.

Pushing up abruptly out of the chair, he straightened his cuffs. Sauntering to a large gilt mirror, he adjusted his cravat. 'I'll take the money, thank you, Edwina.' He was speaking and frowning at his own reflection rather than hers. 'Now, if you'll excuse me, I'm journeying to Kent this afternoon and want to arrive before dusk.' He was halfway to the door when he asked, 'How soon can I collect a banker's draft?'

'As soon as you produce the marriage lines,' Edwina shot back, on a wickedly triumphant grin.

Pettifer approached the chamber door, silently turned the key in the lock, then knocked.

Elizabeth threw down her knitting, rolled to the edge of the bed and scampered to the door. 'Grandmama?' she hissed angrily, not bothering to try the handle.

'It's Pettifer, Lady Elizabeth. Your grandmother would like to speak to you in the parlour.'

Elizabeth yanked at the door, stumbling backwards as it unexpectedly opened. She glared at Pettifer, who looked back kindly, she thought. Looked almost as though he might say something soothing. Should she upbraid him for leaving? Beg him to stay? No. It wasn't his fault her grandmother was a fool. Besides, the wagers were already done and won. What use in that? Restoking her anger at her grandmother, she gripped her skirts, streaked past Pettifer and rushed down the stairs.

She found Edwina sitting sipping Madeira by the fire. With a deep, steadying breath, Elizabeth carefully closed the parlour door. 'I am not going to argue any more, Grandmama,' she stated in a tone that was quietly adamant. 'But I should like to know why you locked me in my room in such an unnecessary and puerile fashion. Did you anticipate I might flee like a frightened rabbit after listening to that daft tale? Why…it is just a laughable fiction. Now I have had time to reflect on it, it is so transparently false that I am amazed you and the Viscount bothered concocting it at all.' She gave a scornful little laugh, paused and awaited her grandmother's comment.

Edwina simply frowned as though weighing up what she'd heard, before moving the glass to occupy her mouth.

'So,' Elizabeth blurted, a trifle disconcerted at the lengthening silence, 'I shall apologise for shouting at you earlier and take it that you have either been under the influence of too much alcohol or too much of that savage heathen's company.'

Uncharacteristically, Edwina, again, had nothing to contribute. Elizabeth eyed her grandmother anxiously as she sipped her Madeira. Tentatively she asked, 'Have you over-imbibed, Grandmama? Or has that scheming rogue intimidated you? You need not be frightened of him! I have every intention of writing this very afternoon and letting him know exactly what I think of his ridiculous attempt to embezzle us. As if you would ask him to loan you a penny! You have money enough to buy and sell half the *ton*! Has he forced you to sign some document? Coerced you? Be assured I shall write and…'

'There's no need for that, Lizzie,' Edwina interrupted, placing down her empty glass and savouring the sweet stickiness on her lips. 'You can reprimand the Viscount in person. He's in the drawing room.'

'I hope that's a joke!' Elizabeth whispered, her eyes huge violet pools in her alabaster face.

'He used exactly the same phrase, no more than twenty minutes ago,' Edwina said with some satisfaction. 'You think alike, Lizzie. That's a good sign. Perhaps on meeting him, you might no longer want to tell him off.'

Elizabeth glared at her. 'He is here? *Now?* And without you even allowing me notice of his arrival?'

'You would have refused to see him, Lizzie, you know that. Actually, he has kindly loaned me money and repayment is overdue.'

'This is the outside of *enough*! I'll listen to no more of your Banbury tales! I know you have no need of a loan from anyone. You have stock bonds and investment documents spilling from your bureau. You must be insane if you think I shall be taken in by woeful tales of some imaginary poverty we are soon to endure.' Elizabeth flung her hands in the air in hopeless despair. 'To broker a marriage with a gentleman would be bad enough. To bribe a rogue to take me....'

'Gentleman rogue,' Edwina interceded with a nod of her head. 'And handsome too...'

'Enough! I'll listen to no more!' Elizabeth gritted through teeth so firmly set she was in danger of taking the pearly edge off them.

'Come, Lizzie,' Edwina wheedled. 'The Viscount is here...in the drawing room...and he is prepared to defer his travel to give you a brief audience.'

Lady Elizabeth Rowe pivoted back very slowly to meet her grandmother's innocent expression. '*He* is prepared to give *me* an audience,' she faintly echoed, her face rigid, bloodless from furious indignation. Once more in her mind's eye she could see those mocking dark eyes catching her peeking at him ten years previously. She could sense his ennui, his laughter at her inexperience as confident, voluptuous women vied for his attention.

Edwina studied her granddaughter's proudly tilted little chin and began relaxing into the chair. Suddenly, she felt more content than she had all day. 'He is a busy man, Lizzie,' she sighed. 'He bade me impress upon you that he cannot tarry long. But he has agreed to spare you a few minutes of his time, before he is away to his Kent estates.'

Lady Elizabeth Rowe's full, soft mouth tightened into a hard little knot. 'Has he? How exceedingly good of him,' she murmured in a voice a-quiver with rage.

'Your gown is a little crumpled, your hair a bit wispy...' Struggling from her chair, Edwina bustled over, circled Elizabeth, tutting as she began winding silky soft blonde tendrils back into their pins with one hand while fussing at rose-pink crepe with the other. Two angry high spots of matching cerise now adorned Elizabeth's otherwise flawless ivory complexion.

'Ross is used to keeping company with beautiful, stylish women. He is not seeing you to best advantage. Most days, you could easily compete with any of them…even the youngest. But I suppose today you look…well enough. The years hardly show…'

Elizabeth snatched herself from her grandmother's touch with two crisp backwards steps. Her whole being felt as taut as a coiled spring. She wasn't sure when last she had been in the throes of such all consuming white-hot wrath. And she wasn't sure on whom to vent it: her idiotic, well-meaning grandmama or the pompous, egotistical villain in the next room. What she *was* sure of was that she didn't now want him to quit the house before she'd had the opportunity to impress on him a few things. She stalked to the door and pulled it open with such violence that, Edwina, just behind, had to catch at it to prevent it damaging her cream silk wall.

As Elizabeth marched the few yards to the drawing room, her quivering fingers found some pins in her hair and yanked them out. So, he was used to keeping company with beautiful, stylish young women, was he? She tossed the pins carelessly aside, then messed the trailing pearly locks into snarls. When satisfied with that disarray, she scrunched the expensive material of her skirts in her fists, just stopping short of ripping into it in her fury.

She halted before the drawing room door, oblivious to Edwina a few paces behind hissing at her, flapping her hands in wild gestures, then watching her, transfixed. Elizabeth closed her violet eyes, took a huge breath, then reached for the handle…

She made her entrance fast, before her courage deserted her, her eyes fixed forward to where she envisaged him to be: either lounging on a sofa or perhaps posing regally by the hearth. The momentum of her pace having taken her a way into the room, her first impression was that it was vacant. The unoccupied sofas, the uncluttered mantel made her thankfully certain that he had deemed himself too important to wait after all. Her head swayed back on her graceful, stalk-like neck, her eyelids drooped and she sighed relief. Dragging forward the few paces to the fire, she warmed her hands against the leaping flames, rubbed her glowing palms along her goose-pimply forearms. The sudden knowledge that she was timorously grateful for his absence, and the reprieve, had her flinging herself around in self-disgust. She had retraced barely a pace when she froze.

He had actually stationed himself on the right-hand side of the room, by a window adjacent to the double doors. Once the doors were opened, the narrow casement was obscured from view to anyone entering. He was still turned slightly towards the glass as though he had been observing the street scene. Now he was looking at her.

For what seemed a small eternity, yet was probably no more than seconds, she stared at him, her heart in her drying mouth while all manner of disjointed messages raced through her mind. It *was* him. Although all trace of youth was gone from his hard, rugged features, this was the same man who had held court amid a band of wild Corinthians a decade ago and occasionally bestowed on her an idle mocking glance on catching her spying on him. He *was* gypsy dark, his hair bronze-black and long with a slight curl where it rested on his collar. Sartorially, he was all stylish elegance. His powerful broad-shouldered frame was garbed in shades of brown: buff trousers, tan tail coat. An amber stone glowed in the intricate knot of his sepia silk cravat. With a skipped heartbeat she realised the tiger's eye resembled the hue she could discern between his close black lashes. He seemed taller than she remembered; if she stood against him she guessed the top of her head would barely reach his chin. The thought of being placed that close to him jerked her out of her trance and into awareness that she was openly staring. A fact that had not gone unnoticed by him: a corner of a finely chiselled mouth had tilted in acknowledgement.

Heat stung into her complexion. But despite her embarrassment, she became aware he was assessing her equally closely. A sardonic, hooded gaze was roving her tangled blonde hair, her crumpled rose-pink gown. Spontaneously, a hand jumped to attend to the self-inflicted damage. She forced it to clench before it could smooth one ruck, undo one snarl. It returned to her side, then slipped behind her to be joined by the other. Her fingers gripped together and her chin tilted, her beautiful flushed visage a study in hauteur.

'Have you had an accident?'

For no reason she could understand she flinched at the sound of his husky, baritone voice. At that moment, she hated him simply for the lazy humour in his voice, in his eyes, as he alluded to her disarray. She moistened her lips. 'Accident?' she echoed as though attempting a foreign tongue.

'You seem a little…dishevelled,' he mentioned taking a step towards her.

Elizabeth took a step back. 'Oh, that.' She launched a freezing smile at him while an unsteady finger worked its nonchalant way into a blonde tangle. 'I have been reclining in my chamber, but thought you would prefer me not to tarry and primp in your honour. My grandmother said you impressed upon her your eagerness to soon leave. So here I am, come directly to impress upon you how well that suits me.'

A slight movement of his dark head acknowledged the insult, as did his dry tone as he said, 'I'm greatly obliged.'

'Good.'

So here she was, indeed, Ross mused wryly to himself. The one place he hadn't expected to find the blonde beauty he had glimpsed in the street, was within Edwina's house…within her family. Her granddaughter had figured in his imagination as a dumpy, uninteresting young woman: an insipid version of Edwina. A sense of chivalry had made him stay and at least meet her. He couldn't have been more wrong about it all. And he couldn't have been more right, thinking he'd seen this woman somewhere before. Such exquisite loveliness was rare, unforgettable. It was also, oddly, unmarred by the fact that she looked as though she'd been dragged through a hedge backwards. If only he could bring to mind where and when they'd met. 'I'm afraid Edwina has left me a little at a loss. I don't know your name…Miss Sampson…?' he ventured.

'Lady Elizabeth Rowe,' Elizabeth stated, her voice wobbly but her tone strong with pride. Her worst fears were realised; she felt her stomach tumble at the immediate intelligence in his eyes. Oh, she knew what caused the strengthening smile, his lashes to droop to conceal the base interest…

His memory finally served him correctly and everything had suddenly become crystal clear. Not least, Ross realised, cynically, why Edwina had omitted revealing her granddaughter's identity and was so damned keen to buy her a husband. He had imagined the chit to be impeded in the marriage stakes by homely looks, not by her ruined reputation…or her age. Not that she looked approaching thirty, but he guessed she must be. If she'd been seventeen at her debut she'd now be in her twenty-eighth year.

Edwina Sampson, he laughed inwardly, really was the most unpredictable woman. He'd never known of her connection to the Thorneycrofts: a less likely mother-in-law to the late Marquess, he couldn't imagine. Now Edwina wanted her sullied granddaughter wed and thought she had found the perfect sap to take her…in him. In fact, despite the lady's haughty disdain, they were probably in cahoots. They wanted to manipulate him to get her off the shelf and respectable before she got too much older and started losing those beautiful looks. And she was desirable…barely five minutes in her company and his body was already impressing on him just how badly he wanted her.

Elizabeth could sense his contempt! But she knew his interest was growing. But then gentlemen were always more interested once they'd discovered her identity. She had come beneath lingering male appraisal too often to be ignorant of what excited it. Because her stupid temper had made her burst in like some unkempt virago, he would now brand her every manner of slut. She scoured her mind for some insolence to send him quickly on his way, for she was horribly afraid she might not manage to brazen it out today…with him. She could feel her throat closing, feel ice shivering her lower lip. She clamped teeth into it. She would not bolt from the room, hide away ashamed…

'I hear you do good works.'

'I hear you don't,' was flung back at once with a childlike defensiveness, even though he had spoken conversationally.

Ross smiled. 'Our sovereign might challenge you on that. He seems happy enough with my services.'

'How well a King so easily pleased befits this great nation,' she sneered.

Ross laughed and his head fell back a little. He frowned at the ceiling. So much for polite chit-chat. 'Look, I'm trying to make this easier for both of us,' he said affably. But his steady gaze, as it levelled on her again, was quite devoid of amity or humour. 'As you appear to disdain small talk…and most other things…let's get straight to business. I imagine you're aware that your grandmother owes me a sum of money?'

'I'm aware that you allege she owes you a sum of money.' Elizabeth slanted a contemptuous purple stare at him. Softly, fluidly, she announced, 'However, there are things, sir, you should be aware of: firstly, I do not believe any transaction has taken place between you and my grandmother. I think you have bamboozled her in some way to lay hands on my dowry. You may fool her, you will never fool me. Secondly, the whole matter of money loaned or borrowed is of no consequence whatsoever. I have no intention of marrying you, now or at any other time. You will need to look elsewhere for money to embezzle.' She turned her face from his. 'I think that is all. Oh, now you may go,' she added with an idle wave of a slender hand at the door. Although she had shown him her back, she knew he was yet there. The silence was deafening. Unable to bear the tension longer she gathered her creased skirts, tossed her shaggy head and, chin up, headed for the door.

She barely saw him move but somehow he had managed to station himself in the middle of her escape route. She made to sweep first one way, then the other around him. Whichever way she stepped, he seemed to block her path.

Backpacing from his proximity, she raised flashing eyes. 'Come, my lord. I thought you were in a tearing rush. Please go before me, if you'd rather impress me with your status and quit the room first. Conscious of your aggrandisement, I did offer you the opportunity…'

Ross took a moment before lowering his face to look at her. He then gave her a smile so laden with deceit, so obviously unmeant and threatening, it took her breath away. As did his eyes. They were cold as metal yet extraordinarily beautiful in hue: green-flecked gold and fringed with thick black lashes that were incongruously childlike in their length. *Her face quickly lowered. I do just reach his chin,* scuttled deliriously through her mind as she blinked at the cleft in it.

'Are you naturally this rude? Or have you been practising insults in my honour, instead of…primping…wasn't it?'

Despite herself, Elizabeth turned scarlet. 'Remove yourself from my way. I wish to leave this room…right now,' was all she could manage in response.

'And I wish to receive back my money…right now,' flowed back, honey-voiced.

'You're lying! My grandmother has no need of your money. She has more money of her own than she knows what to do with,' Elizabeth spat at him.

Ross smiled coldly. She was a damn good actress. And very aware, he was sure, of the effect she was having on him. His fingers itched to touch her, slide her gown from shoulders that looked as fragile as milky glass. They clenched at his sides. Barely two feet separated them. He was so damned aroused that if she locked the door and gave him a taste for an early wedding night on the sofa, he'd get a licence this afternoon.

'I don't doubt Edwina's lying about her ability to repay,' he gritted, angry and frustrated. 'Nevertheless, two weeks ago I was foolish enough to be taken in by some bleeding-heart story concerning the loss of her butler to a rival and her eagerness to try a little deviousness to outwit the woman and keep him. In short, she persuaded me to loan her ten thousand pounds to fund the chicanery.' He withdrew a parchment from his inside pocket. 'The contract states that repayment was due yesterday. Patient soul that I am, I have allowed her one day's grace already.' He moved the document, indicating Elizabeth should take it to check his story's veracity.

Elizabeth eyed the proffered paper as though it might bite. From sounding like lies, it now all sounded horribly plausible. How would he know of Alice Penney poaching Pettifer unless Edwina had related it all? Why would he bother mentioning their domestic arrangements at all unless he had a vested interest in them? Why would he let her read the contract? Her hands seemed welded together behind her back. Suddenly they sprang apart, snatched at the paper. Swishing about, she ran to the fire and fed it to the hungry flames. Her defiance was almost palpable as she put up her chin and shook back tangled locks from her sculpted white face.

'I'm lucky in my man of business,' she heard him say in a voice that dripped irony. 'He's thorough…sometimes tiresomely fussy. He sets a clerk to duplicating documents and nothing else. And Mrs Sampson was obliging enough to sign the set…even that spare lodged in my safe.'

'I don't care,' Elizabeth gasped through the mounting rage and fear tightening her chest. She was behaving with reckless abandon. More stupidly than she had in a long…long while. It seemed the more patient and polite he was, the more rude and abrasive she became. But she couldn't seem to stop. Everything was running out of control. 'I won't marry you. I will never marry you,' she stormed.

'Progress at last,' Ross drawled. 'We've come to something we agree on. You appear to be under the misapprehension that I have proposed. I don't recall doing so, or ever intending to do so. I am done, my lady, with enduring your puerile insolence and disdain in the hope we might amicably solve this problem. I want payment. To be honest, I would much prefer the cash, but I'll take retribution in its stead.'

Chapter Five

'What do you mean?' Elizabeth forced out through her sandpaper throat.

'Well, I'll tell you my dear. I think that the lady doth protest too much. I think you are an accomplice, possibly the instigator, in this feeble plot to trick me into marrying you. I think your pathetic insults are perversely intended to endear you to me in some way.' He walked away from her, braced a hand against the window sill. It looked heavy and dark against the narrow white-painted ledge. Idly he looked down, scanning the street, then up at the clear blue sky. 'You may tell Edwina it might have worked. It's true I like women who are novel and present a challenge. But not that much. If you were planning to ride back into the *ton* on my wedding coat tails, I'm afraid I'm about to disappoint you. Forgive me for being blunt, but I'd never take to wife a rude, supercilious little bitch ruined by scandal.' His sweeping gaze relinquished the heavens and he pivoted about to lean back against the wall. His hands were thrust into his pockets, an indolent look levelled at her. 'I also mean that it's in your best interest to persuade Edwina that you both now act sensibly. Concede defeat. Return my money and the whole trifling matter is at an end… finished.'

He couldn't be sure if her chalky pallor stemmed from shock or fury at his explicitness. More gently he added, 'I'm not a fool, neither am I a vindictive man. I don't want to give credibility to my infamy as a ruthless swine by finishing your grandmother in a debtor's cell…or finishing you in my bed. And I will bring you down…' Between them was catastrophic silence, absolute stillness for a moment. 'If I'm generous and allow you to work off the debt at two thousand a year, including interest due, that's six years service. You might be a trifle sullied now; after a lengthy stint as one of my paramours, you'll be a professional courtesan approaching her mid-thirties. It would be a kindness if I took the trouble to prepare you for meaner partners before ejecting you. Eventually you'll have nothing left but base standards and spoiled looks. You'll be grateful to scrape a living as a tavern whore in Whitechapel.'

Elizabeth moistened her lips, swallowed, tried to speak. No words formed. Dumbfounded, she couldn't find a voice. Never in all her life, even directly after that horrible shame he alluded to, had anyone spoken to her with such deliberate brutality.

But she couldn't fault his honesty. She had encountered similar wretched specimens of womankind as those he alluded to almost every week on visiting Newgate or Bridewell. Sometimes she saw them at a mean liberty, lolling hollow-eyed against a wall in Barrow Road or its environs. At first glance they seemed no different from the rough trade they now lived amongst. Then there might be a hint of once-graceful deportment, or a cultured inflection to an overheard word, and they were betrayed as once having known gentility. And she would try to glimpse, beneath grey, gin-cracked masks, the pride and vivacity that must once have sparkled beneath. And he wasn't being vindictive. His words were harshened by impatience, not malice. His desire to be elsewhere, his indifference, made it all so much worse.

She accepted it now. He was owed a fortune by her grandmother and he wanted it back. Dealing with her was just a vexing waste of his time. She wanted to shout at him that she wasn't involved, that she had known of her grandmother's plot less time than he. Instead she simply stared at him, unblinking, her glossy violet eyes huge in a face that was cold, milky, immovable as marble.

'Persuade your grandmother that a banker's draft for ten thousand pounds would do well to find its way to Grosvenor Square by four this afternoon. I'll forgo the interest for now. Inform her that the cuisine at the Fleet leaves a lot to be desired and she's in danger of fading away. I'm told by disgruntled paramours that my selfishness leaves a lot to be desired. So you choose,' he offered dulcetly. 'But know this, my lady. I want what's due. Parting with the cash might be relatively painless. In your position, that's what I'd choose. That's all I mean,' he stressed in conclusion.

Elizabeth finally unstuck her tongue from the roof of her mouth. The shuddering, indrawn breath she took was barely perceptible. 'Thank you for that explanation, sir. I do now know exactly what you mean.' Her voice strengthened from thready whisper to gruff choke. 'Perhaps I might be permitted to trespass on your precious time a few moments more and let you know what I mean.' Her tousled blonde head came up and she stalked away from the fire towards him, suppressing the shock and bitter humiliation that had moments ago threatened to humble her, crumble her like a rag doll at his feet as his lazy contempt withered her bones.

She approached him, emboldened by a wrath that tightened her fists into quivering, knife-edged balls. She forced them close to her sides lest they lashed out at him, beat at his arrogant, heathen head. She half-circled him at a distance, looking his powerful physique up and down. 'Firstly,' she enunciated carefully, frowning in concentration, 'I must congratulate you on your excellent memory. Yes, I was compromised ten years ago; yes, I have been shunned by people who class themselves as better than me. People like you who shield their disgusting habits behind sham morals and manners. Secondly, had I any wish to sneak back into the *beau monde*, I would choose nobler coat tails than yours to cling to. Perhaps in your conceit you believe I should be grateful…flattered, even, at having been propositioned by an upstart Viscount; a thug who has managed to brawl his way into favour. I'm afraid I must now disappoint you. I've had far better offers than yours. Over ten years, two dukes and two earls have pursued me, along with numerous less eminent but often wealthier gentlemen. A coal merchant once offered me the freehold of a house on Park Lane, together with all the servants, clothes and carriages I could use. Oh, and an allowance of two thousand a year.'

She stared, vivid-eyed, into middle distance. 'The Earl of Cadmore is less generous but more persistent. Just a few weeks ago he wrote again to let me know how greatly I would benefit from allowing his ardent attention.' She spun about to gaze at her tormentor as though he had crawled from the wainscotting. 'And you…a paltry Viscount…a paltry, parsimonious Viscount at that, think to stable me amongst your mongrel harlots? Are you really so stupid, so vain, that you imagine a Marquess's daughter, even a sullied Marquess's daughter, would ever contemplate a union with a Cornish brigand? If my silly grandmother hadn't made the circumstances so tiresome, I swear I might die laughing at your pathetic fantasies…'

She got no further. Two hard, brown hands gripped the tops of her slender, ivory arms, abbreviating her jeering tirade. The speed and ease at which he lifted her made her sure he would jerk her up against him so their faces were level. But he dropped her just before him, abruptly, as though she had become scalding. Her silky, silver head grazed his dark chin, then recoiled to rest inches away.

'Quiet! Or I might now share those pathetic fantasies…just for the hell of it. I promise you won't laugh,' he added with a hint of apology that chilled her.

Elizabeth back-paced, rubbing at her arms as though removing taint. 'Oh, I believe that. I was being ironic, of course. Anyone less diverting than you I cannot imagine,' she sneered, contempt sliding from beneath dusky lashes.

'Well, let me imagine for you,' he whipped back mellifluously. 'How diverting did you find Lieutenant Havering? Was it his pathetic fantasy or yours that you play mongrel harlot for some gentlemen of the road?'

Elizabeth stumbled to a halt. Her pale complexion lost what little colour stained her cheeks. She ran a dry tongue over arid lips. So there it was. He had to let her know that he recalled all her disgrace. Every sordid part. And at that moment it seemed as though the raucous guffaws that had echoed in her ears as she and her stiff-backed papa quit Caledon Square in their elegant carriage were rolling within this room. The walls seemed to undulate with the vicious male amusement that accompanied the start of their journey back to Hertfordshire and thence into exile. Ross Trelawney might not have bothered witnessing her banishment with those crowing dandies, but he was gloating now, determined she understand how equally he despised her. A shaking hand went behind to grip at the sofa-back, as her legs weakened. Slowly her chin came up. 'I have considered it. No, I still cannot imagine anyone less entertaining than you,' she whispered.

Threat of retribution savaged the mockery in his eyes making her sure he was about to come after her. It shocked her out of petrification and into a tottering retreat. 'I must again impose on your patience, sir,' she croaked distractingly. 'Please wait here. It is in your interest to stay for I hope to return in a moment with something that ensures neither of us need ever again endure the other's company.' Without awaiting his agreement, Elizabeth swished about and sped from the room.

Ross watched her go. He stared at the door for a moment before closing his eyes. He felt shattered. He'd limped away from battlefields with more energy and better spirits. A grunt of laughter scratched at his throat as he looked about the sedate, cosy room with its tasteful mix of blue and gold furnishings. But this was a war zone and no mistake. And he had the feeling, despite holding the high ground and an arsenal of weapons, he'd just lost and made an implacable enemy. And for some reason that wounded him to the core.

And then it came to him, sidled into his mind and wouldn't leave. She hadn't withdrawn to find a gun to level at his head, or even to collaborate with Edwina on better strategies. She wasn't involved in Edwina's scheme to get her wed at all. She was innocent of that and he was guilty of barbarism. She'd retreated to fetch something valuable to offer as loot rather than risk his revenge. He smiled ruefully, hoping she wasn't about to struggle back with a sackful of family silver. Idiotically, he didn't even want her to return with a banker's draft…not yet. So much for tactical, wounding words and manoeuvring to keep distance between them. He hadn't resisted the lure of her small, sensual body. He hadn't managed to keep his hands to himself. Now his palms seemed to tingle with the loss of satiny skin beneath them. The fragrance of flowers that had wafted up from her tangled pearly tresses teased his nostrils anew, the infinitesimal stroke of silky hair against his jaw made him irritably toss his head to prevent another phantom caress. The memory of her was narcotic. He wanted more. Now. He wanted her back so he could look at her again…touch her again.

He'd called her a bitch and, innocent or not of plotting with Edwina, his opinion hadn't much altered. Yet Lady Elizabeth Rowe aroused something in him Cecily never touched: few women stirred his mind as well as his body. She fascinated him. He wanted to know everything about her. Everything that had occurred, good and bad, since the first time their eyes met at Vauxhall Gardens. He placed a hot palm against cold glass, then curled it into a fist as his thoughts weaved back through the years to a sultry summer and a blonde debutante.

He'd wanted her then too. But she was too young, too popular…and so was he. He'd known if he approached her, joined that band of fools awaiting a kind glance, permission to call…to dance…to flirt, it might have finished him. For as she had just rightly proclaimed, daughters of marquesses, especially those of rare beauty, didn't forge unions with sons of Cornish freetraders. They married aristocrats; and she hadn't exaggerated the number of noblemen who had pursued her. She had constantly been surrounded by the bluest young bloods. So that summer he'd steered himself clear of her innocently provocative glances, too youthfully vain himself to face enduring the rebuff that was sure to come.

At that time he had wealth but no status...apart from a reputation as a marauder. But there were always women, some classed as ladies, who wanted him because of his rough lineage rather than despite it. Women who were excited by his piratical looks and cavalier manners, who liked him to relate tales of sea skirmishes and plundered cargoes while they traced the marks on his body with sharp fingernails and shivered naked in his arms. The only time they were disappointed was on realising he was happy to stimulate any number of them and no one in particular. It was pleasurable and easy that way and, at twenty-three, he saw no reason for strife or self-denial.

Yet, along with the rest of society, he'd been wrong in guessing Lady Elizabeth Rowe to be ambitious in the marriage stakes and stalking a title and wealth. Her lover had been the youngest son of a baronet and impecunious to boot.

Their reckless elopement had floundered into disaster. En route to Gretna Green, the callow youth was alleged to have panicked and fled, abandoning Elizabeth to a couple of highwaymen who'd stopped his carriage. Her father, so the tale went, eventually tracked her to a tavern in Cambridgeshire where she'd been found partially clothed and alone. A natural conclusion had been drawn to her fate once given over to the felons' tender mercies. And apparently she'd offered no defence to that. Neither had her father.

The scandal had rocked society. Ross first learned of the affair at White's, while playing Faro with Guy Markham and his brother Luke. The redolence of cigar smoke and stewing beef mingling, hanging thick in the air, filled his nostrils. He recalled losing heavily as the ribald jesting crescendoed around him. Inwardly he had felt the angry sorrow of desecration. Outwardly he had chipped in some cynical comment about the sanctity of virgins.

From that moment, for about a month, the gentlemen's clubs had resounded with ever more salacious conjecture on the circumstances of her abasement and how best to tempt the lady back to town for an encore after such a promising debut. And many a titled rake had put his money where his mouth was and offered her his protection. He assumed, from what she'd said, none had tempted her sufficiently.

But one had persevered. He could believe that: Linus Savage, Earl of Cadmore, was known as a man to hold grudges. He was also once known as the man believed to be leading the field in Lady Elizabeth Rowe's affections. A decade ago their betrothal had been expected. When it was discovered she had played a rich peer of the realm for a fool, using him to camouflage an affair with an indigent officer in the army, the Earl became a risible figure, too. Ross could imagine Cadmore to be unremitting in his need for vengeance, even though years had passed and he'd since wed an heiress.

As Lady Elizabeth was guessed to be in the marriage mart to lure a fortune to reline her papa's pockets, Cadmore had seemed a natural choice. When it foundered into farce, in every sense the Marquess was sure to have been disappointed. Thus, for a while, wild predictions on his jezebel daughter's fate were bandied about. He would incarcerate her in the nearest convent; he would despatch her to some remote relative; he would negotiate a discreet deal with a wealthy gentleman prepared to take her as concubine or, paradoxically, borrow the means to buy her a modest husband and respectability. But the Marquess did nothing of the sort. The last Ross heard, as gossip faded for want of any fuel to fire the rumours, was that the Marquess was still devoted to his lovely daughter and they were living a reclusive life at Thorneycroft.

A woman of gentle birth was to be congratulated for retaining her pride after such degradation. Ravished and ostracised, maybe, but she had spirit. She despised him and was quick to let him know it. And there had been no reason for him to know it, or to have met her again at all and now be brooding over ten-year-old tragedies and regrets like a sentimental fool. His teeth met. 'Damn you, Edwina,' he muttered irritably into the mellow afternoon.

Her fingers were shaking so much it took several attempts before the key slotted into the lock. Jerking open the secret drawer in her grandmother's escritoire, Elizabeth withdrew the burgundy velvet roll. Her first instinct was to open it out, feast her eyes one last, private time on the treasure within. She resisted, simply snatching it up, and within a moment was rushing headlong down the stairs. The thought that the beastly bastard might leave without a settlement being reached today; that she might toss and turn the night through, uncertain if the vile man was firmly banished to her past, made her burst through the double doors in a most unladylike fashion.

Although Elizabeth ignored him, and slowed to a graceful walk, she did utter with cool civility, 'Thank you for waiting.' It was honest gratitude and helped to steady the quivering of her fingers as they hovered, then reverentially laid bare her peace offering on the sofa table.

The diamond-and-amethyst collar glittered as sunlight dappled over it. As always when she looked upon it, its magnificence caught the breath at the back of her throat; as did memories it evoked of a certain person. She took a few steps back and tossed up her head, meeting green-gold watching eyes.

A nervous gesture indicated the heirloom. 'It was my mother's,' she brusquely explained. 'Now it is mine. It was Edwina's gift to my mother on her twenty-first birthday. Soon after that she married my papa, the Marquess of Thorney-croft.' She hesitated in reciting the gem's provenance as she became aware of him approaching. She moved away to the other side of the table, wordlessly inviting him to fully appreciate its opulence.

'You might be thinking it is not worth ten thousand pounds. I expect you are.' Elizabeth hastily removed his need to scorn her sacrifice. 'And…and that is quite true. This piece was last valued at two thousand guineas.' She glanced at him, at intervals, searching for signs of anger or impatience.

He raised his eyes from the superbly matched violet and white stones and gazed into something similar. Her eyes were equally cold, equally beautiful. 'Your mother looked like you…' he stated with a half-smile.

Elizabeth blinked, swallowed, half-turned away from him. 'How could you possibly know that?' she demanded, angrily, absently dragging fingers through her tangles. 'This is her necklace, not her portrait.'

'It was bought by someone who loved her…to reflect her beauty. You've the same eyes. I'm guessing you look like her in other ways, too.'

Elizabeth glared accusingly at the collar as though it had betrayed her. It lay glistening between them, shieldlike, protecting a flimsy treaty. Ignoring his astute personal observation as best she could, she recommended stiltedly, 'My papa was pleased with how well this suited my mother and wanted to add to it. He had a matching suite made by the same craftsman and presented it as my mother's wedding gift. It includes a bracelet, two styles of eardrops, a brooch and a small hair ornament. I believe the parure was last valued at approaching eight thousand pounds. It must be worth more now. A decade has since passed. All the pieces, save this one, are kept in a bank vault. But they are all mine. I own it in entirety so you need not fret they are the property of the Thorneycroft estate and will be reclaimed. My mama left them to me. Edwina likes to keep this one here. As she purchased it originally, I saw no reason to deny her the pleasure of looking at it from time to time.' She met his watching gaze, trying to glean from his expression whether he intended rejecting her proposal.

'Are you expecting me to feel too ashamed to take it?'

Elizabeth sensed her face flame but said icily, 'Not at all, my lord. In our brief acquaintance there's been nothing that would let me credit you with a conscience. Your reputation as a heartless villain is quite safe with me.'

His smile strengthened, the crinkles at the corners of his

eyes and mouth deepened. She realised he was, for the first time, genuinely amused. 'That sounds like a challenge to prove equal to such trust, my lady.'

'I should like a receipt…' Elizabeth burst out.

That made him laugh. 'Of course. And how shall I lay my pillaging hands on the other pieces?'

Elizabeth moved to the small writing desk by the window and selected quill and parchment. She dipped, began to write, tutted as her unsteady fingers caused a blot of ink to mar the paper. She hesitated, dithering over whether to crumple it and restart. She finished quickly, in a few sentences, sealed, then immediately proffered the note. 'That gives you the right to remove and dispose of the set as you will. No doubt Sir Joshua will first contact me for verification. It is an unusual occurrence….'

Ross took the letter she was holding by its very edge and slipped it in a pocket. He rolled the velvet into a cylinder again, obliterating her inheritance with deft casualness. The rich, red cloth looked lost in his large dark hand.

'Receipt…' Elizabeth whispered, realising that he could walk away now with all her financial security…her most precious possession…and no one would ever be the wiser. She held out the quill towards him. 'Please…' she forced through a clog in her throat, while her mind chanted, *I'm sorry, mama…I'm so sorry…so sorry…*

He wrote fast, fluently, then placed the pen back in its rest. Her rigid fingers stabbed the paper, drew it towards her as though frightened he might take it back. She looked blankly at him. 'Thank you,' she murmured in the tone of voice that let him know she'd sooner curse him as a devil.

A tiny movement of his head acknowledged her faux gratitude. Unable to take a polite leave of him, any sort of leave of him, she stood, backed off two steps, then turned immediately for the door.

'You'll want it returned,' was addressed to her stiff back. 'Persuade Edwina to be sensible and repay me within a week and I'll let you have it. After that time, I can't promise anything.'

Elizabeth swallowed. She should face him, thank him again, but the two simple words burned like acid in her throat. She felt her eyes fill with needling tears. Without another word or glance, but with dignity in every endless step that eventually brought her to the door, she left him.

'I thought you were long gone, Stratton!'

Ross tore his eyes from leaping flames and turned. He removed from the mantel the glass of whisky he'd helped himself to from the decanter on the sideboard. Sipping, he looked at Edwina over the rim.

'Thought you had to be in Kent before sundown.' Edwina consulted the clock on the wall. 'Doubt you'll make it now…' At his continuing silence she mentioned drily, with a flick of a fat finger at the tumbler now held low by a muscular thigh, 'I see you found the decanter.' She smiled. 'Or perhaps m'granddaughter remembered her manners and served you refreshment. She can be a charming hostess. Did she look after you?'

Ross's smile was intensely sardonic. 'I think you know damn well she didn't.' He assessed her from under low lids until she shifted uneasily. 'You know when I arrived here earlier, Edwina, I was worried you were losing your mind and didn't know what you were about.'

Edwina adopted a shocked look. 'No! What made you think that?' she asked, humour quivering her voice.

'Oh…just some odd notion that you might be foolish enough to intend defrauding me.'

'And what do you think now?'

'Now I think you're an extremely devious woman with an extremely…intriguing granddaughter. I imagine that's exactly what you want me to think.'

'So, how did you like my sweet Lizzie? Pretty girl, isn't she?'

Ross laughed at glowing logs. *'Pretty girl?'* he echoed sarcastically. 'You'd never have bothered putting a pretty girl in my way, Edwina.'

'That's true.' She paused before opining innocently, 'I believe you already like her.'

'No, I don't like her. But we both know that's immaterial, don't we?'

Edwina's eyes narrowed. 'I'll pay out on marriage only, Stratton. No wedding, no dowry. I don't want her settled in any other way. Her papa could have arranged that other way ten years ago. She could have arranged it for herself last week. She's still in demand, you know.'

'I'm sure,' he drawled drily.

'Well, don't keep me in suspense. What occurred? Have you proposed?'

'No. But we came to an acceptable arrangement.'

'Which is?'

'She's paid me.'

Edwina stalked forward. 'She's done *what*?'

Ross placed his glass down on the mantel and withdrew the velvet roll.

Edwina looked at it resting on his palm, then at him. Quickly she shielded her frustration with her sparse lashes. 'She must truly dislike you, Stratton. I believed never in this world would she part with that necklace.'

'She's parted with the rest of the collection, too.'

'Then she's frightened and that's not like my courageous Lizzie.'

'No doubt you'll do the decent thing then and buy them back for her.'

'Oh, no,' Edwina said airily. 'Why should I? I've not given up hope of you doing the decent thing. After all, you're still here, aren't you? And you so busy 'n all, and desperate to get to Kent. I would hazard a guess, Ross, that you've behaved boorishly and now you're feeling guilty. After all, you might not like her now, but tomorrow...'

A tight-lipped smile quirked his sensual mouth, his dark brows hiked with sceptical enquiry. But the way he then shot whisky down his throat, slammed the glass onto the mantel and brushed past, made Edwina indulge in a secret smile before she turned to follow at a careful distance. She watched as he strode out into the hallway, his steps cracking like gunshot as he neared Pettifer. He took his coat and cane from the butler without slowing pace.

'Tomorrow you will…' Edwina murmured slyly at the closing front door.

'Are you not going to talk to me, Lizzie?'

Lady Elizabeth Rowe placed down her breakfast coffee cup and gave her grandmother her attention. 'Are you going to repay that man his money?'

'I cannot. You know I cannot. I have explained about m'funds at present.'

Elizabeth snatched up her cup, raised it to her mouth. 'Then I am not going to talk to you. There is nothing more to say.'

'Lizzie, dear…' Edwina cooed in her most wheedling tone. 'Come, it is two days now since Stratton was here and still you punish me. You have had time to sulk and berate me as a foolish woman. And I have said m'sorrys. It is true I hoped that you and the Viscount might like one another. But if it is not to be…' She shrugged as though it mattered little. 'You cannot blame me for wanting to settle m'debts with money that's just mouldering in the bank. Neither can you blame a fond grandmama for wanting to introduce her granddaughter to such an eligible gentleman. Besides, why take against him so? Don't you find Ross handsome? Charming? Be truthful now. All the ladies sigh over him…'

Elizabeth scraped back in her chair and jumped to her feet. Forgetting her speech embargo, she snapped, 'Handsome? He looks like a romany who has thieved himself fine clothes. Charming? He called me a rude, supercilious little bitch!'

'Did he?' Edwina barked, more surprised than outraged. 'You never said so before. He is usually unfailingly civil to the fair sex; even to those creatures who hardly warrant it.' She sniffed, recalling Cecily Booth boldly soliciting his company at Maria's soirée. 'You must really have got under his skin, my dear, to upset that courteous nonchalance he maintains. Were you…?'

'Was I what?' Elizabeth demanded, peering through the parlour window.

'A rude little bitch. I know you can act haughty at times.'

Elizabeth flushed, leaned her hot forehead against cool glass as she gazed into the gardens. If honest, she knew she had behaved badly. No, worse than that: with anyone else she would have felt thoroughly ashamed of her conduct. Not with him. Never with him. He deserved all her rancour.

Yet there was an irritating niggling in the pit of her stomach. Had she been pleasant, perhaps he might have been so, too. But she had acted purely on aggressive instinct. She never used feminine wiles now. It was ten years since she had flirted and acted girlishly to get her own way. But now she was tormented by regrets…missed opportunities.

It would have been a shrewd move to flatter his pathetic conceit and angle for a little more time in which to nag Edwina to pay him. It would have been wise to batten down her stormy emotions. But it seemed the more cool sophistication he displayed, the more fraught she had become. She still couldn't quite believe that while in the throes of temper she had forfeited her mother's treasure…her treasure.

'Well, were you rude?' Edwina's query cut sharply into her pensiveness.

Elizabeth spun about at the window. 'I had every right to be as unmannerly as he was. For all his failings, Stratton's memory doesn't lack. He was at pains to let me know just how well he recalls my disgrace.'

'And were you at pains to enlighten him to the facts of the matter?'

'Why should I tell him anything so personal? He is of no consequence. I don't need his approval,' Elizabeth flared, sculpted chin arrogantly tilting.

'So he knew of your misfortune, yet was still reluctant to go,' Edwina muttered to herself. Noting her granddaughter's haughty expression, she added lightly, 'Well, if you peered down your nose at him like that, I can see how he might arrive at such a description.'

'In case you have forgotten,' Elizabeth snapped, 'your nasty friend now has my mama's jewellery in his grubby possession.' She covered her face with her hands. 'Oh, why did I do it!' Her head shook behind her palms before they curled into fists. 'I should have never agreed to meet him. I should never have allowed him to browbeat me into settling your debt. I should have let him dun you as he threatened. It is what cheats deserve. You have made a grave mistake in this, Grandmama, and you must put it right. Give him the piffling cash. Please! The Thorneycroft parure is irreplaceable!'

'Don't think badly of me, Elizabeth. I don't always get things right. Neither do I often get them wrong. I would never jeopardise your keepsakes, or my sweet Valerie's memory. The Viscount is an honourable gentleman. I'm as confident of that as I am of seeing you again wearing those amethysts. To tell the truth, they have lain idle in a metal box too long. In a way, I'm glad Stratton has them. At least they will see the light of day again.'

'Oh, yes,' Elizabeth choked. 'No doubt they will also reflect candlelight: strung about one of his naked doxies! How will you like *that*?' She flung furiously past her grandmother to quit the room just as Harry Pettifer was entering. The butler jumped aside then tilted backwards at the waist and turned his stately steely head to watch Lady Elizabeth fly along the corridor.

'Come, tell me, Pettifer, am I right to persevere in this? I swear I need a little proof this might succeed or I shall give it all up, right now,' Edwina sighed.

Pettifer raised the salver he had dropped close to his leg to prevent it catching the young mistress as she burst upon him. Stooping agilely, he swept up from the floor a letter and placed it back upon the silverware. 'Never fear, Mrs Sampson; I think a timely confirmation that you're on the right track has just arrived,' Harry said with a twinkle in his blue eyes and a chuckle rumbling in his throat.

Chapter Six

He would like the opportunity to speak to her again, would he! With a view to reaching a more congenial settlement this time—perhaps negotiating the return of her family's heirlooms. How noble of him! And what would he like in their stead? Elizabeth wondered acidly. Perhaps her head on a platter. Or more likely, her naked body on his bed. How odiously predictable these men were, she inwardly scoffed, flicking aside the letter with brave disdain. But the sudden, fierce pumping of her heart forced her up jerkily from the edge of her bed. Linus Savage always used similar phrases in his little notes: opportunity to negotiate…compatible terms…

Dropping onto her velvet dressing stool, she dragged a brush through her thick flaxen hair for a few moments before impatiently discarding it onto the polished wood of the dressing table. Its clatter masked her deep sigh.

She studied her face in the mirror, raised a finger to touch a small laugh line close to her pouty mouth and wondered why she'd not noticed it before. Wondered, too, how she'd come by it. She'd done precious little laughing recently. The finger moved to press against a frown line between her delicately arching brunette brows. That tiny furrow was probably less an imperfection than her moods and history warranted. Yet, on examining each feature by angling her head back and forth, up and down, she realised her appearance was barely touched by the years that had passed since her come-out. She'd been proud of her looks as a debutante…quite vain, she accepted, dropping her tilted chin and grimacing humility at fingers gripping the edge of the dresser.

Since then many men had attempted to make her life squalid and ugly. And now there was another to add to their number, and what terrified her was that of them all he might know how to succeed…

Her mouth pursed with indomitable spirit. She wanted her jewellery back. She wanted it so much, her stomach clenched into a hurting cramp. 'If I reclaim the Thorneycroft parure I swear I'll never again let it go…' she promised her dead parents in a vehement whisper. But she could dredge up no devious plan likely to outwit a mercenary and make him forfeit his booty. If he returned her jewellery, she rather imagined it would be on his terms…

Pushing it all determinedly to the back of her mind, she concentrated on the day ahead. It was Sunday and, after attending morning service with Edwina at St Mary's, there would be barely time for a quick change into serviceable clothes and a bite to eat before Hugh Clemence arrived and they made their way to Barrow Road Sunday School.

She picked up a pen. Replaced it on her writing desk. Picked it up again and tapped at paper with the nib. She firmly, neatly, put it back and pushed the parchment away. She would reply later, when she'd had time to construct a suitably scathing rebuffal to his impertinence.

'Reverend Timms seemed a little peaky, I thought.'

Elizabeth nodded. 'I thought so, too. I hope his wife has just a chill and talk of influenza is unfounded.'

Edwina leaned forward in her sumptuous barouche to raise a gloved hand at a neighbour just emerging from the churchyard. 'Look at that ridiculous turban,' she hissed at Elizabeth from a corner of her mouth. 'Have you ever seen such a concoction of feathers? I swear she has a whole farmyard roosting atop her head. Of course when one is as sparse-thatched as she, a little borrowed plumage is understandable.'

Elizabeth glanced at Mrs Vaughan, a woman of her grandmother's age, and her two gangly nieces accompanying her. Her soft lips quirked at one corner. 'You can be very unkind, Grandmama. Very duplicitous, too. I heard, with my own ears, you praise her rig-out when she settled on the pew behind us.'

Edwina chuckled, then slid her granddaughter a look. When Elizabeth refrained from rebuking her over more serious duplicity, and appeared content to inspect passing scenery, she mentioned casually, 'Pettifer tells me you received a letter today. He says it was delivered by a young footman in very smart livery. He believes it to be the new Viscount Stratton's colours. Black and gold…'

'How vulgar. Obviously it *was* his servant, then.'

'Have you received a letter from him, Elizabeth?'

Elizabeth turned a pansy-blue stare on her grandmother. 'I'm sure if I have, t'would be my own business.'

'Come, don't be missish! You're m'granddaughter,' Edwina huffed. 'I've a right to be interested in what goes on between you and m'friend.'

'A little late with your worries, I think. But, yes, indeed, a fond grandmama should be concerned,' Elizabeth said sweetly. 'And, yes, I did receive a letter from your good friend. In it, he insinuates he is willing to re-negotiate terms of payment. The lure to meet him is a hint at immediately returning my jewellery…'

'Well, that's mighty nice of him. You see; I told you he was a gentleman.'

'In exchange for being so nice, I imagine he will require my immediate agreement to another of his propositions.'

Edwina shot her granddaughter a sharp look.

'Oh, did I not say?' Her tone was all innocent apology. 'The Viscount was exceedingly obliging in offering various options should I be unable to persuade you to give him back his cash.' She unfurled slender, white fingers and ticked them off. 'There was the Fleet for you; and Gin Alley for me. For him, first of all, of course, came my services as paramour to pay him in kind. He calculated six years before he was done…and so was I.'

'I'll speak to him,' Edwina spluttered. 'Enough is enough. The matter is at an end.'

'Because you say so?' Elizabeth choked a despairing laugh. 'No. You told me he was a powerful and influential man and I didn't want to believe you. Unfortunately, now I do. I think money is not so terribly important to him now. He didn't mention the cash in his letter. He wants reprisal. It appears you have outwitted him and he will not be bested in this.' She jerked her head away, staring sightlessly into September sunshine. 'I believe you meant well and hoped to see me safely settled with him, but…' Elizabeth sighed a sigh that seemed to well from deep within. 'But I think your friend has his own ideas. I think he will make a bad enemy. What *have* you done, Grandmama?'

Elizabeth held her breath as she leaned over the child's scrawny shoulder. Valiantly ignoring a stirring in his wiry hair and the acrid smell of his unwashed clothes, she gently took the piece of chalk from his bony fingers. 'Samuel is spelled with the *u* before the *e*,' she told him, correcting his work by writing his name again beneath his own spidery effort. She returned his chalk, and with a smile moved on. Clara Parker was next in line. She was about ten years old and Elizabeth was aware the little girl hero-worshipped her. Glassy grey eyes were adoring her while a dirty finger twirled a stringy strand of mousy hair. 'Have you finished your writing, Clara?' Elizabeth asked on a smile.

'Yes, m'm,' Clara responded gruffly with an unobtrusive little stroke at the blue wool of Elizabeth's oldest, least fashionable pelisse. 'I'd like my hair in curls,' Clara added shyly, twirling faster at her rat-tail tress, while gazing admiringly at Elizabeth's pearlescent ringlets peeping from beneath an old felt bonnet.

Elizabeth's hand hovered over the child's head. Gingerly she took a section of limp hair and wound it round and round a slender finger. Carefully she withdrew her digit from the loose spiral. 'Now do some letters,' she whispered at the girl's glowing, grubby face. Clara immediately cradled the treasured curl on a palm. 'Come, attend to your lesson or the Reverend will be cross!' Elizabeth looked at Hugh as, hands clasped behind his back, he leaned forward to listen to a youngster falteringly reading the few lines of scripture he had chalked on his slate.

Conscious of Elizabeth's petite figure moving closer, Hugh arrowed her a smile and straightened. Taking out his watch he tapped it indicatively. It was time for school to end. His double clap brought heads up. Then the score or more pupils filed forward at the signal and handed their boards and chalk to the Reverend. The warehouse emptied slowly, the children becoming jocular as they emerged into welcome evening sunshine that warmed their chilled little bodies. Finally it was just Hugh and Elizabeth left in the cold, dingy interior of the warehouse.

'It's a shame this window doesn't face south and let in more light and warmth,' Elizabeth observed as she peered up at a small pane of glass and the uninspiring sight of a neighbouring warehouse's sooty wall.

Hugh grimaced agreement as he locked away the few precious articles into the cupboard. 'Without Mr Grantham's benevolence in allowing us this room, the school would have to shut. It's here or the vicarage, and I don't think Mother would relish the thought of twenty mucky urchins shedding lice on to our carpets.' He laughed a trifle uneasily at the uncharitable admission. 'If only there were funds to build a parish hall…' he sighed.

Closing and locking the warehouse door, he gallantly drew Elizabeth's arm through his to aid her progress as they started negotiating a path over uneven, slimy cobbles. In front of them lay a ten-minute walk through the back lanes of Wapping to the vicarage. Once there, Elizabeth would graciously accept a cup of tea and a slice of dry cake from Hugh's elderly, widowed mother, before being taken back to Connaught Street in Hugh's gig.

Hugh touched a gloved hand to his hat as a woman shouted a greeting from a doorway. She was lounging comfortably, basking in a shaft of dying sunlight that glossed a paint-peeling, bottle-green doorway and mellowed crumbling brickwork. As she exposed her face to the soothing warmth, the pipe gripped in her teeth angled skyward. A child, barely knee high, huddled into her skirts, two tiny thumbs lost in its mouth.

Before they had properly passed the tranquil scene, a man dressed in vest and patched breeches appeared. Grabbing the woman's arm, he shoved her inside with a string of slurred curses concerning the lateness of his dinner and her sluttish ways. She answered him in some colourful language of her own, but slunk away into the darkness with the child wailing in her wake.

Hugh shook his head and increased his pace.

'Lady Elizabeth…?'

The call was so buffered by neighbourhood cacophony that at first both Hugh and Elizabeth herself missed being hailed and continued discussing the likelihood of an influenza epidemic.

'Lady Elizabeth Rowe…?'

The questioning shout strengthened, bringing both Elizabeth and the vicar to an abrupt halt. Extracting her arm from Hugh's, Elizabeth falteringly approached the nearest tenement doorway. Several pairs of eyes swivelled to her. Even after all these months of hurrying back and forth through these alleys on a Sunday afternoon, she still drew curious stares from the locals. The women, especially, picked over with jealous eyes her blonde hair and fine features and her clean serviceable garb. Hugh was a more prosaic sight to his parishioners. Elizabeth knew that her safe passage through the slums was wholly attributable to the respect these people had for their local minister. But never before had anyone addressed her directly. Never would she have expected them to.

'Did someone call me?' Her pupils widened, blackening her eyes as she squinted into the dim interior of the building. The unwholesome stench of rancid food and unwashed humanity had her retreating a pace. In any case, all that was discernible was a broken stairway and a few huddled figures propped against the newel post. About to turn thankfully away, sure she had been mistaken in thinking she'd been summoned, a woman slid from behind the splintered doorframe and simply stared at her. Elizabeth stared back. She knew her. Beneath the sallowing bruise on her face that extended from brow to lip and the matted dark brown hair that tumbled wildly about her thin shoulders was a person she should recognise. But she couldn't fit a name to that poor, gaunt visage.

The woman laughed wryly at the confusion on Elizabeth's face, but the sound couldn't escape her bobbing throat. Her head fell forward into one quivering, cadaverous hand. 'You don't remember me, do you? That's not surprising: I like to think I don't look the same.' It was a cultured voice, just a hint of cockney dialect taking the edge off the vowels and running words together. She shook back her snarled hair, squinted sideways at Elizabeth, a poignant arrogance in the slant of her mouth, the tilt of her head. ''Ere, take a proper look. Know me now?' she challenged, adopting the local nasal twang for all its worth. 'Ain't a pretty sight no longer, wouldn't you say?'

'Jane? Jane Dawson?'

'As was. I married Colonel Selby, remember? Did well, didn't I?' she gutturally mocked herself. She stared at Elizabeth with eyes like wet black pebbles. 'I certainly thought I'd done better than you that year,' she commented slyly and chuckled as the colour rose beneath Elizabeth's pale complexion. 'Never can tell how things'll turn out...' she added with a toss of her tangles. She cocked her head to take a look at Hugh Clemence who was hovering a pace or two behind watching, listening to their exchange. 'You married now? To him?' Jane demanded, cuffing her nose and sniffing. 'You a parson's wife?'

'No! No, the Reverend and I teach Sunday School together. In Barrow Road,' Elizabeth explained with a hand flick back the way they'd just come. Aware that this unusual discourse between a lady of quality and one of their own had drawn inquisitive bystanders, Elizabeth placed a hand on Jane's thin arm and drew her outside to shelter behind the open door. 'What on earth has happened? Where is your husband? Is the Colonel dead?' Elizabeth asked with a perplexed frown.

'Damned if I know,' Jane said on a dull guffaw. 'It turned out he wasn't my husband after all; he wasn't a colonel either. It transpired, my lady,' she mocked in a soft, precise drawl, 'that the bounder already had a wife in Yorkshire and another in Portugal.' She blinked rapidly and bit her lip before choking, 'I think he married the foreigner while in the army during the war. He lied about being invalided out and his rank and regiment. He was a sergeant who had been cashiered from the infantry for cowardice and thievery. I never did any better than you, with that Lieutenant Havering. Army bastards!' She spat. She looked Elizabeth up and down, her glittering black eyes lingering covetously on her fair, classical features. 'But that's not right. You've done well enough by the looks of things, if not as well as you ought. Looks like scandal slid off you like water off a duck's back…'

Elizabeth managed a wan smile. 'Not quite. But I've been lucky in that my grandmother—my maternal grandmother, that is—has never shunned me. In fact, without her, after my papa died a few years ago, I don't know how I would have survived…'

'Same way as me, I expect.' Jane's light spite transformed into a conversational, 'I heard that the old Dowager Marchioness cold-shouldered you.' She leaned forward, giggled conspiratorially, 'She always was a toffee-nosed, miserable old biddy. Do you remember our first time at Vauxhall, when you and Sally Treacher and me got lost in the walkways?'

Elizabeth bit her lip and laughed. 'Yes, I do. The Dowager nearly had an apoplexy!'

'So did my mama. She accused me of losing more than my shawl in the bushes that evening! That silly cow, Mrs Treacher, told her that Trelawney and his band of lusty chums were spotted in the same grove. They both needed reviving with hartshorn after that. When I found out we'd missed them, I was bloody angry…' she exclaimed on a ribald laugh.

Aware that Hugh had moved closer on hearing mention of that particular gentleman, Elizabeth demanded in a low tone, 'But what on earth has happened to you? Why is it come to this, Jane? What of your parents? They surely don't know how you're living?'

Jane put a hand to her trembling mouth, spoke from behind it in gasping bursts. 'They wouldn't care if I was dead. No, that's not true. They'd prefer it if I was. And it's come to this…because I loved him. Because when my father told me…he had discovered sordid details…of Frank's past…I wouldn't believe it. My papa told me to choose…return home with him…or stay with my bigamist…in which case they no longer had a daughter. So I chose…because I was sure he loved me…but he's gone…abandoned me…and our son.'

'You have a *son*?' Elizabeth whispered, aghast. 'Living *here*?' She shot an anxious glance at Hugh who was frowning back, listening intently to all that passed between the two women.

Jane nodded. 'Upstairs.' She jerked her head to indicate the doorway. 'Dosed little Jack with laudanum this evening. Keeps him quiet and out of harm's way.'

Elizabeth closed a firm hand on her friend's wrist. 'That is too much! Fetch the little lad now and come home with me to Marylebone. I shall see what can be done.'

Jane wrenched from her grip and backed off, eyes wild with terror. 'I can't do that. You don't understand. I can't do that. He'll never let me…not till I pay him…'

'Who? Who do you mean?'

''S'pect she means me,' came drifting in an oily drawl on the river-pungent air.

Elizabeth spun about to see a stocky man, sallow of complexion, with greasy-looking dark curls corkscrewing on to his wide forehead. His eyes were an incongruous bright blue, the edges a sunburst of creases as he squinted foxily at them. He slid along the wall as though he might have been spewed from one of the many doorways agape in the rotten brick. Reaching Jane, he slung a possessive, brawny arm about her shoulders. His hand clenched into a thick fist, making the muscle in his forearm jump beneath a matting of wiry hairs. Jane seemed to shrink, become ever more brittle beneath the mean embrace.

'Aren't yer goin' t'intradoos me to yer friend?' he silkily enquired. ''Course me 'n the Reverend's 'kwainted.' When Jane remained quiet with head lowered, he gave her thin body a brusque shake. 'No manners, gel? 'Oos the luvlie lady wiv the vicar?' The cap pushed to the back of his head at a jaunty angle was doffed in a travesty of respect. It was swept low towards his dirty dark trousers, before resting against a dapper corduroy waistcoat.

Hugh laid a heavy hand on Elizabeth's arm and determinedly drew her away. At the same time, he said coldly, 'I see you're at your old tricks, Leach. No dock work to keep you? Have you tried earning your own living?'

''S'not me, Reverend,' the man whined craftily. 'S'these bad girls wot know the tricks and get's me inta trouble. You ask 'm if'n they don't. Badgers me ta look out for'm, they do. So that's wot I do, 'cos I'm a carin' sorta feller.' He shook Jane masterfully again. 'Tell the vicar jus' 'ow good Leachie looks out fer yer.'

Jane raised wide, jet-black eyes. 'He does,' she whispered. 'Go away. I'm sorry…I shouldn't have troubled you…I beg you not to come back…' Grabbing her grubby skirts in her fists, she pulled out of the man's restraint and was swallowed by darkness inside the dank portal.

'Come, Elizabeth!' Hugh's voice was aquiver with urgency and anger.

'No!' Elizabeth swivelled back to glare at the swarthy man who was leering unpleasantly at her. She watched his tongue tip protrude, then work its slow way about his fleshy lips.

Heavy lids weighted over eyes that crawled her primly dressed figure while rough, wiry fingers thoughtfully massaged an unshaven chin. 'Don't yer go takin' no 'eed o' Jane now,' he growled. 'She's poor wiv manners at times. I've 'ad ta speak sharp wiv 'er over that 'afore. 'Specially when *she's* sharp wiv the gents 'oo want ta treat 'er right. You come back an' see Leachie offen as yer like…'cos I've a notion there's plenty a gent might jus' luv ta treat you right. Might even be me.'

Elizabeth opened her mouth to flay him with her disgust but could only think that, if she did, Jane's plight would be that much worse. Her impotent rage put her teeth on edge, curled her shaking fingers.

Leachie recognised her angry frustration and smirked, then laughed raucously, bending over at the waist. Elizabeth turned away and blindly groped for Hugh Clemence's arm so he could lead her away.

'Be sensible, Elizabeth. Listen to what Reverend Clemence is telling you. These vermin are not to be trifled with. They are vicious miscreants who have their own codes; their own underworld hierarchies…'

Elizabeth continued shaking her head at her grandmother until Edwina flung her hands up in despair. She glared at Hugh Clemence, who was still standing close to the door as though uncertain whether he would be welcomed further into the parlour. 'Oh, you speak to her again, vicar. But know this: I hold you responsible for it all. You should never have begun this nonsense of encouraging a gentlewoman to slum visit. See what you have done! Oh, never mind.' She illustrated her impatience with his red-faced distress by flapping a fat hand. 'For now, just impress again on Lady Elizabeth the dangers of associating with this lowlife. And that she must never return.'

'I do not need to again be told,' Elizabeth enunciated angrily. 'I do not need you to blame Hugh for my behaviour. I am a woman of nearly twenty-nine and quite capable of making up my own mind about helping the needy. Today I have sincerely understood just how important it is that such work continues. I have seen with my own eyes just how squalid and mean life can be. I have had paraded before my own eyes living proof that there, but for the grace of God, go I. And if you think for one moment I am about to abandon an old friend, and her son, to that foul man…'

Hugh hastened forward. 'Listen, please, Elizabeth. It is not simply a case of rescuing a…er, fallen woman and her child. Men like Leach tie the wretched creatures to them with debts as well as fear.' An unsteady hand scraped through his brown hair. 'I doubt you have heard of Old Mother Leach. I pray you have not. She is a notorious fence and a bawdy-house keeper. Her name should bring trepidation to the hearts of all decent folk. Nathaniel Leach, whom you met today, is her son and in the same line of business. He knows nothing else. That isn't to excuse him, it's simply the truth. They deal in prostitutes and pickpockets. They are parasites of the worst kind.'

'I don't care!' Elizabeth raged, her beautiful eyes sparking blue flame.

'Please listen,' Hugh again begged. 'As hard as it must be for you to accept, the sad truth is that Mrs Selby is very much in his power and unlikely to leave. Leach will have gained her trust by posing as a concerned friend when she was vulnerable and isolated. He might have presented food or clothes, insinuating they are gifts, then introduced her to an usurer when it is time to pay. He will have told her how easy it is to borrow to settle her dues; how soon she and her son will be able to escape to a better life if she only does as he bids. He will have snared her with her own hope. None of it ever comes about. Only the debt collector comes about. So does Leach, to take what she earns from clients he finds her. He'll give her a little back, keep a tally and encourage her to borrow more. So the debt mounts and the trap closes. She will never have the means to break free; Leach will make very sure of that. And inhuman as it may seem to you, her parents will never now want to know how you found her…or where…'

'Give me some money, Grandmama,' Elizabeth demanded, turning her back on Hugh's pained expression. 'I am begging you as never before to allow me some of my inheritance to help someone far, far worse off than I have ever been.' Heartfelt appeal throbbed in her voice, blazed in her violet eyes.

Edwina stalked away. 'This is madness, Elizabeth. Have you heard *nothing* the Reverend has said? You cannot help in these instances. Do you think I will allow you to involve us with such scum? Do you imagine this Leach is likely to allow you to steal his meal ticket from under his nose without a fight? If he discovers we are two women living alone save for servants, he might send his evil accomplices to rob us blind. He might murder us in our beds!' Edwina pointed a finger at Hugh Clemence. 'Am I not right in m'fears, vicar?' she asked loudly, daring him to contradict.

'Possibly, Mrs Sampson,' Hugh admitted on a lingering sigh. 'And, forgive me, but there is no peace in agreeing with you.'

Edwina nodded vehemently, her salt and pepper ringlets dancing crazily. 'I'll listen to no more foolishness from you, m'girl. I forbid you to go back there. If you defy me, I swear you will be sorry!'

The door slammed after her grandmother's dumpy, bristling figure. Elizabeth looked at Hugh. He needed no more encouragement than that doe-eyed glance. Approaching her, he took both her small, cold hands into the warm comfort of his. 'I'm so sorry, Elizabeth. It's my fault. Your grandmother is right to reprimand me. Involving you in a project in such a stew was not wise. Had I not done so, this evening's chance meeting with Mrs Selby would never have come about.'

'I'm glad it did,' Elizabeth interrupted quietly, squeezing at his fingers. 'At last I feel there is an opportunity for me to truly make a difference. And please don't feel guilty. I volunteered to become involved in Barrow Road. And I want to continue helping. More so than ever now.'

'If you truly mean that, Elizabeth, you must allow me to protect you properly,' Hugh uttered hoarsely. 'You must let me shield you with every means in my power. I would be so very honoured if you would allow me to protect you with my name and my humble vocation...'

Elizabeth squeezed his hands more firmly to make him stop. 'Please don't say any more, Hugh. Just know that I am greatly obliged to count you amongst my true and loyal friends.' Disengaging her hands, she choked a wry little laugh. 'It has been rather an exhausting day, to say the least. I think retiring early is in order. First, I suppose I had best find my grandmama and make my peace. 'Twill in some small part help me sleep.'

Hugh managed a wavering smile and a fleeting touch of his lips to her fingertips before she gently withdrew.

'No, the long-sleeved one, Josie. There seems to be a chill in the air tonight,' Elizabeth told her maid. Obediently, Josie folded away the frothy sleeveless nightdress and replaced it in the clothes press. She removed another and began shaking out heavy brushed cotton that dragged on the floor.

Elizabeth wandered to the fire in her undergarments, holding the fragrant warmth of the washing cloth flat against her face. With a sigh, she moved her face up and down against flannel-covered palms, scouring away the day's grime. It dropped from her fingers to plop back into the shallow bowl, slopping splashes of steaming water onto her writing desk. Retrieving and wringing out the cloth, Elizabeth wiped her arms, dipping her head as she washed a shoulder, reached beneath her heavy hair to scrub her nape. Her lowered eyes encountered the note on her bureau. She immediately relinquished the cloth and picked up the letter, her heart missing a beat. With all the commotion and consternation surrounding her reunion with Jane Selby, she had forgotten about the Viscount and her own problems. But then, in comparison with what she had witnessed today, her feud with Stratton paled into insignificance. She had a doting grandmother, enough food to eat, clean clothes and bedding. She had no problems.

Water droplets had swirled with ink to form a small black pearl upon the paper. She touched a fingertip to it; withdrew it to read again the curt suggestion they once more meet. *Perhaps return your family's jewellery* was untouched by greyish smears. The words were clear and precise and seemed to leap significantly out from the paper. And what came to her next was so simple yet so shocking that she clutched at the bed edge and sat down.

If she could brave the pitfalls of Wapping on a Sunday afternoon, she could do this. What had she to lose? No good name and no keepsake. Both were already gone. And if she didn't act immediately, while the horrors of Jane's predicament still churned her stomach and the thought of a small boy drugged into oblivion on a filthy bed sent bile to her throat, she might never in her life act from true, selfless compassion at all. The seed was in her mind, needing just a sprinkling of stalwart courage to help it blossom.

The note drifted from her quivering fingers onto the bureau. Elizabeth stared out of the window into the gathering dusk. Treetops swayed close to the glass in a stirring breeze. It wasn't so late. Barely nine of the clock, she guessed. She knew Edwina had already retired. She had said her goodnights to her grandmother in her chamber, kissed away her grumpiness and smoothed her soft cheek with appeasing fingers.

She glanced at Josie; her maid turned the nightgown she was holding up before the fire to air it. Satisfied it was cosy enough, Josie approached, holding out the snug garment.

'Not that one, Josie,' her mistress said with a note of hysterical humour. 'My blue velvet gown and black satin cloak…the one with the hood. No, not in which to retire.' A shrill giggle escaped her as Josie gaped in astonishment. 'I must yet go out; and, I'm sorry, but you must accompany me, I'm afraid.'

Chapter Seven

If he deemed it unusual for a lady to arrive, unexpectedly, at nearly ten of the clock; then demand to see his master, the man kept the surprise to himself.

Elizabeth seated herself on the chair the butler indicated, a gracious dip of her head his only thanks. In turn she indicated that Josie take a seat, too. Josie obediently sank down, but with her goggle-eyed stare clinging to her mistress's face. Elizabeth was conscious she had stupefied her maid by acting in such a bizarre manner.

'I shall see if Viscount Stratton is available to see you,' the butler intoned, pessimism barely discernible. Elizabeth again inclined her blonde head in haughty acceptance of his cool courtesy. Perhaps the man's sang-froid indicated that it was fairly customary for women to turn up at late hours, soliciting an audience with his lordship.

The fact that the Viscount was at home was both alarming and reassuring. From Marylebone to Mayfair, she'd been alternately fretting or praying that her reckless sortie might be in vain. Once out and upon the road in a hired hackney, her daring had ebbed a little. Logic had flowed in its stead.

A hedonist such as Trelawney was unlikely to spend his evenings at home alone twiddling his thumbs. If he wasn't abroad, it was likely he might have a pack of cronies around him, which would only make things so much worse. Well, it was too late to demand to know if his master already had company. She peered after the smartly uniformed butler disappearing into the heart of the quiet house.

Elizabeth refused to be impressed by the splendour of this residence. She refused to look about at all to admire the soaring marble pillars, or the glorious paintings, or the chandeliers that blinded with diamond-fire as scores of candles flickered amid icy droplets.

She had been reared amongst such grandeur, she reminded herself. In her papa's heyday, they had leased just such wonderful residences as this. During her come out, they had rented a Nash townhouse in Caledon Square which was the envy of all who were invited within. Wellington had visited; so had numerous other dukes, earls and titled families. She was unmoved by evidence of a hefty chandler's bill, she decided, sweeping a jaundiced eye over stately mahogany furniture and a huge gilt-framed mirror. Her attention was arrested by the pretty unicorn central to its intricate carving.

So, she had been correct in thinking the Viscount wasn't on his uppers. Which meant her theory, voiced earlier to her grandmother, was sound. Stratton wanted retribution. The fruits of his ill-gotten gains were displayed all around. Porcelain artefacts resting on polished surfaces were probably priceless spoils from confiscated cargoes. Her meandering eye returned to a delicate jade figurine close by. Her suspicions as to its provenance were interrupted by the sound of footsteps. The butler had reappeared; behind him came two footmen and a maid. All were dressed in the same neat uniform of black with dull gold embroidered waistcoat and braid trim. Quite a sober livery, she had to admit, as she recalled denigrating it as vulgar earlier today. The servants appeared industrious, while giving her discreet glances.

Elizabeth had witnessed few housemaids dusting so late. Either the Viscount was a hard task master or his menials were curious for a glimpse of the bold hussy visiting a bachelor at his home, uninvited, at such a late hour. She frowned at Josie, gesturing at her to straighten in the chair and look less cowed by the whole affair.

'The Viscount will see you now.'

Elizabeth identified vague surprise lilting the butler's adenoidal tone as she got to her stylishly shod little feet. Her chin edged up; only the rim of colour accentuating her sharp cheekbones might have betrayed how jittery she actually felt. 'Good,' was the sum of her acknowledgement to the favour. Then, 'Please find my maid a little refreshment while she waits for me.' She ignored his raised eyebrows and Josie's quivering. She knew the poor girl simply wanted to be left alone to shrink against the wall.

I am not afraid, neither am I ashamed…beat through her head in time with her footsteps as she followed the butler over a plush carpet. As he came to a halt, pivoted precisely to open the door, then marshalled her within, she clung to the haunting image of Jane Selby and her little son. What was her own humbling compared to their pitiful predicament?

The Viscount was ready to receive her. He was standing, with one arm propped against a high mantel, one booted foot resting against an ornate brass fender. On a table close to a fireside chair was a brandy balloon containing a considerable amount. A book had been placed open, face-down, as though he had just reluctantly relinquished it to gain his feet. It was such an unexpectedly homely scene and one that she would never have associated with Ross Trelawney, bounty hunter, that for a moment she felt disorientated…tempted to apologise for disturbing him. The words were swallowed unuttered.

She realised, with a wrench, that the cosy tableau reminded her of Thorneycroft and her dear papa: a glass of cognac, a weighty tome laid open by the blazing logs. How many quiet evenings had they spent so, happy in each other's company, in their countryside retreat, before her stepmother's arrival? But for her papa's need to remarry and produce a male heir to prevent his detested cousin gaining the entailed estate, it might have continued so… Had she only been born a boy, things might have been so different…for both of them…

'Come in…please,' Ross invited, breaking into her wistful thoughts. He extended a hand to welcome her further into the oak-panelled small salon.

Elizabeth felt herself flushing at his unfazed manner and civility. To cover her confusion at what she knew was a shameful intrusion and breach of etiquette, she blurted out, 'I know I should not have come. I realise it is quite outrageous behaviour. But…but as you and I have no good reputations to keep, I thought…as there is nothing to lose, you would not mind.'

He smiled a lop-sided smile. 'I don't mind.'

Elizabeth nodded, moistened her lips. 'It is important, or I would not have come.' Small, white teeth sank into her lower lip. She was repeating herself unnecessarily. He had already gallantly accepted her explanations. *The lady doth protest too much, I think*…echoed in all its sarcasm, in her mind.

'Of course it's important,' he soothed.

She looked at him, really looked at him, but in glances that quickly strayed. Yet they lingered long enough on his broad shoulders clothed in fine white cambric, his dark, angular features and dusky hair, to come to a profoundly disturbing conclusion. At first sight, he would appear the perfect man. Any woman ignorant of his dubious reputation and lineage would simply see before her an imposing, handsome gentleman who enjoyed a quiet evening reading amid the trappings of his wealth. It would have been unremarkable if, in the other fireside chair, his refined lady wife worked at her tapestry.

She had supposed him an ill-educated oaf, yet she had no proof it was so. And this domesticity wasn't stage-managed for her benefit. He had no warning of her visit. Even if he had, why would he bother seeking the good opinion of a rude, supercilious little bitch? She had simply caught him unawares about his private business. She was seeing the man, not the myth.

'I take it you received my letter earlier?' he prompted, interrupting her startling insight.

'Yes. 'Tis why I'm here.'

He nodded. 'Thank you for responding so quickly.'

She shot him a sharp, violet look, searching his face for sarcasm.

'Would you like some tea?'

'No,' she snapped. 'No, thank you,' she amended, recalling her manners. 'I think it best to get directly to business.' She flushed again as she saw his smile at her bluntness. 'That is…I cannot tarry.'

'I understand.'

He was being too polite. Far too polite. It was as though the ruthless stranger who had menaced her with abuse and a harrowing future had never existed.

As though exactly reading her thoughts, he volunteered quietly, 'As you've found the courage to come here this evening, my lady, I must find the humility to apologise for my crude behaviour when last we met.'

'I'd rather you did not,' she rebuffed him immediately, increasingly unsettled by this change in him.

'Why not? Because my apology might demand yours?'

'I've no need to apologise!' she burst out hotly.

'Yes, you have,' he mildly corrected. 'I imagine you feel as ashamed of your conduct as I do of mine.'

'A rude, supercilious little bitch ruined by scandal never feels obliged to say sorry,' she whipped out icily, but her face was flaming beneath his unwanted perception, his unwanted chivalry.

'We'll leave proprieties till later then,' he said drily, but with an indulgent smile.

'Proprieties are not required between us at any time. This is not a social call,' she retorted, flustered by this bewildering need to keep him in the role of uncouth lout. 'I said a few days ago that I hoped never again to endure your presence. My feelings have not changed.'

'So, why are you here?' He pushed away from the mantel and took two steps towards her. As she back-paced in time with his advance, he halted and swung his head sideways to frown in defeat. 'If my company is that odious and you already regret coming, go. Go away now. I'll not stop you.'

If only she could do just that: whip about and storm out! But she was a Marquess's daughter and above being dismissed by a barbarian such as he! Elizabeth's insides somersaulted with frustration and humiliation. She wouldn't go…couldn't go. How could she leave without the necklace when it had taken every ounce of audacity she could summon to come and fetch it?

Ross watched colour ebbing and flowing beneath her translucent complexion. He could sense her turmoil as she strove to curb her temper and force herself to be pleasant. And as his eyes discreetly roved her alluringly garbed little figure, her pearly hair, he felt the crazy need to stalk her down, corner her…just so he could take her in his arms and comfort her. For the moment, though, he judged keeping his distance and tendering another olive branch might be the best move. 'If you want to stay, come and sit down. I can't talk business if you're going to hide in the shadows.'

'I'm not hiding…I'm not afraid…'

'Very well,' he conceded softly. 'You're not hiding and you're not afraid of me. That's good. Come and sit down.' He pivoted slowly, watching her evade him by keeping to the perimeter of the room on her way to a fireside chair. He returned to the wingchair opposite, mirroring her pose by perching on the edge. Lifting his glass indicatively, he asked, 'Would you like a drink? Wine? Ratafia?'

'I don't drink.'

'Ah, yes. Good works.' He smiled. 'Are you a member of some temperance society?' He took a long sip while awaiting her reply.

'No. But I've sympathy with the cause,' she said, primly eyeing his glass. 'I've witnessed the damage alcohol wreaks on poor wretches.'

'Where? Where have you seen that?' he asked interestedly, placing down his brandy and frowning at her.

'Bridewell, Newgate, the back alleys about Wapping where

I assist at Sunday School…' She broke off, grateful for that timely reminder of her reason for being here, alone with him, at this time of the night, flouting all decent codes of conduct.

Ross leaned forward to rest forearms on knees. 'You prison visit and slum visit?'

She was aware of the surprise, and the hint of disapproval in his tone. 'I haven't risked fresh opprobrium in coming here this evening, my lord, to discuss the charities I support. Might we please get to business? I am keen to return home before I am missed.'

'Edwina doesn't know you are here?'

Elizabeth gave a slight shake of her head. 'No,' she murmured. 'But I doubt she would raise much objection if she did know…' She dropped her eyes, unable to meet the humour lurking in the hazel depths of his at that unguarded observation.

The silence lengthened and she glanced at him from beneath a curtain of lashes, then again more openly. He held her gaze easily that time, moved his glass, gesturing that he was ready and willing to listen. Now the time had come her mind seemed to have frozen. She had lost all her clever phrases, all her rehearsed persuasiveness. All that battered monotonously at her fraught mind was the need to recover her precious necklace. So, unembellished, that's what tumbled out.

'I want back my necklace.'

'I know you do.'

'May I have it?'

'Yes.'

She stared at him suspiciously.

'Now you'd like to know what I want in return.'

She nodded, a jerky movement that swayed silverish tresses against the graceful column of her alabaster neck.

He watched her eyes clinging to his. They both knew what he wanted. She'd spurned his sweet talk, so now it was time to get down to brass tacks and proposition her properly. Yet he couldn't immediately do it. And he wasn't sure why. God knows he'd had enough practice taking on mistresses over the years. Perhaps it was that poignant look of resignation making him hesitate. Of course, she'd heard it all before, lots of times, from other men. He noticed her pearly teeth sinking deeper into her lower lip to keep it still…but that might be simply to prevent a tirade of disgust hurtling at him. She was conquering her pride, solemnly awaiting the further indignity he was about to deliver. That's how she would see it; just as she read his attempts at conciliation as calculated sophistry now he was on home territory. He took an abrupt swig of brandy, noting that his prevarication was unnerving rather than reassuring her. Her fingers were in knots in her lap. He sensed a gentle protectiveness washing through him, again making him want to comfort her. Intense irritation swiftly followed. She'd come to him, uninvited, risking, as she'd rightly said, all manner of censure. She was here to barter. She knew exactly what he wanted. So why couldn't he open negotiations? What the hell else did she expect he might say? Marry me?

'I've decided that Edwina's original offer to settle her dues wasn't such a poor suggestion…' He heard the words and supposed they must be his.

Elizabeth frowned, trying to bring to mind, in her numbed state, what that offer was. Then she remembered. Her violet eyes widened expressively on him. 'She won't release my dowry for your sake. I've asked her several times before to advance a small amount to me but she refuses. She really is a tight-fist,' she confided on a sweet, self-conscious smile.

And that did it. Gentleness was back with a vengeance. She was actually looking at him with something akin to shy camaraderie. For the first time she was letting him see the real woman behind the defensive shell of hauteur. And he knew it was what he'd been waiting for: just a glimpse of the lovable, vivacious creature he'd watched from afar a decade ago. For the first time, too, he felt more kindly disposed to Edwina for getting him embroiled in this mess. 'I'll agree to your grandmother's terms,' he said hoarsely. He cleared his throat, then added, 'It's what she planned all along.'

'She planned getting me wed all along,' Elizabeth contributed to the conversation with the same trace of amicable confiding in her voice and smile. And then, barely established, it was gone. She finally comprehended his meaning. She moistened her lips, waiting for him to scoff at Edwina's idiotic presumption he might take a scandal-wrecked woman to wife. Just as he had before, at her home. But he didn't laugh; he simply looked at her, his golden eyes merging mesmerically with hers. Her gaze fled to her lap; slowly she rose to her feet, one hand behind her steadying against the chair as though frightened her strength might collapse.

So he wanted money after all, not retribution. He wasn't quite the noble savage she had thought. And she wasn't sure whether she hated him more or less. He believed she had come here to brazenly broker a marriage. He had told her, had he not, that he judged her the instigator in this derisory plot to snare him as a husband. He probably thought he was doing her a huge favour by succumbing to the lure of her fortune. Thus, he would not laugh now, during the prelude to his proposal, but he was sure to later when he recounted to his chums how she had come begging him to make an honest woman of her. He would laugh harder on boasting how well he would upkeep his riotous life-style with her dowry and the plump annuity that came with it. She felt her heart thumping achingly slowly, her pride smarting equally painfully. If he imagined she was just some risible toy who would allow herself to be sold, then show gratitude for a soulless sham of a marriage, he was much mistaken.

'If you would allow me two weeks' grace, my lord,' was forced out of her stiltedly, 'I promise to persuade Edwina to be sensible. She is already wavering over the whole stupid affair. I know you have been patient, but if I might again beg your forebearance, I vow she will soon relent.'

Having looked at her, listened to her, Ross stared at the toes of his boots for a moment before pushing to his feet and immediately walking away. He was seething mad, yet simultaneously felt crushed, drained.

So much for being a sentimental fool and taking the honourable way. She'd refused to even acknowledge his tentative overture…his pathetic fantasy, as she no doubt still termed a union between a Cornish brigand and a Marquess's daughter. Having spent all his adult years studiously avoiding the marriage trap, he'd actually begun to propose, and before the words were properly out, it was made very clear they were unwelcome. A double-handed grip tightened on the mantel's cold marble. 'Very well. Two weeks only. If no firm decision is reached by then, I'll dispose of the suite. I'll get a servant to escort you home,' he clipped out curtly.

Violet eyes flew to his rigid, dark profile as he strode determinedly towards the door. He was going to make her leave, empty-handed. She could sense exasperation in him beneath that icy courtesy and guessed that it sprang from having been denied early access to her money. She had no time to further ponder its cause: he was reaching for the door handle. Instinctively she pursued him, raised a hand to detain him, fearful he might dismiss her right now. 'No, you don't understand. I want…that is…I hoped that you would let me have back my necklace.'

'So I shall, when settlement is reached,' he growled, his eyes riveted on the slender, white hand straddling the breadth of his forearm.

'No…tonight. I must have back my necklace tonight…'

'Why?'

Elizabeth's timid violet gaze floundered beneath the narrowed hawk's eyes just visible between those long black lashes. A gleam of curiosity was darkening into something else. Something that alarmed yet oddly reassured her. She swallowed and stared fixedly at his abrasive chin. He might want her out of his house…but he did still want her. Her hand slipped unobtrusively from his shirt-sleeve, as though she hoped he might never have noticed it spreadeagled there. 'I have come here specifically to collect my necklace…please don't make me leave without it. I swear to you I can persuade Edwina to give you back your money, if you will only be patient a while longer.' Her voice was light and breathy. Only the colour creeping beneath her skin betrayed her desperate uneasiness.

'That's not good enough. I want a firm contract before I'll let you have it. You can't expect me to give you back what little collateral I hold,' he reasoned in a voice of gravelly velvet. 'I only have your word that there is anything at all of value in a bank vault.'

'You've had time enough to find out. I would have imagined a grasping opportunist would already have done so,' she sniped, uncontrollable frustration making her insolent.

'I've been too busy grasping other opportunities,' he returned silkily.

The small space between them seemed to throb with tension yet she couldn't seem to withdraw. When she finally managed a step back, she knew before his hands moved that he would bring her close again. His touch felt warm, firm, yet not callous as he swung her about, stranding her between his body and the door.

Her heart seemed to have jumped to her throat; she could sense the wild pulse there. Her tongue tip wet her lower lip, then hid. She peeked up into his thick-lashed watching eyes, wishing he'd say something. He did, and she immediately wished he'd not.

'Tell me why you came here tonight.'

'I've already told you: to collect my necklace.'

'And you imagined this hard-hearted villain would simply hand it over? I don't think so. What did you plan offering me in exchange?'

'A sincere promise that I would extract your payment from Edwina,' she whispered, frowning at the onyx stone set in his snowy cravat.

'You could have written that in a note. Besides, it's not much of an incentive for a hardened rake. I'm afraid I still don't think so,' he purred. A tanned hand spanned her ivory chin, jerking it up. 'Shall I tell you my theory?' He shifted his fingers so their length caressed a cheek as she nodded.

'I think, my lady,' he said softly, 'that you came here, in person, with every intention of tempting me to take a few liberties with you. And you would allow me to take just a few, wouldn't you? Whet my appetite and my trust that you'd deliver what I wanted another night…so long as I delivered what you wanted tonight. You seem desperate to get back home with that necklace, which gives me quite a bargaining stake. So, promise me something else…something convincing, and we'll play it from there. Perhaps we might both end up satisfied.'

She jerked back, clattering her heels against the door. But her face burned where he'd touched it. Burned, too, because he'd put into words something she'd not allowed herself to acknowledge. From the first moment she'd scrambled into fine clothes, prettified her hair, misted her body with her favourite perfume, she'd been…primping in his honour…before quitting the house. 'You're despicable,' she whispered in a shaking voice.

'You've never believed me anything else. Have you?'

Ross observed raw emotion tightening her lovely features. He could tell she was torn between stamping and demanding he give her what she wanted, or ceding and giving him a taste of what he wanted. She was favouring trying just a little flirtatiousness, but didn't know if it would work. What made him smile so wryly was that he knew. And he'd settle for that, because it was a game at which he excelled. If he chose to, he could lead her from one kiss to heaven…or hell. He could make that soft, silky skin that had shivered beneath his palms burn with passion, turn her choked little insults into moans of pleasure. Maybe…he mocked himself, as his eyes wandered her fragile, stony face, her eyes alight with purple fire. Tonight, for his ego's sake, he would take just one kiss, then take his future wife home. Those were his terms, his only terms.

'One kiss,' Elizabeth bit out. 'One kiss only and then you give me the necklace.'

'One kiss?' Ross echoed scornfully. 'I thought I said be credible…'

'One kiss!' Elizabeth wailed, a sob of panic in her voice.

'Very well, if you insist.' There was barely a hint of triumph in his eyes as he drew her forward.

Her eyes were closed tight by the time she was against him. After a heart-stopping moment, when there was nothing other than the sensation of being held against a warm, male body, they fluttered open again.

'Put your arms around me,' he said as she met the hot golden glow in his eyes.

She hesitated for a moment, then her arms rose to rest woodenly against the sides of his broad torso.

'Not there. About my neck,' Ross instructed with all the ardour of a man tutoring a pupil in combat skills.

Elizabeth obediently moved her hands to slide up the front of his muscled chest and hover on his shoulders. But her mouth clamped in a hard, mutinous little line.

'About my neck…'

'You're too tall, I can't reach,' she snapped.

'I've had no complaints before…'

'Well, now you have mine…' she commented icily.

'Perhaps if we sat down…'

'No!' Elizabeth cried, flustered, fretting he might lead her to the sofa set back against the wall. It was long enough to take someone supine. She guessed it might be her. With that disturbing knowledge motivating them, her hands shot up past his powerful shoulders and linked behind his nape. She felt the stroke of his long thick hair against her quivering fingers.

'See how easy it can be, Elizabeth,' Ross murmured. 'Now you've learned to curb that temper, and take a little good advice, you'll make me an excellent, dutiful wife…'

Her violet eyes flew open, her jaw dropped in absolute astonishment. He smiled crookedly at the unwitting invitation of her soft, slack mouth. 'Just a joke…I'll take you the way you are,' he murmured before his lips swooped to cover hers.

This isn't right, was all that paraded back and forth through her head as her knees buckled. No one had kissed her like this before. She had been infatuated with Randolph Havering for two months, and he had never kissed her with such tenderness, such devotion that her bones began melting. Never before had she deliciously shivered beneath male fingers trailing her nape, her collarbone, her ears, every available exposed part of skin, while a careful onslaught of caressing lips and teasing tongue on her mouth made her sigh at its seductive sweetness. Never before had any gentleman during her short debut taken a liberty and made her feel as though her body was swirling in such honeyed pleasure she might die if it stopped. She was losing her mind. And that's why she drew a shuddering breath from his mouth and made it stop.

Working her lips back and forth, she endeavoured to break free from the dangerous magic, while her head chanted, *It's seduction…just sly seduction…* For a moment she was sure he would let her go. The long fingers lost in her hair withdrew to curve over her fragile shoulders. Their mouths unsealed, his tongue tip lightly trailing her lower lip as though in parting salutation…then it was plunging back. This time she wanted it to stop at once; fought to make it stop. His mouth was hot and hard and hurting. This was no subtle wooing. This was selfish lechery: savage and punishing, and the more she twisted her face to free it, the more cruel the assault became. Finally she stood rigid in his arms and within a moment he lifted his dark head.

Two small palms flattened against the rock-like wall of his chest, then pushed. He remained unmoving but, unanchored, the momentum sent her back against the door. A hand went to soothe her throbbing mouth. Her eyes glittered odium. But all she could lash him with, was, 'I said just one kiss.'

'It was one; one for you and one for me.'

His expression was hard, sardonic. He was unmoved by either kiss, she knew. He'd gained little satisfaction from pleasing her or himself. It was all just an exercise, a lesson for her benefit: be amenable and I will be too. Show your claws and that suits me equally.

'Fetch my necklace, at once,' she commanded.

He ignored her demands. Reaching past her, he opened the door. 'As liberties go, my lady, I've taken better,' was all he said.

Elizabeth flung her petite frame back against the door, slamming it shut. 'My necklace!' she squeaked, almost incoherent with fury at his louche, insulting attitude. A small foot stamped down on polished mahogany. 'Fetch it now! You lying…cheating…bastard! You said I might have it. I swear I won't leave without it!' Tears of frustration sparkled in her night-blue eyes, her graceful, slender body a-quiver with temper.

Ross leaned a hand against the door, moved the other to touch her cheek, pursuing her evasive headflicks with idle doggedness until she gave in and allowed the caress. 'I don't recall ever being held hostage in my own home before. It's something I've always fancied: being held captive by a beautiful, belligerent woman. There…we've shared one pathetic fantasy already.'

Elizabeth shook free of his fingers, glared at him through misty eyes.

'If you're determined to wreck my reputation and remain here the night, the least you can do is make an honest man of me.' His thumb caught a sprinkling of tears sliding towards her mouth. 'Come,' he soothed, 'be sensible. I want to return your jewellery. In truth, I'd rather not have the trouble of selling it. But I also want back what I'm owed,' he added reasonably. 'Your dowry is what Edwina wants me to have. I'm not too proud to take it.'

'But you know it won't come unconditionally,' Elizabeth jeered on a watery choke. 'I'm surprised at you, my lord. You'll stoop to take a sullied woman to wife just to lay hands on her money. For a short while this evening, when I saw how well you live, I deemed you a gentleman of some standing.' She paused to sniff. ''Tis all show, is it not? I doubt you can call one candle your own. Now you want to procure my portion to squander!'

'Will you marry me, Elizabeth?' Ross asked quietly.

He watched the conflict on her face. Watched her large, luminous eyes raise upwards, slide sideways away from him as she delved deep to find a way to outwit him. She was weighing up whether to feed him false promises again; tell him whatever he wanted to hear, then rescind it all tomorrow. Would he be gullible enough to let her leave with her necklace on those terms?

'I should be pleased to accept your marriage proposal,' she finally ground out, in a voice throbbing with bitterness.

There was such resentment in her tone that it seemed natural to conclude she had decided against chicanery in the morning. 'I'm greatly honoured,' he said softly. 'I shall call tomorrow and speak with Edwina about the financial implications. But now, it's high time I took you home.'

'I shall return as I came: in a hackney cab, accompanied by my maid. I wouldn't dream of imposing on you. Fetch my necklace now,' was all she deigned to answer him.

'No.'

'No?' she gasped. 'No?' Her small fists flew up. Immediately they were covered by two large hands. She tried to jerk them free, crying, 'If you think I will let you treat me like this…'

'How am I treating you? Far better than you deserve, I think, Elizabeth. Do you really imagine I'll allow my fiancée to travel at night in a hired rig with a valuable gem in her possession and a maid for protection? I'll bring the necklace with me tomorrow when I meet with your grandmother.' He watched her eyes, saw the confliction of reason and vexation. 'You'll just have to trust me to do it. Come, I'll take you home.'

She opened her mouth to fling his courteous offer to escort her back in his face. She managed to bite that back, but not the note of sourness in her voice. 'If you are to kindly escort us, then I trust such a renowned warrior is man enough to protect me and the jewellery?'

Something in the amused twist to his mouth told her he

was anticipating the barb. 'It's nearly eleven o'clock at night, Elizabeth. What are you planning to do with it at such an hour? Wear it to a ball? Stake it at the tables? Pawn it?'

Elizabeth spontaneously coloured, yanked at her hands within his. A dawning comprehension in his eyes had them hardening, as were his fingers on hers. Abruptly he flung her hands aside with a muttered oath.

Once more at liberty, Elizabeth was soon out in the corridor and hastening towards the brightly lit vestibule. Although he let her alone, she knew he was following behind on the thick carpet. He had won, was all that beat repetitively in her aching head. She had come here to get something valuable and leave nothing but empty promises in her wake.

He had turned the tables on her so completely! She had agreed to wed him! Now he had her dowry and her jewellery. He was also suspicious of why she wanted the necklace so desperately. She had nothing other than the word of a re-nowned rogue that tomorrow he would return it to her. She had utterly failed herself and, more importantly, Jane Selby and her little son. She was a fool! An incompetent fool!

Chapter Eight

'I'll see you safely within doors.'

'There's no need!' Snatching her hand from his, Elizabeth swept disdainfully past and up the steps of Number Seven Connaught Street.

Ross signalled to his driver to wait and followed her to the base of the steps, where he braced a foot idly against the lowest. 'Elizabeth,' he called in a voice that was at one and the same time discreetly quiet yet authoritative.

An indefinable inflection accented her name, making her hesitate. Turning majestically by the door, she bestowed a quizzical look. Inwardly she felt piqued that she couldn't continue to ignore him, as she had on the journey. She had felt childishly triumphant at not once having yielded to glancing his way, despite being very aware of his saturnine features facing her. She hadn't thanked him for his escort, or for the use of his luxurious carriage, or even for his gallant assistance in handing her and Josie both in and out of it. She was not, by nature, unmannerly. The fact that he caused her to act so out of character just added to her sense of squirming exasperation.

His expression was concealed by shadow: the flickering coach and porch lamps did little to augment the glow misting about the street lanterns.

'Come here.'

'I'm tired.'

'Come here.'

Grinding her teeth, and with her fingers flexing furiously on air, Elizabeth flounced down three steps, then stopped, so that her pearly complexion was level with his dark face.

'I expect a little more gracious goodnight from my betrothed than the one I've just received. I think it as well to start as we mean to go on.'

Elizabeth's eyes glittered pure disgust but, with a toss of her fair curls, she lilted, 'And I, sir, will witness a cold day in hell before taking lessons in gentility from an upstart Vis—'

'Scapegrace! Minx!'

The sudden sibilant screeching directly behind had Elizabeth jumping on the spot and only Ross, steadying her against his solid body, prevented her stumbling down the remaining steps.

'Where have you been? What have you been doing? Do you know I have sent Pettifer twice along to the vicar to see if you had gone there?' Ignoring Josie cowering by the door, Edwina flew out of the lighted hallway, night rail flapping about her stout legs, and peered down at her granddaughter's back. 'Where have you been? Don't lie now. I shall know if you lie. Have you been to see that drab of a friend in the stews?'

It was at that point that Edwina's myopic vision located a man's muscular figure behind that of her granddaughter. She noticed, also, that the two of them seemed to be locked in some sort of embrace. With a scandalised gurgle, she thumped herself on the breast bone, a pudgy hand searching for support from the wrought iron balustrade. 'Oh, my God! Now she really *is* ruined…'

'Lady Elizabeth has been with me.'

'Stratton?' Edwina barked, astonished, recovering remarkably quickly. 'What are you about? Have you seduced her? Oh, never mind. Come inside, all of you, before we give every nosey parker enough gossip to keep them up guessing all night.' Without another word Edwina shuffled about on her slippered feet. She huffed back up the few steps she'd descended and disappeared into the honeyed glow behind the half-open door.

Gently, Ross put Elizabeth's quaking form from him. With a hand lightly on her elbow, he urged her up the steps. Drained of further resistance by jangled nerves and dismay at the utter failure of the entire evening's enterprise, Elizabeth allowed his assistance.

'Thank Heavens it's you she's been with, Stratton! For a moment there I thought dearest Lizzie had taken leave of her senses and gone slumming at dead of night!' Edwina burst out when they were all inside the drawing room. She managed a relieved little snort of laughter as she wrapped her thick, cord night rail snugly about her embonpoint.

Elizabeth glared at her grandmother. Personally, she deemed it preferable for a spinster to be discovered doing good works at close to midnight than clinging to a disreputable rogue's neck on her own doorstep.

Oblivious to her granddaughter's theory on impropriety, Edwina continued to flap a hand and smile as she relaxed. 'I've been fair frantic since discovering you abroad when I imagined you safely tucked up in bed.'

'You may retire, Josie,' Elizabeth quietly directed her maid. The girl needed no second telling; speedily she slipped from the room, her nervous backwards look speaking volumes. Pettifer, however, impassively traversed back and forth, lighting candelabra and coaxing the dying embers of the fire into a cosy blaze, as though just such catastrophies were commonplace.

'You know, the silly thing is, Lizzie,' Edwina rattled on with the verbosity of stupendous relief, 'I came along an hour or more ago to your chamber, with m'good idea to help your wretched friend, and dam' me if you haven't had the exact same one. Although I didn't know it then, of course, and have been out of m'mind with worry…and twice resorted to m'salts. And I do think, dear, t'would have been wiser and a lot more seemly to wait till morning to seek the Viscount's good advice…'

'Please be quiet, Grandmama,' Elizabeth gritted over her grandmother's rambling.

'Pray, continue, Mrs Sampson,' Ross contradicted, arrowing a brooding look at his uneasy fiancée. 'I should, of course, still be pleased to help, once I know a little more of the problem.'

Edwina stood with her back to the fire, warming herself. 'Do you know I was foolish enough to think that Lizzie might have gone to that revolting rookery tonight? And taken with her something of value to buy her friend's freedom from her fancy man. I was convinced enough to check m'silverware in case she'd absconded with a candlestick or two.'

Ross's dark expression became ever more sardonic. 'I take it from these few odd clues, Edwina, that your granddaughter has a friend languishing in a slum somewhere in very unhappy circumstances. A friend she's desperate to help…at any cost?' Although the conversation seemed to be flowing between the Viscount and her grandmother, Elizabeth knew that every word he uttered was directed at her.

'Well, of course! Has she not told you anything? Have you not told the Viscount anything?' Edwina demanded with a perplexed frown at her granddaughter.

Elizabeth managed a tight little smile for her interfering grandmother before turning a particularly impudent look on Ross. 'Did I not tell you anything?' she echoed, all surprised apology. 'Well, let me make amends, sir, and tell you now. The reason I acted with such temerity tonight and bothered you at home was…not what your arrogance led you to believe at all. I hope that hasn't wounded your conceit too greatly. Goodnight.' With a cursory little bob she immediately turned for the door.

'It would take more than a puerile subterfuge…which, by the by, didn't succeed…to deflate my ego. And before you retire, my lady, I think we should let your grandmother in on our happy news.'

Elizabeth swished about, attempting to freeze his words and his person with a purple glower. But he kept on coming until his powerful physique was towering over her petite figure. 'You should have been more honest, my dear. I just might have been sympathetic.' The words were light, his expression leaden.

'Now, it's my turn not to think so,' she sourly muttered. 'There is no news to impart to my grandmother,' she added in a more audible underbreath. 'As I have just said, nothing tonight was what it seemed. Especially your understanding of my motive in visiting you. I apologise for taking up so much of your evening.'

'I'm glad you did. Now that we are to be married, it would be churlish, indeed, to deny you an hour or two of my time; or assistance with any problems you may have.'

Edwina hurried closer. Although Ross had spoken in an intimate tone, it was obvious from the woman's rapturous smile she had overheard. 'Married, did you say? You have agreed to the match, Elizabeth?' she demanded excitedly. Her glowing eyes spontaneously swerved to Pettifer, loading logs onto the hungry flames in the grate. He acknowledged her triumph with a quirk at one corner of his finely moulded mouth and kept on about his work.

Elizabeth fidgeted beneath a tawny stare. She knew he was challenging her. She could revoke her consent and risk his displeasure and his revenge, or she could honour their agreement. She could deny ever having agreed to wed him; but that would be an outright lie and she knew she was not capable of that. She wanted him to generously release her from their pact. She also wanted him to generously return her gems. She wanted too much, she knew. Nevertheless, she raised her jewel-bright eyes.

'No,' Ross murmured to her unspoken entreaty. He refused to look directly at her, smiling privately in wry acknowledgement of her persuasive powers.

Edwina demanded again, 'So, you have agreed to the match, m'dear?'

After a further silent moment, replete with inner wrangling, Elizabeth muttered, 'Yes.'

Edwina seemed oblivious to the bad grace which accompanied her answer and hugged Elizabeth, delighted. 'Oh, that is wonderful. Quite the best news I've heard in an age!'

Elizabeth kindly reciprocated the embrace, patting at her grandmother's rotund back. Her eyes looked huge in her wan face; dulled with weariness. They livened enough to dart violet arrows at the man who was watching the emotional scene with an amount of rueful amusement.

As Edwina bustled away to direct Pettifer to fetch champagne, Ross approached Elizabeth. Taking both her hands in his, he raised them, bringing first one then the other to briefly touch his lips. His fiancée couldn't summon the energy to snatch them back. She allowed his thumbs to brush soothingly back and forth over the backs of her small fingers.

His eyes held hers and for a moment she thought she glimpsed a look of tender praise in them. But all he said was, 'You must be keen to retire. I'll not keep you longer.'

Elizabeth could do no more than nod at their touching hands while, way back in her mind, she was fretting that perhaps she should have lied after all: he looked too content. He was congratulating himself on his victory. He now had her fortune. He had her, too: a minor encumbrance was doubtless how he saw that. Perhaps he was already planning to banish her to his Kent estate, while his life in London, funded by her money, carried on regardless. Oh, yes; he had what he wanted! He had won! And the crushing knowledge made her lower lip wobble while her lashes fluttered low over glistening eyes.

As though cognisant of the reason for her distress, his fingers tightened on hers and he jerked her gently forward. They were so close she felt his words stir her hair. 'Everything will be fine, Elizabeth. Trust me.' Abruptly she was released. 'We'll celebrate another time, Mrs Sampson, if you don't mind. It's been a hectic night for us all. I'm sure you must be more than ready to retire.'

At the door he executed a polite bow to the two ladies. 'If I may, I should like to return tomorrow and discuss a few details concerning the wedding and so on. You might like then to tell me more of this unlucky friend's plight. Oh, one other thing,' he added conversationally. 'I'm sure Elizabeth would be interested in seeing just what sort of Cornish stock I spring from. My mother and eldest brother are due to arrive in London tomorrow, as are a few close friends. I would be honoured if you would both dine with us one evening soon. If you are agreeable, I shall announce our engagement that night. Thereafter a notice will be put into *The Times*.'

'That sounds delightful!' Edwina gushed.

'Elizabeth?' Ross said quietly.

'Of course, I must come; I should very much like to inspect your pedigree,' she retorted with all the bitter sweetness of lamented defeat.

'I still cannot believe you were that rude!' Edwina rebuked next morning at breakfast. Her knife plunged angrily into the jam pot.

Elizabeth couldn't believe it either, and her face grew hot at the memory. It seemed that, lately, never a day passed without her feeling ashamed of some aspect of her behaviour. The reason for her cringing was always the same: Stratton! She was sick of the man! 'The Viscount and I are well used to exchanging insults,' was all she offered in mitigation. 'It is a bad match, Grandmama. You should never have interfered. I can only hope he will eventually come to his senses and release me from my consent.'

'He is not likely to do that, no matter how objectionable you contrive to be,' Edwina spluttered through a mouthful of toast and jam.

'No, indeed! Not with so much money riding on the wedding lines,' Elizabeth commented caustically. 'I'm sure he'll put up with any amount of my slights, so long as you pay him to take me.'

'I've a notion, m'dear, that Stratton would wed you whether I paid him or not.'

Oddly, that lightened Elizabeth's mood. She gave a little guffaw. 'And I've a notion, m'dear, that you must have been early at the Madeira, to say so,' she returned in a droll approximation of her grandmother's gravelly tone.

The affection and gratitude she felt towards her grandmother prevented her ever staying mad at her for long. If only she hadn't taken it into her silly head to get her wed! It was idiotic! It was infuriating! It was Stratton's fault! she unreasonably judged as she gave her grandmother a fond peck on a chomping cheek. 'I'm going to fetch my pelisse. Sophie wants to choose dress material. I said that Evangeline might accompany us. She likes a carriage ride and a scout through the warehouses.'

After a frantic swallow, Edwina choked, 'You're surely not going out today?' She snorted her disapproval. 'Ross will be here this afternoon. He sent word he is to attend us at three. You must ensure you are home.'

Elizabeth faced her grandmother again, ivory ringlets a-sway about her graceful neck. 'I must do nothing of the sort! I'd rather not be present to oversee my sale.'

'Ross will expect you to be here…'

'It's as well, then, that I shall be absent,' Elizabeth announced petulantly. 'Stratton has yet to learn that I have no intention of fulfilling his presumptuous expectations.' Her small mouth slanted contumaciously as she recalled him yesterday evening requiring her apology, requiring her answers, requiring her gracious goodnights. He would soon learn not to treat a Marquess's daughter so high-handed, she decided on sallying forth, chin-up, from the room.

Sophie widened chocolate-brown eyes on Elizabeth's face. 'You have received a proposal from Viscount Stratton?'

Elizabeth nodded, simultaneously grimacing understanding of her friend's shock. Evangeline continued knitting as though deaf to the riveting news. She was simply glad to be invited on an outing with two lively young ladies...or so the earnest pair seemed to her.

'But, Elizabeth, isn't he the one...the rather savage gentleman?'

'Yes,' Elizabeth admitted calmly. 'The very same. But I have to own the tale of breakfasting on an adversary's liver seems a trifle *de trop*. Grandmama has had him for dinner, so to speak. She maintains he's table-trained.'

'Well, I don't see how you can joke about it, Elizabeth!' Sophie scolded squeamishly. 'Is he terribly handsome?' she immediately demanded. 'I've heard Mama talking about him. She and her crony, Mrs Talbot, seem to think he has a raffish appeal...like a corsair...'

'Or a gypsy...' Elizabeth added with a curl to her lip. Offhand, she said, 'I suppose he might pass as good-looking. If one likes sallow men.' The injustice of that bitchy remark made her shift on the upholstered seat. He wasn't sallow-skinned. He had acquired a healthy tan from being outdoors in the elements. He was handsome...*very* handsome. He was impeccably well dressed, too. Yesterday she had deemed him the perfect man.

The memories of her clandestine visit, that blissful kiss, that hurting kiss, made her stare sightlessly out of the carriage window while heat bled into her complexion. With a stubborn set to her soft mouth, she determined to wriggle free of this stupid betrothal at the very first opportunity. Yesterday evening, when tired, she had allowed defeatism too much rein. Now refreshed, she rallied her pride and confidence. He might have won that battle, but he had not yet won the war!

'Have you accepted him?' broke into her pugnacious thoughts. It was the second time Sophie had posed the question, while leaning across the carriage, gazing into her friend's faraway amethyst eyes.

'I have...but not irrevocably. My grandmother has landed herself in a financial mess with Stratton and my dowry has been dangled as settlement. The engagement is still unofficial.

I'm hoping they will both discover what idiocy it is trying to manipulate me.'

Sophie frowned. 'I see,' she said, when she quite patently did not. The last she had heard from her own mama concerning Mrs Sampson's financial mess was that it involved wagers with that harridan, Alice Penney. Slumping back against the squabs, Sophie asked, 'What of Hugh? Have you told him?' She pulled a little face. 'I'm quite sure, Lizzie, he is harbouring hopes of his own, in that respect.'

'I've not seen him to explain,' Elizabeth said truthfully. But again her thoughts were troubled. She had written Hugh a brief note this morning, and despatched it with a servant. In it she had apologised for Harry Pettifer twice bothering him yesterday evening. She had lightly implied her grandmother's eccentricity was to blame, and left it at that. It was rather unjust; it was also unlikely to appease Hugh for long. When next they met, he would expect proper explanations. It was another reason why she was so keen to be abroad today. She would wager—if she were a betting person, of course—that at some time in the next few hours, Hugh would pay a visit to Connaught Street. The way her luck was running, it would probably coincide with the Viscount's visit. She banished all thought of it. She was determined to enjoy this shopping expedition with Sophie. She needed a little peaceful interlude with a good friend before anxiety again dominated her life.

Having alighted at Harding, Howell & Co.'s warehouse in Pall Mall, the two young ladies, with Evangeline in tow, entered an Aladdin's cave certain to enchant any modiste. A wealth of fabric bolts in every conceivable weight and hue were shelved to ceiling height behind polished wooden counters flanking two long walls of the shop. From mahogany poles, interspersed in the room, silks and satins, lace and damask flowed in a confusion of fabulous colours.

The friends slowly promenaded, turning their heads from left to right, up and down, to survey the shimmering array. From time to time their attention was arrested enough by a sheen or shade to pinch a piece of material between thumb and forefinger and test its quality.

'Have you anything particular in mind?' Elizabeth asked her friend.

Sophie stopped by a roll of coffee-coloured velvet, cocked her brunette head. She unrolled a little, smoothed her fingers along its luxuriant pile, then with a negative sigh, walked on. 'I thought perhaps apricot satin, but I have seen nothing that is quite right.'

Elizabeth caught at her friend's arm and urged her between milling customers to the opposite counter where she had spied a length of peach voile. The gauzy material was woven through with gold and silver string ribbon. A length was swirled off the roll, ready for cutting by the draper.

'This is beautiful,' Sophie enthused. 'The best I've seen, if a little too transparent. But as it is to be a splendid ball,' she chattered on about her parents' forthcoming anniversary celebration which was to mark their quarter century together, 'I fancy something a little daring and eye-catching…'

'I must say, so do I,' stressed a drawling masculine voice. 'And, lucky dog that I am, I believe I've spotted the very thing,' was whispered at the back of Elizabeth's neck, disturbing her flaxen curls and making her skin crawl. 'How are you, my dear? Did you receive my billet-doux?'

Elizabeth marched sideways to escape the interfering fingers on her small rounded buttock. Even through the thickness of her velvet pelisse she could feel the heat and determination in that kneading hand. Furiously twisting about, she glared absolute loathing at the Earl of Cadmore.

He simply grinned at her disgust. 'Still my proud beauty, I see; that's good,' he taunted in a low, familiar tone. An idle glance slid to Sophie, who had only just become aware of his presence. He mocked her look of arrant distaste with an exaggerated dip of his head. 'Send your priggish little friend on with the old woman so we can talk,' he muttered. He leaned his snake-narrow hips back against the counter, seemingly quite confident of Elizabeth complying with his orders. She did; merely to prevent Sophie and Evangeline witnessing her acute embarrassment or suffering likewise on her account. A few quick, quiet words and an explicit look soon had Sophie leading away a blithely smiling Evangeline.

While Cadmore waited for them to distance themselves, his effeminately thin white fingers flicked open a japanned snuff box. He took a pinch, his lizard-lidded weak blue eyes lingering on Elizabeth's small bosom, heaving visibly beneath the straining buttons of her pelisse.

'Go…*away*! At once!' was all she managed to choke between huge calming breaths. Livid-faced, she spun back to clutch at the counter, her white-knuckled fingers rigid on the smooth wood. She was trembling with such fury at his outrageous assault that her shame was soon suppressed. He had cornered her before, slyly touched her before, but never in such a public place. Never with such blatant intent and disrespect. And then she learned why he was feeling so cocksure.

'I hear Mrs Sampson has been unlucky at the tables lately. I hear Alice Penney is holding her vowels for quite a ridiculous figure. In the circumstances, a dutiful granddaughter ought swell the family kitty. I could be of service there.'

'And in the circumstances, a dutiful husband ought swell his own family. Should you not go home and paw your wife in private rather than molest a stranger in public? For I certainly cannot be of service there,' she bit out through her teeth.

Incensed colour began mottling his face as she alluded to something freely tattled and smirked over: in five years of marriage, the Earl and Countess of Cadmore had failed to produce any progeny.

Cadmore advanced on her with such a ferociously snarling mouth that, for a moment, Elizabeth was sure he would strike her. Barely a foot away, he seemed to gather his wits and recall where he was. He halted, darted a circumspect look about to see if they had attracted attention. A pink tongue tip flicked out between his taut, bloodless lips, then recoiled. He nodded a greeting at a gentleman sauntering by with a female

companion. 'You brazen bitch,' he whispered, still smiling at
the couple. 'I shall enjoy making you take back every one of
your vulgar words. One day soon, you will apologise most
profusely, most abjectly, for that outrageous impertinence.'
Eyes like watery sky narrowed on her, but his set smile didn't
waver. To an idle observer they would have passed as stylish
people engaged in polite chit-chat while shopping, rather than
bitter adversaries trading vicious insults.

'And what of your vulgar words and outrageous impertinence, sir?' Elizabeth demanded in a low, vibrant tone. 'Will
you ever find the good grace to apologise for your appalling
insults to me over these many years?'

'Apologise to you?' he sneered. 'Apologise to a devious
little slut who thought to trifle with my affections and make
of me a laughing stock? Apologise to a harlot who's known
the dregs of society? Perhaps that's why you visit the slums
so often, is it? Have you a taste for rough trade now? Do you
like knowing dockers, as you knew highwaymen: in the bib-
lical sense? Do you? Tell me!' he rasped imperatively. 'Does
the vicar watch as they tumble you in the gutter? Is that what
you like? Have you raised your skirts for the clergyman, too?'
Torturously aroused and enraged by what he was saying, what
he was feverishly imagining, his face flushed and swelled with
rampant lust. His hips squirmed against the counter and his
skinny fingers thrust between his neck and his cravat, trying
to ease a little air to his throat. Huge-pupilled eyes locked on
to her shocked, pallid face, then slithered down her rigidly
held little figure. For a moment he looked and sounded like
a man in direst torment. 'By God, you'll raise your skirts for
me before I'm done.' He closed his eyes, took a deep breath
that pinched and whitened his nostrils. 'I'll have you if it's
the last thing I do…' he exploded in a strangled whimper.

Elizabeth backed away from the naked hunger and hatred
blazing at her from his bulging eyes. In her haste to get away,
she collided with someone just approaching. She had a vague
impression of a pretty, dark-haired young woman, elaborately
garbed and rouged. A strong, sweet perfume wafted, height-

ening her sense of nausea. Begging her pardon for bumping into her, Elizabeth glimpsed glittering black eyes assessing her. Then the woman had swept past to clutch proprietorially at one of the Earl's arms. 'I have found just the thing, Caddy. 'Tis scarlet and there is matching lace…' Elizabeth heard her say before she quickly distanced herself from them.

'Do you want to go?' Sophie asked sympathetically as Elizabeth occupied her trembling fingers by testing various fabrics on the opposite counter.

'No. He shall never cow me,' Elizabeth averred in a choking whisper.

'Vile man!' Sophie muttered with a poisonous glare at Cadmore. 'You would think, would you not, after all this time, he would have got over you rejecting him. What a lucky escape! Mama says the Countess looks more sourly countenanced than ever. And little wonder with such a sickening spouse and no babes to love. It looks as though he has his lightskirt with him.'

'I think perhaps I would like to go after all,' Elizabeth whispered, gazing past Sophie. 'Perhaps we could try another warehouse,' she croaked on a strained smile. Her eyes immediately slid to the entrance again. A strange coldness was dousing the fiery umbrage she had felt at the Earl of Cadmore's malicious assault. She wanted to look away, turn away, but couldn't. She wanted to tell herself she didn't care, but oddly, she seemed to. The queasiness in her stomach was giving way to hurting cramps.

She stared at the couple who had recently arrived. The woman idled by the entrance to inspect a fall of beryl blue muslin that Elizabeth recalled had caught her own eye on entering.

Viscount Stratton was looking at the fabric, too, with very indulgent interest. He appeared to make some favourable comment and the woman smiled beatifically up at him. She was more than simply pretty; she was extraordinarily beautiful and extremely elegant. This was no comely courtesan: the sort of woman with whom Elizabeth imagined he dallied. This was a stylish and refined lady who exuded an aura of gentle serenity. But then there was deep affection between them, that was obvious. Their bodies were close; one of her hands clasped his arm in a touch that was casual yet confidently intimate. They made such a strikingly handsome couple that people close by were turning to look at them. Neither seemed caring of the interest they were generating; their attention seemed reserved for each other. It wasn't. He was aware of her.

Elizabeth's eyes had darted from reluctantly admiring the woman's graceful profile and honey-gold hair, to target her prospective husband's dark visage. He was returning her gaze.

Heat was back. It furnaced, while a detached part of her brain regretted that her shopping trip with Sophie was turning into such a farcical disaster. The last place she would have expected to meet either of the men who were plaguing her was in a fabric emporium. It seemed there was to be no respite, even for a few hours! All that was lacking was Hugh Clemence's presence here, searching for her, and her nightmare would be complete.

'Come, Sophie,' Elizabeth quavered with strengthening persuasion. 'Let us try Baldwin's. I hear they have had a consignment of Brussels lace…'

So, he took his mistress shopping only hours before he was due to speak to her grandmother about their wedding plans. The knowledge trampled her pride with far greater success than anything the Earl of Cadmore had said or done. She didn't care. Why should she care? And why should he not do so? She knew he had no intention of altering his life for someone as trifling as his bride. He was wedding a dowry and being saddled with a wife. She was well aware of that. For her part, she was simply interested in regaining her precious Thorneycroft jewels. She didn't want or need a husband. Or any intimacy. Should this madness run out of control, and the nuptials took place, she would be glad he took his pleasure elsewhere. She wasn't bothered at being brought face to face with the woman he…did he love her? She had the look of a woman cherished.

She refused to think of it further. Her chin tilted and she smoothed her gloves with unsteady fingers. Now he had seen her, she would let him know she didn't give a fig on whom he frittered his cash. On whom he might soon be squandering her cash! That did gall! But still she wasn't about to scurry away like a timid mouse. She would pass them, acknowledge this inopportune meeting, let him know his adultery would be of no consequence whatsoever.

Arm in arm with Evangeline and Sophie, the trio proceeded towards the door. Elizabeth knew he was watching as she drew closer; although still chatting with his companion, he had one eye on her and was well aware of her approach. Without looking directly at them, Elizabeth knew when they moved away from the turquoise fabric. With a penetrative peek from beneath a fringe of brunette lashes, she realised just why the woman favoured it: her eyes were the most wonderful shade of green-blue.

They were about to pass! Elizabeth gripped tighter to her friends for support, obliquely aware that Evangeline and Sophie were swapping idle comments on the shop's stock. Bravely, she looked up, met his eyes squarely for a moment before mirroring his courteous nod.

'Lady Elizabeth…?' The greeting was warm, polite.

'Viscount Stratton…' She matched his words, if not his tone. He was stopping, turning, expecting her to do the same. She swished about. So did Sophie, her mouth agape as she recognised the name of the handsome stranger.

'I'm sorry, my lord, we must hurry on. So many warehouses to visit and so little time. I am expected home shortly for a…tiresome engagement…' Elizabeth watched, exultant, as his eyes and mouth narrowed at the barb.

'Well, I mustn't delay you from something so important.'

'As if you could…even for a trifle…' Elizabeth lightly trilled with such an overflow of honey in her tone that his companion looked from one to the other of them, a small, enquiring smile hovering about her lips.

Close to, Elizabeth could see that she was older than she herself, yet still so breathtakingly lovely that her insides clenched. Why could she not have been milk-maid buxom, or garishly painted? Why did she have to be so…so perfect?

She stretched her lips, hoping it resembled an insouciant smile, before sweeping on. She talked with Evangeline about ribbon, gripped hard at Sophie's arm to make her look away and close her dropped jaw. Turning from one to the other of her friends, she laughed at nothing, aware of everything behind. Especially that she was observed. Then they had gained the door and turned the corner. Out of sight, her shoulders slumped, her eyes closed and just one phrase trudged through her mind: Damn you, Stratton! *Damn you!*

Chapter Nine

'Damn you, Stratton! Damn you!' Cecily Booth muttered under her breath.

The man at her side was also cursing inaudibly on catching sight of the Viscount, but for a very different reason. Far from feeling piqued at being overlooked, as Cecily was, Cadmore was uneasy at being the one to have drawn those lupine eyes.

A few days ago, the Earl would have believed Cecily unavailable to him for two reasons: she didn't come cheap and she was besotted with Ross Trelawney. Being a parsimonious poltroon, he thus looked elsewhere for female company.

It was common knowledge that Cecily had been angling for Trelawney's protection for some while. It must have seemed significant to her that she was victorious just as he received his peerage. Soon she'd felt confident enough of becoming a Lady to broadcast hints of mutual devotion and matrimony. She'd seriously misjudged in applying sly pressure. A few days ago, so rumour had it, the Viscount was ribbed about his aspirant 'fiancée' at Gentleman Jackson's, while sparring with Guy Markham. Before nightfall, his deluded young mistress was in need of a new protector.

Linus Savage made his move while Cecily was still reeling from the rejection and susceptible to flummery and negotiation. Earlier he'd been congratulating himself on a shrewd deal…now he wasn't so sure.

Now he was fretting that that vicious look in Stratton's eyes must mean he still had a fancy for the woman clutching his arm. He attempted loosening Cecily's grip and adopting an air of nonchalance.

Cecily's mouth skewed into a scarlet slash at the sight of the Viscount and his companion. To be replaced so quickly—and with such an exquisitely beautiful lady—was mortifying! Then, recalling how brusquely she'd been discarded, she reminded herself she'd hooked an Earl. What would she miss about Ross? His witty charm? His generosity? His energetic…inventive…wonderful lovemaking? Cecily's feigned unconcern faded into an involuntarily gulp of despair. To cheer herself, she surmised bitchily that the blonde was possibly his own age: a decade older than she herself. That made her feel better. Angling her head coquettishly at Cadmore, she hoped her youthful bloom and vitality were much in evidence. Her simpering smile drooped. She couldn't ignore the contrast between this puny-chested fop and the muscular physique of the handsome, rugged man not three yards away now. The elaborate, padded waistcoats the Earl favoured never quite disguised his lack of girth. She shuddered inwardly, realising that about midnight his fleshless ribs would be digging into hers.

'Stratton…' the Earl of Cadmore ejaculated by way of greeting as the couples finally drew level.

Ross jerked his head in curt response, but remained grim and silent. Cecily bobbed archly, dark curls a-sway, while peeping up at him with mingling plea and accusation. He returned her a perfunctory, preoccupied smile that whipped up her indignation.

'Stratton seems irate…face like thunder…' Cadmore muttered, glancing at the Viscount's broad back. He shrugged, eyed Cecily more purposefully. Perky with relief that Stratton had passed, uneventfully, by, a hand slid her back, skinny fingers burrowing beneath an arm to pinch a full, firm breast. Cecily instinctively recoiled in disgust.

Then she remembered: she'd hooked an earl. She paraded

the feat again through her mind, with much self-congratulation, turning towards him to shield his groping fingers from prying eyes. An onlooker would simply have seen a woman leaning close to whisper tenderly in her beau's ear. What Cadmore's new *chère amie* actually said before she tugged herself free, was, 'The scarlet velvet *I* fancy, my lord, is over this way…'

'I'm intrigued. Two attractive ladies: a beautiful blonde and a pretty brunette, and both looked daggers at you. The gentleman looked scared witless. What *is* going on, Ross?' his sister-in-law enquired with a smile. 'Not still breaking hearts and cuckolding husbands, surely?'

'You thought the blonde beautiful?' was all he said.

'Quite exceptionally lovely, despite that sad look in her blue eyes.'

'They're not blue, they're violet…'

'Ha…ha…' Rebecca chuckled significantly, making Ross grimace ruefully at a stack of satin. 'They are indeed violet. I noticed. So did you. Is there anything else you'd like to tell me about her?' she prompted softly, seriously. After a silent moment, she continued, 'And the brunette?'

He shrugged. 'As you said, she's pretty.'

'Ross!' Rebecca chided on an outraged laugh. 'You really are a callous rogue! Of the two, the brunette, of course, is your mistress.'

'Not any more,' summed up his lack of interest in pursuing the subject. He turned about restlessly, looked back towards the exit, then frowned over Rebecca's head at a drape of lustrous silk dangling off a roll on the top shelf. It undulated in a light air current, iridescent, mesmerising. The shade reminded him of hyacinths…and gems that were nestling on velvet in his safe. He wanted to go there and look at them, then take them to his betrothed. He wanted to tell her that if she'd just stopped for a moment or two, he would have introduced her to his brother's wife. He wanted to tell her that there was no need for her to have looked so hurt. And she had; until she realised he was watching her. Then she'd masked her distress with that haughty expression she'd perfected.

She believed Rebecca to be his mistress. And it upset her. But she didn't want him to know; so she'd brazened it out and confronted him. The message was clear: it didn't matter. It wouldn't even matter when they were husband and wife. That's what she wanted him to think. That's why she'd had to mention the 'tiresome engagement' later that day. But now he knew differently. Just for a second or two he'd seen her stripped of armour, wounded and vulnerable because he was with another woman. She cared. The idiotic thing was, he was glad. And he wasn't sure why. The sensible way would be to foster her apathy. He wasn't certain he was ready to… *relinquish all others*… After all, she was still the rudest, most infuriating little… He exhaled slowly, aware he couldn't even think of her in those terms any more.

But he could think of her. God knows, it seemed he could think of little else. He wanted to be with her; even if it was simply to parry insults. He wanted to tell her he'd seen silk that would suit her, that would match her eyes. He wanted to be shopping with his future wife. He wanted her…God, how he wanted her. She'd been out of sight a few minutes, and he wanted to follow her.

What he wanted, he impressed on himself while his teeth locked so hard his jaw began to ache, was a brain physician. The sensible way, the only sensible way, would have been to seduce her yesterday in the comfort of his own home. Had he indulged his lust for her, he might not now be acting like a moonstruck idiot. He might not be planning a wedding, simply settling in a new paramour. In all his life he'd never toadied to any woman, yet he was constantly modifying his behaviour and humouring this pert madam, sullied by scandal, who took delight in slighting him at every opportunity.

Women of all ages…all classes…liked him; it had always been that way. Since he'd been elevated to the peerage, his popularity had soared yet higher. He couldn't keep pace with the deluge of social invitations he received.

So, Lady Elizabeth Rowe was beautiful and desirable; so were other women desirable…and far more responsive to his blasé charm. So, why couldn't he think of anything else? Anyone else? Why had he, minutes ago, been on the point of inviting Cadmore to step outside, so he could hit him? All the man had done was look shifty and bark a greeting at him. He had no proof the weasel had approached Elizabeth today, let alone annoyed her. The fact that Cecily was accompanying him made it unlikely he had accosted her; as did the fact that they had been sited on opposite sides of the shop. Still he felt tense with the need to find out what had occurred, just in case he had looked disrespectfully at Elizabeth.

'Shall we go? Luke should be finished with his meeting now,' Ross suddenly burst out impatiently.

Rebecca slanted a look at him from beneath lengthy lashes, while still fiddling with fabrics on the counter. 'I'm not yet finished choosing, Ross. You used to like taking me shopping whilst Luke did business in Lombard Street…' She pouted.

'Don't flirt. You know you don't mean it,' he said with a laughing hint of apology for his brusqueness.

'That never used to worry you. You used to encourage me to practise on you. Why won't you flirt with me any more, Ross?'

'*What?* And risk my big brother's displeasure?'

'Luke knows it's he who benefits from your tutelage. Besides, that never stopped you before.'

'Before I was a disreputable rogue. Now,' he informed her on a wry, private smile, 'I'm an upstart Viscount.'

Rebecca nodded slowly. 'The violet-eyed blonde…?' was all she said as, arm through his, she steered him back towards the exit.

A long, dark finger unfurled from his fist lying idle on the desk top. It extended to touch a glossy, faceted jewel. Slowly it trailed alternate white and purple stones, stroking with a sensual gentleness. The amethysts were of highly prized deep, rich colour and perfectly matched in clarity and unusual octagonal cut. The diamonds were cabochon, clear of inclusions, shimmering rainbows in afternoon sunlight. A goldsmith of exceptional skill had crafted the piece. Ross supposed the rest of the parure to be of similar fine quality. If so, she had been right in her estimation: from what she'd described, and what he knew, he'd say about ten thousand pounds worth in total.

He was comfortable with treasures; as a mercenary and bounty-hunter he had had regular contact with precious arte-facts: Spanish gold, Eastern jade, African ivory, ancient Egyptian pottery… He'd been rewarded in all manner of currency—even recently crafted Sheraton and Hepplewhite furniture—and never turned any down. Now he was paid in diamonds and amethysts and he was devising ways he could give them back…without ceding what he wanted.

He leaned back in the chair, rested his head back into the leather, but the hawkish gleam between his lashes was still on the scintillating collar laid out on the desk in front of him.

Far, far back in his mind, it occurred to him that he ought to be travelling to Kent and directing his architect and his builder on renovation schedules for Stratton Hall. A few weeks ago, there was little else on his mind but building on his new and very gratifying success. He'd been proud of what he'd, alone and unaided, achieved.

His father's original ill-gotten gains had been laundered by the years and by legitimate transactions into an international business empire. As the youngest son he had been last in line as far as inheritance went. But he'd been reared knowing indulgence: by a father who believed in primogeniture yet compensated for it in other ways, by a mother who doted on her wild child, and by brothers who spoiled him through guilt at taking the lion's share of the family businesses and property. It didn't worry him. He let them all know it didn't worry him…not a bit. It was fair: Luke and Tristan worked harder and gave more time and commitment than he was prepared to sacrifice from his hedonistic life. He'd make his own way…and he had, very enjoyably, ignoring convention and morality along the way. He had his own codes: he never did more than flirt with women his brothers or friends cherished. He was loyal and protective to those he cherished, if unwilling to be restrained or tamed by their reciprocal concern and affection. Until now. Only there was no reciprocal affection. He was making marriage plans with a blonde temptress who disliked him. And he hadn't the vaguest notion why he was so adamant he would marry her. It wasn't the money. But he had to tell her it was, for both their sakes. It was all that was sensible to believe after such a short, stormy acquaintance. It was all she'd believe: that he was a hireling who was owed payment and was not shy of taking her dowry…or taking her as his mistress should she withhold consent to the nuptials. She was haughty, rude and defiant, yet something in her touched his soul…because he recognised the sham. She was bleeding still from a ten-year-old wound and vulnerable to the salt society used to season its contempt. He sensed a poignant wistfulness that made him want to fight alongside her, shield her from male lust and female spite. The instinct to care and protect had subtly, swiftly circumvented his lechery and a wry smile was all that rued its passing.

He sat forward, rested his elbows on the desk. One broad palm supported a tanned, concave cheek as he frowned thoughtfully at the sparking gem. Which brought him to just what the little fool thought she was about by consorting with harlots and pimps in some East End hovel. He wasn't about to have a wife of his risking assault or disease roaming amongst God knew what sort of squalid low life.

From what Edwina had artlessly disclosed, he guessed the situation to be thus: Elizabeth had risked further disgrace last night from selfless motives. She had come to collect her necklace with the sole intention of using it to redeem a fallen woman. She had planned to buy a friend's freedom with her inheritance. His eyes closed and something leaden settled in his stomach. If he'd given in to her pleas and allowed her the necklace, she would have taken it straight there. She would have actually journeyed, unescorted, into the heart of the stews with a couple of thousand pounds' worth of jewellery in her pocket. It didn't bear thinking about.

A slight smile softened the hard set to his sensual lips. He didn't think she'd want to hear that within a week of being ransomed, the drab would be back in Wapping searching for her fancy man and touting for business. Or that meanwhile her precious heirloom would be sold off stone by stone for the price of the freshest young doxy to be had, or a keg of geneva.

Her rescue plan had an almost charming simplicity. It also relied heavily on honest reciprocation from reprobates. It was naïve…very innocent behaviour…and something about that was discordant with what he knew, or thought he knew, along with the rest of society, about her past. And there was something else, something odd he recalled Edwina muttering when he'd brought Elizabeth home… His reflection tailed off and he glanced at the clock as it chimed half past two.

Palming the collar, he let it drape glittering over his bronzed skin for a moment. Was he going to hand it over to her now? Or was he going to prevaricate a while longer? He didn't want to renege on his promise to return it today. But when he'd said he would, he hadn't known why she wanted it.

He stood up abruptly and replaced the gem in his safe. She might have slipped under his guard when he wasn't looking, but he wasn't completely overwhelmed. Strong men made weak by beautiful women were worthy of the utmost contempt, so he'd always thought. Besides, if anyone was short-changed at present from this crazy deal, it was him. Edwina owed him; Lady Elizabeth Rowe damn well owed him. He'd kept himself leashed last night. One kiss they'd pacted and she'd withdrawn. He knew she'd been enjoying it. So had he…too damned much! It had started out as an ostentation of his seductive powers and finished with him luxuriating in the pure sweetness of it all. Just like some novice libertine. He'd keep the necklace awhile, and prove to himself he wasn't acting like a novice libertine. He was still in control.

* * *

Having dropped Evangeline at her door, Elizabeth and So-phie now sat in the small salon of Sophie's parents' cosy townhouse in Perman Street.

Placing down her teacup, Sophie pulled out of its wrapping the length of silver lace, then draped it over the chair back. She peered at it from different angles.

'It's just right,' Elizabeth reassured her. 'So delicate…like a cobweb… It will suit you wonderfully.'

Sophie giggled that she hoped that didn't mean she resem-bled a spider, but her eyes were speculative as she looked at her grave-faced best friend. 'What has upset you the most today, Elizabeth? Being accosted by that rat, Cadmore, or meeting the Viscount with a…um…lady friend?'

Elizabeth immediately sipped from her cup. It clattered back onto its saucer. 'Neither bothered me,' she blurted with a bright smile.

At Sophie's ironically winging eyebrows, the corners of Elizabeth's mouth drooped. 'Oh, very well; I admit that I certainly would have preferred missing both of those *gentle-men* in that warehouse today.' A shapely, slender hand wor-ried at her brow. 'I hate Cadmore! He's a detestable lecher. And I hate the Viscount because…' She tailed into silence. 'I'm quite sure he's a detestable lecher, too. But I've, as yet, no proper proof, so I'll say I hate him because…because… Oh, I just hate him! He has insulted me and threatened me and done various other things.' A hand flap concluded the explanation as she slumped back into the sofa.

'He's extraordinarily handsome, Elizabeth,' Sophie ten-dered mildly. 'Not at all as I would have imagined. I don't think he looks rough at all. Quite the reverse. He seems…sophisticated and polished. And he wanted you to stop and talk to him.'

'I doubt his companion did,' Elizabeth remarked sourly. 'She was very beautiful, wasn't she?' was added on a twisted little smile.

Sophie grimaced agreement. 'Very. But then so are you, Elizabeth. I've always envied you your wonderful eyes and hair. You're younger than she is. You could easily outshine her, if you wished.'

'But I don't wish,' Elizabeth lilted. Picking up the lace, she draped it about her friend's slender shoulders, cocking her head to assess the effect. A violet glance arrowed at the stately burr-walnut case-clock in the corner. It was almost five-fifteen. She would leave at six of the clock. She calculated the Viscount and Edwina would have concluded their meeting by then. She calculated, too, her absence from home adequately conveyed her resistance to the 'tiresome engagement'.

Perhaps Stratton's lady love might object to his marriage and persuade him to retain the status quo. She didn't look the sort of woman to allow herself to be relegated. In fact, Elizabeth, thought dully, she looked the sort of woman who might be a little like herself: a little too proud. Wandering to the window, she scanned the busy street but saw nothing. She trusted he would leave her necklace with Edwina. She believed him a man of his word on that score. She just hoped Edwina's untimely revelation last night hadn't made him too suspicious about why she desperately wanted it. In any case, the truth shouldn't unduly bother him. Whether she kept or disposed of her jewellery would be of no interest once he had her dowry promised in its stead.

'I hate to see you looking so anxious, Elizabeth. Is something else troubling you?' Sophie asked quietly, on joining her at the window. She slipped a comforting hand through the crook of a soft-skinned arm.

'Actually, yes,' Elizabeth admitted. She sighed. 'I saw something awful when returning from Sunday School with Hugh…'

'You must stop going! You are being too reckless entering that slum to teach those poor little wretches.'

'No, it wasn't the children,' Elizabeth reassured, facing Sophie. 'I encountered a lady I once knew well. She had her come-out the same year I did. I classed her as a social equal and a friend. She has fallen on such terrible…harrowing times, Sophie.' Her voice broke and she sensed tears needle her eyes. 'Truthfully, it makes me feel so ashamed for even thinking I have problems. I must help her! But I'm not sure how.'

Sophie quickly steered her friend back to the sofa and sat beside her. Taking Elizabeth's hands in hers, she pleaded, 'Tell me, at once! What on earth has gone on?'

Some minutes later, Elizabeth had recounted all that had passed between Jane Selby and Leach and Hugh and herself late on Sunday afternoon. Sophie flopped back into the plump cushions with her neat little hands covering her lower face. Mingling horror and astonishment was very apparent in the brown eyes widening above her fingers.

'How…*awful*!' Sophie finally exploded. 'The poor woman. To be deceived so. And by a man she believed loved her. And the poor babe!'

'I didn't see him,' Elizabeth quietly explained. 'I've no idea how old he is: whether a babe in arms or a young child. What can be done, Sophie?'

Sophie helplessly shook her head. 'It seems this repulsive Leach wants money or he'll not let her go. I have a small amount left from my allowance,' she volunteered immediately.

'I think he will want a substantial amount. Hugh said that Nathaniel Leach springs from a family of thieves. His mother is a notorious bawd and a fence. They will doubtless let Jane and little Jack go free if the price is right. But *then* where are they to go? Jane maintains her parents have disowned her, and Edwina is loath to help, let alone take her in.'

Getting into the spirit of the drama, Sophie leapt up and raced to the door. 'I shall see what I have to pawn.' Some minutes later, she was back with a reticule stuffed with odd pieces of jewellery. They were tipped onto the sofa between them and picked through: silver combs and earrings, a pearl ring and a broken gold bangle. Sophie disentangled a small gold locket and pulled it to one side. 'Not that.' She smiled apologetically. 'It was Fiona's,' she explained, referring to her elder sister who had died of smallpox, aged fifteen.

Elizabeth laid a hand on her arm. 'It's very good of you, Sophie, to part with anything at all. But I'm not sure this vile man will be moved by anything less than a substantial bribe.' She sighed in exasperation. 'And Hugh will not be of any help at all! Not only is he intimidated by Edwina—she has forbidden me to go back there—but he believes it is too late to help Jane, in any case. He insists she will never leave her fancy man…that she is somehow in his thrall! What nonsense! What do men know of these things! They are all such conceited creatures. Yet I believed Hugh to be different.' She tutted her disgust. 'And Grandmama endorsed his male chauvinism; simply to frighten me into staying away, I'll warrant. But I'll not be so easily put off!' She paused for breath. 'You must keep it all confidential. Please don't breathe a word that I intend to somehow help Jane and her little son.'

'Of course!' Sophie stressed. 'And I shall assist in any way I can. 'Tis the time to do the deed.' She suddenly interjected, in all seriousness, 'Mars…planet of action…is currently midheaven. It's a good sign.'

Elizabeth gave a little choke of laughter. 'Well, we're certainly going to need all the good auspices we can get!'

'Well, miss, what have you to say for yourself?'

Elizabeth removed her bonnet in the hallway, then shook out her crumpled, pearly locks. Slender fingers combed casually through them. 'What have I to say for myself?' she echoed with mock pensiveness. 'Ah, I know, what you're hinting at. It concerns the Viscount's visit, does it not?'

'Indeed it does!' Edwina shrilled in high dudgeon.

'Well I shall oblige you then and say: did he bring it?'

'Did he bring what, may I ask? A big stick with which to beat his graceless future wife? Who could blame him if he did?'

'Did he bring my necklace?' Elizabeth enunciated, overlooking her grandmother's boiling physiognomy.

'Well, if he did, he took it home with him again. And serve you right if he did do that. Had you scraped the grace to drag yourself home before he left half an hour ago, perhaps he might have handed it over! If, indeed, he had it with him.'

Elizabeth's mouth pursed into a rosebud. The relief that she had avoided him by such a narrow margin was barely acknowledged. 'He said I might have it today!' she exploded as her foot stamped on marble.

Edwina ignored the tantrum. 'We are to dine with Ross and his family on Friday. The documents are signed pertaining to the dowry. The marriage is to take place in three weeks…' she listed out.

Elizabeth's violet eyes darkened as her pupils grew large with shock. 'Over my dead body,' emerged in a croak.

'That can no doubt be arranged. The Viscount looked murderous, I can tell you, when I said you were not yet home. By the time we had twice taken tea and talked of trivialities and he realised you had no intention of putting in an appearance, I thought he might take himself off again without concluding the deal. Even Pettifer said he'd never seen him look so fuming.'

'More likely he was aggrieved at having cut short his shopping trip with his mistress,' Elizabeth snapped into her grandmother's censure. But she couldn't ignore the writhing in her stomach on learning how well she had succeeded in annoying him.

Edwina looked sharply at her granddaughter. 'You saw him out today?'

'Indeed. He was shopping with his doxy in Pall Mall.'

Edwina's face softened, and for the first time since her granddaughter had walked through the door with September sun silhouetting her petite figure and haloing her glorious hair, Edwina felt kindly disposed towards her. She took one of Elizabeth's small hands in a pudgy palm. 'You don't want to get upset over that vampish brunette,' she cajoled, patting at white fingers. 'Trollops like Cecily Booth are soon forgotten by the likes of Stratton. She might be younger, but she can't hold a candle to you in face or figure. Ross will never give her a second thought once he has you as his wife.'

'Oh, indeed! You're absolutely right about *her*, Grandmama,' Elizabeth dismissed on a shrill laugh. 'The trollop I was referring to is actually a little older than me, I should say, and blonde and very beautiful. Mayhap, he'll not be quite so eager to cast her off. How many in all do you imagine there are?' Without awaiting a reply, she made for the stairs, aware of her grandmother stunned into speechlessness for a change. She had given her something to chew on, she knew. In a determined show of nonchalance, and ignoring her stomach's squeamishness, Elizabeth began swinging her bonnet on its ribbons as she lightly ascended the stairs. But the same phrases tumbled through her mind as had earlier that afternoon in the fabric emporium: Damn you, Stratton! I just don't care!

'I'm glad you chose that gown: I've always thought it suited you.'

Elizabeth managed a smile at the compliment. She fussed over pushing a pin more securely into her elaborate, lustrous coiffure. A slender finger wound a smoky-blonde tress into a tighter ringlet, then twiddled the damson-coloured velvet ribbon threaded there. Abruptly she sat back against the squabs, gripping her fidgeting fingers in her lap.

'Are you nervous?' Edwina asked as they rattled over cobbles in her luxurious barouche heading towards Grosvenor Square.

'Of course not!' After a moment a glossy-eyed glance slanted across the dusky interior of the coach. Elizabeth noticed her grandmother was smiling. A small, reciprocal smile slanted her soft mouth. 'Well, perhaps a little. It is a while since I socialised with anyone other than Sophie and her parents. Or Hugh and ladies from the Society of Friends.'

'You call that socialising?'

Elizabeth ignored the dry comment. 'I'm a little out of practice, that's all it is,' she explained away her uneasiness at dining with the Viscount's guests. She soothingly smoothed her unsteady fingers back and forth against the rich, plum

velvet of her stylish gown, while restoking her agitation by
wondering whether any of those who were to be present tonight were cognizant with her history.

Edwina had told her before they left Connaught Street that
the Viscount's mother seldom left Cornwall where she led a
quiet life. It was unlikely she would have bothered herself
with *beau monde* scandals. His brother, although a wealthy
aristocrat, now resided in Brighton with his family and used
his Mayfair townhouse but rarely. Edwina had then com-
plained she wasn't sure which other people were to be present,
although she guessed Guy Markham might, and that failing
was all Elizabeth's fault. Her last meeting with the Viscount
had been so strained due to Elizabeth's non-appearance that
she had forgotten all the little essentials over which she had
meant to quiz him.

Elizabeth tilted her chin. She didn't care, in any case, which
of his piffling friends were due to attend! If they liked him,
that obviously cast their own characters under grave suspicion! She didn't care, either, whether they knew about her
disgrace. She had no intention of playing the pariah for any
parvenu cits! In fact, she had had no intention of playing
along with this foolishness at all. She found herself travelling
to Grosvenor Square this evening not primarily to dine or
meet his friends and family, but to retrieve her necklace.

She had been quite certain that, once the Viscount's temper
cooled a bit, he would make contact during the week. After
all, they were now unofficially betrothed. But he had not. She
had not seen or heard a word from him. Thus there had been
no opportunity to revile him for keeping her necklace. And
she had balked at the idea of again scandalising all concerned
by visiting him to demand he return it. Which left just writing
a note: which he would doubtless ignore, for he must still be
very angry with her for again snubbing him. He hadn't even
contacted Edwina; her grandmother had been a little chary of
the absence, lest he was brooding on breaking the contract,
and this dinner date. Elizabeth, too, had been moderately re-

lieved he had not, for she needed to accost him tonight and wrest her jewellery from him.

In direct contrast to the Viscount's absence had been Hugh Clemence's many visits. The first one had her inwardly groaning, wondering how to deflect questions over her odd disappearance from home that had occasioned him being twice roused from his bed by Pettifer. Edwina had unexpectedly come to her rescue. Usually the vicar's arrival prompted her grandmother to disappear in the opposite direction. This time, she was all affability.

'Sorry about harrying you the other night, Reverend,' she had barked. 'If you must tick us off, blame m'granddaughter. She has this habit of secreting herself in odd corners of the house. And m'eyes aren't all they should be. Can you wonder at m'fears when she wasn't in her bed, but potting ferns in the conservatory at such an hour? I think this business with the slum dwellers is badly affecting her.' The dark hint and head tapping that accompanied the remark had been laden with accusation.

Hugh had looked mystified at being obliquely to blame for his own disturbance. On seeing his hurt bewilderment, Elizabeth had comfortingly mouthed, 'Eccentric…' with a couple of meaningful grimaces for good measure.

Whatever her grandmother said, she was determined to go as usual with Hugh to Sunday School. And she would make it her business to track down Jane Selby and rescue her. So she would need a valuable item to take with her…

Her musing was curtailed as she realised the carriage had stopped. Elizabeth noticed two flare-toting footmen, resplendent in their dark livery and moth-bright powdered wigs, approaching their carriage door. Her final reflection, before disembarking, was that the cheating, lying host she was about to be presented to presently held that necessary valuable item. But not for much longer. It was hers! And she was determined to have it!

Chapter Ten

'I've always been a tiny bit in love with Ross...'

The confession emerged in a conspiratorial sigh. Rebecca wrinkled her neat little nose at her friends, then glanced across the opulent drawing room at their darkly handsome host talking to her beloved Luke.

'I think we all feel that way about Ross, Becky,' Emma Du Quesne admitted, but her exquisite topaz eyes were on her tall, blond spouse, grouped with the Trelawney men, and no doubt discussing their copper-mining consortium. Sir Richard Du Quesne had propped a negligent elbow on the magnificent Adams' chimneypiece, while emphasising some point to his Cornish colleagues with the crystal goblet he held. His silver gaze slid sideways, merged with his wife's; it was a second or two before a private smile passed between them.

There was a third lady, resting comfortably between Rebecca and Emma on a plump-cushioned gilt-framed sofa. Viscountess Courtenay trailed an oval fingernail across delicately painted cherubs on her gauzy fan. 'It's as well our husbands trust us so much,' she contributed to the romantic debate. Victoria slanted a fond look at her dear David, chivalrously bringing to Demelza Trelawney a glass of ratafia while her sons socialised by the hearth.

All the people in the room were joined by family or deep friendship. All were enjoying this fine opportunity—while awaiting the arrival of Ross's other guests—to catch up with news on subjects as diverse as business and babies, as well as airing all the other myriad little domestic matters that were gladly heard by people whose opinion and advice were valued.

'They trust Ross, too. That's why they let us flirt with such a dangerously attractive bachelor,' Emma said. 'They've all been acquainted such a long time. Richard told me that Ross has ever been a successful charmer. I doubt it's exaggeration! In the short while I've known him, I've witnessed all manner of females fighting quite immodestly over him.'

'I feel privileged to have had his escort on occasions,' Rebecca added. 'It's been very agreeable. I'll miss his teasing remarks and wicked glances...I shall make Luke take over where his brother has left off!'

'That was quickly achieved, Lady Ramsden!' Emma drolly announced, noticing Baron Ramsden's dark eyes targeting his vivacious, blonde wife.

'What makes you think Ross might now deprive us of his delightful gallantry, Becky?' Victoria interjected. 'The few days I've been here in London, I've noticed no change in him.'

'Oh, it's hard to be specific,' Rebecca bubbled, very conscious of her husband's ardent gaze. 'He just seems different: a little preoccupied and impatient at times. He lacks his usual devil-may-care attitude to every single thing. I think perhaps he is at last taking his responsibilities seriously: he did tell me there is a mountain of work to be done at Stratton Hall before it is properly habitable. And then again he seemed very...interested in a fair lady we saw when out shopping. I think he is possibly in the process of...' Her voice became whisper-soft. 'Delicate negotiations with a new *chère amie*. We also came face to face with a brunette he had just put off! The blonde is so much lovelier...refined, too. I believe Ross called her Lady somebody or other. Mayhap she is a young widow. But I couldn't prise out of him much at all. And you know how he usually yields to a little coquetry.' She nodded meaningfully at Emma and Victoria, and as one, they all slanted a speculative look at Ross who was consulting his gold hunter.

Irritably, the case was flicked shut and he looked at the clock on the mantel, as though checking the time.

'Is Guy Markham late?'

Ross stared blankly at his brother for a moment.

'Is Markham late for dinner?' Luke repeated with slow stress. 'Dammit, Ross, you're acting like a blockhead. You've had your watch out three times in three minutes. Who are you waiting on? Markham or this Mrs Sampson you've invited?'

'More likely to be Mrs Sampson, I'd have thought,' Dickie Du Quesne chipped in drily before sipping from his glass.

'Mrs Sampson is a very old friend…in more ways than one: she's over sixty years of age,' Ross informed Dickie with a grin.

Dickie choked into his aperitif. 'Over sixty?' he gasped. 'Good God! That's a little too mature even for your all-encompassing taste. You mentioned her granddaughter might accompany her. Perhaps she has you on tenterhooks. Is she squint-eyed and stalking you?'

It was Ross's turn to choke on his drink. He grimaced while soothing his furrowed brow with hard, dark fingers.

Reading nothing positive in his friend's skewed expression, Dickie guessed gloomily, 'Oh, perfect! She's not just out of the schoolroom and liable to get all giggly if anyone attempts conversation with her, is she?

'Well, whoever it is we're waiting on, I wish they'd hurry up,' Luke growled. 'I'm ravenous!' Barely pausing, he continued, 'And Mother is signalling at you…for the second time. By her look, I'd say maternal advice is in the offing. First, a little brotherly advice,' Luke continued soberly, with a staying hand on Ross's arm. 'Tell her what she wants to hear. For some reason, she's been more anxious than usual over you, of late. She was determined to come to London and see how you do. And you know how much she hates to travel…'

With a sigh, Ross retrieved his goblet from the mantel and

dutifully strolled towards Demelza Trelawney's chair. As he hunkered down beside it, Lord Courtenay removed himself from where he'd been perching on the arm. With a parting smile, David strolled to squeeze onto the sofa beside his darling wife, Victoria, and her friends.

Demelza placed a delicate hand on her youngest son's lean, tanned face. 'Are you happy?'

Green-gold eyes lifted to hers, gazed deep into their gentle brown depths. He smiled. 'Of course…yes, I'm a Viscount, in favour at court. I've this fine townhouse and a magnificent estate—or at least it will be when I'm done with it. You must come and see it; next week, if you feel like a carriage ride to Kent.'

'You've told me what you've achieved, Ross, not what I asked,' his mother mildly reproved. 'Being a Viscount with a grand home is nice. Being content with that would make it wonderful. You're still not content. You've craved danger and excitement all your life and I've watched you indulge it way too much. Now I feel I should have been firmer with your father…with you all…and curbed it when you were younger. Oh, very well, tried to curb it,' she amended with a little moue as she read his ruefully amused expression. 'But it's gone on too long now; restlessness…inconstancy…seem natural to you.' She angled her head, attempting to lure her son's evasive feral eyes.

She gazed at his dear profile until it wavered out of focus and in her mind's eye stood a child; wild as the rugged Cornish coast, as the wind that cowed the grass along the cliff tops. Never still, never sated, never hurt. Sometimes he would come to her, out of childish duty, raise torn elbows and knees, while fidgeting to be free again. Momentarily, he might tolerate her fingers forking into his thick, sleek hair, her lips kissing better his wounds, before his wiry little body wriggled away. And then he would be gone, running…running…long dusky locks tangling with the briny breeze, his beautiful dark face once more animated…laughing…always laughing. And now…now Ross was hurt again and it was nothing a mother's kiss could soothe. Ross was in love.

Aware of her eyes on him, Ross glanced up, humouring her with a crooked smile.

'You helped Luke discover tranquillity and I know you'd like to find it, too,' Demelza resumed slowly, choosing her words carefully. 'But its lack never worried you, before. It only worried me.' She punitively waggled his square, shady jaw, emphasising her vexation. 'But now…you're different, my love; there's melancholy in your eyes. I think perhaps you finally know where it is, but still it's eluding you…'

Ross removed his mother's cool palm from his face. He looked at it, fleetingly pressed his lips to it, before linking their fingers and skimming her pale cheek with the back of his dark hand. He smiled at her appealing, fine-boned features. Her skin looked as soft as it felt: little marred by the years of coastal living, and her raven's-wing hair shining with silver skeins, rendered her still strikingly attractive at sixty years old. About to give spurious reassurance while inwardly cursing her maternal perceptiveness, Ross suddenly became aware of her eyes slipping away from his and a static silence crackling in the room around him. It was the serene curve to his mother's lips that snapped his head about.

'Mrs Sampson and Lady Elizabeth Rowe…' Dawkins, his butler, droned nasally.

Elizabeth sensed herself rooting to a spot barely a yard into the drawing room. Blood drained from her complexion until it prickled icily, and those old, terrifying demons that she thought conquered and long banished to her past, danced with devilish abandon in the pit of her stomach.

The scene was a decade old, yet frighteningly familiar. *Parvenu* cits? Her disparaging description returned to mock her as she gazed, panic-stricken, into a room that was all dignified elegance…as were its occupants. One skittering, scouting look had impressed on her these were charmed people; people of influence and gentility…and fabulous wealth. And they were all staring at her…and she couldn't bear it.

She was obliquely aware that only a few seconds had passed since she and Edwina were announced; the butler was still in the process of bowing sedately out of the room, pulling closed the enormous doors as he went. Only seconds had passed! But in a moment she would hear the whispers, see the sneers, and squirm beneath their scorn as she strove not to turn and flee.

As though Edwina sensed she might bolt, a preventive hand grabbed her elbow, attempting to urge her forward. Encouragement was hissed warmly against her ear. But her legs felt stiff and leaden, her chest too tight to drag in breath. Her violet eyes began flitting agitatedly over blonde…brunette… male…female…sparkling gems…sleek silk; never lingering long enough to register anything or anyone clearly, yet scouring, desperately seeking. Where are you? wailed plaintively in her head. More than anything in the world, she wanted to locate his strong gypsy face, his broad, brown-clad body. She needed him…now…so much…

Her bated breath whimpered out between her compressed, chalky lips as his movement amid the stillness arrested and held her eyes. He rose slowly, sinuously, from the side of a chair and was walking towards them. His eyes never once relinquished hers and she held to that comforting, honeyed gaze as a castaway might cling to a piece of driftwood.

'Mrs Sampson…Lady Elizabeth…I'm very glad you could come…'

The welcome was warm, sincere. His attention was courteously with Edwina as she addressed him, but his touch was immediately with Elizabeth. Slowly, discreetly, he drew her towards him, his firm familiar fingers on her cold, quaking arm. She felt the warmth of a thumb smooth back and forth, back and forth, and another shuddering little sigh escaped her. He shifted casually closer, and it seemed the most natural thing in the world to move to meet him, seek the lee of his large, solid body.

Within a few seconds of listening to discourse about the changeable weather, in particular the rainstorm earlier that had knocked the petals off Edwina's favourite crimson rose, and the ensuing sunshine that was so welcome but did nothing to repair the damage; Elizabeth was calm enough to again be fretting. This time her fears were that he would think her a socially inept nincompoop to be standing so mute and trembly, and so clingingly close to him. She took a very small step back; it was the most she could manage.

Another superbly attired, handsome gentleman strolled to join them. Ross introduced she and Edwina to his brother, Luke. She believed she murmured an adequate response to a convivial greeting from this stately aristocrat who looked older than Ross by some years, but so resembled him, that the family connection would have been obvious. Then Baron Ramsden was gallantly leading Edwina away to meet the other guests.

Elizabeth blinked rapidly at Ross's shoulder, unable to look anywhere else. She was sure they were the focus of many pairs of eyes, and that she was foolishly engendering further interest, and thus her own uneasiness, by her obvious reluctance to quit his side. She despised herself for her timorousness, but it was far too soon to relinquish the relief and security she found stationed so close to this man.

'Don't be nervous, sweetheart,' he encouraged with such husky affection in his tone that Elizabeth's head jerked up.

There was amusement gleaming in his tawny eyes but it wasn't scornful; it was gentle, understanding…and prompted an immediate defensive indignation. She wouldn't be pitied! Not by him! About to retort that she wasn't nervous and he had no right to suppose she might be, the words withered, unuttered, on her lips. The discreet caress on her arm was again working its lulling magic; also she read from his wry expression that he was anticipating the rebuttal. But primarily she remained silent because she recollected him calling her sweetheart and, even if it was mere meaningless cajolery, she liked it.

His smile strengthened into a throaty chuckle that acknowledged the piquant mingling of belligerence and vulnerability purpling her eyes. 'Good; I can tell you're now a little more relaxed, Elizabeth. You look almost the shrewish little madam I've come to know and love…'

Elizabeth stared at him, unable to draw breath, drowning in his golden gaze replete with a mockery that wasn't quite genuine. Her eyes dragged away and her tongue tip moistened her lips. 'I…I'm sorry if I seemed a dumb idiot just then when you introduced me to your brother.' Desperate to appear confident and capable, she flicked her bright, burnished head, setting her curls dancing, while rushing on, 'It's just…I rarely socialise in…I'm a little out of practice with people of…I rarely go out now.' She tailed off, feeling her complexion heat. 'I don't like to be stared at…' she defensively concluded her justification.

'There's not a soul here who means ill by it, Elizabeth. It's just that it's impossible not to stare when you look so outstandingly lovely. When you arrived, you stunned me into gawping at you, too, for a moment. And I'm acquainted with your ravishing looks.' His eyes became heavy-lidded, a veiled honey gaze flowing over her lush, petite body sheathed in taut plum velvet.

A hand instinctively fluttered to her low neckline as though she could shield from view the frantic rise and fall of her pearly, satin-skinned bosom.

He took the fingers, placed them in the crook of his arm, as he turned them into the sparkling warmth of his opulent drawing room. As far as her little reconnoitering glances could detect, nobody was staring, or even looking their way now.

'Come, let me quickly introduce you to everyone. Then I should like to speak to you privately before dinner.' His voice had lost its intimate, indulgent edge and become brisk.

Elizabeth felt chilled again, although her composure was consolidating. Of course, he would be businesslike now he had steadied her nerves…made her presentable. This was, after all, business, however attentive and chivalrous he contrived to be in front of his kith and kin.

When this invitation had been issued at the beginning of

the week she had presumptuously believed he was eager his family and friends should find favour with her. Now, she was more inclined to think the reverse was true. Doubtless, he wanted *her* approved by these imposing people before irrevocably committing himself. He intended she play the part of an agreeable, prospective spouse. Pride and indignation wedged a blockage in her throat. Well, she would have little choice but to cooperate tonight, even if she never did so again! And she expected him to reciprocate by playing the part of an honest gentleman and returning her necklace when she demanded it!

With a huge, settling breath, her sculpted chin tilted confidently just as they reached a sofa. She steeled herself; she was fine and ready; she was a Marquess's daughter. And then she looked down into the smiling, turquoise eyes of the lady her intended had taken shopping.

She had not realised just how literally he meant…*quickly* introduce. Within what she guessed to be under fifteen minutes, Elizabeth found herself being returned, by her host, to the double-doors of the drawing room she had so recently entered. Her head was reeling from the effort of remembering names, from an amazement at the sincerity and warmth of the welcome she and her grandmother had received from these people. She could discern no sly looks or whispered asides from the ladies as she passed by the sofa. None of the gentleman had ogled her, although she understood the approval in their eyes as they took a look at Ross in that subtle, meaningful way men had. And all present were so astonishingly good-looking! Even his gracious, doe-eyed mother was still attractive. She couldn't ever recall being in a room with so many beautiful people.

'Mr Guy Markham…' boomed out close behind them, startling Elizabeth out of her pleasant reflection.

Guy swept in, looking a little overheated and harrassed. Spying his friend at once, just inside the door, he blurted, 'Sorry, Stratt, to be so late. Blasted axle nigh on departed company with the carriage in Oxford Street. That footman of yours who's handy with the tools is giving my man some assistance with it…' Giving proper attention to his friend's companion, he suddenly declared, 'Well, Lady Elizabeth Rowe! And not looking a jot different from when last I saw you! How have you been?' He found one of her hands and gallantly raised small, white fingers to his lips.

'Very well, sir, thank you,' Elizabeth said amiably, with a little dip of her smoky-blonde head. Feeling now quite light-hearted, she was about to return the courtesy and ask how he did, but found that she was being backed through the closing doors by Ross, while Dawkins, his butler looked scandalised by his master's undignified behaviour: squeezing them a path past him through the aperture.

'Find yourself a drink, Guy, and then speak to my mother, would you? She was only asking after you this morning,' Ross sent casually back over his shoulder.

'Oh…right….' Guy said, bemused. He tilted his nut-brown head to watch his friend disappearing from sight.

'Dinner is ready to be served, my lord,' Dawkins informed his master in a cautionary tone once he had closed the doors with a precise flourish.

'Not quite yet, Dawkins. I'll tell you when…'

Dawkins inclined his head in acceptance of the dictate and marched, arms swinging, away along the carpeted corridor.

Aware of being studied, Elizabeth glanced up very quizzically from beneath her lush, brunette lashes. She looked down again, heart hammering in response to a wordless discipline she read in his eyes. A tentative move to re-enter the drawing room was blocked. Instead she found herself being steered determinedly along the corridor by a firm hand practically spanning the back of her tiny waist. He released her, swung open another door, and tersely gestured for her to enter.

His aloof manner made her exceedingly apprehensive, yet she knew she needed a little discreet conversation with him if she was to recover her necklace tonight. Inside the room, a roving inspection registered that it was a study with book-lined walls and an imposing desk spanning the entire area beneath a wide casement window. Beyond the glass, stars studded a black sky.

She turned quickly about, heart pumping. 'I know my reputation is tarnished already, my lord, and I know I have previously engineered just this sort of private tête-à-tête, but I really think, as you have company, it is best we are not alone like this.'

He had not moved away from the door and stood resting back against it, arms crossed over his chest, watching her. Some silent seconds later Elizabeth dropped her prim gaze from his hard face. The aubusson carpet, the walnut panelling, seemed less unyielding.

'I'm very angry with you.'

The bald admonishment, delivered dispassionately, rendered her speechless. She had believed he had tolerated her initial lack of social graces. She had demonstrated impeccable breeding ever since. To now remind her of her panic, fling it in her face in that…that careless manner… Glossy, violet eyes blazed at him as she chewed at her lower lip.

'I believe you owe me an apology, my dear…once again.'

Elizabeth opened her mouth to speak. Humiliation blocked the words in her throat. Her lips quivered then pressed closed. She had allowed him to lead her here imagining that, prior to announcing their betrothal, he wanted to impress upon her that the sordid details of their wedding contract be kept confidential. She had been certain he wouldn't want these eminent people to know he'd been outwitted by a wily old woman.

'I…I have already apologised,' she finally burst out in a tight little voice. 'I did not mean to act with such…such crass dependency, or embarrass you, if that's what you feel I have done. I think it more likely I have made a fool of myself. Nevertheless, as you wish to hear it one more time: I am sorry. I am sorry for ever coming here tonight—'

'Ah, I see…' he broke into her fierce defence. A small smile quirked his mouth. 'No. I didn't actually mean that, Elizabeth. Your insecurity and vulnerability don't bother me.

In fact, it's quite endearing. I like you close to me…needing me.'

'What, then?' she whispered, unable to hide her astonishment at that revelation.

He pushed away from the door. 'What, then?' he mimicked. 'What, then…about a *tiresome engagement* we had arranged earlier in the week that you failed to attend. Does that strike a chord? I'm quite happy for you to feel ashamed of that crass behaviour. Do you?'

Elizabeth bristled beneath his sharp, sardonic censure. 'No,' she snapped.

'Why did you deliberately stay away from home and avoid contributing to the wedding plans? Because you thought I had been shopping with my mistress earlier that afternoon?'

Elizabeth blushed to the roots of her silky, silver hair. 'I…I thought no such thing!' she burst out. Her complexion, if possible, became hotter, not only because it was an arrant lie but because the elegant lady she had just met, and learned was his sister-in-law, Rebecca, had greeted her with such sweet friendliness. And she had referred to her to Edwina as a doxy!

'Why, then?'

'I…I was upset by…by a certain…event. And I had more important things to do!' And all of that was the truth! she exhorted herself, remembering how shaken she had been by Linus Savage assaulting her in the fabric warehouse. She also recalled she and Sophie investigating ways to raise money for Jane Selby that afternoon after their shopping trip. Without doubt, her time had been far…far more vitally spent in that charitable occupation than in returning home to pick over a venal marriage contract with this hateful…hateful man!

'What certain event upset you?' he asked as he came closer.

'It's a private matter…'

'That you can share with your future husband. I've told you…I take an interest in my betrothed's problems.'

'Please don't,' Elizabeth rebuffed him frigidly. 'For I shall deal with all of them alone.'

'Even those that necessitate you slumming around Wapping docks to find this friend fallen on hard times?'

Elizabeth swallowed, froze beneath his astute scrutiny. 'Yes. Especially those…' she eventually forced out. He was barely a foot away now, and she was aware of his hot stripping gaze flowing over her body, lingering where the tonal velvet pile was rippling alluringly at breast and hips.

His fingers curled by his sides before disappearing to clasp behind his back. 'There are times, Elizabeth, when I'm not quite sure how I keep my hands off you.'

She shot a startled glance at him, then at the door as though measuring its distance.

His expression was bemused, self-mocking. 'Then again, if I yield to it, there's a possibility they might go straight for your throat. Such a waste…' As if to remove temptation, they were shoved into his trouser pockets. As if to remove her inclination to flee, he abruptly walked away. 'So; let's try again. What upset you that afternoon. Was it Cadmore?'

Another artless blush betrayed her.

Ross swore beneath his breath, at her wordless confirmation of his suspicions. 'Did he speak to you? Insult you? I saw him, too, whilst I was in that shop. He looked guilty as hell. Did you tell him we are betrothed?'

'Of course not! Why should I tell him any such thing?' Noting the intelligent, speculative glitter in his eyes, she blurted, 'I can deal with the Earl of Cadmore. I have been doing so for almost a decade.'

'Yes, I know. And I've just witnessed how that constant *doing so* has taken its toll on you. What did he say?'

Elizabeth dropped her eyes, her stomach churning again with sick shame as flashes of that venomous stare, that muttered invective, bombarded her mind. She didn't want to recall it…she wanted it forgotten.

'Tell me…' he insinuated silkily, sternly, into her turbulent thoughts.

Elizabeth jerked her head to frown at the comforting glow in the hearth. 'It was nothing…nothing much at all. I for-

get...' She choked an acrid laugh. 'He is never very imagi-
native. I'm sure you must know what men say to women in
such circumstances.'

Ross walked close and a hand spanned her face, gently
bringing it to look into his. 'No, I don't know. What did he
say?'

Compliance came suddenly, unexpectedly. 'He said I was
a brazen bitch who had known the dregs of society and that
he would make me pay for my insolence and have me if it
was the last thing he did. There! That is what he
said...amongst other things. I told you he was not very original and you would already know the gist of it. Did you not
say something similar to me yourself? Are you satisfied now?'
She jerked her ashen face from his fingers and backed away.

Ross stared at her, his face seeming a tense, fleshless mask,
as though his skin had tightened on his bones. Then he
frowned as though in profound puzzlement. She noticed white
bracket his mouth, a muscle close to it pull spasmodically.
'Thank you for telling me,' was all he said.

'Can we go back to the others now?'

'No.'

Elizabeth gestured futility with a pale, graceful hand. 'Why
on earth not? What is to be gained by staying here alone? It
can only lead to further bickering between us.'

Ross rested his weight back against the desk, braced his
hands either side of him. Abruptly snapping his head up, he
gazed at the ceiling. 'Come here,' he requested. When she
remained still, he dropped his face to look at her and extended
a hand. 'Come here.' His fingers beckoned.

She looked warily at those long, tanned fingers that a few
days ago had so gently skimmed her skin, scorching fever in
their wake.

'Come...'

She recognised the edge of command in that final, short
summons. Slowly she approached him, halting just out of
reach. Rocking forward, he grabbed her by the upper arms
and hauled her between his spaced feet, holding her until she

ceased straining. She was aware of his shady dark chin close to her forehead, aware of the spicy, sandalwood scent of him, the warmth of his hard masculine body.

'I'm sorry. I'm very, very sorry that I ever said any of that to you. I wanted to apologise before but got distracted. You do that to me. Make me forget things, make me say and do odd things. You've turned my world upside down... I don't know why I shall go into my dining room in a short while, and face people I care about, to announce my marriage, when privately I know my fiancée dislikes me. Unless, in a way that defies logic, I care more for her than anything else, and sense it's worth the risk carrying on because I'm hoping...chancing...that in time, she will like me...'

Elizabeth slowly raised cynical violet eyes. 'It's not the money,' he said in response to that look and the unspoken words souring her full, sweet lips. 'God knows, it's not the money. I don't need it...leastways, not that much.'

Elizabeth plumbed his eyes, searching for his soul... searching for deceit and sophistry. This was Ross Trelawney, a frantic part of her brain reminded her, as she sensed her scepticism melting beneath his liquid gold gaze and her body tilting towards his. Viscount Stratton was really Ross Trelawney, the bounty-hunter, hellion and seducer par excellence, she rigorously impressed upon herself. A decade ago she had witnessed snippets of his wild carousing with her own eyes, had heard gossip of much, much more. Only a few days ago, her grandmother had let slip he kept a vampish brunette mistress, and she had wondered how many others catered to his pleasure. He was a hard-hearted villain and a hardened rake, as he had described himself not a week since, while in this august house in a room very similar to this one. Yet he wanted her to believe such a man held tender feelings for her? That he didn't intend wedding a scandal-wrecked spinster simply to recoup the fortune a crafty old woman had tricked out of him? Only recently he had mocked her presumptuous expectation that he might propose marriage, then callously given her unchoosable options to repay him.

'If you like me, and repayment isn't important, give me back my necklace,' Elizabeth challenged in a breathy voice.

'So you can do what with it? Hand it over to a pimp in the naïve hope he'll hand over your friend? Life isn't that simple, Elizabeth.'

'It is! It's that simple!' she choked. 'Whatever you say, I know it's that simple. Just as I know you're lying when you say my dowry isn't important to you. It's everything to you. At one time you threatened me with abuse and my grand-mama with gaol simply to lay hands to it! But now you know for sure you can't have it without me, too. So you pretend to care. You're as calculating and crafty as Edwina, but to her I owe so much, not least my affection. To you I owe nothing. You don't like me! That's not what you feel at all!'

Ross looked at her. Then laughed, a bitter sound that grazed his throat. 'Very well; we'll do it your way. I'm motivated by lust and greed. In which case, you can have the necklace tonight after you give me a kiss. Not a very equal exchange, but as I've guests in the house and little inclination to scan-dalise my mother, I'll allow you to satisfy my lechery another night. Then we'll go in to dinner; pretend we're blissfully happy and I'll announce we're to be married in three weeks.'

'No.'

'No?' His dark brows hiked idly, as though he really couldn't care any more.

'Not three weeks… It's too soon…'

'Not for me it isn't,' he drawled drily. 'Three weeks.'

Elizabeth licked her full, soft lips, while she considered. He closed his eyes.

'Get my necklace.'

'When you've kissed me.'

She looked at his lean, dark face. His eyes were still closed, black lashes fanning his cheeks…child's lashes, she thought hysterically as she marvelled at their length and the slight curl to them. Unobserved, she studied the incongruous beauty of his rugged features: thick black brows, wide forehead above, softened by lengthy strands of glossy mahogany hair; straight, strong nose, flaring slightly, well-moulded lips that were a little narrow. She hastily suppressed the urge to touch a finger to the cleft in his chin and curiously test the abrasiveness of shady masculine skin along his honed jaw. His breathing was easy; his powerful chest, resplendent in figured cream waist-coat, was expanding towards the plum velvet curving over her bosom. He was composed; he couldn't give a damn whether she complied or not. She could walk away. She had wanted to before. She had been ready to forfeit angling for her neck-lace earlier just to escape to the drawing room and other company. Now, that seemed unbelievably craven and selfish. Jane Selby and her little son had been easily abandoned; yet she was their only hope. It was that simple!

'What sort of kiss?'

His lashes raised. 'What sort of kiss?'

'One for you or one for me?' she gravely enquired.

His mouth twisted wryly in comprehension. 'One for us, Elizabeth…' he said, adopting her solemn tone.

She looked again at his sensual mouth and he watched her. She fidgeted on the spot a little. He watched her. Her hands began to raise as though to touch him, then clasped in front of her uncertainly. She pressed her lips together. Her eyes met his.

'Come closer, you can't reach from there,' he pointed out.

'Oh…yes…' Elizabeth said on a faint smile.

He returned her the same sort of faint smile.

She shifted further forward between his spaced feet. Her hands brushed unintentionally against the twill-sheathed iron muscle of his inner thighs and recoiled. She tried to nonchalantly rest them on the desk, by his, but found it too far away. The movement left her tilting precariously off balance. She clutched at his sleeves, steadying herself, her face against his shoulder. Her eyes squeezed shut in mortification. 'I…I'm sorry but I'm no good at this. It's been too long since I…when I was last fond of someone…in the manner of wanting to kiss them, that is…it was…very long ago.'

'Are you talking about Havering?'

Elizabeth relaxed a little, not wanting to move. It felt so comfortable, so easy just being warm and close to him. But it wouldn't last, of course, he didn't want her comfortable and easy laying against his shoulder. But for guests in the house, he would have her pandering to his lechery. 'Yes,' she simply answered his query.

'He's married now,' he said in the same cool, neutral tone.

Elizabeth swallowed, closed her eyes against the soft wool of his coat. 'Yes, I know.' She pushed herself back, unwilling to discuss any of it further. 'You could do it,' she said. 'It will be more to your liking and quicker; your guests must be wondering where on earth their dinner is. Edwina said she was most looking forward to her dinner…but then she always does, of course. She guessed fifteen courses or thereabouts and was hoping that pheasant and salmon and syllabub would be amongst them…' She trailed into silence, a vague smile fading away to nothing, as she stared at his intricately folded cravat, stark white beneath his dusky chin. Suddenly she tipped against him, kissed him full on the lips.

It was shy, soft and soon done. Then, because she realised how boring and inexperienced it must seem, before breaking contact she touched her tongue tip to his mouth, as she recalled he had done when kissing her. She felt his lips part allowing it to flick inside and she was petrified into stillness, unsure what to do next. She knew if she raised her lashes, he would be watching her, probably in a scientific, calculating way. She had confessed to not having kissed in years; she wondered how long it had been since he had encountered such gauche clumsiness from a woman he desired. She doubted Cecily Booth, the vampish brunette, kissed him this way…

With that forlorn thought, she pulled back, face flushing. Immediately she walked away. 'My necklace, please…' She hoped the request sounded cool and compelling. Inwardly, she was writhing. If he laughed at her, scorned her pathetic effort by saying it came nowhere near to earning her back her jewellery, she knew she might fly from the room…from the house.

She heard the slide of wood on wood as a drawer smoothly opened, then his footsteps closing with her. The unexpectedness of cool fingers on her febrile skin made her flinch. He moved her hair from her nape, then the sleek coldness of gold and precious stones slid against her throat. He fastened the collar, then carefully smoothed her moonlight-fair hair into place before both dark hands slipped downwards to enclose her pearly upper arms.

Elizabeth raised unsteady fingers to glide against the gem she had last worn at her début ball. 'Thank you...' she whispered, her lids drooping in sheer gratitude that she once more had it.

He turned her slowly about. A long finger trailed the drape of a silky spiral of hair laying against a fragile jut of collarbone, before sliding to her face. Wordlessly he lowered his mouth to hers, courting her in just the same sort of sweet, seductive way he had before. It was a kiss for her and she was already drowning in it. Her hands raised, unbidden, slid about his neck, into his hair. Her lips opened beneath his, tracked his, sought his when he started to pull away. So it started again, until this time his mouth strayed to freedom across the satin of her cheek and she lay, enervated against him, eyes closed, mouth sleek and lax.

She felt a large hand stir in her hair, rousing her. 'Believe, me Elizabeth, I do like you...' he said softly as, taking her hand, he led her, dazed, from the room.

Chapter Eleven

Elizabeth might have had just the one relation present, but Edwina had been unabashedly joyous enough for a host of family members. Oddly, that had roused her spirits: she'd wanted to please her grandmama. Seeing her so very happy was reparation of sorts for the shelter, the affection she had needed so desperately from the only fond kin remaining to her. Even her anguish on her beloved papa's death had not softened her paternal grandmother's attitude towards her. The Dowager Marchioness considered her disgraced granddaughter as contemptible then as she had when she first besmirched the lofty Thorneycroft name.

Before the announcement, they had feasted on delectable fare. Or so Edwina described it in endless detail the following morning. As the assembly had settled either side of the stately dining table, there had been a scintillating air of expectancy. Elizabeth knew she'd eaten a little, but of what she could not say. Every morsel had turned to ashes in her dry mouth, directly after that brutal look. She had known then, with chilling heart, that kisses counted for nought; she remained unforgiven and still beholden for the necklace she wore.

She had slighted him again, rebuffed his apology, implied he was incapable of finer feelings. So be it, she'd read in those sardonic, dark-as-molasses eyes that had adhered pitilessly to hers. I can be motivated by lust and greed. Expect that of me and I'll willingly oblige.

Thus she had understood, as he'd intended she should, the cruel ambiguity in his speech. Yet it had been sublime… subtle…significant only to her. With an easy eloquence that had demolished for ever her estimation of him as a philistine, he'd conveyed that a bond of deep affection existed between them. Yet never did he actually say so. He'd managed to make her blush and everyone chuckle—she did too in mild shock— with a teasing remark that the fair faces of his children would be attributable to his wife. The ladies had blinked dewy eyes, the gentlemen had looked wise and empathetic. In his mother's gentle countenance she'd read a profound welcome; a tiny sanctioning dip of her head had held no condescension but a hint of female conspiracy.

He had publicly aired his aim to get children on her and gloated over his fortunate choice of marriage partner… Only she knew it was a fortune that had been her grandmother's bequest. The private message was clear: he was happy enough to take her body and her dowry. He had no complaints…yet she might…

A stab of piquant pain accompanied the realisation that, but for different circumstances, it might have been the happiest day of her life. Could she have chosen her in-laws, it might well have been people just like those who counted him as family or friend. Could she have chosen how her husband might look, how he might deport himself on just that occasion, it might have been as Ross Trelawney had that evening. The devastating irony was not lost on her as she was again put in mind of how perfect he could seem. Strong… handsome…witty…polished: no woman could possibly ask for more in a consort…and yet it was all so false.

During their bitter-sweet tête-à-tête he had declared he soon expected her to assuage his lust, then kissed her with mocking tenderness. He had professed to liking her, yet constantly tormented her by look or word. He had said money wasn't his prime concern, yet it didn't alter the fact that only days previously, he and her grandmother had pored for hours over the terms of transferring to him her dowry.

And nothing altered the fact that it was the Sabbath. For the first time in over a year, when Hugh Clemence had come to collect her to take her to Sunday School, she had sent him away, pleading a migraine. Or rather, Edwina had; even in that she was lacking valour. Had she spoken directly to him, she would have felt it incumbent on her to tell him of her engagement…and she couldn't—not yet. She had forsaken the children and Jane and her son because she was an abject coward, she inwardly railed as Hugh's gig turned the corner of the street and finally disappeared from sight.

With a hopeless sigh, she let the curtain flop back into place and wheeled into the room. She had not yet vowed to honour and obey. She was not even betrothed two full days, yet already she was dutiful! She was disgusted with herself!

'I'd hate to discover you've again concerned yourself with East End harlots against my express wishes,' had been his quiet parting shot as she and Edwina took a harmonious leave of his guests. She had dismissed the injunction with a low flippancy that it was her express wish he concerned himself with his own harlots.

She had been determined to carry out her rescue plan…especially since she now had something of equal value with which to barter that would keep safe her mother's precious necklace. Reflexively, she moved a hand and the diamond dazzled blindingly, looking enormous on her small finger.

She had been astonished when he gave it to her. Their short walk back along the corridor to the drawing room had passed in silence. But he had kept her hand in his, as though he had believed she might yet attempt to bolt and embarrass him. Moments before they rejoined the others, he had stayed her; drawn the ring from his pocket and slipped it onto her finger. The ritual seemed to crystallise the enormity of what she had pledged to do. It was serious; it was real; she *was* to marry this gentleman rogue.

And it was superb: a pastiche of the style of her Thorney-croft collection. The large central stone was a diamond rather than an amethyst but it was cut octagonally to match her jewellery. The surrounding smaller stones were cabochon amethysts, eight in number. It must have been specially made for her. She had intruded far enough into the life and mind of this itinerant Cornishman for him to have spared time to consider the specific design of the betrothal ring he gave her.

That evening, at the dinner table, blushing beneath his quiet articulate compliments, branded by the unaccustomed weight on a hand in her lap, she had felt suddenly close to tears at the horrible hypocrisy of it all. Tell them! had throbbed in her mind. Tell them all that my true attractiveness lies in a bank and comes as a lump sum on production of the marriage lines; thereafter as an annuity each January for as long as I survive…

And the hysterical thought that at least he wouldn't give in to the temptation to throttle her, no matter how she riled him, had elucidated something else. *Such a waste*…had been his reasoning for keeping his hands from her throat earlier that evening. Suddenly she had understood what he meant. Such a waste, indeed! Quite absurd, in fact, to lose out prematurely on ten thousand a year…

Elizabeth irritably twisted the heavy gem on her finger. And now, instead of finding a certain equanimity with Hugh's poor parishioners and wretched Jane Selby, she was awaiting the arrival of her silver-tongued fiancé. He had yesterday sent a formal note to say he would call today at two of the clock and take her for a drive. How very civilised a courtship it had become. How very confident he was that she would not be at Sunday School but heedfully at home awaiting him. And so she was…

She ripped the ring from her finger. She would leave it in her room. It was a paltry show of defiance, but a show none the less! And tomorrow…tomorrow, she would go to Wapping instead, seek normality, and concern herself with as many harlots as she pleased!

'Are you not going to get changed?' burst in on Elizabeth's fuming thoughts. Her grandmother was gawping her distaste. 'You can't go out with the Viscount dressed like *that*!' Edwina flicked a scornful finger at her petite figure. 'That old dun serge is what you wear when you slum visit!'

'I know…'

'Well, don't just stand there like a…a bedraggled pauper,' Edwina barked. 'Ross will be here at any minute. Last time he set eyes on you you looked like an angel in that velvet gown and your amethysts. You can't venture out with him on your first public appearance together looking like…like…'

'Like a woman ready to teach Sunday School?' Elizabeth offered sourly. 'If that's how I look, then I'm glad. That's exactly what I intended to do today. It's what I always do on a Sunday. And how I wish Hugh would return on some pretext and give me another chance to do just that!'

Her grandmother's pale eyes widened and she cocked her head. Then she was wobbling to the window. 'It's Stratton's barouche…and what a corker it is, too…and it looks like rain… Good; he's got the hood up. Quick, get your black silk cloak: 'twill conceal all that tat you're decked in…hurry! Oh, and find a pretty bonnet, too…'

Elizabeth felt her heart start to hammer. He was here. He was actually here and she wasn't ready. Not that her modest garb bothered her, but she had hoped to mentally prepare herself. She uncurled her hand and looked at the jewel on her palm. Her ring finger stretched meekly towards the golden circlet, then abruptly joined the others in forming a fist. She dropped the opulent gem carelessly into a pocket of her old dress.

A moment later, Harry Pettifer announced in his grand way, 'Viscount Stratton…'

'I'll make excuses for you and occupy him while you change,' was hissed from a corner of Edwina's stretched mouth.

Elizabeth barely heard the instruction. Her eyes were drawn immediately to her fiancé's tall, powerful physique. Despite herself her heart lurched at the splendidly handsome sight of him.

He was dressed in a black tail coat and buff trousers. The tiger's eye stone blinked in a cream silk cravat. The snowy, razor-sharp collar of his shirt slashed a stark contrast against his lean, tanned jaw. Black calf-top boots resembled ebony glass. He looked cool elegance incarnate as he strolled forward to bow to and greet Edwina. His inscrutable dark visage turned then towards Elizabeth. Eyes like tawny agate slipped down her slender mouse-coloured body before returning to her exquisite porcelain features crowned by a chignon of sleek ash-blonde hair. Blood suffused her cheeks as she squirmed beneath a look that was pure quizzical amusement. Her chin edged up and petulance pursed her mouth. She didn't give a fig what he thought of her appearance!

'I'm honoured, Lady Elizabeth,' he murmured gravely. 'It seems it was a close-run thing who you graced with your presence this afternoon: me or the vicar. I'm very glad you were sensible enough to let me win.'

Elizabeth bridled beneath the latent mockery; it barely veiled the threat narrowing his eyes and slanting his mouth. 'You've not won!' she snapped in a low breath, excluding Edwina from the dialogue. 'And I've not missed my true vocation this afternoon simply to do your bidding.'

'Of course not. I'd never think such a thing…'

Elizabeth's small fingers spasmed at her sides at his smooth irony, but as he offered her a suave arm, and a head flick indicated that he was ready to leave immediately, there was very little hesitation before she complied.

'Are you ashamed of me?'

Ross stretched out his long legs in front of him and settled back more comfortably against the luxurious hide squabs, the reins loosely held in one large hand. The perfectly matched greys were impeccably behaved and the barouche glided evenly on. 'Ashamed of you?' he echoed on a frown.

'I thought we were to take a drive in Hyde Park, or perhaps

St James's. We have been out a full hour and still this is not Hyde Park or St James's. Are we going to Richmond?' A sideways glance darted to his impassive, dark profile before she resumed sweetly, 'No? Well, I imagine you are avoiding popular places lest we are spotted by the Town Tabbies. And I understand your fears, my lord. Speculation might start as to why an eligible nobleman would squire a scandal-wrecked spinster…with very poor dress sense.' She feigned concern. 'Heaven forbid, but a scurrilous rumour might circulate that said nobleman is in fact a scavenging *parvenu* out for an old lady's blunt…'

The abruptness with which he swung the barouche off the main track and onto a wide grass verge had Elizabeth tipping against him and gasping. She scrambled up, straightening her clothes and looking about nervously. She had been so lost in introspection, castigating herself for deserting Jane Selby, and blaming him for everything, that she had been oblivious to how properly rustic the scenery was becoming. The hedgerows either side loomed lofty and dense; in the distance, up an incline, woodland was fringing the horizon. This didn't look like a pleasant little pastoral oasis in the sprawling metropolis. This was deep, desolate countryside.

Elizabeth felt her heartbeat pick up tempo. Quickly, she stabbed an assessing look at him. He swivelled on the seat and leaned back against the carriage, watching her in a way that did nothing to appease the alternating exasperation and anxiety that had engendered her foolish sarcasm in the first place. She ought to be working charitably and harmoniously with Hugh, not baiting this dangerous and unfathomable man. Was he brooding on that undercurrent of antagonism that had simmered between them at their betrothal dinner? Was he still angry with her for refusing to contribute to the wedding plans? He seemed quite mellow…but then it was hard to tell his mood. From past experience she knew he could treat her with unexpected gentleness at one moment, yet act like a ruthless ruffian the next…

At one side of his powerful shoulders, she spied a clutter

of cattle close to a gate, bovine-ringed noses thrusting through rough planks. 'Where are we?' she abruptly demanded.

'Just outside London…'

'Outside London?' she parroted, horrified. 'Well, turn about at once. I didn't give you permission to take me outside London.'

A white smile transformed into a choke of laughter. 'Have I your permission to take you inside London, my lady? If so, I'm more than ready to immediately recross the boundary line.'

She flushed scarlet and rammed herself backwards against the carriage, so they sat face to face. The knowledge that she was still under obligation for the return of her necklace pounded the forefront of her mind. Surely he was not so mean and vile as to have brought her into the wilds today for that? It was yet daylight! 'Take me…return me home now! This instant!'

She was aware of his green-gold eyes roving her face, her petite figure, and instinctively gathered the black silk cloak more tightly about her.

'You told me once you weren't afraid of me…'

Huge violet eyes flicked up to his. 'Neither am I… Why should I be?' she challenged hoarsely.

'I don't know, Elizabeth. Why should you be? Unfortunately, I get the distinct impression that you are…most of the time…even now when we are soon to be wed. I don't want that. I don't want a wife who's afraid of me.'

'Oh, well, in that case I'm terrified…' she muttered.

'My God, you're an infuriating little…' The reproof concluded, unfinished, in a sigh as he reached for her.

Elizabeth slapped out at his hand. 'What are you doing?' she hissed at him, flattening against the carriage again.

'What do you think I'm doing?' he asked softly. 'I'm preparing to kiss my fiancée—'

'Well, don't!' she shrilled, raising a guarding hand in readiness to defend her. Her eyes darted from him to the road as though seeking another vehicle. ''Tis time to turn about any-how. 'Twill soon be dark.'

'I'll turn about when I've achieved what I set out to do and not before.'

Elizabeth tensed, raked his face with purple eyes. 'Which is?'

'I want to talk to you. Properly talk to you. There's a great deal we need to discuss in depth and in private. This is private enough.' He gave her an encouraging smile. 'I'll start the conversation by answering your earlier question: no, I'm not in any way ashamed of you, Elizabeth. I don't give a toss about polite society or what it thinks of me or you. It can ostracise us both for all I care. I've no time or inclination to bother with Janus-faced bores. I have all the family and friends I need. As for your clothes: the first time I saw you at Edwina's you looked oddly dishevelled, intentionally so, I imagine…as now. Unfortunately, a shabby gown doesn't de-tract from your allure.' That mockery was directed more at himself. 'You look delectable, however done up. Besides, it's what's underneath that interests me. Your character and per-sonality,' he explained with studied gravity as a suspicious look was cast on him. 'But, you guessed correctly: I avoided the centre of town because I'm not quite ready for our rela-tionship to be made public.'

When she said nothing but continued staring sulkily at the hedges, he asked drily, 'Would you care to know why that is?'

'No. I can guess.'

'And?'

'You're ashamed of me.'

Ross swore beneath his breath. 'Do you ever listen to what I say?'

'Oh, yes. But I seldom believe you sincere.' She barely paused before jibing, 'I told you to return me home. Do you ever listen to what I say?'

'Oh, yes. But I seldom believe *you* sincere.'

Looking away was impossible; she tried, but her gaze was

again adhering to eyes the colour of caramel. This time as a
hand came out slowly towards her she simply watched it,
unblinking, as a rabbit might mesmerically eye an approaching snake. A solitary dark finger brushed downwards over the
silken contours of her alabaster cheek, stroking, soothing.
'So…now it's your turn. I'd like you to talk to me. Tell me
things…important things about your past. If you like, I'll tell
you important things about my past, too. We'll share those
secrets that husbands and wives should know about each
other's history.'

Thick lashes screened violet eyes. She felt her heart thump
painfully slowly, her lungs ache with little use. It was what
she'd been dreading, yet expecting. Buried in her mind had
been a thread of hope that he might be different. Yet she knew
all along he wasn't. For all his clever phrasing…all his sly
vocabulary of sharing and caring, all he wanted was crude
titillation, as they all did. He wanted her to tell him things…of
course he did.

'I need to know, Elizabeth,' he said gently. 'I don't want
there to be any secrets between us.'

'You're so…so utterly predictable! Such a despicable
lecher!' she spat. 'You're no different to Linus Savage or any
of the others. Shall I tell you how many men have sidled up
to beg or buy a few explicit details? Would you like to hear
that? Did you think your smut original? Unique? I'm surprised
at you, my lord! With all your filthy experience should you
not have a little imagination when it comes to sordid…
sordid….' The words suffocated, jammed in her throat by fury
and fear. She blinked rapidly, endeavouring to quell the sob
she could sense tightening her chest. A hand scrabbled desperately behind for the door, searching to liberate her. She
was prepared to shelter in that herd of bulls if it meant es-
caping him. From the corner of her eye she noticed him slide
on the hide seat towards her and she twisted to lash out
blindly with both fists.

A vice-like grip crushed her hands in his, keeping them

utterly still. She couldn't move one bone in one finger, yet strangely they felt unhurt.

'If you're determined to continually throw punches at me, Elizabeth, you should learn to do it properly,' he said quietly. 'All this girlish hand flailing is far too provocative…and far too ineffectual.' He forced the left hand up, the other down and positioned slightly behind it. 'Keep your thumbs in to protect them; feint with your left, then bring the right through.' He jabbed the hand towards him, allowing her soft knuckles to graze his abrasive jaw. 'Keep your guard up all the time or you'll leave yourself vulnerable.'

As his tutoring tailed off and he relaxed his grip, she flung him off so savagely she tumbled back onto the squabs. Within a second she was recovered enough to launch herself forward again, angry humiliation puckering her features and curling small digits into claws. He was quite ready for her. Dark hands banded about her wrists, driving them back against the carriage. He slid them together above her head, anchored them there with five lean, insolent fingers while five more moved leisurely towards her unprotected face. The fork of his hand fitted over her pointed little chin, forced it up so she couldn't avoid his mockery, before slipping to straddle her willowy white throat. A thumb softly traced her mouth. 'Why don't you ever listen?' he chided, but a rueful smile just touched his mouth.

'I'll kill you,' she choked, twitching her face away from his indolent caress. 'I swear I'll kill you the first chance I get. You'd be a fool to marry me, even for a fortune. I'll catch you unawares and you'll never live to squander it. So you might as well strangle me first…before I shoot you. I've got a gun…'

'What sort?'

Elizabeth sniffed and blinked at him, momentarily shocked out of hysteria. 'What sort?' she echoed in a breathless gasp.

'A duelling pistol? A blunderbuss? A hunting rifle? What sort?'

'Oh, I don't know!' she cried. 'What difference does it

make? It's good enough to shoot you. Oh, I'll…I'll stab you then! I've a silver dress dagger that was once my papa's. I know it's a valuable Jackson and sharp. When I was fourteen I cut myself on it.'

'Did you? Where?' he asked softly, barely smiling.

Elizabeth screwed shut her eyes to deny his warm honey gaze. 'My knee. It fell out of my hand,' she whispered.

'You didn't listen to your father, either, did you? I'll wager he told you to keep it sheathed or leave it alone.'

'You think you know everything, don't you?' she hissed at him, mortified at his perception on something so precious and private. She began struggling to free her hands, still enclosed in his, over her head.

'No. I don't know everything. Some things I know. Some things I can guess. Some things I'd like you to tell me. I'd like you to tell me why Edwina said *now she really is ruined* the night I took you home. It seems an odd thing to say, all things considered. Why would your grandmother say that, Elizabeth?'

Elizabeth composed her face into a supercilious mask, flicked up her lids. 'I've no idea, my lord. Why do you not ask her?' she sweetly suggested. Then snapped, 'Let go of my hands.'

'I'm asking you. If I let go, are you about to scratch… gouge…slap? I'm getting tired of restraining you this way. That other way is far more pleasurable.'

'What other…?' The words tailed off as languid-lidded eyes dropped suggestively to her softly parted mouth.

She jerked her hands and this time he let them free. The momentum whizzed them dangerously close to his face. She panicked, snatched them away and controlled them, letting them fall to her lap where they clasped demurely.

He smiled at her. 'Very good,' he praised. 'You're taking good advice again. See how easy it can be?'

She turned her head, haughtily tilted her chin. 'I hate you,' she declared with great aplomb.

'No, you don't.'

'I do!'

'No, you don't. You can't. My mother says you're just right for me.'

Elizabeth stared at him. 'Your mother? You've been discussing me with your mother?'

'Shouldn't I? She's soon to be your mother, too. She thinks you're enchanting: sweet and mannerly and beautiful…just right for me.'

Elizabeth scoured his face for irony. So far as she could discern, his wry grimace seemed to mock his entitlement to her charms rather than her right to lay claim to them. The awful incongruity of his mother's opinion considering her recent bad behaviour made an uneasy flush singe her cheeks. Her tongue tip circled her mouth and she frowned and squirmed a little on the seat, disconcerted. 'Well…well you must thank her for her kind compliments. I…I very much liked her, too. I liked all your family and your friends. You're very lucky to have such agreeable kith and kin. I'll own to being surprised you could call them such,' she couldn't help qualifying her concessions with a sniff.

'I'm glad you like them. I hoped you would as they're soon to be your kith and kin. Everyone present said how engaging they found you. Where's your ring?' he asked without pausing. He raised her left hand from her lap and looked at the nude fingers.

Elizabeth had the grace to blush again after learning of such pleasing plaudits from such fine people…his people! She thought fast and said quickly, 'I put it in my pocket. 'Tis a fraction too large and I'm afraid to lose it. Wearing it to Wapping seemed a little ill advised.'

'Indeed. Going there against my wishes would have been equally ill advised. I'll have it made smaller for you.'

She snatched back her hand and inspected her manicure. His hand slid, palm up, into her line of vision. Speedily she retrieved the ring from her pocket, then placed it on his palm.

'Do you not like it?'

Elizabeth's head jerked back and she met his steadily

watching eyes. Part of her resented him for asking, even if it was a quite pertinent enquiry. Every passing moment was making her feel increasingly chagrined and churlish. She could tell he genuinely wanted to know if his gift pleased her. 'Of course I like it. 'Tis a magnificent ring, but…'

'But I gave it to you. Had Havering given it to you, no doubt it would have remained constantly on your finger.'

Elizabeth swallowed and said nothing.

'Do you pine for him still?' he asked harshly, returning the ring to its rightful place with a slow, sensual stubbornness.

'Of course not,' she answered quietly, studying the glowing jewels that seemed to obliterate half a slender digit.

'Of course not? Am I supposed to understand how you feel about him now? All you show me, Elizabeth, is a prickly surface. All I see is a little girl huddling, wounded, behind an armoury of pride. Talk to me. Tell me how you feel…share it with me!'

Desperation coarsened his voice and it curled her stomach, made mute the reflexive cry that she wasn't wounded and how dare he say she was. He sounded as though he cared. He sounded as though he would comfort her, salve the pain… With an instinct honed from ten years' injury, she reinforced her armour, put up her shield. 'I like it best when you talk to me.' An idle hand movement scattered a fragmented rainbow from the diamond. 'How am I to know how you feel about Cecily Booth if you never say?' she parodied. 'Why do you not tell me about her?'

'What do you want to know?'

She stilled and stared ahead. She had anticipated her outrageous impertinence would have him blustering, bawling her out, then, disgusted, taking her home. Young ladies—even damaged young ladies—did not acknowledge the existence of any gentleman's arbitrary amours. It was a taboo subject never broached by the decorous. But then she had been branded anything but that. Carelessly, she tossed her blonde head about, then looked into his narrowed hawk's eyes. 'What do you think I ought know?'

He grimaced thoughtfulness, while remaining totally dispassionate. 'Perhaps that she's nowhere near as classically beautiful as you. But she's pretty enough. She's some years younger, I should say, some decades more mature…more experienced…'

Elizabeth felt the same odd writhing pain as she had when she'd first seen him with Rebecca in the fabric emporium and imagined they were lovers. Well, she had asked about his mistress; and he was uninhibitedly telling her. And she wished he wasn't. She no longer wanted to know. 'How ideal she sounds!' she exploded breathily. 'As you insist you're not a fortune-hunter, I really think, sir, you ought make an honest woman of her, not me.' She had again wrenched the ring from her finger whilst speaking. About to throw it back at him, she noticed the latent triumph in his eyes, and it stirred her vexation to new heights. He understood very well how mention of his paramour had affected her. The need to thwart his arrogance helped her retain a tenuous grip on her self-control. Carefully, very carefully, she let the ring drop to the leather seat between them, then, head high, turned away. She even managed an insouciant smile at the thrush starting to warble atop the hawthorn hedge and tilted her head this way and that, examining rain clouds gathering in the distance, verdant, damp countryside: everything spied from her side of the carriage held a certain fascination.

'What makes you think she's ideal or that I might marry her?'

Elizabeth darted a quelling look at him, then found, again, she couldn't drag her eyes away. Silently, soulfully, she ceded…begged him to stop. She was not equal to this. She had again stupidly started something she was not fit to finish. She was no more able to win this verbal battle than she was able to beat him with her puny fists. Shamming indifference while he listed his mistress's attributes was beyond her. As he had pitilessly impressed on her while drawing comparisons, she possessed no such sophistication. 'Take me home, please. I…I feel unwell…I had a headache earlier…' she murmured, closing her eyes against the pretty bird bobbing close by. There was no mistaking she had made an utter fool of herself. What was he seeing now? A damaged little girl, or a cowed little mouse? A risible spectacle in either case, she was sure.

'Does it hurt?'

Unsure to what he referred, she hesitated in replying. Then, with aching perception, she realised ambiguity was intended. Did Cecily Booth hurt? Did her erstwhile, callow suitor's abandonment hurt? Did her ostracism hurt? Did her head hurt? Yes! she wanted to scream. Yes! Yes! Yes! She simply frowned at the first fat raindrops spoiling the dusty earth. They trailed the window like slothful tears. She nodded. He could make of that caitiff's response what he would.

The hand that slid beneath the pleat of hair at her nape felt warm and firm. Gently he urged her towards him and, a little token stiffness apart, she went to him. Her head drooped on to his shoulder and when his arm came across, pulling her properly close, she made no objection. Soothing fingers massaged at her neck and his head dipped until his mouth rested against her silky silver hair. 'There's one other thing you ought know about Miss Booth…' He tightened his hold on her, anticipating that her tension meant she might try to free herself. 'And I didn't intend telling you this, Elizabeth, because…' she heard the smile in his voice '…because, my frustrating, infuriating little love, there's a part of me that likes you jealous…likes to know you're not as indifferent to me as you'd have me believe.' As she melted against him, gentle fingers resumed the soporific stroking at her nape. 'But then caring about you, wanting to protect you from hurt, seems to have come out of nowhere and taken over my life. So, whichever fool has told you she's my mistress is a little out of touch with current affairs. I finished with her a while ago.'

'You don't have to tell me…I don't care…'

'I know I don't have to tell you,' he answered drily. 'God knows, it's not the sort of thing any man relishes discussing with his future wife.' As though to reinforce her status, he gently slid the ring back onto her finger, then curled it, as though locking it there. He brushed a thumb across the gem. 'But you did ask and I don't want something so trivial causing you additional pain.'

She grabbed at his arms, pushed back to look into his eyes. What she saw made her breath catch achingly in her throat. For a timeless moment it seemed she hovered in a dizzying limbo, bathed in a gilded, beatific warmth. She could see a tiny reflection of herself in his shining agate eyes, as though he had already absorbed her, used his body to cocoon her against harm. She read the words there, too, and held her breath waiting for them…waiting. She watched his lips, saw them part…then lower to hers. He kissed her and there was such tenderness in his attentive caress, such devotion in the hands that cradled her face, tremored against her flushing skin, that she gave herself up to it, kissing him back shyly with all the sweet gratitude she could muster, while in her mind she consoled herself with thinking the words she had expected to hear. Words no man had spoken to her for ten years: 'I love you, Elizabeth…I love you…'

Chapter Twelve

He had that look about him, Luke realised, a pang of anxiety cooling the film of perspiration on his skin.

Pulling off his visor, he sat on the bench, discarding his foil on the ground by his feet. He roughly dried his face, briskly towelled his damp, ebony hair, then settled back to properly spectate. His brother was advancing using a spare, efficiency that demonstrated he was keen to conclude the contest. With perfect balance and a powerful, easy athleticism, he was driving his adversary back towards the perimeter of the arena. A final riposte, and the tip of his épée threatened a thick, sinewy throat. Henry Bateman, no mean swordsman himself, put up his hands in submission, laughed, shrugged. They saluted and shook hands, then Ross was walking towards Luke, and Henry was folding over at the waist, exhausted.

'Good bout,' Luke mentioned conversationally. 'You slipped under his guard a couple of times. I'm glad the buttons were secure; you were attacking like a demon. Not in training for anything in particular, I hope?'

Ross jerked off his visor, shook his head, sending shaggy mahogany locks back from his face. He inhaled sharply, then blew, slowly recovering from the gruelling exertion. Stripping off his gauntlets, he wiped sweat from his eyes.

'Not in training for anything in particular, I hope…?' Luke

repeated, attempting to break through the deafness of intense preoccupation that, at times, left his brother stranded within his own consciousness.

Ross glanced at him, smiled absently, settled wordlessly onto the bench. Guy Markham strolled over, swigging thirstily from a cup. Having recently finished his own match, he was now eagerly awaiting the clash of the Titans. Dickie Du Quesne and David Hardinge were both skilful, evenly matched fencers. It would make excellent sport; as would a bout between these two brothers, should they decide to engage today.

Sensing Luke's observation, Ross slid him a look, challenge and reassurance mingling in his slitted lupine eyes.

Luke felt his uneasiness increase. 'What is it?'

'Don't worry. It's no problem.'

Ross turned his head away. Humidity had loosely corkscrewed the hair close to his forehead and nape into incongruous little chestnut ringlets. Those by his brow were clinging to skin, sweat sheened to bronze satin, those trailing his neck coiled down as far as the shoulders of his white cotton fencing jacket, now hunched up, as he rested forearms on knees. Luke considered his brother's perfectly composed profile: his mouth a sensual contour, nostrils flaring slightly as he regained his breath, long, sooty lashes slanting parallel with his cheekbone as he watched his foot positioning his épée on the floor in front of him. Almost cherubic, Luke judged with a wry, private smile… Yes, one might almost think that…if one didn't know better. And he, more than anyone else, knew better…

When their father was alive, some nineteen years ago, there had existed a thriving illicit side to Trelawney importing and exporting. The Trelawneys had, for generations, been Cornwall's premier freetrading clan. Then Jago Trelawney died, prematurely, from a wound sustained in a clash with a deadly rival, and, as head of the family, Luke decreed it was time to bury their infamy and lawlessness with his father. His brother, Tristan, had been in agreement, for already he was betrothed and leaning towards a quiet life farming at Melrose, their Cornish estate.

His mother had been relieved; their fleet of traders sailing out of Bristol, and their tin and copper mines closer to home, were all showing handsome profits; risking it all for criminal activity seemed pointless. Ross, alone, had seen a point to it, and had carried on regardless, traversing the channel in his own boat. The Trelawney family were by then rich enough to pay for whatever luxuries they needed. Ross needed what was unpurchasable: the skirmishing with rival gangs or the revenue, the thrill of the chase. He was just fourteen years old.

But he had first sailed with his father and older brothers on night runs at ten. By the time he was thirteen he had an impressive precocious musculature and height, and could fight with fists or sword as well as most men. By the time he was fifteen, he was a superior shot, too. By the time he was seventeen, their mother was in despair and Luke was worried. Neither mining, shipping, land acquisition nor any of the other commercial activities that constituted Trelawney enterprises at that time soothed Ross's restless spirit in the way that did smuggling. Yet he was far and away the most naturally intelligent of the Trelawney children, if not the most scholarly. Luke and Tristan had worked heedfully at their lessons, and conscientiously attended university lectures; Ross shrugged his way through to graduation.

He would shrewdly invest ill-gotten money in legitimate Trelawney transactions, then squander an awesome profit on gambling or carousing with women he seemed to barely want or use. Again, it was the chase he desired—surrender defeated him. And therein, Luke brooded, now lay the crux of the matter. This dangerous mood was a lot to do with transition and reform. It was everything to do with a woman he very much wanted but couldn't use…even supposing she surrendered. He was defeated until she loved him.

Lady Elizabeth Rowe was beautiful, and without a doubt there existed between them a chemistry of explosive proportions. At one point, when Ross was announcing their engagement, Luke had visions of the dining table going up in flames, so fierce were the sparks flying from one end of the mahogany to the other. Never before had he seen his younger brother so intensely aware of any woman's presence. Even later in the evening, when post-prandial chatter had them socially grouped yards apart and facing in opposite directions, still Ross was absorbed with the petite blonde who wistfully twisted a priceless gem on her betrothal finger.

Obviously, there existed between them, too, highly charged problems. Whether those related to her past misfortunes and the scandal that surrounded her banishment from London, he couldn't say. And Ross, it seemed, wouldn't say. His brother had not mentioned a solitary thing about her history to anyone present that evening. Yet he obviously realised, at the very least, that all the gentlemen would know. Sir Richard Du Quesne and Lord Courtenay had been rogues about town during that era and, if not engendering outrage themselves, were well aware of who was. Guy Markham had been with him and Ross when the news first broke in the clubs that the Marquess of Thorneycroft was taking his daughter home in disgrace. Luke got the distinct impression that Ross's silence was a test for them: they could judge her on hearsay or they could accept her as his chosen partner. And there was no doubt in Luke's mind where his youngest brother's loyalties now lay. If need be, he would turn his back on them all for her.

Quietly, Luke said, 'When I met Rebecca…for a while, the coward in me wished I hadn't. I knew, from the first sight of her wading in that pond, that I was lost. I couldn't do without her…I couldn't leave her…it came out of nowhere and shattered me. That's the thing with falling in love, there's no calling card…no time to prepare, and once you're in, you never know if you'll come out the other side whole.'

Ross arrowed him a humorous look.

'At times, I thought I was going insane,' Luke resumed nostalgically.

'I remember…'

Luke grimaced at his brother's dry tone. 'It's an odd feeling: suddenly being in bits, knowing she's the only one who can put them back together.' A circumspect look slanted sideways. 'Is that how it is with you and Elizabeth?'

Ross flicked his head. It was almost a nod. He kept staring ahead. 'Yes…she's the only one.'

Luke cleared his throat. He shifted a bit on the bench, then tendered hesitatingly, 'I'm here…you know…to talk…if you want…'

'I know…thanks,' Ross said, a twist of a smile softening his mouth at his older brother's gruff concern.

With that out of the way, Luke gladly turned his attention to the two swordsmen circling, lunging, parrying, and was about to make some comment on their friends' technique, when he glimpsed Ross's stealthy movement. He had dipped sinuously to collect the rapier at his feet. Luke's eyes darted to his brother's face; it was a mask of brutal satisfaction. Blowing out his cheeks in resignation, Luke looked up at the gaggle of dandified newcomers who were loitering about the arena to watch the sporting spectacle.

Without a word, Ross stood, sauntered towards them.

With stabbing little looks, Linus Savage, Earl of Cadmore, watched him approach. In fact, he'd been expecting his presence, and that of his Corinthian colleagues, at this venue. These renowned sportsmen performing here today were the reason for he and his friends stopping off at all at Harry Angelo's Fencing Academy. Cadmore felt unthreatened. Stratton was with respectable company; he was with his own eminent cronies.

Since that encounter in the fabric emporium, he'd not seen hide nor hair of the Viscount. Had it been any lingering lust for Cecily Booth that had prompted his hostility that day, it must surely, by now, have petered out or he would have taken her back. With smarting resentment, Cadmore knew the man could do just that, if he wanted. Cecily still pined for him, and the mewling, vicious little cat was not averse to hinting at shortcomings in his bedsport skills compared to her rugged Cornish lover's. A bauble or two soon stopped her complaints.

But Cadmore knew he was already becoming bored with the avaricious jade. If it wasn't for the fact Cecily knew a novel little trick or two designed to steady a man's roving eye, he would by now have discarded her. Perhaps the Viscount had schooled into her those special delights; perhaps he should thank him, he chortled inwardly. Outwardly, he greeted him affably, 'Stratton; how goes it with you, my dear fellow?'

Ross moved the gleaming rapier in mocking salute. 'It goes very well with me…now I've set eyes on you.'

Cadmore laughed, a trifle shrilly, unsure what to make of that. Was it a threat? A compliment? This man had never before sought his company. In fact, he got the distinct impression Trelawney had always despised him. For his own part, he was wise enough to tread softly about such an enigmatic warrior. 'We heard that there were to be some fancy bouts. Thought we'd call in *en masse* and take a gander.' A languid hand emphasised his entourage.

Ross seemed unmoved by any number of his foppish cronies and slung a powerful arm, terminating in a lethal weapon, about the man's effeminately narrow shoulders. He drew him slightly to one side. 'I was counting on it that you would hear and would come,' was drawled close to Cadmore's large ear.

The Earl attempted to wriggle his bony frame from beneath the controlling arm, disquiet curdling his stomach. He glanced about, noting that Stratton's black bear of a brother was swivelled on the bench, arms crossed over his chest, watching the pair of them through slitted eyes.

'You wanted to see me? About what?' he protested.

'About a woman.'

'Cecily?' Cadmore snorted, disbelief plain.

'No…not Cecily,' Ross said, mildly disparaging. 'I want to talk to you about Lady Elizabeth Rowe.'

Cadmore gawked at him, as though unsure he'd heard right. Then, slowly, slowly, comprehension dawned. A sly leer distorted his fleshy mouth. Of course! Why had it not occurred to him before? Ross Trelawney was notoriously popular with the ladies and notoriously fond of a challenge. That haughty whore would be a prime target for his fastidious but jaded eye. She was high born and would doubtless prove a trial, even for such a successful womaniser.

Over the years, fine sport had been got wagering who would be the first buck to bring her down to earth and strip her of disdain. In his arrogance, and with his luck running so sweet, the Viscount probably thought it would be him. He probably thought she'd fall like a ripe peach! He was newly ennobled, in favour with his Majesty, and to top it all, just to trumpet that he could, he wanted that frigid bitch pleasuring him in bed. What a fine joke! Cadmore barely suppressed a snigger. He would hazard a monkey that the erstwhile cool Cornishman was in hot pursuit of the lady.

Stratton moping about in a fabric warehouse had nothing to do with the lightskirt he'd discarded; it was everything to do with the one he'd set his sights on. Lady Elizabeth Rowe had been in that shop the afternoon this man had looked daggers at him. He must have been irked at seeing them together. It was no secret that he had been stalking her himself for years. Just as it was no secret that she had made a laughing stock of him, playing up to his court simply to disguise her interest in that snivelling puppy she'd run off with. Cadmore surfaced enough from malicious memories to spy wolfish eyes preying patiently on him, analysing his reaction. Why not encourage him? He wasn't renowned for lengthy liaisons. If Trelawney succeeded in seducing the ice maiden, he'd make sure he was handy when the thaw set in. He wasn't too proud to shun a peer's cast-offs. After all, for ten years past, he'd been chasing what a pair of gentlemen of the road had ditched.

So what was it this man wanted? Cadmore ruminated foxily. Was he going to warn him off? Demand a few salacious snippets about her? It was common knowledge that he had followed the scandal with fanatical relish. The poor fool wanted a favour or two. Perhaps, he might just oblige him.

'What is it you'd like to know about the…erm…fair *lady*?' Contempt stressed the title; a smirk was circulated for those of his chums who were cocking an ear to glean some gossip from this unlikely tête-à-tête.

'What is it you'd like to tell me?' Ross rejoined softly, staring over Cadmore's fussily crimped head at nothing.

'Well, let's see… To start,' Cadmore lectured, 'if you're interested in offering her your protection for a time, I'll warn you that she's deuced difficult to approach. That is your intention, I take it?'

'Oh, yes,' Ross said. 'That's definitely my intention.'

Cadmore nodded, licking his lips; he was enjoying himself, playing up to the attention he was generating. 'Well, you obviously know that I am…er…have been interested in doing likewise; with little success. It's not easy; she has an unconscionable high opinion of herself, has lovely Hoar Frost.'

Feral eyes, looking like green-flecked jet, sprang to his face. Dark brows lifted, demanding an explanation.

Cadmore obligingly expounded, while grinning at a couple of friends who were in on this private joke, 'Just a little pun. The sobriquet stuck at the time of her…umm…unfortunate escapade. For, lord, with that silver hair and wintry way she has, who'd ever think she'd been broken in by a couple of hot highwaymen. Mayhap, that night, they felt like riding a different sort of mare…' He guffawed and a few of his friends snorted humorously too. Most, however, looked a little uneasy on noting that the man Cadmore was hoping to impress seemed singularly unamused.

Wiping tears of mirth from his prominent eyes, Cadmore patted a fey hand on a solid shoulder. 'Let me know how pleasurable it is in that particular saddle, won't you now? If anyone can rein her in, I reckon you can. Anything else you want to know?' he asked chummily, still smearing wet from his eyes.

'Yes. How do you want to die? Your choice of weapons. Five o'clock tomorrow morning, Wimbledon Common.'

The next minute seemed to spin endlessly in time. Gentlemen, who moments ago had been dissecting superlative fencing skills as demonstrated by Sir Richard Du Quesne and Lord

Courtenay, now stared at the stupefied Earl of Cadmore and his vicious-eyed challenger. For a short while the metallic swipe of steel on steel continued, then lessened until there was no sound but echoing silence.

Ross walked away from Cadmore, drooping grey-faced in disbelief, and into the group of macaronis. He smiled slowly, thoughtfully, in a way that had some of them fidgeting, looking about nervously. He started an easy stroll about the loose circle, making it open as gentlemen shuffled back, giving him a wide berth. All were exceedingly conscious of the silver blade in his brown hand and of this man's craft with it.

'Has anyone else got any interesting anecdotes about my fiancée?' Ross asked quietly. 'Anything that I should know about Lady Elizabeth Rowe's past, or their part in it?' He halted, pivoted on a heel, eagle eyes swooping to rake an arc over slack-jawed faces. 'Come…don't be shy. There must be something: an insult…a grope…a proposition, that I'd like to hear about. No?' He read sarcastically from ruddying, perspiring complexions. Fingers were being thrust to loosen collars, frantic glances were shooting at Cadmore, lingering, fascinated, as though seeing the man for the final time. Facial expressions ranged from numb horror to mischievous relish.

Luke paced stealthily closer; Dickie and David and Guy followed. In harmony, without a passing look or word, they positioned themselves about the ring of men and waited, grim-faced. Not that any one of them believed Ross to be in any danger. Far from it. In fact, as he seemed to be the only one armed, both with weapon and lethal intent, protecting him from his inexorable quest to avenge seemed the most pressing need.

Linus Savage, darted an arid tongue about his parched mouth. 'Fiancée?' he managed to shrill with a sickly grin. 'Why did you not say, my dear fellow? Of course, I'll apologise for any misunderstanding about your interest in the lady, and for any offence unintentionally given. Naturally, I'll never again approach her. I'll not accept the gauntlet on this occasion.' He started a backwards glide towards the door, ignoring the frank looks of astonishment and disgust from his comrades as they observed him desperately trying to wriggle free of the hook. He might be, literally, fighting for his life, yet the expectation was that gentlemen should resign themselves with dignity to their fate, and preserve their own and their family's good name at any cost. Death before dishonour was a truism scrupulously adhered to.

Lord Grey, a longstanding acquaintance of the Earl's late father, inclined towards him and hissed furiously, 'Think what you are doing, man! How can you refuse him satisfaction? We all heard what you said about the lady. It was unequivocal defamation! If you fight shy now…think of the disgrace! I'll stand as your second; Beecher will, too.' He indicated a younger man with a dip of his balding head.

The Earl of Cadmore did think; he thought as hard and as fast as his scrambled brain would allow. And came up with nothing good. Death, maiming or ostracism were already his. All he had to do was choose. The situation seemed nightmarish…unreal, as did the venom that started spitting through his teeth. 'That bitch has plotted this.' He was unable to control himself, even when Ross reacted to him colluding in his own destruction by laughing. 'You're probably not even betrothed to the trollop. Has she hired you to kill me? Are you bounty-hunting for me dead or alive? Run through or ruined? Are those your orders?' He snickered in shock, for a corner of his mind retained lucidity and was screaming at him to cease, or he might be right here, a dead man. 'What's your fee? A tumble in the gutter with the whore? She likes rough trade: thieves and dockers… She'll go for you.'

In a fast fluid movement, Ross faced him, pinned him to the wall with his blade through Cadmore's coat. It effectively cut off his escape route and his raving. The Earl visibly shook and looked as though he might retch.

Slowly, deliberately, Ross took his fencing gauntlet and swiped it, with insulting lightness, about one of Cadmore's sallow, quivering cheeks. 'Just to formalise matters,' he said softly. 'Tomorrow, Wimbledon Common, five o'clock. Grey and Beecher have offered as seconds.' Ross indicated his own men with a backwards flick of his dark head. 'Ramsden and Markham stand as mine. Your choice of weapons. Now you can go.' He jerked free the blade.

Luke frowned, watching the last of the subdued gentlemen troop away. Before going, some had sidled over and mumbled their disgust at Cadmore's astonishing vitriol and base cowardice. Others had simply swayed their heads, solemnly acknowledging the gravity of what had taken place here today, while exiting at speed. Doubtless, they were keen to begin circulating this juicy gossip in clubs and salons peopled by the *beau monde*.

'He's going to choose pistols and shoot early,' Luke warned.

'I know…' Ross replied.

'You could try for rapiers,' Guy chipped in. 'You're undoubtedly the injured party in this and could exercise the option to choose.'

'He'll never go for that,' David said drily. 'Cadmore knows close combat would be a massacre.'

'And over in thirty seconds,' Dickie added. 'Whatever the outcome tomorrow, even if Cadmore fails to show or fires early, Ross has finished him here today. Everybody knows that, including him.' He looked at Ross shrewdly, and with not a little admiration in his silver eyes. 'You crafty bastard! You planned it that way. You got us here this afternoon—arranged these bouts—just to draw him in, didn't you?'

'Would I do that?' Ross drawled, as, whistling, and apparently unperturbed at the thought of stopping a cheat's bullet, he strolled off to change.

'I don't know whether I ought to tell you this, Elizabeth…'

Elizabeth glanced at Rebecca with a small enquiring smile.

'I feel embarrassed at ever having thought such a thing.'

'Well, *the thing* sounds intriguing. I think you now must explain.'

Since being formally introduced a few days ago, the two

women had spent time together shopping or taking tea or a carriage ride in the park, and had settled into an easy camaraderie. Elizabeth had met the Ramsdens' two delightful little sons at their beautiful townhouse in Burlington Parade. Today they were strolling along Bond Street, chatting and window shopping, oblivious to their differing blonde looks drawing admiring male glances and envious female scrutiny.

'As we are soon to be sisters-in-law, and I already like you very much, I shall tell you.' Rebecca giggled. 'Besides, if I do not, Emma or Vicky might let it slip at some time—for I told them both,' she said with a backwards peer at their companions strolling some paces behind. 'Then I would really be in a fine pickle for not owning to once having imagined that you…'

Elizabeth felt a slight chill creep over her. Was Rebecca hinting she had heard tell of a scandalous Lady Elizabeth Rowe from years back? Was she about to embarrassingly say she couldn't conceive her to be the same person?

'When I saw you fabric shopping last week,' she broke into Elizabeth's anxieties, 'and I noticed Ross paying you such particular attention, I imagined you and he…that is, I believed you might be his…*chère amie*…' Rebecca pulled an apologetic little face, but her smile was wicked.

Elizabeth choked a laugh in her relief at that news. 'Well, Lady Ramsden, as you have been honest, I must be, too. I imagined you already filled that role when I spied you with him. I almost dropped through the floor in shock and embarrassment when you were introduced as a relative.'

Rebecca squealed with laughter. 'You believed *me* to be his mistress? How famous! He is rather gorgeous…' She grimaced. 'Oh, sorry! I meant nothing by it, of course. It's just—with Luke's blessing, naturally—I have grown accustomed to flirting innocently with Ross over the years. He has been the best ever brother-in-law; so interesting and amusing. And his nephews haunt him when he visits; Troy, that is, for Jason is but one and a half and not yet able to play soldiers and pirates or ride a pony. But he laughs happily when he spies his uncle

Ross. Ross is a natural with horses, and knows exactly which ingredients to mix as poultices for swollen fetlocks and so on. All the grooms are most impressed by his herbalism…Miles, too. Oh, he's our butler and a sweet old cove…' At Elizabeth's continuing quiet, Rebecca ceased her chatter and groaned regret. 'I imagine you must be heartily sick of females fawning over your future husband. How tactless of me to go on so. I shall caution Vicky and Emma, for they both adore him, too.'

'Say nothing to them.' The clipped words were followed by an insouciant smile. 'It doesn't matter. I'm barely aware—or caring—of his popularity. Besides, knowing he is kind to children and dumb animals is most welcome.'

Rebecca smiled at the wryness in Elizabeth's tone. She had just last night discussed with her darling Luke the tension that seemed to exist between this couple. 'Nothing worth having comes easily, sweetheart,' Luke had reminded her huskily with a meaningful look that made her blush and reminisce about their own very bitter-sweet courtship.

'Oh, Ross does have his gentle side,' Rebecca communicated archly. 'I am never more aware of that than when he looks at you, Elizabeth.'

Elizabeth retrieved her neutral smile, while pointing at an interesting window display. She urged Rebecca towards it.

The three ladies strolling a few yards behind joined them in inspecting glorious fabrics draped into enticing approximations of the newly arrived Paris fashion plates depicted. Victoria, Emma and Sophie were also enjoying a stroll along this busy street this fine September afternoon.

'Do you think our husbands will have exhausted themselves fencing and soon be home?' Victoria asked. 'Lucy will expect her papa to be energetic enough to take her on his back and gallop around the floors,' she said, referring to her three-year-old daughter's predilection for using her doting father as a pony.

'Heavens! I hope they won't be too tired out,' Emma said,

aghast, causing Rebecca and Victoria to exchange a look, then chuckle.

Emma, not long married, blushed prettily then tutted her mock disgust. 'Oh, I give up with you two vulgar hussies,' she fondly chided. 'I simply want my husband in a fit state to visit my parents. When we pluck up courage to go to Cheapside, I assure you Richard needs all his wits about him to fend off their importuning. Papa for money and Mama for invitations to Silverdale.'

Elizabeth felt at ease with the casual banter between these sweet, unassuming ladies. The thought of Lord Courtenay down on all fours with a child atop his broad, elegant back was enough to have her chuckling, too. Her amusement soon faded. There was a woman's reflected image visible in the shop window to one side of her. She seemed familiar. Yet this was the West End of London. The last time she had spied that gaunt profile, framed by dark curly hair, she had been dockside with Hugh Clemence! With careful casualness Elizabeth half-turned to slant a look.

Jane Selby was hovering close to the road, a child's hand gripped in hers. On this occasion, she was dressed quite neatly and soberly. She certainly didn't look out of place amongst the Quality promenading along Bond Street. But the furtive peeks that were sliding from beneath her bonnet brim at the shoppers were definitely suspicious. The boy by her side looked to be about five or six and he, too, was tidily turned out. But his expression was anguished: he was gazing up at his mother with such huge sorrowful eyes that Elizabeth felt her heart ache. What she saw next was still more disturbing and caused an icy shiver to hurtle through her.

Although no one stood with them, they were not there alone. And, by now, Elizabeth's clandestine observation led her to believe that they might be up to no good! Jane was nodding at a young girl, perhaps fifteen years old, who was stationed some yards away. In response, the girl tapped at her pocket, then flicked a sly finger towards a lone matron promenading.

At the signal from her accomplice, Jane pulled her hand free of her son's and whispered in his ear before pushing him away. The child swayed his head and looked at his mother with supplicant's eyes. She rejected him with a terse brush of a hand. With tears on his face, he sidled to the target, skimmed inconspicuously against the woman's ample hip and came away with a scrap of lace in his hand. It was quickly scrunched into his small fist as he took a circular path back to his mother on spindly legs that were visibly shaking. He immediately offered up to her his booty.

Aware, suddenly, that Rebecca was talking to her, asking her if she would step inside the shop with them, Elizabeth swayed her blonde head. It was the most she could manage. She felt mute with shock at what she'd witnessed. 'I've a slight headache; it's uncommonly warm,' Elizabeth blurted. 'Please, browse to your heart's content. I shall stay here, in the air, with Sophie.'

Sophie scoured her friend's face, having read an unspoken plea in her violet eyes and the breathless tenor of her voice.

'We'll be but a short while,' Victoria said as, arm in arm, the three ladies proceeded inside the shop.

Before they were properly out of sight, Elizabeth had urged Sophie into a recess between buildings and discreetly indicated Jane Selby and her son. Frantically, she whispered who they were and what she had just seen. She concluded with, 'They are teaching the little lad larceny and he looks barely six…and so distraught! How can she be so cruel and stupid! I shall tell her I know what she is about. It's a wonder no one else saw him pickpocket and raised the alarm! They might all be before a magistrate tomorrow!'

Sophie had her wide, brown eyes riveted on the mother and child. 'Good grief! Quick, approach her now, Lizzie, for I do believe she is about to send him thieving again!' she squeaked.

Elizabeth did move then, faster than Sophie could keep up with her. Weaving, almost at a run, through the strollers, and ignoring their curious looks, she was soon at Jane's side.

The woman's black eyes were wide and apprehensive as she recognised the beautiful woman who seemed to have materialised from thin air. Elizabeth grabbed the child by the shoulders as he began his stalking, and gently directed him back to his mother. 'Your son, I imagine, Jane?' she enquired by way of greeting. 'Little Jack, I believe you said was his name?' She looked down at the small boy's solemn, tear-streaked face. 'He seems distressed…'

Jane's astonishment at being thus accosted vanished; wariness instead pinched her wan features. Her eyes darted vigilantly about, then hovered on one spot and naked fear dilated her pupils.

Elizabeth turned her head to investigate and immediately saw why the wretched woman looked so terrified. The girl who had been loitering as look-out had disappeared. In her place was a man Elizabeth instantly recognised. Nathaniel Leach, dressed in dapper dark garments, had his slitted gaze on them. He touched his hat in insolent salute then, crossing his arms over his brawny chest, adopted a menacing stance and continued staring fixedly.

Elizabeth drew a deep breath; he might frighten Jane, but she wasn't so easily intimidated! she exhorted herself, and with a haughty toss of her head, ignored him. 'I saw you sending your son to pickpocket. What on earth are you about?' she demanded angrily. 'Even if that vile Leach has you in his power, how can you use your own son so? He is so young! So vulnerable!'

'Go away and leave us be!' Jane bit out, jerking her son back by the shoulders and into the shelter of her skirts. 'You're making things so much worse for us both.'

Elizabeth laid a comforting hand on her thin arm. It was immediately shaken off. 'Don't you realise the jeopardy he is in?'

'Don't *you* realise the jeopardy he is in?' Jane bitterly countered. 'You know nothing! You with your kindly, rich old granny and your doting pious vicar and your fine clothes and your fed belly! What do *you* know of any of it?' she choked out in despair.

'Jane, please listen…'

'No! *You* listen,' Jane croaked across her words. 'If he's to survive, he's to toil. And this is how we must earn. For if Leach sells him to a sweep, as he's threatened to do, he'll not last this winter out. This way, he's close to me,' she breathed fiercely. 'This way he won't burn or starve…not before I do.' Her fingers reflexively bit into her son's fleshless arms, making him whimper and look up. 'Now away with you. And your friend,' she spat, jerking her dark head at Sophie who was hovering close by, tears glossing her eyes at what she'd heard.

Elizabeth felt impotent rage thickening her throat, as it had once before when she'd learned harrowing details of this woman's predicament. 'It can't be! He wants to sell your son to a chimney sweep? No!'

'Oh, yes! Why should he keep the snivelling little runt? he says. He's old enough to make a bob, he says.' Jane swiped moisture from her eyes.

'How much do you owe him, Jane? How much can it be that keeps you tied to such a monster?'

Jane shook back her head and sniffed before grunting a mirthless laugh. 'How do I know? He's bribed the bailiffs on my account. Paid my fines and my debts after the bigamist left me. Sometimes he's kind like that…fights my battles,' she explained with a poignant seriousness. 'I lost count at four hundred. Must be more now what with the laudanum and the interest. He knows I'll pay any price for Jack's laudanum. If you want a reckoning, ask Leachie…he's the tally-man,' she concluded with an impatient snap.

As they stared at one another Jane murmured wistfully, 'I really thought you'd come back to Wapping, even though I told you not to. I thought you meant what you said, about helping, being as you'd had bad luck, too.'

Elizabeth winced; felt the pain filter from her throat to her toes. Her fecklessness whipped at her like a thousand scourges. She wanted to impress on Jane that she had not forgotten, that since their first meeting in that hovel, never an hour passed in any day when she did not recall the horror of her plight and fret over how she could help.

Such empty sincerity! The truth was that she was as much a man's puppet as Jane was. Lord Stratton's threats might be smoother, more sophisticated, but it was manipulation just the same. He had forbidden her to visit this wretched woman in the stews…so had her grandmother…but it was him she was chary of defying. He was the reason she was shopping with genteel friends; he was the reason she had simply locked all charitable thoughts to the back of her mind while she made idle excursions to furnish a trousseau.

She felt utter shame swamp her as she looked deep into Jane Selby's despairing black eyes. There but for the grace of God and a fond grandmother went she. How soon she had forgotten that maxim. Immediately she turned and walked away.

Chapter Thirteen

As Elizabeth strode purposefully closer, Nathaniel Leach peered furtively about, slack-jawed in disbelief. In truth, *she* couldn't credit either her audacity in approaching him so openly. An ocean was roaring in her ears, her ribs quivered with the pounding beneath them. But her mind's eye was focused on Jane and her son, and this man's part in their dismal lives, and she forced her wobbly legs on.

'Do you know who I am, Mr Leach?' was bitten out with cold fury as soon as he was within earshot.

Brackets deepened either side of his mean mouth and sunbursts radiated from slitted sky blue eyes as far as his hairline. 'I do h'indeed, Lady Elizabeth,' he enunciated with mocking humility. 'Marquee's daughter, 'n't yer? Jane told me a foo int'resting fings about yer. Now 'oo'd've fawt such a top-lofty gel bin in such bad trouble? 'Course…we all makes mizdakes…I understands that…an' never judges folk.'

Elizabeth glared frigidly, unabashed by his smirking innuendoes. 'Yes, I am a Marquess's daughter,' was all she icily confirmed. 'And I shall make life very difficult for you if you don't do exactly as I say.'

'An' what exackly do yer say, my lady?'

Her stomach squirmed at his sinister purr; she knew he would very much like to cow and bully her as he did Jane. Nevertheless she bit out coldly, 'I say, Mr Leach, that you immediately give Jane and her son into my care or you will be very sorry.'

Stout fingers scraped at his chubby, stubbly jaw. 'Well; now…'s'up to Jane what she do. She's as free as you'n me. Soon as she pays 'er reck'nin' she can be on 'er way an' good riddance. An' the nipper…'

'How much is her reckoning?'

He smiled…really grinned in amusement. 'A lot. A lot even by your fine standards, m'lady. 'N all noted 'n signed fer. She's a greedy little gel, is yon Jane. 'S the trouble wiv shabby genteel…they want luckshriz. They gotta pay fer 'em…everyone gotta pay. Now, shall I tell yer what I say, my lady?' he sneeringly parodied her words. His black beaver hat brushed her face as he inclined close to slyly leer at her small, curvacious body. 'I says that I was right about yer firs' time. I could tell from them knowin' eyes o' your'n you'd 'ad a little ruff 'n tumble in yer time. You should've come back to see Leachie…we'd deal right well togevver. I could intradoos yer to a foo of me Quality gents…set yer up right good. Betimes this turns proper grey…' He tweaked one of her smoky-blonde ringlets where it draped close to her bosom. 'Yer'll have a tidy nest egg…me 'n all.'

Elizabeth shot him such a poisonous look that his grin drooped and his impertinent fingers withdrew to twiddle on air. Sunlight was making a beacon of the dazzling diamond being spun agitatedly on her finger. His eyes swooped and greed tautened his face. A crafty peek slanted up at her from beneath his shaggy eyebrows. 'Might jus' do it…' was all he croaked, snapping down his chin. 'More'n a fousand pounds is doo…'

Her finger curled protectively. 'No. But I have something of equal value…a necklace…' Instinctively she had opted to lose her heirloom rather than her betrothal ring and that astonished her to such a degree she hardly noticed his uncontainable excitement. His Adam's apple bobbed as he fitfully swallowed, he shifted from foot to foot, he assessed her with his craggy face cocked this way then that, keen for her to elaborate.

. Surfacing from her daze, Elizabeth blurted sharply, 'I can't meet you later today, I have an appointment. I'll meet you tomorrow; at dawn at St Mary's. Bring Jane and her son and I shall let you have the necklace.'

His mouth pursed in suspicion; he scratched at the mottled skin on his neck while considering, but she could tell avarice was winning. Enticingly she allowed the ring to escape concealment in her skirts, and flashed it back into view. 'And I require proof Jane's debts are paid, too.'

'Fair 'nuf...' was all he grunted.

Spying, through milling shoppers, Sophie hesitantly approaching them, she slipped past to prevent her coming closer, and under this evil ponce's scrutiny. 'Five o'clock in the morning. I shall be with Reverend Clemence so don't think to try and cheat me or browbeat me, for it will be the worse for you,' was launched at him, low and fluent, before she finally hurried away.

Now that they were betrothed, Edwina deemed it permissible...nay, necessary...that her granddaughter privately get to know her fiancé. As soon as an elegant hessian trod over the threshold of Number Seven Connaught Street in the evenings, Edwina made herself scarce.

Elizabeth did learn more about the Trelawneys, too. Ross had told her about his brother, Tristan and his sister, Katherine, both of whom she had yet to meet; and of his clutch of nephews and nieces. Each of his siblings had two children and she could tell he was indeed fond of all of them and proud that Katherine was soon to make him godfather to her baby son.

He told her of Melrose, the family's Cornish estate that spanned the clifftops at Pendrake. With a quiet passion that held her captive, he'd described breathtaking views with such evocative eloquence she was sure she could hear the ocean's shingle-sucking hiss, its rock-battering roar; she was blinded by the glare of sun on water, by spectral mists rolling in; she could smell and taste the tang of fish and brine.

He was content, he'd said, that their new home, Stratton Hall, had its southerly aspect facing the Kent coast. Elizabeth had been oddly pleased that he already considered it her home. She found herself telling him that she, too, was lulled by the sound and sight of the sea, and had enjoyed trips to Lyme Regis and Brighton with her papa.

When it was her turn to contribute a little family background, she told him of her mother's premature demise after a fall on ice that fractured her pelvis, and that she still missed her beloved papa dreadfully since his death, a few years ago. She also admitted to seeing little of her father's relations since his funeral. The very same day he was interred, she had travelled from Thorneycroft to London to live with Edwina. A pause had followed that statement, but she had simply resumed by stating that she missed her young half-brother, Tom, and feared that at seven years old he might eventually forget her. That had left her gruff-voiced and dewy-eyed and, to deflect his steady attention, she'd boldly asked whether he had killed many men and had a partiality for liver for breakfast.

He'd looked unruffled, as he always did, by her impertinence while telling her that in his trade sometimes killing a man was the only way to stay alive, and that, personally he preferred ox kidney for breakfast. With a defeated flounce she'd then taken herself off to bed. But since that first, ice-breaking session, they had settled into an easier rapport. Even when she retreated within herself to ruminate again on his motives for wanting to marry her, and nothing much was said, silences passed comfortably. He'd never again told her that her dowry wasn't important. He'd never again sought to justify himself at all, and seemed content to remain quiet while she brooded, as though allowing her to privately make sense of it. Inexplicably, that piqued her; as did the lack of any flirtation. He flirted with his sister-in-law, with his friends' wives, but not with her!

'I hear you went missing today, whilst out shopping,' was

dropped into this particular cosy quiet, curbing her introspection.

'Oh…oh, y-yes…that's true,' Elizabeth stuttered, thinking that silences were definitely preferable at times as she recalled the reason for that absence. 'Sophie and I simply spied another acquaintance a way along the street. When we returned to the draper's, Rebecca and the other ladies had gone. Possibly they thought we had already set off home. For I felt unwell…' she disjointedly explained. 'I shall apologise to them. It was rather rude to go off and chatter for so long without saying.'

'No harm's done. You're safely home…and better now?'

Elizabeth bestowed on him a small smile, and nodded, while flicking over pages of the journal on her lap, and wondering how soon she could encourage him to leave. She wanted him gone so she could fly to Hugh, yet every evening when he left at about ten o'clock, she felt restless and wished he'd stayed a little longer. She soon missed him. He could be amusing and interesting company; just as Rebecca said he was. Just as, no doubt, his other female admirers would describe him, she thought acidly. A soundless sigh escaped. Why had she just wasted a perfectly good reason to curtail his visit by answering in the affirmative when he asked if she was well?

Ross settled his powerful shoulders back into the chair, a polished boot raising to rest atop his knee. 'Did Madame Vallois attend you this afternoon for a dress fitting?'

'Yes,' Elizabeth said with a spontaneous, sweet smile as she dwelt on the beautiful silk shift that was being prepared for her wedding day. Earlier, with Edwina and the modiste clucking and fussing over her, she had got caught up in the infectious excitement of it all. As Edwina directed first this, then that luxurious fabric be draped about her undergarmented body, she was soon as absorbed as they by embroidery and lace and net covered with seed pearls. The need to steal away and speak urgently with Hugh about their meeting with Leachie early in the morning had soon slipped her mind.

'What sort of material did you choose?' Ross enquired casually, his eyes on a newspaper spread open on a side-table. He sipped from his teacup while awaiting her answer.

'Is the announcement of our betrothal in the paper today?'

He smiled at her evasion. 'No; but be prepared for a deluge of attention tomorrow,' he warned, his smile wryly distorting. No doubt the gentlemen's clubs were already awash with varying versions of the furore at the fencing academy. Over the years he'd issued or taken up a score or more challenges. All of them had been appointments with worthier opponents than Linus Savage and he'd walked away from each. Yet the Earl was a passable shot, and he was probably not going to wait for the call. It was odd; settling down was having an unnerving effect on him. He'd been confident enough of his technique before when facing cheats.

Elizabeth was also ruminating on a dawn rendezvous: fretting that Hugh might refuse to get involved, and she was certainly chary of meeting the blackguard alone. With a guilty pang, she reassured herself that Hugh was quite easily wound about her little finger. If only this man was…

'What sort of fabric did you choose?'

Elizabeth started to her senses. 'Bridegrooms are not supposed to ask such things,' she demurred. 'You're supposed to be totally enchanted with the vision of loveliness I present as I walk down the aisle…whatever I wear.'

'And so I shall be, sweetheart,' he said huskily. 'Totally enchanted…I'll be surprised if it's not white silk.'

Elizabeth jerked the journal up from her lap to study a mediocre hat. She lightly laughed, 'Please don't probe, for I'll not tell you.'

'You don't have to, Elizabeth. Some things I know…' he said softly.

'Were the fencing bouts to your liking? Did you win?' she blurted.

'They were very much to my liking, thank you. And, yes, I won,' he said with such a hint of wry humour in his studied politeness that a violet peep slanted at him from beneath a curtain of dusky lashes.

Her shy look elicited such an affectionate smile that she began agonising again whether to confide in him. Might he be sympathetic if she told him of Jane Selby's plight? Might he perhaps offer to escort her instead of Hugh in the morning? Certainly, that beast, Leach, was more likely to keep his side of the bargain if this striking man was present… No! it was out of the question! She scathed herself for being swayed by his mellow mood. He was an enigmatic, unpredictable man. He might get angry on learning of this dangerous escapade and again forbid her consorting with East End harlots. She wasn't sure of him, didn't quite trust him; yet the idea of returning to fearing and despising him as she once had was also out of the question.

In a way she wished she could resuscitate her passionate dislike; at least it was unequivocal and relatively painless. Now she no longer knew what she felt for him, other than it was bittersweet and frustrating. Her equilibrium was ruined: her thoughts constantly dragged to him, whatever she did, wherever she was. She had reasoned that discovering his opinion of her might help. She wanted to specifically know whether he regarded her as good, bad or indifferent.

He had admitted to liking her and wanting to care for her…but that wasn't enough. There had to be more to it than that…or less. Horrified, it occurred to her that sympathy might play a dominant part. Perhaps he pitied her still paying for her youthful folly a decade on. She knew he'd been livid on learning of Cadmore's abuse. Well, she had looked after herself thus far and had no wish to receive as well as bestow charity! Especially not from an upstart! She winced at her unwarranted meanness. Besides, now she knew him, and his fine connections, it was an ill-fitting description.

She stared at the side of his gypsy-dark visage, cocked to one side, as his fingers flicked over the newsprint. She was no longer convinced he was a fortune-hunter who wanted to fritter her dowry on licentious living. He seemed to possess an innate dignity that would disdain something as vulgar as money or revenge dictating whom he married. Or would he? She willed him to look up so she could scour his beautiful green-gold eyes for clues in her hunt for the truth. Before she succeeded in luring them, his mouth tilted, almost as though he could sense her observation…her neediness. She melted contentedly beneath the honeyed caress that bathed her from between long, curved black lashes, for it couldn't disguise a smouldering neediness of his own. Whatever else he felt for her, he still wanted her. The knowledge no longer alarmed her as it once had. In fact, for the first time in ten years she was exulting in being found desirable.

Blushing, she dropped her eyes to the journal in her lap. It was astonishing they were the same couple who a short time ago had met in this room and traded vicious insults. She'd resentfully given him her necklace and cursed him as a devil. He'd made no attempt to disguise his despising either. She'd been very conscious that he'd wanted to demean her; punish her haughty insolence by dragging her to a sofa, and putting her on her back.

Now he'd only need to kiss her once and she'd willingly walk there, she mocked herself, recalling a few days ago reclining languidly on to a hide seat and allowing him unlimited liberties with her person while dusk discreetly curtained them, and birdsong serenaded them, and a patter of drizzle hit the hood of the barouche, contributing an earth-scented ambience.

She had been…a wanton at his mercy that afternoon. And he had been…the perfect restrained and respectful fiancé. It was he who had imposed boundaries on their passion, he who abruptly lifted her upright, straightened her clothes with unsteady hands while muttering it would be prudent to head home. As the memories swept through her, sensations tantalised too. Her flesh fizzled in reaction to the haunting touch of brown fingers on white skin. Her stalwart inhibitions had been no defence against such insidiously sweet sensuality.

Even though he'd not once said he loved her, she'd willingly cuddled up to him on the way back to London. Almost as far as her own doorstep, she'd clung to him, vine-like, with the witless abandonment of one intoxicated. The euphoria endured for some hours after he saw her within doors, then departed.

By the time she was soaking in her tub at bedtime, she was soberly assessing her behaviour and feeling stupid. Randolph Havering had never touched her so intimately, yet he had declared undying devotion at least a dozen times a day. An infamous womaniser showed her a little contrived gallantry and she wanted to believe he was in love with her. She'd believed herself adept at rebuffing amorous males. Pitted against his expertise, hers failed dismally.

He could have succeeded where so many others had failed, but had chosen not to. She supposed it was enough that he now knew he could…and she did too. Of course he would employ a little of his seductive charm to sweep away lingering bitterness and aggression between them. He seemed a gentlemen who would exact a certain civility from his wife and a certain physical compatibility. Thus a harmonious household would be enjoyed, as would getting those many heirs he wanted. It was all very respectable and sensible. Not virtues much previously associated with Ross Trelawney, Cornish hellion. But, now, of course, he had left notoriety behind and was fêted by the *beau monde*. Such an ironic reversal of her own situation!

'Why are you sighing so?'

Elizabeth looked up from sightless perusal of the journal, to see he had folded the paper and was watching her. 'What are you thinking about?'

'Oh, nothing!' she rebuffed with unwarranted sharpness, frantically fluttering pages as blood stained her porcelain complexion. 'What are you thinking?' she demanded quickly.

'The same as you, I imagine…judging by your blush…' he said, gently amused. 'It was madness, I know…'

'What was?' she snapped, afraid to look up and see mockery in his eyes.

'Acting the perfect gentleman.'

'And so out of character,' she sweetly scoffed.

'Indeed. But, as I've said before, you make me behave oddly, Elizabeth.'

'So sorry,' she jibed, still inexplicably smarting.

'Not nearly as much as I am, I'm sure.'

'I hope you're not out for sympathy tonight.' A page tore beneath her furious fingers and she tossed aside the journal.

'No…' He laughed. 'Actually, I'm out to rectify matters tonight.'

Violet eyes sprang to his face, and she nibbled at her soft lower lip.

'I want to marry you…'

'Indeed…I thought you were to, sir…' was quipped breathily.

'Now. I'd like to marry you now. I've got a licence.'

Elizabeth stared at him. He seemed quite serious. 'What…what do you mean? Elope? W-why?' was all she could stutter.

'I want to marry you tonight…because tomorrow…who knows what tomorrow might bring? I want you as my wife now…tonight. Shall we get married tonight?' Too late, Ross understood why she looked so stricken. She'd heard something similar before. Havering had probably used much the same pathetic phrases when coaxing her to elope with him…and look where that indecent haste had led. But he couldn't tell her he wanted her immediately protected by his name, his reputation, because tomorrow if things went awry she might be prey to some lecherous bastard again. Even the idea of it locked his jaw, made him silently vow to exact a promise from Luke tonight that he would always watch over her should the need arise. And way ahead of all the worthy practicalities, was a basic need to possess her…an atavistic urge to impregnate his chosen mate with his seed. He wanted a chance to gift her a legitimate child, because, on some subliminal level, he understood that there was nothing she needed more than a baby.

Elizabeth was in shock. Her good opinion of his recent

honourable conduct seemed to disintegrate into dust. He was slipping through her fingers…and the tragedy was she yearned to hold on to him despite suspecting what he was now offering was no better than Jane had got from her colonel; that had been no real marriage either. 'Are you now proposing the sort of union that reaps you all the benefits and none of the drawbacks?' she demanded in a voice raw with hurt and loss. 'The sort of ceremony conducted by a charlatan that might pass muster and get you your money and your wedding night…followed by an annulment at some later date when certain legalities are found to be lacking?' Her wide, violet eyes attacked his. 'Why do you not simply ask me to sleep with you…as all the other men do?' She jerked to her feet, tilted her white face, slashes of angry colour accentuating her winging cheekbones. 'It is late, my lord. I wish to retire.'

'I want to make love to you, Elizabeth…'

'Goodnight!'

'I love you, Elizabeth…' flowed out low and vibrant.

She hesitated by the door, flung herself about to glare at him, dithering over whether to jeer at the untimely, pathetic lie, or fly back and hit him for daring to stoop so low and use it. She managed neither, simply stared, glazed-eyed, at him. His face dropped and a grunted curse emerged through his fingers, followed by a despairing laugh.

He shook his head back, addressed the ceiling. 'It's the truth…but go to bed anyway. I'm sorry I made such a mess of telling you. That's how you affect me, Elizabeth. I'm barely able to pass muster as a bumbling idiot.'

She had her hand on the door knob behind, felt sure she would quit the room before he reached her, but something in his slow weary pace kept her spellbound. A dark finger traced an alabaster cheek, persevering when she flicked him off. 'Don't believe anyone who tells you I'm a practised philanderer, will you? I can be the veriest callow youth about you.' He lowered his head and she immediately swung hers about so his lips grazed her soft platinum hair.

'Please…'

She heard the catch of need mingling with his wry humour. 'One kiss…one for you…' he cajoled.

She faced him, mouth pursed tight. Invective, battering to be vented, died on her lips as she noticed a suspicious sheen burnishing the gold of his eyes. The anger on her face transformed into a look of mute disbelief. And then his mouth was slanting back and forth with silky heat over her rigid lips. They slackened. Her hands climbed his chest in weak pulls, then linked at his nape and her body pressed reflexively against his. He lifted her abruptly, as though she was featherlight and instinctively her thighs opened, her calves clasped him. And far back in her mind she thought that if only the callow youth she had entrusted herself to ten years ago had been like this one, things might have been so very different.

Freeing his mouth, his thumb slid comfortingly over her slick lips as they immediately sought his again. 'Go to bed… It'll all come right in the morning,' he said huskily, and gently placed her down behind him before he quit the room.

The last time Luke had seen that look of savage composure, had he but known what it heralded, he would have shackled him to the stairs.

But since he was a small boy, there was no helping and no hindering Ross.

He'd been standing on the clifftop when Luke eventually came upon him that morning having searched and shouted for him for some while. His brother had been needed at Melrose to help with a particularly bad foaling that was defeating the stablehands, but might just prove a mere half-hour's inconvenience for Ross, on this his nineteenth birthday.

And something in the way he'd been balancing there, so still, so close to the edge, had choked the raucous cries in Luke's throat. For with Ross it was impossible to tell if the quest for novel stimulation might at some time take him to sanity's outer edge.

It was seeing him shoeless that had made him panic. Then he'd noticed how little else he had on: dark breeches, white shirt, his glossy locks knotted by a summery breeze. Ross had flicked his brown countenance clear of snarls, laughing in that exasperating way he had when nothing could be done.

Luke remembered crying out, as in a nightmare, when all the horror is there in abundance, but no sound quits the throat. His own feet had seemed rooted to turf as he watched his brother launch to soar like a swallow before he swooped gracefully and was falling like a stone.

Madly, he had raced to the cliff edge, gaped at nothing, sped to the path and slithered, slipped, scrambled to the beach so fast. It seemed like hours, not minutes, later he was racing along it. Ross was there. Dripping wet and with his hands pillowed behind his sleek, black head he lay on smooth rock, grinning up at him. 'Told you it could be done,' he'd said.

Luke had beaten him; in relief and fury he had thrashed him, until Ross felt he'd allowed contrition enough. With one punch he'd freed himself. 'Don't tell Mother,' he'd said and walked away. Then he'd turned, pacing on backwards through salt-stained, sinking shingle. 'Try it,' he'd called. 'Nothing in the world like it. But stand where I did. There's nowhere else. When the tide's high, that's the spot.' Then he was gone; and the foal was fine, the mare, too.

And Luke did. He tried it. Loved it. There was nothing like it. The exhilaration...the thrill...the rush of breathtaking atmosphere before a quiet tranquillity, before the icy sting of brine. There was nothing like it: diving over a hundred and fifty feet into the Cornish sea.

And he had realised one day as he lay, drying off, hands pillowed behind his head in exactly the same way he'd found Ross that first time, that it had been no wild whim that took his youngest brother to the edge of the cliff the day he turned nineteen. It had been, in all probability, the end of many months of observation, of stringent calculation of water depths, of trajectories, of tides.

Ross was an adventurer by chosen trade; assessing the odds on survival and coming through was his business. And nobody did it better. And now…this misty September dawn…he was looking scientific again.

'Hair-trigger flintlocks are unpredictable bastards,' Guy Markham muttered.

Luke nodded, but his black eyes were fixed on the men pacing away from each other. He shot a look about at silent figures: the surgeon, Dickie and David by the hedge, still as statues. Lord Grey and Lord Beecher and various others…Cadmore's men. His eyes jerked back as they reached the marker and began to turn. He watched Linus Savage with a ferocious fascination as he immediately swung up his arm, and a shot rang out.

Ross staggered, somehow kept to his feet. The surgeon sprang forward. Cadmore's seconds looked at each other, shook their heads in disgust. He'd fired before the call. Luke's lips curled back from his teeth in impotent rage as he saw a crimsoning on the snowy cambric of his brother's shirt. He heard Guy's savage string of curses, glanced at Dickie and David as they separated in a seething, aimless perambulation.

With a jerk of his head, Ross dismissed the fussing surgeon. He turned his attention to Cadmore quaking on the spot. The spent weapon in his hand still smoked, flopped to point at the floor.

Slowly, carefully Ross transferred the pistol from his useless right hand to his left. He raised it all the way up until it was levelled at the Earl's head, then pulled the trigger.

'Are you warm enough? Here, take this rug.'

Elizabeth smiled at Hugh. 'I'm quite comfortable,' she said, but draped the proffered travelling rug over her jittery body. Her gloved fingers dashed away a cold nervous sweat on her top lip. She forced herself to settle back into the gig. 'What time is it, Hugh?'

'Five thirty…'

Elizabeth nodded, frowning into the chill morning mist. Her fingers crept to the heavy stones in her pocket, needlessly testing for the hundredth time that she had brought the jewel. 'I'm grateful for your escort, Hugh.'

'You know I'd do anything for you, Elizabeth,' he harshly responded. He choked a bitter laugh, 'Even what I shouldn't. Your grandmother will probably kill me for aiding and abetting…if your fiancé doesn't…' Mournful brown eyes slid sideways at her. 'Why could you not tell me yourself? Why did I have to learn from Sophie that you were soon to be wed? And to such a man as he?'

'He…the Viscount is a good man,' she championed quietly. 'And I…I would have told you, Hugh. It's just…oh, everything has been such a muddle. First I thought I would not marry him…then I would… Now I…now I think I shall…' A restless hand went to her head, worrying at her cool, creased brow. 'Please don't ask me to explain; I hardly understand it myself.'

How horribly true that statement was! What was she to make of what had occurred last evening? He'd wanted her to elope with him at eight o'clock, for no proper reason. He'd called himself a callow youth for declaring his feelings with such a lack of finesse. How then out of such ineptitude had he drawn her surrender? And her love? With an awful remoteness she had realised she loved him and that if he asked her again to go with him, she would, and devil take bogus clergy, sophistry and anything else.

She just wanted him. Even knowing other women did too, and might have been similarly won over by seeing him look so uncharacteristically vulnerable, made little difference. Was playing the dilettante just a subtle skill in his seductive repertoire? God knows it worked!

Was she just an infatuated fool? She was here, now, with Hugh, cold and nervous, because she was endeavouring to save a poor wretch broken by circumstances she had again contemplated embracing herself. Jane Selby's unwise trust and unrequited love for a trickster had brought her and her son to the brink of disaster. What reason could there be for Ross to want to marry her with such indecent haste? Surely, none other than base selfish motives? She sighed it all away. For the present she must simply endeavour to help Jane. It suddenly came to her that for a decade she had been doing that: concentrating on others' misfortunes; helping the poor and needy because she couldn't bear to closely examine her own barren life and situation.

'If I thought Stratton could make you happy, I would bless the union myself,' Hugh piously pierced her perceptiveness. 'But what I have heard of his…gross licentiousness gives me no hope to think he will make a worthy or even a discreet spouse. Of course you might overlook his misdemeanours. I hear he has a persuasive way with the fair sex…' His stricture broke off as he squinted into pastel morning light. Elizabeth heard the vehicle, too.

Within a moment, a hackney cab drew up close by. Before it was properly stopped, Nathaniel Leach jumped down, leaving the door swinging and, hands in his pockets, swaggered over to them. Elizabeth's eyes were immediately swerving past to the two pale ovals visible at the aperture. Mother and son were staring back at her.

Leach doffed his hat. 'Reverend…m'lady,' he greeted affably as though no inhuman trade were about to take place and he was simply emerging from Sunday service.

Hugh was barely able to acknowledge him, so huge was his antipathy. After a curt nod, he snapped, 'Bring Mrs Selby and her son closer.'

Nathaniel Leach beckoned to the cab's occupants, while sliding a look at Elizabeth. 'Believe yer've got a little summat fer me, my lady?'

Elizabeth withdrew the necklace from her pocket, but held it fast in a clenched fist. Leach's eyes were like limpets on the treasure. Even in the insipid dawn light it sparkled its magnificence. He raised thick fingers and beckoned impatiently as Jane helped her young son alight. A small dog-eared book was dropped on the seat of the gig. 'Tally book fer yer, as y'arst. All fair 'n square.'

Elizabeth simply nodded, reluctant to relinquish her heirloom even though mother and child were now by the villain's side. Their blank, bleak countenances loosened her grip on the necklace far sooner than any of Leach's threats might have.

Nothing escaped Leach's cunning comprehension. Jack was lifted and plonked on the seat next to Hugh. 'There y'are. Be a good boy fer the lady…' he cooed while holding out a casual hand.

With an unsteady breath rasping her throat Elizabeth placed the jewel on his flat palm. His fingers sprang like a trap as soon as gold touched skin. Within a moment it was lost to his pocket. Elizabeth shifted to make room for Jane on the seat, swallowing the bitter bile in her throat. It really was done. She'd lost her mother's necklace to this loathsome man.

'Be on yer way, then…' Leach said with a triumphant smirk.

'Jane, too…' Elizabeth swung about to gaze appealingly at Hugh. 'He said he would free them both.'

'I said nought but I'd let yer pay 'er doos. Yer've got the tally…an' the nipper. Yer can't 'ave me wife. 'S' not right nor legal ta separate a man 'an 'is wife. 'N't that so, Reverend?' he taunted, then laughed aloud at the defeat that lowered Hugh Clemence's strained features towards his clenching fingers.

Chapter Fourteen

'I have vital news, Mrs Sampson.'

Edwina leapt up from the breakfast table, linen blotting her mouth. She frowned; her butler looked agitated and breathless as though having sped to the dining room. That agitated her. Pettifer could be relied upon to cope imperturbably with any eventuality—good or bad. It was customary for Harry to damp down the fire, she supplied the bellows.

'What is it, man? For God's sake, tell me, before I expire from the suspense. Remember m'age.'

Immediately, he launched into, 'The whole town is abuzz with gossip of a duel…between Viscount Stratton and the Earl of Cadmore. Allegedly, the challenge was issued yesterday by the Viscount and the meeting took place at dawn today on Wimbledon Common. The first account has it that Cadmore fired before the call and injuries were sustained. I have returned immediately to tell you, but will try and glean more details…'

Edwina sank back down to the table, a plump hand pressed to her heaving bosom. The other reached for her knife. Feverishly she began buttering her toast. 'You have frightened me witless for that! Of course there's been a duel!' she snapped testily.

'You were aware of it?' Pettifer's usual baritone trebled in astonishment.

'Oh, I've heard nothing. But I've been hoping Stratton would call the blackguard out. Indeed, I've been relying on it that he would. I knew he'd live up to m'expectations.' She shot Pettifer a wicked smile, it transformed into a gleeful, triumphant chuckle. Happily she crunched on toast.

Pettifer stared at her, his firm jaw sagging. 'Injuries were sustained, although no specific news as to whom or the severity. Are you not overset that the Viscount might be mortally wounded by that caitiff's bullet?'

Edwina waved an airy hand. 'I have every confidence in m'new grandson. God knows he's certain to have kept appointments with cheats before. I've heard tell he's blazed successfully so many times gunsmiths outdo each other supplying him with fancy pistols, gratis. Good for business, I suppose. He'll never countenance a weasel of Cadmore's calibre drawing his cork!' She snorted sheer disbelief. 'It's as like the reverse might be true and Cadmore's soon to push up the daisies!'

Harry Pettifer sighed, shaking his stately grey head.

'Don't look so Friday-faced, man! Apart from ridding ourselves of Cadmore, there's a little added bonus to this morning's work.' An arch look slanted at him. 'I was confident enough of the Viscount seeing Cadmore off to bet on it…with your new mistress. She sniggered in my face when I wagered that before the end of the month Cadmore would be less welcome in town than a dose of the pox. Can you guess what I persuaded her to stake?'

Harry Pettifer allowed a smile to quirk his lips. 'I believe I can, madam. Although I had no intention of staying with Mrs Penney longer than the six months I signed for, in any case.'

'You probably wouldn't have summoned the stamina to do so…' Edwina sourly muttered. Then, loudly, 'Well, now you're not to go at all. I've saved you from a sordid fate. You're once more my man…'

'I've ever been that, Mrs Sampson,' Harry said quietly. 'That's my fate…'

Edwina looked at him; her chewing slowed and dawning comprehension flushed her chubby cheeks. 'Is m'granddaughter still a'bed?' she spluttered.

'I believe she must be. I've not yet seen Lady Elizabeth this morning.'

Edwina glanced sideways at him. An odd feeling stirred. She shook herself mentally. She'd not thought of *that* since her beloved husband died. Heavens! She must be as wanton as that bad Penney! Her blush grew hotter. She sought refuge in hearty conversation. 'It might benefit if this news reached Lizzie's ears. She's softening towards the Viscount. Perhaps a little shock might clearly focus her affections and Stratton's fine qualities. He's done this specifically to coincide with the announcement in the paper.' The knife's hilt thumped on *The Times* folded by her plate. 'He's made public his honourable intentions towards her and restored her position and reputation.' She grinned mischievously. 'A little side bet? I'll wager that before the day's out we're lining up visiting cards and invitations on the mantel. Come, a guinea says…mmm…six by noon!'

Fifteen minutes later, Edwina was going upstairs, mightily pleased. In a pudgy hand was the first proof that Harry's guinea might soon be hers. She started to hum while again reading that Lady Regan hoped Mrs Sampson and Lady Elizabeth Rowe might this afternoon grace her little salon at Brook Street with their most welcome presence.

'Where are you off to with that?' she suddenly barked, spying her granddaughter's maid hurrying along the landing with a tray of food. Josie screeched in surprise and jumped on the spot, slopping milk on to the carpet. Edwina stomped on up the treads to join her. 'You clumsy chit. What are you doing with it? Is Lady Elizabeth to breakfast a-bed?'

Josie goggled at her employer and simply nodded her head affirmatively.

Edwina's eyes hovered over milk, scrambled eggs, toast, butter and jam. She frowned. 'Is she ailing?'

Again Josie's head quivered confirmation, her eyes a passable imitation of the saucers she was carrying.

'Well, she can't have much to complain about if she intends tucking all that away. She's not fancied scrambled eggs for breakfast since she was a youngster.'

Josie gulped audibly, making Edwina shoot her a look. 'Here, I'll take it. I want to speak to m'granddaughter.' There ensued a see-sawing tussle for possession of the tray which occasioned milk to again puddle the floor. Retaining a contesting grip with one hand, Edwina's other delivered a stinging smack to one of Josie's, thereby further depleting the milk jug. 'What are you doing, you insubordinate hussy?' Edwina roared. 'Are you keen to be shown m'door without a character in your pocket to warm you on your way?'

Josie wobbled her head in denial, her bottom lip trembling. She burst into tears and abruptly let go of the tray.

Edwina tottered backwards; the crockery tilted, but she managed to find her balance without mishap. 'Cease that blubbing and make yourself useful,' she growled. 'Open Lady Elizabeth's door for me.'

'What is all the commotion, Grandmama?' Elizabeth emerged from her chamber and shut the door behind her. She was dressed in a powder-blue embroidered night rail, her pearl-fair hair cascading shimmery tendrils to tip about her tiny waist.

'Oh, nothing,' Edwina snarled. 'Just this saucy minx making me cross.' She turned her bulk sideways, looked expectantly at Elizabeth.

'Thank you, Grandmama.' With a vague smile Elizabeth took the tray.

'Oh…I'll come in and sit with you while you eat, dear. I've some very interesting news for you. What's ailing you, in any case?' she demanded with a scouring peer at her granddaughter's wan complexion. 'You've more mauve in the hollows beneath your eyes than in them. Did you sleep badly?'

'Yes, I slept ill,' Elizabeth immediately conceded. 'I've been feeling queasy. I shall rest a while longer, then come

down in an hour or so and you can tell me your news.' She
gave her grandmother a sweet smile. 'Josie,' Elizabeth called.
A small head movement indicated to her maid to attend to the
door.

Before disappearing inside the chamber, Josie's triangular,
goggle-eyed face peeked back through the aperture. Edwina
scowled and reflexively the maid slammed the door shut. Elizabeth grimaced warningly, a finger to her lips, as Josie took
a shivery breath about to recommence blubbing for having
been twice unintentionally insubordinate.

On the other side of the door, Edwina slid her head sideways on her chubby shoulders and pressed an ear to the panels. She shrugged, looked at the invitation in her hand and
strolled off, smiling, to inspect her wardrobe for fitting attire
for an afternoon salon in Brook Street.

'Are you hungry?' Elizabeth asked kindly.

The small boy simply stared solemnly at her.

She crouched close to him and took one of his tiny hands
in hers. 'Come, Jack, eat a little of this and you will feel so
much better.' She watched his eyes fill with tears and his lips
quiver and immediately cupped his mouth with a gentle hand.
'Don't forget…this is a game…like hide and seek…and who
is quietest wins. But…if you are to win…and get the cake I
promised…you must be as quiet as a mouse.'

'Don't want a cake. Want my mam,' the boy choked miserably.

'I know, my love. I promise I will try and get her for you,'
Elizabeth said with a fierce glower into space. Lifting him off
the small pallet where he'd cat-napped on the floor by her
bed, she put him on his feet.

After an awed gawp at the laden tray balancing on the
dressing table, Jack's hunger overcame all else and his fingers
stole towards the toast. Soon the eggs tempted him too and
he shovelled them up with a spoon.

Josie was clutching double-handed at the bed post, transfixed, as though in the presence of a spectre.

'We must bathe him, Josie. He looks a little…'

'Scummy…' Josie supplied, uninhibited by the delicacy that limited her mistress to wrinkling her nose, and with unaltered pop-eyed entrancement.

'Fetch hot water and fill the bath. My grandmother will be away in her chamber at this hour. She will not spy you.'

Keen to avoid the old harridan, Josie fled to do her mistress's bidding. Within five minutes she was back with the first pitcher of water. Within ten minutes, Jack had cleared the tray and the tub was half-full and steaming.

Coaxing him from his clothing, Elizabeth realised, was to be no easy task. He was eyeing the water, and the soap in Josie's hand, as though it might be poisonous. Elizabeth groaned inwardly. If only she had been able to persuade Hugh to give the boy shelter until they could fathom what next to do! But although the vicar claimed he would do anything for her, it didn't extend to donning the trousers in his own house. His elderly mother had no qualms in ejecting the lad before he'd set both feet in the hallway of the vicarage. Strict directions were given to the closest foundling hospital, as though her son might have forgotten the location since Tuesday when last he read scripture there! Sheepishly Hugh had offered to drive them either to that bleak institution or Connaught Street. Elizabeth had no intention of little Jack exchanging one miserable existence for another, so had brought him home.

Prising Jack from his mother to take him anywhere had been a heartbreaking feat. Nothing would sway Leachie into letting Jane go. Not her son's howling, nor Hugh's appeals to the man's conscience, nor Elizabeth's irate insistence that he honour his word to do so. Quietly resigned to sacrificing her own health and happiness for her son, Jane had begged them to go and keep Jack safe from sweeps and pickpockets. The lad's fate if left behind was inducement enough for Elizabeth to concede defeat. Besides, demanding back her necklace from the duplicitous devil would have been quite futile. He would have laughed in her face. So, home she brought Jack, with him sobbing all the way. Hugh passed the time muttering the marriage was probably a sham and Leach was simply keeping Jane to put her back to work.

Her grandmother was still abed and, thankfully, the only two servants in the vicinity of the side doorway were Josie and Peter, the youngest groom. They were sweethearts and had been bestowing a hearty good morning on each other away from prying eyes, as Elizabeth and Jack slipped in at seven o'clock. They had been equally disconcerted at the untimely encounter and were easily sworn to silence. In all, things could have been worse. With that encouraging thought, Elizabeth confidently advanced on Jack. He backed away to the window. 'Your mama will want you to be a nice clean boy when you again see her. I shall tell her you've been very good.'

It seemed to strike a chord. With his sweet solemn face lifted to hers, his small fingers picked at his buttons to undo them and the toe of one boot fastened over the heel of the other to remove it. Gratefully, Elizabeth sank to her feather soft mattress and, as slowly, shyly, he revealed a skeletal, milky body filmed with grime, she felt enraged that it might so easily have been crusted with burns; or blackened with soot…or bruises from Leachie's fist should his stepson's pick-pocketing fail to satisfy his avarice.

She knew she couldn't keep the boy secreted indefinitely and there was only one person left to turn to for aid: Ross. He had asked her to share her problems with him before and she had rudely rebuffed him. Now she wished she had confided in him yesterday. He had the strength and experience to know what must be done. He would doubtless be cross she had disobeyed him…but…she needed him now. She must humble herself and beg his help in finding a solution to this regrettable fiasco.

'It is a miracle he is alive.'

'He has sharp reflexes. How do you think he has survived so long in such a perilous trade?' Edwina remarked, while tipping her head this way and that, assessing her butler's contortions.

'Rumour has it that Cadmore was so early with his fire he could have shot him in the back!'

'What are you doing, Pettifer?' Elizabeth asked from the parlour doorway, while frowning at the spectacle of their sedate butler standing sideways with his lofty frame bowed and one of his arms up as though he were taking aim at an imaginary adversary.

Pettifer straightened his shoulders and his black uniform. 'Er…I am…er…demonstrating a particular method of protecting one's self whilst engaged in a duel, Lady Elizabeth. It is, by all accounts, no mean feat to master the art whereby a ball needs to pan all the way up the arm before touching a vulnerable part.'

Elizabeth chuckled. 'Are you to duel then, Pettifer? With whom, may I ask? Have you and Grandmama been at odds again?'

'Why, no, Lady Elizabeth. Your grandmother and I are…ever harmonious…' That elicited a blush from Edwina…and a smile from Harry when he saw it. 'Besides, my technique may not match Mrs Sampson's. She may have received tuition from her friend.'

'Good. The Bow Street Runners might arrest you both. Duelling is stupid and criminal, too!'

'Also heroic,' Edwina interjected, patting the sofa cushion invitingly. 'Especially when life is risked to avenge wrongs done a lady.'

'I'm sure the lady would rather not have such barbarism on her conscience…' Elizabeth's voice faded, her skin crawled fearfully.

Harry abruptly busied himself clearing away the coffee pot and the depleted dish of sweetmeats. Quietly he quit the room. His retreat seemed diplomatic. It also seemed to confirm Elizabeth's dreaded suspicions. 'Who were you talking about, Grandmama? Which friend might have taught you a duelling technique?' Before Edwina could reply, she resumed in a panic, 'What was it you wanted to tell me, earlier?'

'Well, m'dear, am I right in thinking you've grown a little fonder of the Viscount recently?'

Pansy-blue eyes grew dark and large in a snow-white face. She simply nodded jerkily and small teeth sank into her lower lip.

'Your good opinion of him is overdue but well deserved, Lizzie. Ross has put life and limb in jeopardy returning you status and respectability. This morning the announcement of your betrothal is in the paper; it coincides with him meeting Cadmore on Wimbledon Common...'

Elizabeth heard no more. Her heart had vaulted to her throat where it pulsated crazily. An anvil was pounding in her fragile head. She grasped at the nearest chair and lowered herself stiffly into it. She could see her grandmother's mouth working, realised she was explaining about the cards she was fanning out on the sofa-table. There looked to be at least eight. Edwina was tapping a fingernail on one of them.

'So of them all, I think we ought go to Lady Regan's first, then on to the Braithwaites' later. Unless you've a preference for one or two of the others.'

'Is he dead?' exploded in a whisper.

'Ross? Dead? Of course he's not dead!' Edwina snorted. 'He wouldn't be wounded but for that lily-liver getting a shot off early, but...'

Elizabeth sprang to her feet. Her complexion was now ashen, her eyes bright with tears dammed by shock. 'Badly wounded? Are surgeons attending him?'

'It's a flesh wound, I've heard. As Pettifer was demonstrating—quite admirably, I thought—there is a technique whereby one can use an arm as a shield to cover oneself. Obviously Ross has long ago mastered it...'

'What of Cadmore? Is he dead?' Elizabeth breathed.

'He deserves to be. Ross shot off his hat, by all accounts, when all present believed he would put a bullet between his eyes.

'Thank God, he missed…'

'He didn't miss!' Edwina scoffed. 'Ross spared him. He's given the skunk a stripe straight across the pate, so rumour has it. Cadmore's branded as the poltroon he is. Not that he's likely to again show his face in public. Ross is a marksman…even left-handed,' Edwina said on a proud, emphatic nod.

'Where is he? I must see him…' Elizabeth gasped, twisting about agitatedly on the spot.

'I believe he is with his brother. Luke will ensure he gets the best physician. You would not want to see him all bloodied. I understand the surgeon has extracted the bullet.'

With nausea bubbling in her throat, Elizabeth stuffed a fist to her mouth and turned and fled.

'Open this door at once, Lizzie. Do you intend to stay in there for ever?'

'I'm staying home this evening, Grandmama. I'm tired.'

'Tired? You've slept the clock round these past few days. How can you still be tired! You must venture abroad this evening,' Edwina wheedled. 'Look…it is the most prestigious invitation yet,' she enthused. 'From the King's favourite: Lady Conyngham. Now what do you say to that?' The thin card was slipped under the door.

Elizabeth retrieved it, saw it boasted an Italian diva performing at a notable Mayfair address. Listlessly she dropped it onto a sidetable to join a pile of others with which Edwina had recently tried to lure her out.

'Is the Viscount yet back in town?' Elizabeth asked huskily. There was silence for a long moment from the other side of the door.

'I don't think so; but men always take themselves off for a while after such scandals, Lizzie. Gentleman that he is, Ross is probably allowing Cadmore time to scuttle back to his wife in the country before he returns to town to be fawned over. As his fiancée, *grandes dames* are falling over themselves to secure your presence at their little functions. Bets are being laid as to who will first manage to tempt you out. We could lay a discreet wager and collect a tidy sum…'

'Has he a fever, Grandmama? Has the wound become infected, do you know?'

Edwina let out a mighty sigh. 'No, I do not know! But he has fought battles with soldiers, with smugglers, with the revenue, with drunken cronies and come through them all. He's as strong as an ox and has taken more stitches over the years than you'll count in your bridal gown! Besides, not so long ago, you would have filled him with lead yourself, given the chance! Oh, I shall go with Evangeline then,' Edwina mumbled and was heard rustling away.

Elizabeth sighed; her grandmother regretted resorting in pique to that last accusation. She was equally ashamed, for it was quite valid. She leaned her head against the door panels, again tortured by the vision of him raddled with ague and poisoning of the blood. She might never again look upon his gypsy face, never again hear his voice, feel his strong, dark fingers fasten gently on her. She might never have the opportunity to apologise for her rudeness…and say she loved him…

Edwina stomped, muttering, down the stairs. In truth, she was a mite worried herself now. Little was known on the grapevine of Ross's recovery or his whereabouts. She frowned, wondering whether to call at Grosvenor Square on her way out to Lady Conyngham's and see if he was yet at home. She was spared the need. In the hallway, Harry was in the process of taking her prospective grandson-in-law's coat.

'Where have you been?' she barked at Ross, sheer relief making her irritable. 'It's as well you're here! M'granddaughter's acting very strange. Even before she knew of the duel she was pasty-faced and ailing. She's barely quit her room since discovering you were hurt…' Enlightenment abruptly dropped her chubby jaw, and she gawped at the handsome, virile man who had his fierce agate gaze angling up the stairs.

Edwina's gimlet eyes attached to his dark profile while she reflected on the time her Lizzie had disappeared from home. She'd been brought back close to midnight by this charming romeo. 'Morning sickness…damn!' she groaned to herself. 'Why did it not occur before? Blast that Wapping drab! It's her fault! No wonder Lizzie's fretting so. Not yet wed and really ruined…'

'What?' Ross frowned, obliquely aware of Edwina glaring and mumbling.

'You'd best get her respectable as soon as maybe, or I'll fill you full of lead m'self. See if I don't!' She flapped a hand. 'Oh, go on up. Third door on the left. No point in standing on ceremony now. I'm off out to hear Signora Favetti…' trailed back at Ross who was taking the stairs two at a time.

If Josie's short double tap at the door seemed a little heftier than usual, it didn't disturb Elizabeth enough to stir her from her comfy spot on her bed. A call to enter vied with a yawn as a slender finger touched a lock of hair away from Jack's brow. She smiled tenderly as he snored; in the short while he had been with her he looked healthier, with colour in his cheeks. She was sure he had even put on a little weight. He rather resembled her little half-brother, Tom, she judged, assessing his small regular features and mop of flaxen hair. And of a similar age, too…

'Is that the problem? I'm too old for you?'

Elizabeth's finger froze by Jack's head. Abruptly she squirmed on to her stomach on the counterpane. Pushing back on her elbows, her satin-sheathed derrière poked provocatively into the air, before she made it onto her hands and knees, where her eyes were immediately level with muscular buff-coloured thighs. She swallowed, her violet gaze sliding upwards over blatantly hardening masculinity before skittering hurriedly on to encounter an elegant chestnut coat. She stared up at him, unblinking, as though he was a ghost, and a small hand actually fluttered out to test his arm. Her weak prod blunted on healthy muscle. The light, hungry touch transformed into a furious slap. Platinum tresses danced about her slender shoulders as she shook back her head to get a good look at him. 'You…you absolute devil! Why did you do that?' she squeaked. Instinctively she'd lowered her voice to avoid waking Jack, yet her tone quavered with despair.

'Why did I do what?' he asked huskily, his eyes hot as molasses and coating her curvacious body. Her breathing was coming in sharp bursts and her nipples were clearly visible beneath the sleek negligée. With a groan he reached for her, but she reared back onto her heels away from him, then scrambled to the edge of the bed.

'What did I do? Startle you? I'm sorry…'

Elizabeth drew herself up to her full five feet three. He seemed larger and darker than usual; apart from that he was perfectly normal. The agonies she'd endured imagining putrefied flesh and amputated limbs seemed now so wildly unnecessary. She rushed to the table, strewn with invitations and grabbed a handful. 'This!' she hissed. 'This is what you did!' She advanced back towards him, bristling like an angry kitten, then lobbed them up at him.

Ross turned his face and the cards fluttered about his long dark hair before scattering on the floor.

'You risked your life to get me this?' she choked. 'You thought I'd be impressed by some…some grand gesture allowing me to ride back into the *beau monde* on your undertaker's coat tails? I don't want society invitations!'

'What do you want?' he asked immediately, softly.

She could feel the pull of his eyes on hers, insisting she look at him. The small space between them was cramming with heat, with tension, with unspoken words.

'Come, tell me,' he said. 'You can do it…you're a very brave woman. Tell me what you do want, Elizabeth…' His voice was low, hypnotic and drew a single, croaky syllable from her.

'I'm all yours, sweetheart,' he said with hoarse contentment. 'And I did it…because it needed to be done, that's all.'

'I thought you might be dying of fever or poisoning,' she gasped.

'I'm fine. I've been at Stratton Hall for a couple of days. I usually go to the coast when I'm wounded: sea water's healing.'

She backed away, tears sliding her face, sticking silky curls to her cheeks, scraps of shock and anger still writhing in her.

He cornered her and exasperatedly she flung up her fists. They froze in mid-air. 'Where are you hurt?'

He smiled down at the top of her smoky head. 'Everywhere...' he purred as he lifted her up so her face was level with his. 'Where are you hurt?'

'Everywhere,' she echoed.

'Good...it'll all need kissing better...'

With a defeated sob she wound her arms tightly about his neck and ran her lips fleetingly over his face, covering his skin from bronzed brow to abrasive jaw. It was tender, at odds with the punitive fingers that twisted in glossy mahogany hair.

'Have you something else to tell me? Something I'd love to know?'

Elizabeth opened her eyes and, past his head, Jack stirred in his sleep. 'Promise you won't be angry...he's a good little boy.'

'I didn't mean that, actually, sweetheart,' he said wryly. 'But now you've mentioned him...is he your half-brother?'

Elizabeth looked at his frown. Her tongue tip nervously moistened her lips. She struggled to free herself, to act decorously when she explained. As she pushed against his right arm he winced. Immediately she was still and hugging him. 'Sorry...oh, I'm so sorry for everything, Ross. Promise you won't be angry with me...' There was raw plea in her voice for she so wanted to build on this new harmony and affection, not destroy it with her revelation.

Ross sat abruptly in the armchair. Gently, deftly he manoeuvred her to face him so her knees straddled his thighs. As she attempted to sit more demurely on his lap, he stopped her, took her mouth in a slow loving kiss that drained her of energy or will to move at all. She flopped against him, breast against breast, her pert behind tilting ceilingward.

Ross abruptly curtailed the kiss, as though his mind had been working throughout. 'Who is he?' he asked mildly, but she recognised the suspicion and intelligence in the question.

Her arms tightened about his neck, as though to restrict his temper. 'His name is Jack; he's the son of an old friend of mine…the one who presently…who is unfortunately…'

Loosening her grip, he firmly held her back from him by her wrists, so he could see her face. His dark countenance was a study of ironic disbelief. 'You've abducted a harlot's child?'

'No! She begged me to take him. Jane was to come, too, but that monster wouldn't let her go. Edwina doesn't know of any of it, or that Jack's here.'

He swore beneath his breath. 'Life isn't that simple, Elizabeth, is it?' The sheer fear of what she might next admit to having done coarsened his voice to a gravelly explosion. 'Have you been back to the docks to barter with a pimp? Alone?'

'No…with Hugh…Reverend Clemence. He's a good friend of mine and very obliging to me… Don't be angry!' She banned his annoyance in a whisper, blazing appeal in her jewel-bright eyes.

For a moment his expression didn't alter, he simply held her gaze with its odd mix of meekness and defiance. He studied the perfect contours of her fine-skinned face, the lucidity of her grave amethyst eyes. Despite his best attempts at sangfroid, his blood was boiling, dragging his appreciation lower, to the soft, rounded body tempting his. His half-smile was self-mocking, already defeated as he said thickly, 'An upstart Viscount wouldn't be lenient…would he?' He felt his loins answer before she did.

'I…I don't know, sir,' she answered coyly, hiding her blush against his shoulder. Her breasts throbbed, felt heavy and full; the apex of her parted thighs grazing his body seemed hot and dewy and these new sensations were exciting…and terrifying her. 'My Viscount is a brave and honourable gentleman who would never abuse his position of power, even if sorely tempted.'

'He is sorely tempted, sweetheart…'

'I know…' Excitement won. She instinctively pressed her hips forward and her lips to his, just as a knock came at the door.

Josie was in the room before Elizabeth had time or mind to scramble from straddling her fiancé's lap. The maid stopped short, brought her dropped jaw together with an audible clack of teeth and garbled, 'Pettifer says as there's visitors to see you, Miss Elizabeth…' Her goggling eyes blinked once, then she was gone in two precise backwards steps. With contained hysteria Elizabeth realised that Josie no longer had the capacity to be scandalised.

Chapter Fifteen

'You!'

Elizabeth advanced into the room, her expression tight with wrathful disbelief. She glared accusingly at Hugh, then turned her back on him, causing him to redden and abandon explanation.

Josie had fled before Elizabeth could discover the identity of the visitors. She had told Ross she suspected it might be Hugh and Sophie come to see how Jack fared. They were both aware of his presence at Connaught Street and timed their visits to coincide with Edwina's social sorties. She was half-right! It was Hugh…and with him was Nathaniel Leach! She understood how he had got past Pettifer's rigorous scrutiny. Soberly turned out in smart, dark clothes, clean-shaven and with slicked-down hair, she barely recognised the villain herself. He could have passed muster as the vicar's apprentice, he looked so meek and mild!

Ross had quit her chamber first, giving her time to hurriedly pull on a gown. She guessed he was being diplomatically discreet in allowing her time alone with her friends in the drawing room while he kicked his heels in the parlour. She was sure he wouldn't go without saying goodbye. She found herself hoping fervently that he had not.

'Why on earth have you brought him here?' she heatedly demanded of Hugh.

'If I've mistaken your commitment to Mrs Selby's welfare, I apologise,' Hugh said with pained primness. 'Mr Leach came to the vicarage in a panic, saying he had urgent news concerning Mrs Selby's health but would only recount details to you personally. I thought you would be overset if I did *not* immediately act on it. I ensured your grandmother was out before calling.'

Elizabeth hoped to God Edwina didn't return early. She would have a purple fit on finding this rat infesting her drawing room. And how credulous Hugh was! Or perhaps a few unhappy dealings with this trickster had made her a cynic! A glacial glare accompanied her snapped, 'I've nothing more to give you, if that's your intention in coming here, Mr Leach.'

He gestured unctuous apology with the hat in his hand. 'Fergive me, m'lady, fer the introoshun. Beein' as yer've suffered some too, an' come from sim'lar stock as Jane, I 'opes yer'll be kindly disposed ta listen. She's frettin' so over the little lad, she's dosed 'erself nigh to deaf wiv laudanum. I'm at me wits' end. She's fadin' afore me eyes,' he intoned with theatrical gravity. 'She'll only rally, I reckons, if 'er 'n' the nipper can be togevver.'

'Have you brought her with you, then, so mother and son can be reunited?' His Haymarket histrionics seemed to vindicate her scepticism; she was sure all that ailed Jane was this vile man's rapacious greed.

'No, 'cos I'm sure yer'd agree that a man deserves compensatin' fer losin' 'is wife,' he crooned.

'She's no more properly married to you than I am!' Elizabeth furiously remonstrated.

'That's a relief…' was drawled from the doorway.

Ross walked into the room, a half-filled brandy balloon cradled in his hand. He set it down on a side-table before assessing the men with calm, feral eyes.

Both Hugh and Nathaniel Leach were statue-still, gawping warily at this imposing gentleman who had quietly, confidently joined them. Hugh shot Elizabeth a stern look: the roguish Viscount seemed quite at home, while Edwina was away. Nathaniel Leach was also eyeing her, but with approval. She knew exactly what he was thinking, too: she'd found herself a Quality gent without any help from him.

'Are you not going to introduce us, my dear?' Ross gently prompted as her guests began shifting uneasily beneath his appraisal.

'This is Viscount Stratton,' Elizabeth announced, feeling very pleased as Leach's hooded lids unshuttered. Obviously Ross Trelawney's reputation preceded him even to the further reaches of the East End. 'Reverend Clemence is a good friend of mine and is vicar at St George-in-the-East. Mr Leach is no friend of mine and is responsible for cruelly separating Mrs Selby from her son.'

''S'why I'm 'ere, m'lady,' Leachie whined. A vigilant eye stayed on the Viscount. He was unsettled by Trelawney's unnatural stillness, his profound, impassive attention. 'You've got me all wrong: I ain't an 'ard-'earted cove.'

'You'll be keen to immediately return the lad to his mother then.'

'No!' Elizabeth cried, rushing to her fiancé, her stricken face turned up appealingly to his. 'If Jack goes back to Wapping, he'll be forced to pickpocket again, or be sold to a sweep…'

Leach looked equally disconcerted at the idea of being foisted with the brat he'd just offloaded at a tidy profit. Jane was still of some commercial use, but nothing like as valuable as that rock-like diamond he'd seen flashing on this classy strumpet's finger. He'd duped the vicar into bringing him here with the intention of relieving her of it. But now he was nervously cogitating that this infamous rakehell might have given it to her…and that necklace…and he was cursing himself for a dolt coming here at all. He'd thought the mooning-eyed vicar was her beau. He'd plucked out of Jane that m'lady had been ravished and was no longer marriageable merchandise in high society, although many a nob wanted her for a liaison. Had he known she'd secured Ross Trelawney's protection…

He chewed the inside of his cheek, surreptitiously sidling towards the door. Home ground called.

'How much?' Ross asked quietly, lifting the brandy balloon to his lips.

'I've paid him already!' Elizabeth thoughtlessly cried.

After a long swig, Ross replaced his drink. 'The necklace?'

She nodded, colouring miserably. She'd never felt more of an incompetent idiot. Leach had intended this all along: he had no real wish to keep Jane or her son, but desired extracting as much as possible for their release. Having easily parted her from one gem, he'd felt encouraged to return for more.

'I want the necklace back,' Ross stated.

Leachie licked his lips nervously. 'Well now…m'lady give it to me in exchange fer the nipper an' 'er friend's tally…'

'It isn't my fiancée's property. It's mine. I'm willing to negotiate a price for its return. I take it you've still got it?' he enquired silkily. A smile touched his lips at Leach's startled expression on learning Elizabeth was properly under his protection.

Leachie nodded slowly. His interest was quickening, so was his caution. *Fiancée?* 'Struth! Yet he'd rather not have the bother of prising stones from gold to sell for a fraction of their worth. It was too much of an exquisite, noteworthy piece to fence whole.

Exactly reading his thoughts, Ross interrogated, 'Is it undamaged?'

'It is, m'lord.'

'Good. I'll do business with you tonight. Do you know Cinnamon Wharf?'

'I should think I do,' Leach smirked. 'It's my manor…'

'Good,' Ross repeated in a satisfied drawl. 'I'll meet you there at ten o'clock. I'll show you out.'

Elizabeth recognised the deceitful smoothness in her fiancé's voice and smile from her own early dealings with him. A chill assailed her. There was to be dangerous trouble and Ross was already injured…

Leach kept a respectful distance behind the tall, athletic

figure striding easily along the hall. By the door, Ross curbed the instinct to accelerate the slimy toad down the steps with the toe of a boot. Instead he said, 'Ten o'clock, then. Don't be late or make me come looking for you…'

'I'll be there,' Leach vowed. 'Might I be so bold as to ask…what sorta price, yer lordship?'

'No,' Ross said and shut the door.

'Do I need to show you out, Reverend, or do you know the way?' Ross asked quietly, on re-entering the drawing room.

The fading heat in Hugh's cheeks re-ignited and, mumbling farewell to Elizabeth, he curtly nodded at the Viscount before hastily removing himself.

Elizabeth started after him, hissing, 'Did you have to be quite so rude?'

'Yes, I did. What's the man thinking of, bringing a thieving pimp into the house? If I hadn't been here, Leach might have felt inclined to help himself to a few valuables before he left. A few virtues, too. The vicar would have gone down with one punch.' He blocked her way, preventing her pacifying Hugh.

Elizabeth stiffened in shock. It had not occurred to her that Leach might cause such havoc. There *were* several attractive female servants in residence, and personally she was very vulnerable to his savage spite…

Ross swore beneath his breath and enfolded her close, rocking her soothingly in his arms. 'I'm sorry…I shouldn't have said that.'

'No, you're right! He is a fiend! I don't want you to meet him later. He's going to try and trick you. He might bring accomplices and beat you and rob you and you're already hurt…'

'Hush…it's a simple enough exchange.'

'What of Jane?'

'I'll do what I can. The boy needs his mother. I've no intention of starting married life with a ready-made family. I'd rather make my own…' He kissed her blushing cheek and with a rueful sigh put her away from him. 'I had every hope of a quiet, romantic evening…' was his wry farewell.

Cecily Booth emerged from the shadows and watched the curricle pull away at speed. Her rouged lips pursed as she stared malevolently across Connaught Street at the neat façade of Number Seven. Her recent aspiration to win Ross back and become a Viscountess, or failing that, retain her status as paramour to an Earl, lay in tatters.

She'd tracked Ross here before and believed he was simply visiting the old woman he classed as a good friend. Now, she knew differently. Along with the rest of the literate populace, she'd read of his betrothal to the late Marquess of Thorneycroft's daughter: that virago's granddaughter! To add insult to injury that day, she'd also learned Linus Savage had been socially crippled after a duel with Ross over the same woman.

Cadmore was repulsive but powerful; he'd provided an adequate meal ticket and, as his mistress, she'd gained entry to the fringes of the *ton*. Now, without even a farewell, he'd fled, with his tail between his legs, back to his wife in the sticks. There had not even been a chance, before he'd absconded, to importune for help with unpaid bills and the rent due on her villa in Chelsea. The idea of resorting to fully satisfying the stump-toothed oaf of a landlord she'd recently mollified made her stomach heave.

She'd lost everything! And it was all due to a trollop who was no better than she ought to be. She'd been eavesdropping when Mrs Penney thus maligned Mrs Sampson's high-born granddaughter to that woman's face. A few evenings ago, at Maria Farrow's musicale, the two widows had constantly spat venom at one another behind a potted palm, believing themselves unobserved. Edwina Sampson had bested every insult. Gloatingly, she'd described in fine detail the magnificent betrothal ring her besotted grandson-in-law had lavished on his beloved until, boiling-faced, her enemy bounded away in defeat.

On overhearing it, Cecily had been cut to the quick, too,

yet still she had harboured hopes of being reinstated as his mistress. She was very adept at pleasuring jaded men. Lady Elizabeth, on the other hand, was rumoured to be a virtual recluse, more used to pandering to scum in the slums. But earlier today even the consoling hope of enticing him into a discreet liaison after his nuptials foundered. Stratton had noticed her loitering about his house this afternoon, as he had on many other occasions. Before he would acknowledge her with a bored tolerance. Today there was nought but disgust and irritation in his hard face. She finally saw she was nothing to him. Yet just relinquishing him to the woman who had wrecked her life was impossible. She wanted something in return: revenge, and, ambitiously, a valuable diamond and amethyst ring. That would certainly cosy her way north to Yorkshire and her doting old godfather.

Ross had only been gone a few minutes when Elizabeth had dashed off a letter to Luke concerning her fears that his brother would be ambushed at Cinnamon Wharf by an East End rabble. She was sure that Luke could dissuade Ross from such a hazardous rendezvous when he was wounded. Harry Pettifer had been despatched post haste to deliver the missive to Luke's mansion on Burlington Parade and she was now impatiently awaiting his return.

When the rap came at the door and no footman responded, she dithered over the wisdom of doing so herself. It was dusk; it was possible Leach might have returned for some reason. Opening the door just a crack, she found herself peering at a dark-haired woman who looked familiar.

'May I speak to Lady Elizabeth Rowe?'

'You are doing so.'

Cecily Booth lowered her eyes, shielding her annoyance at her rival's loveliness. Even with so little of her perfect features and lustrous pale hair visible through the aperture, she recalled having spied this beauty with Cadmore in the fabric warehouse. The Viscount had been there too that day. She'd unearthed the identity of the blonde woman he'd been escorting and recalled a smug relief on discovering it was his brother's wife. Now that small comfort was ripped away. Even then Ross had been more interested in this blonde...so had Cadmore. The bitch had her pick of the two men lost to her. 'May I come in and speak to you, my lady?' she asked meekly.

'May I know who you are?' Elizabeth responded coolly. Something in this young woman's flamboyantly stylish garb seemed at odds with her diffidence.

'My name is Cecily Booth...'

Behind the door, Elizabeth flinched as though she'd taken a blow to the stomach. Her tongue darted to moisten her arid mouth; still her voice sounded hoarse. 'Why do you want to talk to me?'

Cecily modestly hung her head. 'I find myself in a...very delicate situation, my lady, as a result of a...friendship with your fiancé.'

Some silent minutes later, Elizabeth was conscious enough of seeming an imbecile to abruptly jerk wide the door and invite her in. An unsteady hand gestured at a hall chair for she'd scraped together sufficient composure to deny her any better hospitality. Cecily seated herself, then threw back her fancy bonnet so her long dark ringlets bounced about her shoulders.

'Thank you for allowing me a little of your time, my lady. I shall be brief and to the point. I read of your betrothal to my erstwhile fiancé. I congratulate you and wish you better luck than I enjoyed with the Viscount. I managed just a few secret weeks as his intended before he demanded I return my betrothal ring, then ruthlessly cut me out of his life. I was devastated...knowing as I do that we will ever be linked by blood.'

Elizabeth felt her world begin splintering apart, yet with admirable, cool civility, she asked, 'What is this leading up to, Miss Booth?'

A sad smile played on Cecily's mouth. 'Unfortunately for us all, it is leading up to the Viscount's first born...in about six months' time. Yet I am nothing to him now, just a discarded plaything, although once he professed to adore me. He refuses me even the token of the love we once had. At the very least, returning my betrothal ring would provide some security for his unborn child until such time as I find employment. I have been left destitute.'

'Betrothal ring?' Elizabeth echoed faintly.

'It was unique; fashioned to reflect the eight wonderful months we'd shared, so he said. A central octagonal diamond surrounded by amethysts.' She choked a mournful little laugh, pressed fingertips to her eyelids. 'I'll own to being a fool. I had heard of his reputation as a pitiless philanderer…but when in love…we women do foolish things, isn't that so?'

Elizabeth was again rendered speechless. The most she could do was touch her ring finger again and again to satisfy herself that this woman hadn't somehow craftily glimpsed the gem. But she knew quite well it lay in a drawer in her chamber. Jack's presence had restricted her to the house for days. How could she describe it so accurately? Had Ross told her about it? Why would he? He'd said he'd finished with her a while ago. Who was lying? He? She? Both of them? Suspicions whirled faster, making a vortex of pain scour the inside of her head.

Cecily Booth *had* had a relationship with Ross; her own grandmother had let slip she was his vampish brunette mistress. She might well be carrying his child. He might well have promised to marry her before Edwina schemed to trap him…for her. The ring might have been made for someone with a slightly larger finger. Was it just a horrible coincidence that it bore a resemblance to her Thorneycroft parure? It was no strict match…

Elizabeth stood silent and still, feeling as though her clothes and the skin from her body were slowly being stripped from her, leaving her raw and bloodied. 'I'm sorry, I cannot help you with any of this,' she announced stiltedly. 'Speak to the Viscount direct about his responsibilities. Good evening.' Rigid-backed, she swept to re-open the door on legs that shook so that, on gaining it, she put a hand to the wall to steady her.

Cecily Booth slid a crafty glance at her successor's chalky complexion, her large shimmery eyes…amethyst eyes. Despite the blonde's dignity she was devastated. A wedge was driven between the Viscount and his love and she revelled in the knowledge. At the very least he would have some serious explaining to do. She hadn't realised revenge could be so sweet. Appropriating the ring had always been an unlikely bonus. Joining Elizabeth at the door, she dredged up a wan smile. 'It seems so unfair, does it not,' she breathed with sisterly concern, 'that men are able to treat us so appallingly and never be marked with scandal they supply. I have heard you experienced similar misfortune when younger, and that you show sympathy to poor wretches ruined by men's lust. My only reason in coming here at all was to beg you understand why I must keep in discreet contact with your future husband.'

Unable to respond to that, Elizabeth closed the door, leaned back against it for a moment before folding over at the waist, her wet face cupped in quaking hands.

'Are you going to call or ogle that redhead all night?'

Guy Markham looked away from the titian-haired temptress who was fluttering her fan and her eyelashes at him and paid attention to the cards in his hand. 'Hearts…' he announced to Baron Ramsden with a meaningful grin.

'If you say so…' Luke responded drily, with an oblique glance at the demi-rep. He examined his hand, shifted cards about into suits.

'I thought Ross was back in town,' Guy idly remarked, laying a Jack of diamonds.

'He is…' Luke confirmed, beating it with the Queen.

'Where is he, then?'

'Where d'you think?'

Guy peered at Luke over a semi-circle of trumps. 'It's a love match, isn't it?'

Luke smiled and his dark eyes strayed sideways to where his own love stood chatting with Emma Du Quesne and Victoria Hardinge. He watched her graceful fluttering mannerisms, the way she laughed with just a hint of mischievousness, and savoured anew her ability to enchant him.

Dickie Du Quesne and David Hardinge had returned to distribute drinks to the ladies. Rebecca turned with her glass at her lips. Meeting Luke's eyes, she slipped away from the group and came over. A slender finger shaved her husband's lean jaw on its way to lay a card for him. Guy immediately trumped it and chuckled.

'Come, hurry up with this,' Rebecca coaxed. 'Signora Favetti is to perform in a few minutes. And I have spoken to Mrs Sampson,' she added conversationally. 'She says that poor Elizabeth is still indisposed and not due to attend. But she is certain tomorrow she will be so much better! I expect it is no more than a malaise brought on by the worry over the duel. Ross is a rogue to terrify her so! I must have been asked a score or more times if Viscount Stratton will attend tonight. How famous! Ross is all the rage. Do you think he will put in an appearance?'

'No,' her husband succinctly supplied, with a smile for his talkative wife. He turned his face so his lips discreetly brushed the delicate wrist bone close to his shoulder.

'Baron Ramsden…an urgent message for you, my lord.' One of Lady Conyngham's bewigged footmen was proffering a silver salver.

Luke frowned and took the note, breaking the seal. His thoughts were immediately with his mother at Burlington Parade. She had not accompanied them to this recital, preferring to spend all her time with the grandsons she infrequently saw. The message *was* from Demelza, simply to enclose another note that had been delivered that evening.

Luke's lips thinned to a tight white line as he read Elizabeth's hastily penned anxieties over Ross's safety at ten o'clock that night. He handed the note to his wife, simultaneously checking his watch.

'Oh, no! You must go to him, Luke! Stop him! Do something…!'

Sensing vital goings on, Sir Richard Du Quesne and Lord Courtenay joined them. Rebecca's stricken countenance and Luke's cards suddenly skimming the baize prompted the two friends to exchange a look then, abandoning proprieties, read the Baron's letter. It was handed on to Guy.

Rebecca rushed to quickly impart news of a threatening catastrophe to her friends.

Emma was soon at Richard's side. 'You must go and help,' she told her husband, her elfin face turned up appealingly to his. She was terrified for Ross. It was too cruel he might be in mortal danger and never know wedded bliss with the woman he loved. She recalled all the drama and laughter they had shared. He had courageously saved her from the clutches of a sadistic suitor, he had protected her, charmed her… helped becalm the stormy passion between she and her darling Dickie in the advent to their marriage. He had ever been the man she secretly would like to have married…could she not have had the man she loved.

Richard's thoughts were treading a similar path to Emma's as he dwelt on the gratitude, the unpayable dues he owed Ross Trelawney, friend, comrade-at-arms, business associate. His lips lingered at his wife's fingertips, then, wordlessly, he was striding behind Luke who was already threading through the throng towards the exit.

'Be careful…' was the sum of Victoria's encouragement to David. He smoothed her raven's-wing hair, smiled as she turned her face into his palm. Then he, too, was gone.

Guy was examining the cards strewn on the table with great interest. Gathering them all up, he laughed. 'I would've won.' The few guineas were scraped together and he pocketed them. An easy smile was flashed at the three anxious ladies watching him. 'No rush,' he said airily, reading their collective thoughts. 'Unless there's a dozen of these dockers, injured or not, Ross'll see them off.' He pushed out of his chair and sauntered away, detouring past the redhead. She smiled, triumphant, as he dipped his head to murmur something to her on his way to the door.

At the first faint sound he crouched instinctively, hands going to cold metal in his pockets. He listened to the low guttural hum become distinct voices, heard the shuffle and pat of footsteps. He individualised them. At least six men, with all the stealth and finesse of a herd of elephants. He grimaced a smile. Sometimes enthusiastic amateurs were the worst to deal with. He had no desire for any carnage. His desire lately seemed to run solely in one direction, he mocked himself as he came fluidly upright then came out behind them. He watched their scruffy backs for a moment: it could be so easy. Like taking candy from a baby. If the runt had brought the candy with him of course. He saw the small woman being pushed in front of a thug toting a torch. A line of yellow undulated on the oily swell parallel to the jetty.

'Leach?'

They sprang about in unison, clumsily…except one. One knew what he was about and was balancing on the balls of his feet, hand at his pocket, already shifting sideways out of weak light into shadow.

Nathaniel Leach stepped forward, holding high a flare. He bowed mockingly but his eyes were up and vigilant, peering past Ross's solid silhouette into a nebulous murk.

'I came alone,' Ross volunteered drily. 'Is that the boy's mother?'

Leach beckoned and a henchman urged Jane forward for inspection. Oddly, the fact that Trelawney was unaccompanied yet undaunted by his burly accomplices unnerved him. Even with the Viscount's reputation as a fearless fighter, one against six was poor odds. Leach could feel the flare's cone sliding as his palm leaked sweat.

'The money?'

'The necklace?' Ross mimicked sardonically.

The glittering collar emerged, sinuously, from a pocket to

swing tauntingly between thumb and forefinger. 'Come and get it, m'lord.'

Ross's long fingers curled about the gun in his right pocket. It was a four-barrelled duck's foot, and he knew, at this distance, he could incapacitate at least three of them with no problem…four if they moved closer together. There again, if they liked the idea of returning him the gem, releasing the boy's mother, and getting nothing in return, they could all walk home. The hackles on the back of his neck stirred, causing him to smile wryly. Obviously it wasn't going to be that easy. He crouched, bringing the duck's foot out of one pocket and a dagger-fitted flintlock out of the other.

'Don't shoot…I'm on your side…' Dickie drawled, emerging from between tarpaulin-shrouded pallets on his left.

Ross was already lowering the weapons and pushing out a string of expletives through scraping teeth. He could identify this man quite easily in darkness. They'd fought side by side too often for him not to react to his stature and pale hair. 'You infernal idiot! I could've given you a belly full of lead!'

'Why…reflexes shot to pieces?'

Ross curled a sarcastic lip at him. There was a troubling truth in that. Other familiar figures were now visible approaching along the wharf.

Close to, Dickie could read the naked disbelief in Ross's eyes. 'Don't blame me,' he said. 'I thought it was just Luke and me didn't like sopranos…'

Ross's dark head tilted back. 'This is embarrassing…' he told the stars.

Luke strode up with belligerent speed. *'Embarrassing?'* he snarled. 'You damned lunatic. You'll only take one direct blow on that arm and the stitches will burst open. That would be bloody embarrassing! The way I feel, I might land you one myself.'

'You could try…' Ross bit out but with conciliation in the challenge. He could feel his brother's anxiety radiating from him with blistering intensity; as it always had his life through when he did something Luke deemed needlessly reckless.

Now he understood: commitment made you cautious. But it was a strength, not a weakness. From the age of twenty when their father died, Luke had been dogged with responsibility. Luke lived to live and provide. Ross had lived to die and provide himself with all manner of self-indulgence until that day…until now.

Coming here alone with a fresh wound hampering him, knowing Leach intended cheating him, had been idiotically reckless. For quite some time now he'd been thinking with his heart, not his head, and it was a foreign and disorientating phenomenon. He didn't want to go back and tell Elizabeth he'd killed or maimed men tonight. He just wanted to go back to her…whole…strong enough to be a good husband and father…in his brother's image. But for his own sake he couldn't return without taking those things she wanted: her necklace and her friend.

'The notorious Ross Trelawney needs a few nob friends to help him,' Leachie sneered, but he was frustratingly aware that his cronies were not looking quite so confidently aggressive now the odds had evened. 'Togged out in fine duds, too,' he mocked the gentlemen's sartorial splendour.

'That's a point,' Guy moaned, sotto voce. 'These threads are new…first time aired.'

'I reckon yer've a yella streak, Trelawney. Yer lucky I'm jus' int'rested in the colour of yer money,' Leach blustered, keen to get the cash in his hand, before incidentals like brawling or chicanery, robbed him of it.

'I don't buy back my own property.'

'Yer said yer would,' Leach bellowed in rage.

'I said I'd negotiate. I'll do so now. I get the necklace in one piece, you get to go home in one piece.' Ross turned to fully face him, conscious of men fanning out behind him.

Leach's lips strained back over stained teeth. He could hear the disgruntled muttering of his pack. He'd promised them a tidy bit of blunt from this night's work. In sheer exasperation he flung his shaggy head about. His savage gaze alighted on Jane, visibly quaking against a backdrop of rocking water. In fury and frustration he strode towards her and slammed the heel of a hand against her breastbone. 'You an' yer fancy friends!' he snarled.

With little respect for his excellent tailoring, Guy hit the Thames within a second of Jane disappearing, with a shriek, beneath the oil-filmed water.

Ross advanced as Leach backed away; they paced in unison until Leach abruptly turned tail and fled. Ross sprinted after him along the jetty, idly tripping and kicking a henchman off-balance and into the river as he tried to block his path.

David Hardinge grinned at Dickie, with one eye on the remaining rabble. They were shifting, goading each other with jeering comments on the fighting ability of the dandies. 'I think they *mean* Corinthians.' David allowed them the benefit of the doubt. 'Shall we oblige them? It's been a long time…'

With Luke sighing resignedly behind them, Dickie and David took off their elegant jackets, discovered the best place on the pallets to lay them, then strolled forward.

'Come away…you'll go blind…' David mocked as Guy gravitated towards a trio of ample-bosomed strumpets lounging against brickwork. The women immediately scuffled competitively as Guy's eyes swept over them. The stoutest flung off her colleagues and began to hip-sway forward, undeterred by the fact that her prospective punter was sopping wet.

Along with a good deal of the other residents of this Wapping tenement, the women had emerged from the building to see what the commotion was all about. The heap of groaning bodies slowly disentangling on the jetty drew few curious glances. Five society gentlemen of obvious wealth and prominence strolling off Cinnamon Wharf, and up the alley, all bloodied and dishevelled, was a far more unusual and intriguing sight.

Dickie shrugged into his tidy coat that a moment ago had hung over his shoulder on a crooked finger. 'Who trod in that heap of dung?' he ribbed his closest friend. 'We all avoided it. I'll buy you a lorgnette…'

At the reminder, David lifted his boot and grimaced distaste at the mucky sole as he hopped along. The foot found the ground again with a scrape of leather against cobble.

Ross flexed his aching shoulder. His other arm drew the shivering, dripping woman close to his side to warm and calm her as they made for his carriage. In his pocket the weight of gold and precious stones was comforting. He felt content. His mind turned again to that blissful interlude earlier that evening in Elizabeth's bedroom. He felt himself growing so warm that he carefully shifted away a little from Jane in case she started steaming, before again allowing himself to picture Elizabeth on his lap. A few more minutes and she would have said she loved him, he knew it. And he would have shown her just how much he loved and wanted her…in a time-honoured way that would have been the first of her many trips to heaven. He thought of her white silk wedding gown and smiled ruefully.

Chapter Sixteen

Ten minutes ago, the chaos of getting Jane out of her wet things, and into a hot tub had taken every scrap of Elizabeth's time and attention. It was paramount that mother and son were settled out of sight before Edwina walked back through the door.

Josie had excelled herself; dealing with drabs fished from the Thames might have been a mundane duty for a lady's maid at Number Seven Connaught Street. Good naturedly the young maid had responded to Jane's plea to know how Jack fared with, 'Little lad's never stopped eating, m'm. You'll hardly recognise him, he's plumping out so.'

But now the hallway was quiet again; the brackish water that had seeped from Jane's hem to pool on the marble was a sole reminder of the pandemonium. It pulled between them now, widening an unbridgeable gulf.

'What's the matter?' Ross repeated, cracking the tense quiet. 'You've barely spoken to me or looked my way since I walked through the door. Has the vicar been back to warn you I'm a godless villain?'

'I don't need Hugh to tell me that!' was snapped out before she could even think, let alone act, judiciously.

Ross smiled. It didn't reach his eyes.

She took a steadying breath, determined to act with dignity and prudence. 'Are you injured?' was the first example of it.

Her eyes scanned his face and body. Apart from a mark close to an eye and his fine clothes appearing torn and muddy, he seemed undamaged. 'I hoped Luke would intercept you. I feared you might be ambushed by a mob.'

'I was. It's cheering to know my safety worries you.' His ironic tone heightened her colour, otherwise she seemed unmoved. 'Had it not been for Luke and the others arriving at the eleventh hour, the outcome might have been very different. As it was, little blood was shed on either side. I owe my brother and my friends a great debt of thanks. And you, too, for sending them after me.'

'And I owe you a great debt of thanks,' she returned with acid equity. 'You've reunited Jane and her son and reclaimed my necklace. But then you had a vested interest. The necklace is part of my dowry, and thus well worth retrieving, and I know you were keen to eject cuckoos from the nest.'

'Are you annoyed because I made some comment about wanting to make my own family? I hadn't intended to sound callous about the boy.'

His patient self-possession simply exacerbated her indignation. As did the unshakeable vision of a host of voluptuous women parading gypsy-visaged children for their father's approval. Her tenuous hold on her composure slipped away. 'I'm annoyed that you hadn't thought to mention you'd already started making your family. Perhaps you deem your first born none of your future wife's concern.'

Eyes like twin gold coins gleamed at her until her savaging gaze turned on the wall. 'Already started? First born?' he selected with silky softness.

'Your paramour came here, inveigling for funds to support the bastard she is expecting. She claims you were once secretly engaged and that you cruelly abandoned her. Was that when Edwina bought you for me?'

The silence was catastrophic. Finally he quietly summarised, 'Cecily Booth came here tonight and said we were engaged and she's expecting my child?'

'Yes.'

'I apologise for her outrageous lies and impertinence. She won't ever again accost you or bother you in any way.'

'I'm sure,' emerged sweetly through clenched teeth. 'I think she's more interested in again accosting and bothering you. I agreed that would be best.'

'Elizabeth…look at me…'

Elizabeth responded to the hoarse plea in his voice.

'Are you going to let something so patently false and malicious poison what you feel for me? Look at me!' he blasted when she swung her face away. 'I'm the same man who held you in your bedroom not two hours ago, who kissed you. What did you tell me then? Say it now! Tell me what you want.'

When she remained silent, staring at the wall, he resumed harshly, 'If she's pregnant—and I doubt she is—Cadmore's the culprit. I know enough about the workings of the female body to be sure she's nurturing no child of mine. She was regularly indisposed the short time she was under my protection.'

Elizabeth flushed; embarrassment fanned her feverish need to hurt him…topple his composure.

Gently he reasoned, 'She'll win if you reject me, Elizabeth. Is that what you want? To let some scheming harlot get the better of you by wrecking your happiness and mine? Come, I'm exhausted and you're overset. It's been a chaotic day for us both. Let's not give credence to this paltry fiction by discussing it further.' He withdrew her necklace from his pocket and held it out as a peace offering. 'Do you not want this?' he asked on a boyish smile that flipped her heart.

Elizabeth stared at gleaming octagonal amethysts. Similar stones to those in her betrothal ring. Was it hers? Was the ring a complement to this necklace or to eight months' fornication? 'No.' She rejected the olive branch. 'You've earned it. Keep it as payment for tonight's work. I intended the necklace should buy Jane's freedom.'

A dark thumb began sweeping the glossy jewels; his eyes

tracked the movement, as though he was lost in thought. 'You'll want it back,' he eventually said.

'You told me that once before,' she mocked.

'I was right once before. Take it now, or you'll come and find me again and plead for it. Think what you're doing. Think carefully, Elizabeth, for I'm done with being honourable and lenient.' He looked up and their eyes tangled, strained, while he waited, allowing her time. A hand hovered over his pocket, then, fascinated, she watched the jewel slink shimmering out of sight.

'My lord?'

Ross pivoted on a heel, close to the door, his face a tense, expressionless mask.

'You've forgotten something, Viscount Stratton. Here.' The ring was whipped from her pocket and thrown straight at him. He put up a hand instinctively, deflecting the missile with a palm. That same hand arrested the ring a foot from the flags.

'Give that back to your whore. She's sorely missing it and the eight wonderful months it represents,' Elizabeth stormed raucously.

A mirthless laugh cluttered his throat as he looked at the priceless ring. Within a moment she was alone.

'You say the Viscount was in on this! I'll skin him alive!'

Elizabeth put soothing fingers to her aching head. 'Please try to understand, Grandmama, they have nowhere else to go. How in the name of Christian decency can they be turned onto the street? I have told you Jack will be forced to pick-pocket or climb chimneys if Leach has his way. And Jane—'

'Oh, I know...*and Jane*...' Edwina mimicked ferociously. Jane coloured miserably and pulled Jack back into her skirts to shield him from the woman's withering glare.

'I have been truthful in apprising you of their presence, Grandmama,' Elizabeth said with just a little blush that her honesty was somewhat tardy. Jane had been in residence thirty-six hours before Elizabeth realised it was pointless concealing them longer. For her own conscience's sake—and,

less worthily, because of mundane practicalities such as pro-
viding them with basic necessities—she had had to own up,
beg forgiveness and appeal to her grandmother's humanity.

'Well, as Stratton involved himself in hoodwinking me, you
can get him to find a respectable lodging for the pair of 'em.
They'll not stay longer beneath *my* roof!'

'I can't do that, Grandmama…'

'Why not? He's your fiancé. You're all but wed,' she hinted
darkly with a peer at her granddaughter's waistline. 'Twist
him a little more about that betrothal finger of yours. Where
is your ring? Give it to me for safekeeping.' Jane and her son
received another dubious look. 'Pickpockets, you say…' she
muttered, a hand diving into the silver dish at her side. A
piece of marchpane was picked then, with an irritated tut,
discarded. Jack, having seen the sweet, crept closer and
peeped into the dish. Edwina glowered as he raised his large
child's eyes to hers.

'I suppose you want it,' she accused him.

He simply blinked.

'Oh, take it then!' She grumpily pressed the dish on him
then flapped a hand to wave him away from her. He whispered solemn thanks and was soon back with his mother.
'Take yourselves off to the parlour,' she ordered Jane. 'I want
to speak in private with m'granddaughter. Leave the dish!'
she bawled as Jane opened the door.

'Why is it you can't do that?' Edwina demanded, one gimlet eye on the silver dish as it was safely replaced.

Elizabeth winced. This was another piece of news she
hadn't relished breaking to her grandmother. Not least because tears needled her eyes simply at the thought of it. She
didn't want to discuss it and be torn to shreds.

'Where was Ross yesterday? Usually he visits every day.'

'We have quarrelled, Grandmama,' Elizabeth said huskily.

'People in love always quarrel.' Edwina flicked a dismissive hand.

Elizabeth swallowed painfully. The lump stayed in her

throat. 'It was a bad quarrel. We are no longer betrothed. I returned his ring.'

'You have broken the engagement?' Edwina looked too shocked to be angry. 'In God's name, why? I know you love him. And little surprise in that! He is the most eligible man around. You are sought after by all the top hostesses…as his intended. He has helped you rescue these…these waifs. *Now* you refuse him?' Edwina was utterly bewildered, but Elizabeth sensed anger, too, simmering close to the surface. 'Has he lectured you on the wisdom of involving yourself with riffraff? You can be stubborn and haughty once you get ideas in your head, Elizabeth.' A plump finger was wagged cautioningly.

'The cause was *his* failings, not mine,' Elizabeth blurted out indignantly.

'His women?'

Elizabeth pressed tight her quivering lips, but her heightening colour betrayed her.

'I suppose that silly strumpet's been following him about again and making a nuisance of herself and you've come to hear of it.'

A sharp, violet look demanded further explanation.

'That blasted brunette is a figure of fun for mooning about after Ross. Even when Cadmore took her on, she still set out to entice Stratton back…and made it very plain. Damned if she wasn't eavesdropping on m'conversations last time I was at Maria's. Everywhere I turned, there she was, watching me. Probably hoping to hear where Ross was to be found. Cecily Booth is a jealous minx up to no good, you mark m'words!'

Elizabeth did. Her heartbeat was painfully slow as she ventured, 'What did she overhear? Were you boasting of my engagement to the Viscount?' An icy suspicion shivered her. 'Were you boasting of my ring?'

Edwina frowned reflectively, then chuckled. 'Yes. That's it. Alice Penney was boiling mad when I regaled her with it all at Maria's.'

'Was he engaged to her, Grandmama?'

'*Engaged to her?* Hah!' Edwina shrieked a laugh. 'She'd like to think so, I'm sure! She let it be known she figured on becoming a Viscountess. As soon as Stratton got wind of it, his lawyers were figuring her a pension fund. Impudent hussy! A month or two warming an aristocrat's sheets and she gets fancy *ideas*?'

'Were they together eight months?'

'Eight weeks more like. Can't say I ever recall Ross spending eight months with the same filly…' Edwina coughed and shifted on her chair. 'Well now, that's enough of that indelicate talk. What I'm saying is…'

Elizabeth closed her eyes in consternation. She knew what her grandmother was saying better than she did herself. She'd been an utter, utter fool. She'd been swayed by malicious lies because she was too sensitive and too woefully haughty. Finally she accepted he had never wanted her for her dowry, but it was too late. He had warned her where acrimony would lead; he had tried to deflect and soothe her jealous hurt before she let a spurned woman wreck their future together. A smuggler's son had the graciousness to apologise for his lapse in conduct, to offer her the opportunity to do likewise when she yielded to temper. Still she resisted behaving properly; a Marquess's daughter was loath to stop being a rude, supercilious little bitch.

Pettifer announced, 'Mrs Trelawney and the Ladies Ramsden, Du Quesne and Courtenay are arrived, madam, with their children. Shall I show them in?'

Edwina frowned at Elizabeth's wraith-like complexion and wide shame-filled eyes. 'Well, Ross has kept news of the rift to himself, that's obvious, if his kith and kin are paying us a call. Thank Heavens! Perhaps you might yet persuade him you're just an impetuous madam…as if he don't already know!'

Ross was in Kent, overseeing repairs to Stratton Hall, Elizabeth had learned from his mother. She implied she knew of his whereabouts, of course, to avoid awkward questions. The ladies had kindly come to see how she fared and whether her indisposition was finally gone. She had felt the fraud she undoubtedly was, and a little tongue-tied with them. Demelza Trelawney had taken particular care to sit close, take one of her hands, and tell her again how glad she was to welcome her into their family. She chatted about the quiet ceremony planned at a local church and how it was drawing close. She said she was sad Katherine and Tristan would miss the wedding and how they had both written to say they were eager to meet their new sister-in-law. Every time Elizabeth met Ross's gentle mother she liked her better and she knew the woman's regard for her was genuine. After recent events and the appalling way she had treated her youngest son, she felt an unworthy recipient of such esteem and affection.

Rebecca's children, Troy and Jason, and Victoria's daughter, Lucy, had played on the floor with a rag doll and tin soldiers while tea and cakes were distributed. Victoria had a second daughter, Faye, but as she was still a babe-in-arms, just months old, she had been left with her nurse for the afternoon. When the children had got bored with that game, Edwina had huffed down there with them and showed them how to flip a coin with another coin into a cup. Gruffly she had bid Elizabeth fetch Jack, so he could play. Jane came, too, and was introduced as an old friend who was staying awhile. Elizabeth had studiously ignored Edwina's dry cough at that comment. All the ladies had greeted Jane kindly, and if they thought her overly diffident or recognised the gown she was wearing to be one of Elizabeth's, they kept it to themselves. If they guessed at her identity from what their husbands had told them of the fracas on Cinnamon Wharf, that kindly went unremarked as well.

But now the drawing room was quiet again. Jane and Jack had repaired to the parlour, obviously deeming it best to avoid Edwina as much as possible.

'Fine people,' Edwina enthused, observing their departure through the window. 'Joining that circle is a privilege not to be lightly dismissed.' She seated herself again in her comfy fireside chair and looked at Elizabeth. 'So where were we? Ah, yes. You've made a bad mistake, m'girl, haven't you? You've overreacted to tittle tattle and you're too proud to admit it.'

'No, I'm not. I readily admit it,' Elizabeth croaked, blinking rapidly.

'Well, that's a step in the right direction. To help you take another...I'll allow your friend and the boy house room for a few days.' At Elizabeth's immediate thankful expression, she added, 'On the condition that you eat humble pie with your fiancé. Yes, he is still your fiancé, I'd stake m'life on it.'

Elizabeth dropped her face into her hands. 'I can't...'

'You can and you must. Are you still feeling queasy in the mornings?'

Elizabeth nodded. God knows her stomach churned and curdled the day through. As a possibility penetrated, she quickly looked up, scouring her grandmother's face with apprehensive eyes. But Edwina seemed unconcerned about following up her leading question.

'No brass-faced baggage is about to ruin m'granddaughter's happiness and good name. A few days ago you had both those things. You'll have 'em again or I'll eat m'wedding hat!' She gave Elizabeth an indulgent smile. 'Go and get yourself ready; Josie can travel with you.'

She heard the ocean before she saw it. The sound of surf rushing on shore kept her still for a moment, straining to listen. A violet gaze swept the meadowed horizons; no blue but the sky was discernible.

Aware that the coachman was hovering for a gratuity, she opened her reticule and counted out some coins. Soon the hired rig was turning on the circular forecourt, then cracking back along the gritty drive that meandered a good half-mile, Elizabeth had judged, to the main road.

Josie was dubiously eyeing a crenellated and slate-slipping roofline that crowned the brick-and-timber façade of Stratton

Hall. Her wide-eyed stare turned on her mistress. She grimaced. Elizabeth forced her faltering smile to strengthen, as she nervously assessed the decaying Gothic mansion of which she might or might not yet be mistress. Josie began creeping towards the curve of stone steps that lead up to weatherbeaten double doors stranded between crumbling portals.

'Wait here a moment longer,' Elizabeth checked her maid. 'I don't want to go in just yet. I must find the sea.'

Leaving Josie encircled by travelling bags, Elizabeth calmly got her bearings, then set out across rough, unkempt grass towards the southerly horizon. She passed through the detritus of what once must have been a fine orchard. Rotting fruit was scattered stickily beneath branches that contorted low to the ground. The lush scent of cider cloyed in her nostrils. Insects fidgeted close to her hem, then flew up to worry her for disturbing them. She flicked her shining head and walked on. She noticed shards of broken timber entwined with bellbind. What remained of the rickety fence swayed in a tepid breeze. She plucked a grass stem from a matted clump, drew the feathery frond through her hand, then abruptly shed its seeds onto the ground. She did so again and again with fierce concentration while weaving a path through thigh-high reeds, her skirts gathering dew from the roots of a confusion of uncultivated wild flora.

As the natural melody penetrated her thoughts again she looked up. Slowly she took the last few steps and stopped and stared. Below, sun-sparkling water was rimmed by the silver sand of a small, pretty bay. Captivated, she watched as an arc of foam plunged to race and recede…race and recede.

Finally she became aware of him, slightly behind and to her right. Instinctively she turned away, smeared wet from her eyes and let the fresh sea draughts dry her skin. 'It's closer than I thought. So close…'

'Move back from the edge. The chalk's crumbling. It's possible the house might cover the beach at some time.'

'That should please you,' she said with a wryness in her voice. She took two careful paces back and turned to look at him. Her stomach tipped over. This wilderness of rough beauty and decadence was his natural habitat. With gnarled applewood at his back, he merged with the landscape, dark clothes, dark hair wind-tangled, golden hawk's eyes narrowed…preying on her. She saw a Cornish brigand for the first time.

'You'll have to excuse the mess in the house. There are few servants at present. Just a few old retainers. If I'd realised you were coming today I'd have got them to tidy up. You're here sooner than I thought.'

She was aware of the hard satisfaction in his tone, the idle triumph. But then what had she expected? *Think what you're doing*, he'd said. *Think carefully, Elizabeth, for I'm done with being honourable and lenient.* But she'd come anyway. She saw now, in his glittering beast's eyes, in the ruthless amusement curving his mouth, that he'd meant what he'd said. Apprehension needled her skin, but proudly she tossed up her head, letting a soft salty zephyr beneath her bonnet to soothe her warm face. 'Are there steps?'

'Yes. But you're not going down there now.'

She heard the implacable note in his denial. He was waiting for her to challenge his ruling. He wanted her to. 'No,' she murmured. 'Not now,' and walked past him and back towards the sombre house.

The red salon was, he'd said, the only reception room in a reasonable enough state to receive guests. Is that what I am? she had wanted to ask him. A guest? But she had not found the temerity to do so.

It was a dusty room, but well appointed with a view through large leaded casements over an expanse of unmowed parkland. It held some quite exquisitely dainty furniture that seemed at odds with the rough, masculine tenor of the property. They were, she realised, the last chatelaine's taste.

Josie had been led away to the kitchens by Maude, a maidservant, the pair boldly taking each other's measure as they walked side by side. Maude had returned, as directed by her master, within a very short time with a tray of tea and cakes for Elizabeth. She had barely managed one sip and swallow before agitatedly rising from her chair and pacing the room.

'I think a pianoforte might suit that corner…' The observation held a brittle gaiety and was met by the sound of glass hitting wood as his brandy balloon found the table. She took a few more forlorn steps about the faded salon, still inwardly praying her tentative rapprochment might elicit some favourable response.

The silence stretched. Her small teeth worried her bottom lip, her pellucid eyes pleaded for a small indication that he was not as unyielding as he seemed; that he might yet forgive her. Her wistful, shy appeal elicited just a small movement at one side of his mouth. He swiped his drink from the table again and downed a quantity while a booted foot rose to balance on the edge of a footstool in front of his worn hide chair. Eyes the colour of the cognac imbibed watched her over the rim of his glass.

With sinking heart, and fingers twining in front of her, Elizabeth continued perambulating. He had no intention of making this easy for her. But why should she expect him to? In London she had taken for granted and abused his respect, his consideration, his humour and patience, secure in some innate female sense that he would tolerate her petulance. Now she was isolated in Kent in a house that seemed as cold and forbidding as its new master. For the first time a fearful uneasiness stole over her. Perhaps Edwina was wrong about her roguish gentleman; perhaps he no longer deemed himself her fiancé at all…

She touched a chipped Meissen bowl on a sideboard; her nervous fingers flicked pages of a leather-bound volume on copper mining in granite. She was tempted to provoke him into conversation on that subject. Little matter that she would understand none of what was said. She moved on. The throbbing atmosphere seemed to dog her footsteps. Her damp palms were dried on her delicate rose-pink skirt. Forcing a little smile, she examined a small clock on the mantel. 'I…I see…understand why you must have been very angry with Edwina…for tricking you out of your money. The renovation costs here must total quite a sum.' In case that sounded like a criticism of his home she quickly added, 'But I…I think it has great potential…'

'It's a derelict dump.'

'You don't like it?'

'I like where it is. His Majesty let me choose between this or an estate in Warwickshire. The house and grounds there were in far better condition, having only recently been returned to the crown. This has been empty for about nine years.'

'You wanted it for the sea?'

'Yes.'

''Twill someday be fine again. I like it…'

He drank from his glass.

Desperate not to let the conversation stop and thus endure that stifling silence, she bubbled, 'I meant to tell you…your mama and your friends' wives called on us. That's how I discovered you were here. I pretended I knew. I thought it might seem odd that you had not told your fiancée of your whereabouts.'

'When last we spoke I got the distinct impression you wouldn't ever again give a damn where I was.'

Elizabeth winced and flushed but felt heartened that he hadn't denied she was his fiancée. 'And Edwina now knows Mrs Selby and Jack are in her house. She said she will flay you for helping me rescue them. But they can stay awhile, so long as I…that is, at least until I return home,' she hastily amended.

'A roof over their heads so long as you keep me company?' he astutely guessed. 'Is there no limit to your philanthropy, my dear?'

Elizabeth swung about to look at him, her chin came up. 'I would have come whether Edwina allowed them shelter or not. It was my decision to come.'

'Was it?'

'Yes!'

'To what end? Tell me what's brought a Marquess's daughter into a Cornish brigand's lair.'

'I…I want to apologise to you. I know now you were right in what you said about…about that woman's malice…and where it would lead…'

'And you've come for this,' he stated, ignoring the reference to Cecily Booth.

She watched as he drew her necklace from the table close to his glass and let it swing between thumb and forefinger.

'I said you'd want it back.'

'I know,' she hoarsely whispered.

'Do you remember what else I said?'

Their eyes locked. After a moment whitish tresses swayed about her alabaster neck as an almost imperceptible nod answered him.

'Good. Come and get it then.'

Elizabeth hesitantly approached. As she came close an idle shove with a foot sent the stool a fraction away from him. 'Sit down,' he directed.

She sank to the tapestry-covered seat before his chair, her fair head low against the broad, dark expanse of his torso.

After a moment he leisurely leaned forward so his elbows rested on his knees and their heads were close. 'Now what I want you to do…' she visibly flinched as the ellipse was deliberately protracted '…is give me one good reason why I shouldn't act the rampaging heathen you've always thought me.' The necklace was draped across the milky fragility of her wrists held neatly on her lap.

'You said you loved me,' she answered him as the glittering manacle blurred into purple fire.

'You said you wanted me.'

'I do,' she affirmed in a weak croak.

'Prove it.'

The small clock chimed, making her start and wonder how much time had passed since his challenge. How long had she sat before him, wanting just a small sign that this callousness wasn't meant; that he would soften, as he always had, beneath her demanding pride and innocence. A hand slid from beneath the precious weight. She placed the necklace on the stool close to her dusky-rose skirt, then stood, smoothed out the silk and took the one pace to his chair. Crumpling her skirts again with trembling fists, she climbed onto his lap with her knees spread, straddling him as he had positioned her before, in her bedroom. She tilted forward, blindly searching for his mouth with hers. Her lips found the lean plane of his cheek, tasted the salt of the sea air, slid down to sweep sweetly over his mouth.

He returned the shy salute with just enough restraint to prevent bruising her lips, with a savage skill that craftily eroticised the pain. She kissed him back. In her own way she persevered with trying to please him while the tears filling her eyes spilled and slipped between them.

She felt cool air then the harsh heat of his mouth on her shoulders as he bared them. As her demure bodice was pulled lower she curved into him, trying to shield her nudity with his body. His hands girdled her dainty rib cage, thrust all the way up until her small firm breasts were raised then covered by his palms, offered up to his tormenting, treacherous mouth.

Her fingers slid into his hair, twisted at the outrageous pleasure that put a moan in her throat and a coil of fire in her belly. Still she made no move to deny him, even when her skirts were ruched up by an insolent hand flowing from knee to buttock. Hard fingers pressed over her thigh; one insinuated beneath the rumpled hem of her drawers, turned so the back of it tormented the satiny skin near the moist core of her.

'Do you want to go home? You've only to say.'

'No,' she gasped.

He wound a hand into her thick soft hair, tilted her head back to look at her tear-smeared face with smoky-amber eyes.

'No?' he echoed tauntingly. 'You want to stay? Is this how you prove you want me? By crying when I touch you?'

'You said you loved me,' she choked fiercely, her vivid eyes accusing, pleading, before snapping closed to stem a fresh surge of brine. 'Is this how you prove it? By being so cold…so insulting?' Then she was tipping forward again, trapping him against the chair, already fearful he might reject her because of what she'd said.

'You didn't like me honourable and lenient, either, Elizabeth. I thought I'd try this instead…'

She heard the hoarseness in his sarcasm, recognised the first hint of her victory and her arms tightened about his neck in thankfulness. 'I'm sorry…I will be different in future, I promise. I liked you as you were…'

She heard the low laugh…followed by low cursing as he fought her gentling him, fought his own male need. His hands fastened over hers at the back of his head as though he would push her back, make available her body. She let her head droop against his shoulder, pressed her bare breasts against the soft wool of his coat.

'Randolph thought they would kill him.' She halted, heart thumping, wondering why she had said it, for she had not been conscious of thinking of anything past. She frowned her confusion at his shoulder, barely aware of a new delicacy in his touch. His hands released hers, moved to splay over her back, warming her goosepimpled flesh. She felt comforted, comfortable. 'I thought they would, too. I shouted at him to flee…but I never seriously thought he'd go completely away. I thought he'd return for me later. The highwaymen had no bullets left and had intended tying him to the tree to steal his carriage…not to execute him. They wanted the gig and money to escape for the dragoons were closing on them. Randolph didn't even have a loaded gun for them to steal. My father was most furious at that.' She gave a watery sniff, knuckling wet from her eyes to keep it from soaking his neck. 'He said a military man should know better than to travel at night without a loaded weapon…' She paused. 'Do you think that?'

'Yes.'

She nodded. 'He was so young…barely twenty. He said he was a bad soldier. His father bought him a commission. It was his sole help. Randolph was for ever cursing primogeniture. He hated the army; he'd rather have studied medicine.

'The Boar's Head was close by and they talked of breaking into a barn. They took me with them for one of them, the leader, thought I might be worth a ransom or useful as a hostage. Also, the dragoons were looking for two men, not three people travelling together. He told his accomplice to find some food while he guarded me. I knew straight away what he intended for he'd been looking slyly at me.' She paused, resumed in a faraway voice, 'By the time his partner returned he had stripped me of my gown and punched me twice...no three times, I think, for I never stopped fighting him. And then...'

She felt long, tender fingers slide up beneath her hair, cradle her scalp. 'His wife was back and hitting him with a shovel. She hit him so hard her hat was knocked off. She had very long hair all wound into a bun and hidden in its crown. I thought at first she had killed him. He was unconscious for some time. She helped me...with her calloused gentle hands...she helped me dress...gave me some food, cursing him for a stupid lecher all the while.

'Then the dragoons were in the courtyard. I could have screamed I suppose; she looked at me, thought I would. Still she left me unharmed...unbound. The dragoons were looking for two men, I reminded her. I took off my dress again...gave her it and my best wishes. They got away, I think. I hope she escaped the gallows or Newgate. When prison visiting or at Bridewell I used to look for her. I shan't ever forget her face.'

After a silent moment, soothed by the fingers moving against her body, she resumed, 'My papa had already started after me...as soon as he discovered I'd eloped. He found me a day or two later. It seemed like a week I was there, hungry...hiding in just my underclothes. I hid in case the dragoons came back to arrest me for aiding and abetting...or to misuse me. I told Papa honestly all that had happened. He never blamed me, but he was so sad, so angry at circumstances, at Randolph, at himself. He blamed himself for not caring well enough for me when no one ever had a better papa. My grandmother, the Dowager Marchioness, said it mattered little what they had or hadn't done to me, I was ruined the moment I set out with Randolph, then returned unwed. She wished I hadn't returned…that they'd killed me, I'm sure, although she never actually said so. I hated her thereafter; just as she hated me for tarnishing the Thorneycroft name. Perhaps I'm too like her: too arrogant and proud.'

Slender white fingers smeared wet from her cheeks. 'Papa was a very private man…although well-liked and sociable,' she explained with a touching earnestness. 'But the scandal…the contempt and abuse from people who once he'd thought were friends, was too much too bear. Even the birth of his son, the heir he had wanted so much to prevent his cousin Cyril having the estate, couldn't cheer him. He didn't see Tom grow. Tom was but three when Papa died. My stepmother hated me too. She blamed me for putting her husband in an early grave, my grandmother blamed me for the loss of her son. They hated me so much.' She gasped in a shuddering breath. 'I deserve it, I know…they were right…'

'It's not your fault he died…'

'I know…' she whimpered.

'It's not your fault, Elizabeth…none of it's your fault. You're brave and selfless and wonderful,' was whispered against her hair, while his hands slid across her back. She felt the wool of his sleeves against her nude skin as he pressed her against him. 'Edwina told me his heart was weak. Your father might have died at any time.'

'But I broke his heart…I know I did…' she shrilled in anguish.

'It's not your fault, Elizabeth…'

The sob, gathering momentum, jolted her violently against him. She buried her face into his neck, keening as though her own heart might shatter into a million pieces.

Chapter Seventeen

Elizabeth woke suddenly, yet remained quiet and still. Her eyes raised, focussing on a faint scar that ran parallel and slightly beneath his jaw. His steady breathing was raising and lowering the burden of her body in a soporific rocking rhythm that weighted her eyelids again.

He was unaware she was awake. His eyes were lost between long close lashes as he stared ahead, deep in his own thoughts. A cigar was smouldering, forgotten, between his fingers resting on the chair arm. Curiously, it was then recollected. She watched his mouth, lips that could savage or soothe, curse or comfort, as the ash glowed a dull red. His head angled lazily, a strand of his dark hair stroking her forehead as smoke was directed away from her and at the ceiling. The pressure of a hand was on her back but not tactile skin. He had dressed her; put up her bodice and smoothed down her skirts while she slept.

She felt too luxuriously content to move; in this shadowy, shabby room she'd found peace and home. This was her home…not Thorneycroft, not Connaught Street: both had housed her in her tender years. This sea-worn mansion was her's. So was this man: this Cornish rogue who had warred and seduced his way to nobility; who'd shed infamy and fecklessness, for her; who'd cradled her carefully in his arms while she wept and slept. He'd believed in her, waited for her, finally taught her to trust enough to let him, with a few simple words, conquer her haunting demons and take her heart and soul. 'Say you love me.'

He didn't smile, didn't look at her. But with a soft vibrancy, an immediacy that denied a need for thought, he told her what she wanted to hear.

'I love you,' she echoed softly.

That did make him smile. 'I know,' he said and brought his tobacco-scented fingers to stroke her face.

Elizabeth turned into the caress, then snuggled closer and kissed his cheek. 'You wanted to elope with me because you knew Cadmore would cheat. You thought he might kill you and I'd again be at his mercy. You wanted to protect me...as your widow...your beneficiary...'

'Something like that...' he said wryly.

'Why didn't you *tell* me?'

'Because you would have stopped me meeting him.'

She gently tested his right arm to see if it still pained him. 'You won't seek out Randolph...not now...will you?'

'No. In a perverse way, although I despise him, I admire him, too. He saw you, wanted you, had the fortitude to persevere knowing there was a good chance he'd be rejected. I withdrew at the first fence...'

'You? You didn't even know I existed ten years ago.'

'Of course I knew...'

At his stinging self-mockery, she sat back on her heels on his lap to study his dark, satiric expression. Dusk was enclosing them as shadows elongated in the quiet, fire-daubed room.

'I always knew where you were to be found. Sometimes I'd allow myself to go there...sometimes I wouldn't. I'd never have let myself endure the humiliation of being summarily rejected. No courage, you see...'

Elizabeth put a soft hand to his hard cheek, devilishly lit by the glowing coals in the grate. 'That's rubbish. You're the bravest man I know.'

'No, I'm not. I'm the most self-indulgent man you know.'

'Not any more. You'd deny yourself anything...do anything...for me.'

He smiled at the truth of it. 'Do you know what really
rankles, Elizabeth?' Silky blonde tangles were smoothed from
her face as he cupped it double-handed, brought her close. 'I
know now you wouldn't have rejected me.'

'You fascinated me then, too. I wanted you then, too,' she
shyly admitted.

'So...what would your papa have said,' he breathed against
her warm parted lips, 'when you told him you'd settled on a
Cornish smuggler's son?'

'Oh, that's easy...he knew people...he'd just have said...
well done...'

He discarded the stick with which he'd patterned the sand
in front of him, and looked at her again. He squinted through
twilight; just a blush on the horizon, dappling glitter on the
grey sea showed there had been a sun.

Ross leaned back on an elbow on the smooth flat rock at
the base of the cliff. Overhung by craggy strata and straggling
brush, it formed a natural windbreak; a shelter from the elements and prying eyes. He watched as Elizabeth sifted
through pebbles for shells by the water's edge. There was
something almost primitive in the way she was foraging, fascinated, her glorious hair already thick with salt and gleaming
like mother of pearl. She resembled a mermaid, he decided
with a smile, the way she was resting on an elbow, with her
legs sideways and hidden in a cone of skirt. Beneath that
cascade of ivory locks she might have been naked to the
waist. She stood abruptly, skirts raised to carry her beach
booty, displaying shapely calves and ankles, tiny feet, putting
paid to his mermaid fantasy. She was about to wander further
away so, as she glanced at him, he beckoned.

She obeyed with an eagerness that was sweeter for being
transient. A few more hours would help restore her proud
independence and he could be patient a little longer. At some
time he'd share a confidence of his own: tell her that he had

been on the point of returning to London to see her and try to win her over, when she'd showed up today. Eventually she would ask where were the builders he was supposedly setting to work.

Elizabeth dropped to her knees before him, scattering an assortment of sea shore on the smooth rock.

'Is that for me?'

'Yes.'

'Thank you,' he said with a gracious dip of his head and a hot golden look arrowing at her.

She laughed. 'You look a little disappointed, sir. Were you hoping for a crab? A fish? A turtle?'

'None of those. Something a little sweeter,' he said huskily.

Elizabeth felt her heartbeat hammering with a wild excitement, a calm acceptance. It was time. Despite the sea-breeze her skin felt febrile, raw with wanting him to reach out and touch. 'Such as?' She shook back her hair from her exquisite face so the heavy tresses separated into rope-like silver skeins.

His low-lidded eyes swerved past hers to stare out to sea.

Elizabeth raised a soft hand to slide along his abrasive jaw, brought his eyes back to hers, exulting in her power in this mating game. 'Such as?' she repeated. She could see his turmoil, his pain and regret for having succcumbed to a vengeful lust earlier, vying with his need for her now. Her fingers went to her bodice, working until it gaped. She was aware of his stillness, his eyes tracking the movement. He dipped his head, watched the heel of his boot score a furrow in sand. She brought his chin up, tilted forward to boldly kiss him. 'I love and trust you. I want you. Let me prove it.'

'You don't have to. I believe you,' he said hoarsely. 'I was acting stupidly when I said that, like an uncouth lout. Or an upstart Viscount, perhaps…'

She moved closer on her knees, slid her arms about his neck, pressing herself against him. He felt hard and hot. So hot that she sensed his torso toasting hers. 'I thought you wanted me, too, Ross…'

The rumbling laugh shook him backwards. He took her

with him so that she was lying atop his tense, pulsing body, then studied her beautiful face, her serene, inviting smile. 'What about your white silk wedding gown?'

The question was unnecessary; she knew from his blackened pupils, his subtle manoeuvring to ease his tortured pelvis, that she'd won. He couldn't go back. 'I won't tell if you don't.'

'I think Edwina already believes you to be *enceinte*.'

Elizabeth giggled. 'I know and I swear she's secretly pleased.'

'And you? How pleased would you be?'

Elizabeth looked deep into his velvet eyes as though the reality had never occurred to her. 'A baby?' Wonderment made her yearning sound ragged.

He turned her gently on to her back, shifting them from hard rock to soft sand. His hands pillowed her scalp, lost in hair that veined platinum on gold. 'You know I'd do anything for you, Elizabeth...' He was still smiling as his mouth merged with hers.

Epilogue

'Damme... She got her way after all,' Edwina said, but with a grin for her grandson-in-law. 'Lizzie was forever trying to spend her dowry on waifs and strays.' She looked up at the sturdy building and read the caption beneath the roofline: *The Lady Elizabeth Rowe Charitable Foundation.* Cast in bronze, it was an enduring tribute to her granddaughter's benevolence.

Ross disentangled his hair from his son's strong grip, slipped a long forefinger into his plump, curled fist. He smiled as it was immediately used to soothe toothless gums. He looked at his wife, wanting to cut a swathe through the town dignitaries encircling her, and carry her off home. The need made him feel guilty and selfish. For weeks she had looked forward to this day, but he wanted to curtail it to make love to her...properly make love to her.

'Here...I've something for you.' Edwina regained his attention. She handed him a document she had pulled from her reticule. 'Thought you might like it...now m'ship's come in.'

Ross shifted his wriggling infant son in his arms. Unfolding the parchment, he quickly scanned it. He frowned. 'This *is* a ship, Edwina.'

'Yes...I know. Thought you might like it. It's a good one...as fine a trader as you'll buy anywhere.' She assessed him shrewdly. 'Why did you never badger me for repayment? You've spent the dowry on this building and pledged the annuity to a charitable trust. You're seriously out of pocket now you've renovated Stratton Hall from your own funds, too…'

Ross's golden eyes raised. He smiled at the Heavens, shrugged. 'It's just money. You gave me far more than I gave you…'

'You're a fine man, Mr Trelawney,' Edwina said with a choking huskiness in her voice. 'And don't even try and give me that paper back,' she threatened as, suspiciously dewy-eyed, she waddled off to mingle with the pillars of society from neighbouring parishes and more local and lowly townsfolk.

Ross threaded his way through the crowds towards his wife. He passed by Guy Markham, chatting to Elizabeth's best friend. 'So what birth sign were you born under?' he heard Sophie earnestly ask Guy.

'Virgo…' Guy promptly answered with a grin. 'I think…'

'Think again…' Ross muttered drily as he strode on.

Aware of a spicy sandalwood scent, Viscountess Stratton turned towards her husband and gave him a blissful smile. Amid the press of chattering, laughing people, their eyes locked exclusively as they stood face to face, each cradling a baby in their arms. 'I'm so happy, Ross…'

'Good. You look it…and quite beautiful…blooming…' A discreet hand moved to touch her, a thumb caressing her arm in an old familiar way.

Elizabeth sensed the tremor in his fingers, the hunger he was still repressing. She lowered her eyes. Her confinement had only recently come to an end and she was feeling stronger every day. Five months only to recover from the birth of twins was exceedingly good going, Edwina had assured her. 'I feel blooming. Very well, indeed,' Elizabeth impressed on her patient, wonderful husband as her eyes merged meaningfully with his. 'Here, take your daughter.' She swapped the chestnut-haired blue-eyed angel dozing in her arms for her bobbing blond-haired son. His alert little eyes were already showing signs of turning the colour of autumn leaves. 'I must just speak to Hugh and Jane…then I should like to return to Grosvenor Square for some papers for my speech later at the Guild Hall. Will you take me there?' she asked with a provocative amethyst glance slipping at him from beneath her lush lashes.

'Of course,' Ross said, softly laughing. 'You know I'll do anything for you, my love.'

Hugh was being led away from Jane Selby by a colleague just as Elizabeth was approaching. Hugh greeted her in passing and smiled at her lively son.

'You're settled here, Jane?' Elizabeth asked, indicating the building in which her friend was now installed as matron. Edwina's initial reluctant few days' hospitality for the Selbys had extended to almost fifteen months harmonious cohabitation. After Elizabeth's marriage, Edwina had been gruffly appreciative of her live-in female companion and her engaging little son. But now circumstances had changed for all of them. Edwina wanted back her privacy. Jane was more than ready for financial independence and self-fulfilment. These were to be gained from managing an institute that provided shelter and an education for orphaned and abandoned children, and refuge to destitute women of the locality. Who better to give support and sympathy? she had said on applying for the position.

'Oh, yes, I'm settled. And Jack, too.' A proud maternal look arrowed to a lively blond boy chasing a few young friends on the fringes of the crowd. 'I can't ever thank you enough, Elizabeth, for what you've done for us.' Jane's voice vibrated with emotion and gratitude. Before Viscountess Stratton could demur or look concerned at her friend's tear-choked tone, Jane quickly changed the subject. She raised a hand to touch the petal-soft cheek of the boisterous infant in her friend's arms. 'You've fine babies; honeymoon twins... How wonderful...'

'Yes,' Elizabeth said with a small private smile as the tang of brine and the sound of rushing surf assailed her senses. 'Wonderful...' And then with a parting wave she was returning to her husband.

'Now go to your grandpapa, my love...' Elizabeth handed

over her precious burden to a stately, steel-haired gentleman who immediately put the child to his shoulder as though practice had perfected the move. Her husband carefully placed their still-sleeping daughter in Edwina's fond embrace.

Settling sedately into their elegant carriage, Elizabeth waited for it to move away along the street before she slid the seat and, giggling, fell into Ross's welcoming arms. She hugged him close. Then with a mother's instinct disengaged herself, angled her head to see through the window, and watched serenely as Harry and Edwina Pettifer hugged their great-grandchildren.

'I'm so lucky,' she whispered to Ross. 'How did you do that? I would have been thrilled with one baby…but two…' The frank adoration and awe in her glowing violet eyes made him smile crookedly before bending his dark head to hers. He touched their lips together lightly, then with a hunger that made her weld against him and encircle his strong neck with silken arms. With a wry modesty he murmured against her slick, soft lips, 'I thought you'd like it that way, sweetheart: one for you and one for me…'

*   *   *   *   *

MILLS & BOON®

Makes any time special™

**Mills & Boon publish 29 new titles
every month. Select from...**

Modern Romance™   Tender Romance™

Sensual Romance™

Medical Romance™   Historical Romance™

MAT2

2 FREE

books and a surprise gift!

We would like to take this opportunity to thank you for reading this Mills & Boon® book by offering you the chance to take TWO more specially selected titles from the Historical Romance™ series absolutely FREE! We're also making this offer to introduce you to the benefits of the Reader Service™—

- ★ FREE home delivery
- ★ FREE gifts and competitions
- ★ FREE monthly Newsletter
- ★ Exclusive Reader Service discounts
- ★ Books available before they're in the shops

Accepting these FREE books and gift places you under no obligation to buy, you may cancel at any time, even after receiving your free shipment. Simply complete your details below and return the entire page to the address below. *You don't even need a stamp!*

YES! Please send me 2 free Historical Romance books and a surprise gift. I understand that unless you hear from me, I will receive 4 superb new titles every month for just £2.99 each, postage and packing free. I am under no obligation to purchase any books and may cancel my subscription at any time. The free books and gift will be mine to keep in any case.

H1ZEA

Ms/Mrs/Miss/Mr ....Initials.....................................
BLOCK CAPITALS PLEASE

Surname ....

Address ....

....

....Postcode...............................

Send this whole page to:
UK: FREEPOST CN81, Croydon, CR9 3WZ
EIRE: PO Box 4546, Kilcock, County Kildare (stamp required)

Offer valid in UK and Eire only and not available to current Reader Service subscribers to this series. We reserve the right to refuse an application and applicants must be aged 18 years or over. Only one application per household. Terms and prices subject to change without notice. Offer expires 31st October 2001. As a result of this application, you may receive further offers from Harlequin Mills & Boon and other carefully selected companies. If you would prefer not to share in this opportunity please write to The Data Manager at the address above.

Mills & Boon® is a registered trademark owned by Harlequin Mills & Boon Limited.
Historical Romance™ is being used as a trademark.